PSYNC

ENCHANTED UNIVERSITY

BOOK ONE

ZILE ELLIVEN

Created with Vellum

DISCLAIMER

Sadly, this is a work of fiction. Unless the men with the lovely drugs and darling white coats say otherwise, all the names, characters, businesses, places, events, and incidents in this book are either the product of the patient—ahem—author's imagination or used in a fictitious manner. Any resemblance to actual persons, living or dead, or actual events is a coincidence. But if you want, feel free to do as I do and believe with all your heart that in some dimension or fairy hill they are in fact real. Because it makes life more fun that way.

To my best friend and the best beta in the world, my Char-chan. Thank you for playing the what-if game with me at all hours of the day and night. All that lost sleep was worth it.

CHAPTER 1
ELI

Hot. It was hot and it was sweaty and it was godawful in the crowded auditorium. Eli's modest stature wasn't doing him any favors as he fought against the stream of students pouring into the stagnant, overfilled room. After an elbow to the face and thoroughly stomped on feet, it was increasingly clear returning to his dorm to retrieve his forgotten folder wasn't happening.

He'd just have to make do.

With a sigh, he turned himself around to go back to his seat, which of course had already been filled with another, smarter freshman's ass. One who hadn't forgotten the information packet.

So instead of getting a seat up front where he could see what was going on, he was going to be stuck in the back—probably behind a ridiculously tall person whose sole job was to take up as much space as possible, so people of modest and very respectable heights were unable to see anything useful.

At this point he was ready to take any seat as long as it

would get him out of the river of sweaty students he was currently trapped in.

Oof!

He'd reached the bottleneck where several rows met and was lifted right off his feet.

Hotcloseawfulhelp!Wrong!

Then hands were at his elbows pulling him out of the crowd and into an empty seat.

"Buddy, you okay?"

Eli looked up dizzily into a boyish set of friendly gray-green eyes and blinked. His attention was snatched away by a piece of paper folded into a fan flapping furiously in his face.

"Of course he isn't okay, dork, he almost got trampled." The fan wielder was a girl with her hair pulled back into a ponytail so tight it made Eli's eyes water in sympathy. Her shirt had a blue, pink, and white flag emblazoned across the front.

The morning had started out so well. He'd left his room with plenty of time to spare and a song in his heart. He'd finally made it. The shadows in his mind were mere whispers in the face of this accomplishment.

Not only had he made it to college, but he'd made it to one with a good language program and on a scholarship to boot. Which meant every dime he had saved could go to living expenses. For once in his life, he could focus only on studying.

However, his wonderful mood of the morning was gossamer in the face of being manhandled by half the student body on campus. At the moment, he'd be proud if he could simply manage to catch his breath.

The fan waved faster in his face, and Eli used it as a

focus to bring himself out of his head. It was dark in there, and sticking around was never useful.

"I'm Alice, by the way." The girl's voice was softer than when she was talking to her friend.

"And I'm Nate. Alice, get that thing out of his face." The boy pushed Alice's arm back.

Eli realized distantly that Nate was leaning back from him, giving him as much space as possible. On Eli's other side there was a nice, safe wall. In front of him, instead of a row of seats, there was a set of railing. He found that there was air in the auditorium after all. "No, it's okay. It's giving me something to focus on."

For a minute, he allowed himself the simple luxury of breathing. Once he was positive all the air in the room would stay where it was supposed to, he unfurled from the ball he'd curled himself into.

"Better?" Nate asked, the worried crease between his eyebrows fading.

"Yes, much. Thanks, I—" What little blood had made its way back to his face drained away again.

Holy crap. He'd just gone full-on nonfunctional in a group of complete strangers on his first day of college. Which was, of course, the one thing he'd been afraid of most. Score one for stress bingo.

Well, at least he'd gotten it out of the way.

"Sorry about that." Eli managed weakly. Perhaps they would turn out to be nice people and allow him the option to pretend it never happened?

"Don't worry about it." Alice poked the fan toward him. "Take it, I can make another."

Eli took it gingerly. Any second now, he was expecting them to give him the cold shoulder after his freak-out.

"Seriously, man, it's okay. You don't have anything on my mom. Once when I was ten, she had a panic attack at the grocery store. I had to wheel her back to the car in a grocery cart. My other mom was so freaked out she wouldn't let her leave the house alone for a week." Nate's hand hovered over Eli's shoulder like he wanted to pat it, but it never landed.

Ah. Looked like today was his lucky day after all. New school, new situation, new people? With his brain, panic was inevitable, and it was hilarious for him to have thought otherwise. No, the luck came from him losing it near the right people when it finally happened.

And with that thought, the rest of the attack drained away, leaving him shaky and giddy in its wake.

"Then thank you. Imagine the embarrassment of snuffing it like that on the first day."

"Oh, I imagine there are worse ways to go," Alice said, busily putting the finishing touches on her new fan.

"Like falling down the stairs during a fire drill because you were trying to put on pants?" Nate laughed and elbowed Alice, causing her to drop her fan.

"I didn't fall down the stairs! And my pants were mostly on. And I didn't die, thank you very much." Alice scooped her fan off the floor and hit Nate's shoulder.

"Sure, sure. And I'll bet it happened to your friend, not you, right?" Nate snatched the fan out of Alice's hands and began fanning himself.

"My sister told you that story, didn't she? I swear . . ." Alice noticed Eli as he did his best to hold back mounting laughter. "I'm sorry, you don't even know us, and here we are raving like lunatics."

"Don't worry about me, I like lunatics. My name's Eli, by the way." He nodded in lieu of reaching out a hand to shake, causing a lock of wavy black hair to fall into his face.

It made a nice little curtain to put between him and the world, so he let it stay. "So, I take it you two know each other?"

Good. This was good. Instead of translating his favorite songs into Japanese to stay calm, he had actual people to talk to until the assembly started. Lucky day indeed.

"Yep!" Alice said merrily and threw an arm around Nate's shoulder. "We've known each other since kindergarten. Fortunately for him, he got into the same school as me, or else he'd be crying alone in the corner." She reached out to wipe an imaginary tear from Nate's face, only for him to shove her hand away.

Eli spent the next few minutes learning about his rescuers. Like Eli, they'd both grown up in the eastern half of the state. They were next-door neighbors and as close as siblings.

Thankfully, neither of them asked him any probing questions like, what's wrong with your brain, or why are you out without a keeper? Instead, they asked about his family. Talking about his mom and sister were easy topics, and it gave him a safe place to spend all of his leftover adrenalin.

"So, your mom raised both of you on your own and put herself through nursing school?" Alice whistled. "Congrats, Eli's mom. Mine doesn't do anything more strenuous than yell at the gardener through the window."

Eli nodded. He was incredibly proud of his mom. "After my dad died in Afghanistan, she poured everything she had into making sure my sister and I had the life they'd planned for our family. I think it helped her deal with losing him."

His phone buzzed in his pocket. The name on the screen read Berry. Speaking of his sister Juniper . . .

• • •

Berry: *Hey jerk, you still alive?*

He put it back in his pocket, but it buzzed again before it even made it all the way back in.

Berry: *Don't leave me on read, assface.*

Eli: *I'm talking to someone rn, fuck off.*

An outsider would think he didn't get along with his twin, but theirs was a special bond. A bond that involved copious amounts of swearing.

Berry: *You made a friend??? I didn't even have to pay someone!*

Eli didn't bother responding. Juniper had only texted him in the first place to make sure he was okay. Any response other than *dear sweet god in heaven send help* was a sign he was fine.

He was lucky she hadn't texted him fifteen minutes earlier when he was decidedly not fine.

"Hey, I think it's starting," Alice said, bringing his attention to the stage.

Several people had filed onstage while the crowd waited, and now an older woman in a smart pantsuit moved up to the microphone. She began what Eli was sure was a rousing welcome speech, but before she gotten too far in, his attention was drawn to a young Asian man sitting in a chair on the far end of the stage.

His dark hair was pulled back in a short ponytail, and he was dressed in gray slacks and a white dress shirt that looked expensive even from this distance. But it wasn't the clothes or the man's strikingly handsome face that caught Eli's eye, but rather the way he was looking around the auditorium.

Unlike everyone else on stage, he was slowly scanning the crowd with an intensity Eli couldn't help but notice. What was he looking for?

"But don't take my word for it, let's hear what students from each department have to say." The woman stepped away from the podium and motioned to a young woman to step forward.

Over the next hour, Eli did his best to focus on what each speaker had to say, but no matter how hard he tried, his attention kept going back to the man at the end of the stage gazing intently into the crowd. It looked as though he was going from face to face. When he reached the row Eli was on, his eyes seemed to linger for a moment before moving on.

Finally, it was the young man's turn to speak, and he took his place at the podium. For a moment, he stood motionless, using his new vantage point to scan the crowd. Again, his eyes lingered on the area where Eli and his companions sat. A lock of hair had fallen artfully in front of his face. It was so perfect, Eli suspected the man had done it on purpose.

The lady in the pantsuit—who turned out to be the Dean—cleared her throat loudly in an attempt to get the young man to continue.

Rather than chagrin, his face showed mild irritation,

but he ceased his search and spoke into the microphone in a deep, confident voice that made Eli's skin tingle. "I'm Haruka from the Language department. If you're one of ours, we'll work you hard, but we'll take good care of you."

Huh. They were in the same department.

Eli waited for him to continue, expecting to hear about the heavy course load he'd read about in his information packet. It had sounded like a shit ton of work, but that was perfect for Eli. The more work the better. If his brain was occupied, it was less likely to make him its bitch. But instead, Haruka bowed sharply and went back to his seat.

The room was treated to the Dean looking flustered and rushing back to the podium to fill in the dead space in the program. She managed to hem and haw her way through the first few awkward moments, glaring in Haruka's direction more than once, until she reached a point where she could close the assembly with a modicum of grace.

Eli's new friends kindly waited for the auditorium to empty, making it seem like they had nothing better to do with their time than to sit and learn all about Eli.

"The guy from the language department was hot like fire. Eli, your job is going to be to help me achieve contact."

"Um."

"Just because you're both in the same department doesn't mean he's your servant, Alice." Nate grabbed his bag and stood up. "Are you two ready to go? I'm supposed to meet my advisor soon."

The rush for the door had thinned to a trickle, which made now as good a time as any to leave.

Eli stood and shouldered his bag.

:*I must be losing it.*:

Eli jerked his head up. "What?"

"I said are you ready to go?"

:*This is ridiculous.*:

"Um . . . yes?" Eli said in response to both.

He turned to look behind him, but the seats were all empty.

In front, Nate and Alice were bickering pleasantly as they made their way down the stairs.

What the actual fuck, brain?

CHAPTER 2
ELI

After his little episode, he'd left his new friends and wandered in a daze all the way back to his room.

Over his short life, he'd gotten used to the random quirks his mind continued to introduce to him. Like the no-touching thing. He'd had that since he could remember. It was close friends with a gnawing sense of emptiness inside, as if he'd been born incomplete somehow. And of course, after The Incident, he'd learned being alone at night was no longer an option for him. According to his therapist, it was normal and he would grow out of it.

He was still waiting on that one.

He'd had a brief, but intense, argument with his mom over whether or not he should have a single room or a double. She wanted him to push his comfort zone and try to learn to sleep by himself. She even went so far as to suggest it would be unkind to inflict his nightmares on a perfect stranger.

Eli had countered her argument by stating his nightmares rarely happened when he wasn't sleeping alone. Then he immediately contacted the student housing people and explained the situation. The man on the phone had been more than happy to find him a psych major who had no problem with Eli's idiosyncrasies.

It turned out better than Eli could have hoped. When they met yesterday, his new roommate Jace had been the first to bring it up, asking Eli about his problem and how it manifested, somehow making him feel at ease and not a total nutcase at the same time.

Of course, that didn't stop Eli from deciding not to mention his recent panic attack the next time he saw Jace.

He took a deep breath and opened the door to his room, slapping on his *everything is fine* face. He dropped it as soon as he realized the room was empty. A note on his bed caught his attention, and he plucked it off his comforter.

Department party tonight. Be home late.

-Jace

Well, at least he didn't have to pretend not to be wired and oversensitive in front of anyone.

He managed to waste thirty whole minutes straightening an already immaculately organized room before flopping down onto his bed.

:*And now there's a rock in my shoe. Perfect.*:

Eli shot off the bed like he'd been electrocuted.

He spun around looking for the speaker but found an empty room. After looking in both closets and under both beds, he sat on the floor and specifically did not hold his head while rocking back and forth. Only weird people did that.

If it had only been a single incident—he'd chosen to count earlier as a single incident since they'd happened so close together—it could be explained away by a million rationalizations. And he'd managed to go through most of them on the way home.

But there was no one around he could conveniently blame this voice on. He was alone now.

Alone and hearing things.

Come on, brain, you didn't think I had enough interesting things to sort through? You had to throw a dash of schizophrenia into the mix just to make things fun? Thanks. Really, from the bottom of my heart.

This was absolutely not going into the list of things he was planning on talking to his therapist with.

You know, once he got around to getting a new one.

Eli wasn't going to let this issue get the best of him. He pulled out the biggest weapon in his arsenal—his favorite language app. The next two hours were devoted to learning grammar patterns, practicing kanji, and leaving absolutely no space for anything else to shove its way through the cracks of his mind.

He barely noticed as night fell. He was so immersed in the world of words and symbols that the growling of his stomach was a distant, ignorable thing, and the dark room around him only served to cocoon him further into his studies.

So, when the door opened abruptly, the scream—a very manly shout of surprise—that emerged from him was completely understandable.

At least that was what his roommate told him as he sat next to Eli on his bed, fanning his neck soothingly.

"I think it would help if we got you a desk light that came on automatically at dusk. It might help you stay connected to your body enough to prevent scares like that in the future."

Eli nodded absently. The last thing he wanted to do right now was talk about his issues. No, what he wanted to do was go to the basement and start digging a hole he could move into for the rest of the semester.

But he was an adult now—in theory. So, he pulled up the shopping list on his phone and typed in: Buy timer for lamp.

"Um, it's okay if you want to switch rooms tomorrow. I wouldn't hold it against you."

Jace's face softened. "Why would I want to do that? You're a fellow weeb, we have to stick together!" He slapped the bed next to Eli's leg. "Besides, you have the potential to become an excellent case study. Who knows, maybe I could plan my thesis around you."

Eli let out a small laugh. One he didn't have to fake at all.

He spent the next two days before class officially started going to freshman events and getting all the things he'd forgotten to buy for his new room.

Today, he was at the mall looking for the light Jace had suggested. Which didn't explain the full cart in front of him. He'd only come here for one thing. How was he supposed to carry all of this up to his room?

He poked though his cart trying to decide between the NASA hoodie and the Dragonball Z button-up when he realized he'd crashed into something.

No, not something. Some*one*.

He looked up . . . and then looked up a bit more. Jesus, this guy was tall.

"Ack! I'm so sorry!" Eli bowed repeatedly, having picked up the gesture from his touch aversion and too much anime. "Are you okay? You came from out of nowhere!"

When his victim bowed back, Eli realized he recognized him. "You're Haruka!"

"I am." Almond-shaped eyes narrowed appraisingly as he took Eli in. "And I didn't come from out of nowhere. I was standing here, minding my own business, until you barreled into me."

"I'm sorry, I . . . wait, were you watching me come towards you? Why didn't you move out of the way?"

"I wanted to see what would happen. I didn't believe someone would be stupid enough to do that." Haruka smiled ruefully.

"Well . . . I . . . hey!" Eli felt his ears burn, and he fought the impulse to cover them. "I've got a lot going on right now, and—"

"Didn't ask for an explanation." Haruka was already turning to walk away, but he paused and looked back. "Watch where you're going next time, chibisuke."

"I'm not short!" Eli's ears were joined by the rest of his face, only it wasn't embarrassment anymore. Yes, he was on the small side, but that didn't mean people had to go and point it out. "I mean, that's not my name."

But Haruka had already begun to walk away. "Didn't ask. Don't care." He threw over his shoulder as he went.

Eli was so busy wanting to curl up in a ball and die that he failed to notice Haruka turning back to look at him once more before disappearing down an aisle.

CHAPTER 3
ELI

Somehow, Eli had managed to pare down his purchases to two large bags. He wasn't made to let go of the large, fluffy blue pillow he'd discovered, which meant he was going to have to endure the dirty looks he got for taking up more than his fair share of the elevator. *So be it, lady giving me the stink eye. My sister does it way better than you could ever dream of.*

Since he was thinking of Juniper . . .

He juggled his bags around until he could use his phone to drop his sister a gif of a cartoon zombie dog rolling its eyes.

He smiled when she immediately sent him one of a busty, blonde anime girl giving the camera the finger. Then he saw the time and cursed. He was going to be late for his faculty event!

He raced down the hall to his room, staying only long enough to fling his purchases in the general direction of his bed before legging it to the center of campus.

He screeched to a stop outside the classroom where all the freshmen were gathered and did his best to make himself look like he wasn't seconds from asphyxiation. Once he looked as normal as he knew how, he went inside and glanced around the room.

Alice was here! He hadn't seen her or Nate since they'd rescued him from death by stampede, and he'd been kicking himself for not exchanging phone numbers.

He'd spent the past two days wondering if they were just being nice when they'd met, or if they'd also gotten the same *instant friend* feeling Eli had.

Alice spotted him, and her eyes lit up. "Eli! We saved you a seat!" She waved her hand energetically enough that Nate, who was sitting beside her, had to dodge to keep from losing an eye.

Eli hurried to the seat she pointed to. "Nate, what are you doing here? I thought you were a Bio major?"

Nate shrugged. "I already finished my faculty events, so I thought I'd keep this loser company."

"Please, he wanted to see you as much as I did. I can't believe we didn't exchange numbers. Here, call yourself, I'm not letting you get away again."

Eli took the pink and black phone shoved under his nose and dialed his number before handing it back.

A silver phone appeared on his desk. "You might as well do mine too," Nate said in a bored tone.

While Eli did the same thing to Nate's phone, Alice said, "Please, Nate, you've talked about Eli at least as much as I have." She put on a much deeper baritone voice than Eli could have managed and made her eyes large and dreamy. "Oh Alice, do you think he likes Sword Art Online as much as we do? Because if he does, we could all watch it together!"

"I do, actually. It reminds me of an episode of this older

anime I watched once called *Tsubasa* where the characters got sucked into a virtual world—"

"He watches CLAMP, Nate. He's mine now." Alice went to grab Eli's arm but stopped just shy of touching and switched to squeezing his backpack instead.

She'd remembered not to touch him and had done it without making a big deal about it. Something inside Eli glowed warmly. For just a second, it eclipsed the ever-present emptiness inside.

Shortly, several teachers filed in and introduced the room to the various department heads in the program. Each took turns explaining how the first few weeks would go for various language majors.

Since Eli was specializing in more than one language, his course load was going to be heavy. Just the way he liked it.

"I can't believe you, Eli." Alice groaned dramatically. "Japanese is going to be hard enough as it is, why would you add more languages? Are you insane?"

"Well, yes, actually, but that doesn't have anything to do with this. I just really have an affinity with learning languages."

"Why are all of them from Asia? I mean, you are very, um . . ."

"White?" Eli wasn't just white. He was *burst into flames after seconds in the sun* white—something his sister, who'd been blessed by the Cherokee genes from their dad, constantly teased him over. "I know, but there's just something about Japan that calls to me. I can't explain it. I've been into Japanese culture since I was little. I guess it was a gateway drug because eventually I fell in love with several other countries in Asia as well."

It was one of the things Eli didn't peer too deeply into. He tried not to look a good coping mechanism in the mouth. Especially one he might be able to make a career out of.

"Eli, do you know that guy over there?" Nate asked in a low voice as he pointed to a blond student scrolling through his phone.

"No, why?"

"Because he keeps looking at you."

Outwardly, Eli smiled and shrugged, but inwardly he cringed. Then he took a deep breath. He was probably overreacting. He was probably, definitely overreacting. Just because he'd had a few mishaps in the past didn't mean the phenomenon would follow him here.

A shadow fell over Eli's desk.

"Excuse me." The blond was smiling down at him in a friendly way. "Are you doing anything tonight? Because some of my friends are having a party and they asked me to invite people." The boy put a hand on each side of Eli's desk, boxing him in. "Your friends can come too."

Nope. Not an overreaction. The Thing had definitely followed him.

Eli wasn't a particularly impressive individual—as far as he could tell. Nothing about his looks, or abilities should have singled him out in a crowd, but for some reason, wherever he went, he had a habit of drawing unwanted attention. Since he'd hit puberty, he'd been the confused recipient of constant offers from strangers to hang out, meet up, have coffee, etc. But due to the Incident, Eli couldn't bring himself to accept.

In fact, one of the main reasons he was so drawn to Alice and Nate was that they hadn't invited him anywhere after they'd met. Plus, they'd seemed to pick up on his no-touching thing super quick, which was incredibly rare.

They'd also asked him all about himself and seemed genuinely interested in what he'd had to say. People under the influence of the Thing rarely wanted to know anything about him other than his number and when they could meet up.

Eli stood up and shoved his folder into his backpack. "I'm sorry, I have plans." Avoiding the eyes of the blond boy, he hurried out of the room.

Heedless that he'd abandoned the event before it finished, Eli didn't stop running until he'd left the building far behind.

In the afternoon, he set out for his appointment with his advisor, this time armed with an oversized hoodie and sunglasses. He'd found the effects of the Thing could be mitigated if he covered up enough. It was easier to do when it was cold outside.

It was not cold today. No, it was a scorching 93 degrees outside, and the only concession he could make to the weather was that he'd picked a white hoodie instead of a black one.

He only remembered at the last second to take down his hood before the meeting with his advisor. He'd have a better chance of convincing her to give him his way if he didn't come off looking like someone hiding from the paparazzi.

He knocked on the doorframe of the cluttered, but cheerful office. "Hi, I'm Eli, your three o'clock appointment."

A middle-aged woman with long auburn curls stood and waved him inside, making the dozen bracelets on her wrist jingle. She reached out a hand bearing a ring on each finger. "Nice to meet you, Eli. I'm Beth."

Eli only paused for a second before taking the woman's hand in a brief handshake.

Wrongwrongwrong.

Ugh. Even braced for it, he couldn't get used to the feeling of touching someone he didn't know.

Eli put on his best business smile. "Nice to meet you too."

"I'm sorry to call you here the day before classes start, but I couldn't help it. When I went over your course schedule, I found a huge mistake."

There was no mistake. And it was Eli's job to convince her of it.

"If you looked at it at all, you must have been freaking out over it, but don't worry, I'm here to help."

"Help me with what?" Business smile stayed firmly in place.

Beth frowned at her computer and tilted the screen toward Eli. "Look at your course load. It's twice what it should be. If you tried to do it all, you'd be burned out after a semester."

"It's okay, I planned it that way."

"You—wait, you planned to burn yourself out?"

Eli couldn't help it, he laughed. "No, of course not. What I meant was that I planned my courses myself. I researched the best way to get the most out of my time here."

Beth's eyebrows were almost touching at this point. It wasn't the best sign. "Eli, I understand you're a scholarship student, but you don't need to push yourself this hard in order to be able stay. I've seen your test scores. You'll still be eligible for a full ride with a lighter course load."

Eli barely suppressed a groan. Why was he so bad at communicating with people? Especially ones who had the power to make decisions about his life. He needed his advisor on board with his plan. Otherwise, his life was about to get much harder.

Time to try again.

"I don't think I've made myself clear here. What I'm trying to say is that I'm planning on testing out of most of these classes in the first week. I've been studying the languages in my major for years, some more than others, but I believe I'll be able to test out of all the 101 classes and most of the 102 classes as well."

Beth's eyebrows softened, and she leaned forward in her seat. Eli took this as an invitation to continue.

"It's my intention to move to all second and third-year language courses by the spring semester. In order to do that, I have to prove to my teachers I am proficient enough in each language to do so."

"I don't understand. Why didn't you arrange this with the school beforehand?"

"I tried, but no one seemed to understand what I was trying to do." He'd spent weeks on the phone getting shuffled from department to department—often being sent back to the same person who'd recommended him to the current one, trying to find someone who could help him skip this stage, but after two rounds of departmental musical chairs, he'd finally found someone who suggested he try a self-guided course of study. After a flurry of research, Eli had finally managed to cobble together his own Build-A-Bear style major. Complete with all the bells, whistles, and hoops he'd have to navigate his way through.

"I like your confidence, but I'm not convinced you are ready for this—that anyone is ready for this much work.

Learning five languages and their cultures in four years is a monumental challenge, even by someone with your potential. I'd be remiss if I signed off on this without some reassurance."

There.

Eli had been ready for this. Had been hoping for it, even.

"Then let me give you some. Let me prove to you I can do this." All he needed was to get into the classes to be able to show his teachers he could test out of them.

"How are you planning on doing that?"

"Pick one of the languages from my schedule. Any of them. Then find a website in one of those languages and have me look at it. If I can't understand at least thirty percent of what's on the page, I'll let you trim some of my classes."

Beth studied him for a moment then nodded. "Thirty percent, bare minimum."

She busied herself at her computer while Eli waited—mostly—patiently. Finally, she said, "I used Google translate to tell me what's on here, so I'll know if you're bullshitting me or not."

She turned the monitor and displayed the government tourist page for Hokkaido, Japan.

Eli was just—only just—barely able to hold in a squee of joy. It was easily his best language after English.

Beth had conceded only after Eli had translated half of the Hokkaido Tourist website, as well as half of a Thai fluff piece on cats, most of a Vietnamese recipe for Pho cuon (which he totally cheated at because he'd researched it for his sister to make less than three weeks ago and was able to guess at what it said), and an article in Hindi on Holi—a festival in India—that he thought he'd mangled, but Beth had seemed impressed enough.

Now, Eli was practically bouncing through campus, high on his success. He officially had a shot at not being stuck in college for the next six years, which was great because his savings would never hold out that long.

Now he wanted to celebrate.

He could do something totally crazy like text Alice and Nate. Or he could be a massive dork and go buy himself ice cream and eat it alone like a schmuck.

His hand hovered over his phone forever before he finally sent off two quick texts and then shoved his phone back in his pocket like he'd done something illegal and wanted to hide the evidence.

He wandered by a small ornamental pond and agonized for about nine thousand years until his phone buzzed twice.

When he opened his phone, he saw that he'd only been waiting for four minutes before getting a group text from his new friends.

mAlice: Yes, please! Meet us at the duck ASAP!

NatetheGreat: She means the bronze statue in front of the big pond.

He sent back a thumbs up and did his very best not to skip all the way to said duck.

CHAPTER 4
ELI

The first few days of class went by in a blur as Eli systematically worked his way through his teachers, wheedling and cajoling his way into testing out of each class. So far, he had three out of five teachers on board.

Somehow, he had fallen into the pattern of collapsing into an exhausted, but optimistic, pile of goo next to Alice and Nate as they ate lunch every day. Sometimes he even managed to find the energy to eat with them.

On day three, he discovered he and Alice were both in the same History of Japanese Religion class, and the two sat in the back rating various Buddhist priests on hotness using a completely arbitrary scale.

Juniper would have loved it.

After class, Nate met them outside and demanded they follow him to his dorm to have lunch. Eli was still struggling to juggle his class syllabus into his backpack when it happened again.

:*Why is it always my right shoe that gets soaked? This happens every day.*:

Eli stumbled and nearly spilled the contents of his bag across the hallway, but at the last second, he managed a—relatively—graceful save.

:*Beautiful moron . . .*:

"Eli . . . hey, Eli!" A delicate hand with intricate nail polish designs in shades of pink and blue waved at him from the doorway as Alice tried to get his attention. "Are you coming?"

"Sorry, just having fine motor control issues."

"Well, hurry up, I need you to defend my virtue if people find out I went to this dork's room alone."

"Um . . ." Eli looked down at himself, then back at Alice who easily topped him by two inches and may or may not have had more muscle mass as well. Petite was the word his mother often used to describe him. Juniper called him travel-sized. He liked to claim he was densely packed for maximum power—on days he was feeling particularly self-delusional.

He gave her a feeble smile in response.

"Don't tease him, I think he's cute." A new voice joined in, followed by a heavy arm over Eli's shoulders.

Wrongwrongwrong . . .

His face froze into a panicked half-smile as he took in the stranger.

He was taller than Nate by an inch and had messy, light brown hair. If Eli wasn't busy trying to figure out how to politely escape back to his room, he might have called the effect charming.

"Eli's having a stressful day, if you need cuddles, go for Nate." Alice said gaily and smoothly lifted the newcomer's arm away from Eli and dropped it onto Nate's shoulder instead.

"Sorry, Eli. The name's Sam." The boy stretched out a hand.

Eli looked at it, feeling a bit like he was being handed an old, dead fish. This was normal. Normal people shook hands. Eli shook hands, even. On good days though. Not after having another brush with what he had started to call the Voice. Just as he was about to suck it up and shake the outstretched hand, Nate intervened, knocking it away.

"If there isn't food in that hand, we aren't interested. We're starving man, you're more likely to pull that thing back as a bloody stump." Nate laughed and pulled on Alice's arm. "Come on, folks. My stomach waits for no one."

Eli bowed at Sam because he watched way more anime than was normal, (but honestly, bowing was such a graceful, noninvasive way to greet people, and it really should catch on in Massachusetts if people were smart) then he turned and hurried after his friends, secretly marveling at how smoothly they'd helped him.

He tended to have mixed results with his touch aversion, ranging anywhere from narrowly escaping a hug with only mild awkwardness to being full-on tackle hugged and smiling outwardly while silently screaming inside.

"Thanks," he said once he'd caught up to his friends. "It's not that I don't like people, I just don't deal well with touching."

Alice said, "Is this all the time? Or is it first week stress?" Her face showed nothing but mild curiosity.

"The stress makes it worse, but . . ." He really didn't want to finish. Exposing his stupid issues to the first nice people he'd met wasn't his favorite idea, but they were friends now. Didn't that mean they had a right to know? "On a regular basis I feel that way all the time, but it's manageable. It's just ramped up right now."

"Any touch? Or just hugging?" Nate's face was calm. Neutral. Giving Eli no clue how the guy was feeling.

"I can touch other people, but, well, it feels wrong. Like, there's something under my skin that activates and says, *Intruder Alert! Man your battle stations!* If I know someone very well, I barely notice, but if I don't know the person, it's pretty unpleasant."

Nate nodded. "Good to know. I'm allergic to shrimp, like deathly. So, if you see me about to eat some, you should stop me." He mimed smacking something imaginary out of his hand. "And Alice doesn't talk to her dad. Ever. So, if a guy comes up to you claiming to be her dad, call me. I'll take care of it."

Alice's sunshine smile dimmed, but she gave Eli a thumbs up. "Everyone's got quirks. Our job is to find friends to help us deal with them. Lucky for you, we happen to have an opening in our group." Her smile turned up to full power leaving Eli a little dazzled.

"That's . . ." Eli choked on his words, and he blinked his stinging eyes rapidly.

Alice continued to smile, and Nate waved, encouraging him to come up the stairs to his dorm.

"I guess I could fit you two into my schedule," he managed to say and summoned up a watery smile.

"Air hug!" Alice mimed wrapping her arms around Eli, and he laughed.

"If the drama is over, I am literally dying of starvation here. Please, just follow me before I keel over."

"Fine, you emotionally stunted freak." Alice sailed up the stairs and beat Nate through the front door, leaving Eli to catch up.

Once ensconced in Nate's messy room, Eli found himself surrounded by a mountain of food, most of which he'd never seen. He couldn't wait to try everything.

"This is all courtesy of my abuelita. She's convinced I am going to starve to death and has no idea just how tiny my fridge is here. So, if you like something, take it home with you. Seriously, you'd be doing me a favor." Nate shoved a Tupperware container into Eli's hands. It held something that looked a bit like vanilla pudding with caramel on top.

Eli tore the top off and accepted the spoon Nate poked in his direction. He dug in and it tasted . . . Damn. He wrapped himself around the container and narrowed his eyes at the room. "I hope neither of you were planning on having any of this."

The room exploded with laughter.

"Oh yes, we're definitely keeping this one." Alice wiped tears of mirth from her eyes. "Don't worry, Eli. I've had Abuelita's flan many times. That one is all yours."

Eli nodded and said, through a mouthful of heaven, "Is she single?"

It might have been Eli's imagination, but there seem to be a pause in the room before Nate said, "Sorry, man. My abuelo could crush you without even noticing. He's even crazier about her cooking."

"Ah well . . ."

"Don't worry, Eli. If you're on the hunt, we'll find someone for you. What's your type?"

Eli was, in fact, not on the hunt—for grandmothers, or anyone, but he played along.

"Well, a good cook is a definite must." Eli searched through the containers until he found tamales. Jackpot. "Nice is also a plus."

"What about . . . physical features?" Alice asked

nonchalantly. Focusing completely on the plate of sausages Nate had just shoved at her.

"I don't really have a physical type, to be honest. I haven't really dated much." Or at all. Ever. And if he was very lucky, he would extend that into the rest of forever.

"But what about—"

"Oh, quit beating around the bush, Alice. Eli, she wants to know if you're a member of the Alphabet Mafia." Nate waved a forkful of fried rice at Alice. "She wants someone to dye their hair pink with her, and she figures if you're gay or bi, she's got a shot. I'm sure as hell not doing it."

It was one of the most unique ways he'd been asked that question, that was for certain. And definitely one of the more polite.

"But you don't have to answer her just because her nosy ass is too cheap to go to a salon."

"No, it's okay. I just . . ." He trailed off. He never knew how to answer this question.

"If you're worried about what I think, I have two moms. I'm an ally if I know what's good for me." Nate winked.

"Is it okay to answer that I'm not anything?"

"Are you ace? Asexual, I mean. It means not attracted to any gender."

"I don't really know." The answer was more complicated than that, but he felt it was good enough for brand new friends. "Is that okay?"

"It's more than okay, it's how you feel! That means it's perfect." Alice gave him another air hug, and this time he awkwardly returned it.

"Thanks." And he meant it. Other than Juniper, until now, this conversation had never gone so well.

His mom was convinced he was a late bloomer. Maybe he was, but since he didn't particularly care about dating, he didn't bother with worrying about it. Everyone else's opinion was slotted into his mental *Other People's Problems* file.

Any other reaction was courting the bad place. And that wasn't conducive to a happy Eli.

"Well, I can't let you dye my hair, but I have experience dying my sister's hair. I can definitely help."

"Wait, what about the touch thing? Will you be okay?"

"Since I'll be expecting it, and I know you, it should be okay." He politely left off the part about wearing gloves and only touching her hair being another useful element to the equation. It just seemed nicer not to mention.

"Yay!" She flung up her hands, unfortunately each filled with an éclair. Both got squashed when they hit opposite ends of the rooms.

"Alice!"

"I'm cleaning it up!" Alice darted away, napkin in hand to deal with the fallout of her outburst. "But really, Eli, you should rethink the pink hair idea. Everyone will know were friends!"

Eli laughed. "Have you seen me? If you add pink hair to this, I'll become everyone's favorite stuffed animal. Hard Pass."

Alice gave him the once over. "You do have a point. Every gay man within three miles would come after you like a starving beast."

"Thanks . . ."

"Well, if you do end up liking guys, girls, or anyone in between, let me know, and we'll help you get them."

"Not likely but appreciated." Even though his stomach was already stuffed to the brim, Eli continued to nibble on his tamale, so he didn't have to talk anymore.

Find accepting friend group at school? Check.

CHAPTER 5
ELI

Cold! Way too cold!:

Eli was jolted out of his dreams by the sensation of being drenched in ice water.

"What the actual fuck?" He was on his feet now, shivering from the cold. He shook himself to get some of the water off, but he was . . . bone dry?

"What's wrong?" The muffled voice of his roommate emerged from the pile of blankets Jace had buried himself in.

Eli looked at the time and saw it was five minutes to six.

"Nothing, man. Go back to sleep."

It was one thing for the Voice to harass him day in and day out, but it had another thing coming if it thought it was going to mess with his roommate too.

Jace was the best roommate Eli could have ever hoped for. He was gone for most of the day, quiet when he was there, and relatively neat. And he was super cool about all of Eli's little quirks. He was so great that Eli was officially terrified of meeting any new people, because the law of averages meant they were bound to be horrible.

A shiver went through him, causing goosebumps to race up his arms. Why the hell was he so cold?

He grabbed a towel and his bath accessories from the closet and made for the shower. He wasn't getting back to sleep now, and it was a great way to warm up.

However, when he got to the shower room it was out of order. He worried at his bottom lip with his teeth. Maybe he could try a different floor?

The one under him was only for girls, so he tried the one below that.

Steam billowed out of the partially opened door.

Score.

He was so excited, he nearly ran head on into a wall of towel-wrapped muscle. His arms windmilled frantically as he fought not to plow face first into a very bare chest. Once he steadied himself, he was about to issue an apology when a drop of water caught his eye as it leisurely made its way down golden skin.

"I have eyes, you know," a painfully familiar voice said.

Eli swallowed and looked up.

It was Haruka.

"Sorry! My shower's broken, and I was just so happy to see this one wasn't. I didn't think—"

Haruka held up a hand to stall Eli's apology. "I don't need your life story. I need pants."

Eli held his change of clothes tightly to his chest. "Well, you can't have mine."

"I don't want your pants, they wouldn't make it halfway up my legs, chibisuke." Mahogany eyes glinted in amusement. "What I want is for you to get out of my way, so I can go get my own."

Face burning, Eli realized he was blocking the doorway. He stepped aside, plastering himself against the wall so

Haruka wouldn't accidentally brush against him on his way by. "Bring your clothes with you next time then."

Haruka paused, then turned to face Eli. "If it bothers you that much, then don't look."

"It-it doesn't bother me!"

An elegant eyebrow rose. "So, you like looking then?"

A sad, strangled sound was the only thing Eli was able to produce in response. How badly would his no-touching thing punish him for kicking a mostly naked stranger?

"You wish!" He finally managed.

Haruka leaned into Eli's personal space with an evil look in his eye.

Eli held his breath and did his very best to squish himself through the wall behind him. His heart was beating so hard Eli thought it was possible it might actually break through the wall all on its own.

Haruka laughed and pulled away. "You're too easy." He raised a hand to ruffle Eli's hair but stopped when Eli jerked away.

"I'm not a pet."

Haruka shrugged and turned to go. "Don't use the first shower, chibisuke. It's busted."

"Thanks . . . I mean, I'm not short!"

The low rumble of Haruka's laughter sounded down the hallway long after he was out of Eli's sight.

Late late late! He was so late!

It wasn't Eli's fault all the buildings on this side of campus looked the same. He'd been inside three before he'd finally found the right one.

And now he was late for his first geometry class. He

barely glanced at the room number as he scurried into the room and squeezed himself into the first free seat in the back.

He opened his bag and pulled out a notebook, doing his best to avoid the teacher's eye as she stared him down for daring to interrupt her class.

"You'll have to share with your neighbor. I'm out of syllabi now." The edge to her voice let Eli fill in the, *If you'd been on time, maybe you would have gotten one*, she'd left out.

He turned to his neighbor, and, to his horror, it was Haruka giving him a smug smile. Eli decided he'd let hell freeze over before he asked to share anything with him.

"Early risers usually tend to be on time," Haruka whispered.

"I don't usually get up that early." Eli ground out tersely.

"Why the special occasion this morning? Was it just to see me?"

Eli snorted and ignored him. For the next few minutes, he used all his compartmentalizing powers on paying attention to the teacher. Since he'd missed the beginning of class, he didn't get to hear the usual introductory speech. The teacher—who's name he'd also missed—had decided to dive right into the curriculum, and Eli already felt lost. This was a 101 class. Why was did he feel so out of his league?

And what was Haruka doing here? According to Alice, he was a junior. He should be well past 101 courses at this point.

His eye fell on the pen his neighbor was rhythmically tapping on his denim-covered knee.

"At least you're wearing more clothes than you were this morning."

The pen paused.

Shit. Had he just said that out loud?

Reluctantly, Eli raised his eyes to Haruka's face and then immediately wished he hadn't. The man had the devil in his eyes.

"I knew you missed me." The slow smile creeping across Haruka's stupidly attractive face forced Eli to look away.

"Who would miss you?" Eli muttered to his desk.

"I know it's the first day, but I want to you pull out *Deductive Geometry* so we can go over chapter one before next week," the still-nameless teacher said. Eli was really going to have to learn her name before the end of class.

Wait. *Deductive Geometry*? He only had *Geometry: A Comprehensive Course*. Fuck, he was going to have to hit the campus store immediately after class, but until then . . .

Apparently, hell was about to freeze over.

"Um." Eli ventured.

Haruka didn't respond, but something about his body language told Eli he was listening.

"I don't have the book with me today."

Haruka narrowed his eyes and sat back in his seat. "So, you were late, need to share the syllabus, and the textbook —" He held up a hand and was ticking off each transgression on his fingers as he went. "Do you want me to take tests for you, too, while I'm at it?"

Eli scowled, and for some ungodly reason this prompted Haruka to smile. One that actually reached his unfairly pretty eyes this time.

"Are you going to share, or do I need to move and find someone else to partner with?"

In response, Haruka scooted his desk over until it was touching Eli's.

They both bent their heads over the book as the teacher went over the material. While Eli fought to follow along, the strangest sensation crept over him—he was warm and tingly, and it felt good. Really, insanely good. He started to sink into it until he realized the warmth was Haruka's body heat.

That was when it finally dawned on him exactly how physically close they were.

Adrenaline coursed through him as he waited for his body's defense systems to kick in and punish him for getting too close to another person. But nothing happened. Maybe it was because they weren't actually touching?

Just to be safe, Eli put several inches of space between them. Haruka noticed and raised an eyebrow at him but didn't say anything.

"Is it just me, or is this a little hard to follow?" He finally asked.

"You're able to follow it?" Haruka asked, faint surprise lacing his tone.

"Well, yes, but it's making my head hurt."

Haruka leaned closer and gave him a measuring look.

When the teacher finished her explanation and told everyone to split in pairs, it only made sense to stay with Haruka since they were already sharing a book. As it turned out, his partner was actually useful. He broke down difficult problems in a way that made perfect sense to Eli. Once he was able to understand the basis of the formula he was supposed to be using, he sailed through the rest of the work, finishing well before the rest of the class, aside from Haruka.

His paper was snatched out from under his hand. "Hey!"

"Partners check each other's work." Haruka placed his

own notebook in front of Eli.

The handwriting was neat, almost like it had been printed from a computer rather than written by hand. Eli went through each problem but couldn't find any mistakes. Instead, he saw one place where he'd gone wrong on his own work. At least he could fix it when he got his paper back.

"Wow."

"I know, I got number 10 wrong, but I know how to fix it now."

"No, I mean, wow, I can't believe you got any of these right, considering you're in the wrong class. You even got the extra credit one . . ." Haruka trailed off as he frowned at Eli's paper.

It took a moment for what Haruka said to sink in. "Wha—wrong class? What do you mean, wrong class?"

"I'm pretty sure you're supposed to be across the hall in Geo 101. This is 209, baka."

Being called an idiot in Japanese went right over his head as the blood drained from Eli's face. "I'm in the wrong room? I missed my first class?" Where had all the air in the room gone? An iron clamp began to tighten around his chest. "Why didn't you tell me?"

"I wanted to see your face when you realized. I thought you'd notice right away when the material was introduced, but you managed to keep up." Haruka leaned forward. "Are you okay? You don't look good." He reached out a hand to Eli's forehead.

Hastily, Eli scooted his desk away, hating the loud, attention-grabbing screech it made as it moved across the floor. "Please . . . don't touch." He choked out. Being touched by a stranger was the last thing he needed right now.

He couldn't miss his first class. He was a scholarship student. He couldn't miss any classes, ever. And if he did, it couldn't be over a stupid thing like going to the wrong class. What if he got sick later and needed to take a sick day? The iron clamp around his chest tightened another notch.

"Hey," Haruka's voice grew soft. "You're okay. It's okay. You didn't do anything wrong. Just breathe."

Just breathe, huh? Easy enough to say, less easy to do at the moment. It took everything Eli had to suck in a thin, shuddering breath.

"There you go, just like that. Good job."

While Eli worked on breathing, he tried to console himself with the fact that he wasn't going to need to worry about Haruka irritating him anymore. After this, the man was likely to turn and run the next time he saw him.

Time seemed to pause as he focused on taking in another breath of air while he listened to Haruka's deep, soothing voice.

As his breathing began to normalize, the rest of the world started to filter into to his consciousness. At some point, class had ended and everyone in the room had left, leaving him and Haruka alone in the room.

"Feeling better?" Haruka had scooted his desk back from Eli's, but he was turned in his seat, leaning toward Eli.

It didn't feel intrusive. It felt protective.

What a stupid thought. No one was here to protect Eli.

He'd chosen a to go to a college that was hours from home, so he could prove he could take care of himself. So his mom could stop looking at him with sad eyes. So his sister would stop overprotecting him and verbally dancing around the Incident. Some days it seemed like everything she said was deliberately designed to not reference it. How exhausting that must be for her.

He sat up and pulled himself together. Pulled the mantle of normality around himself. Then he turned to look at Haruka and smiled. It was his best smile. It was his, *hey, anything you saw just now couldn't possibly be as bad as you thought it was if I can look at you like this now* smile.

"Yes, much better, thanks." He took his notebook and placed it calmly and meticulously back into his bag, making sure it went in the right spot. One thing at a time, with no focus on the past or the future. All he needed to do was the next right thing and then the next so he could get the hell out of here and lick his wounds in peace.

When he stood, Haruka stood too, towering over him, his face serious and not looking remotely like he bought Eli's act.

He might need convincing to let Eli leave here alone—or perhaps not. Eli was nothing to Haruka. Just an annoying kid who'd slammed a shopping cart into him and irritated him during a class.

Eli considered the situation and what he knew of the man. He was smart enough to be put on stage during orientation, but self-absorbed enough to all but ignore the responsibility once he got up there. His expensive clothes and painfully good looks gave more evidence to Eli's theory of Haruka being self-absorbed.

He should be fairly simple to shake. Especially if Eli got clingy.

He was revolted at the very idea. Even if there was some tiny part of him suggesting that not being alone right now would be an excellent idea. Even if there was another, louder part of him that kept remembering how warm Haruka had felt when they were so close earlier.

CHAPTER 6
HARUKA

The beautiful moron was about to bolt. It was as obvious as the panic attack the poor idiot had been suffering through.

Only he wasn't actually an idiot, was he?

The first time Haruka saw Eli, he'd been surrounded by a flock of geese. He'd watched in amazement as the boy sat eating a sandwich, surrounded by a swarm of birds that were clearly about to attack. When he'd finally looked up, Haruka was struck by enormous turquoise eyes that had gone from studious to alarmed between one breath and the next.

Any smart person would have thrown their food and made a run for it, but instead, the kid stuffed his sandwich in his mouth and started packing up his things. He appeared to be in a hurry, but not on the level of *about to be torn apart by wild birds*. It was more like he was trying to dodge a clingy girlfriend.

Haruka had been torn. Should he help the idiot out? Survival of the fittest was a thing for a reason and right now it looked like the only thing the boy had been blessed with was a lovely face. And he wasn't going to get to keep it much longer if someone didn't do something.

"Eliiiiiiiiii!" A voice sounded in the distance.

The boy's shoulders stiffened, and he abandoned trying to put his things away neatly. Instead, he grabbed everything in a big pile and ran, right through a narrow opening in the flock of hungry geese, right past Haruka, and in the opposite direction of the guy shouting his name, now running down the hill startling the flock into taking flight.

The guy got to the bottom of the hill and looked around, trying to find his prey. Haruka pointed in the opposite direction Eli had run.

"Thanks!" The guy said and ran off in that direction.

Something silver glinted in the grass, and Haruka went to investigate. It was a pen that had an engraving on one side. It read: *Happy 18th Birthday, Eli!*

Haruka slipped it into his pocket.

The boy had never even noticed he'd been moments from getting his ass kicked by a flock of birds.

The next time Haruka saw him, it had been at the store. A commotion had caught his attention, and he watched as a dark-haired boy plowed through an aisle of people, causing several to dive out of his way. The entire time, the boy never looked up from the cart he was rummaging through as he walked.

As he got closer, Haruka was certain it was the goose boy from earlier.

Haruka couldn't help himself. He purposefully planted himself in the boy's path, wondering if he would actually run him down, or if he would come back to reality in time to stop.

Either way, Haruka would get a chance to see those striking eyes again.

When the cart crashed into him, Haruka barely felt it. The boy was too small to do any real damage. But he did get to see those eyes again.

It had been worth it to watch them go from dreamy, to shocked, to angry as Haruka teased him. The boy's eyes actually shifted color as his mood changed. They went from light turquoise to sky blue, until settling on a stormy ocean blue.

As Haruka drove back to campus, it occurred to him that he should have given the boy his pen back. It didn't, however, occur to him to wonder why he was carrying it around everywhere he went.

Over the next few days, Haruka had watched as the boy stumbled, tripped, and generally half-assed his way through campus. It really was a wonder the boy was still alive. And it was even more of a wonder that Haruka thought about him at all.

Haruka wasn't here to make friends. He was here to find something. And to get a stellar education. As long as he could ignore certain unwanted interruptions, he would be perfectly happy with his current situation and the small number of people who already hounded his day-to-day life.

But, for some reason, he couldn't ignore the enigmatic eyes of the campus moron.

Then his friend Bryan had not-so-casually told him about the kid whose entrance exam scores had blown Haruka's out of the water.

It wasn't that he cared. It wasn't as if it really mattered. Except . . . those scores had meant something to Haruka. They been his ticket out of the ridiculous circus back in Osaka his aunt kept trying to drag him into. They were proof he was meant to be more than a lapdog.

So he hadn't been able to stop himself from finding out

who had outscored him. He turned up the name Eli Talosa. It could have been a coincidence. He wasn't social enough to be able tell if Eli was a common name in America.

It wasn't too difficult to get a face to put with the name. He wondered if he should have been more surprised to see those vivid, mercurial eyes he'd gotten to know over the past week.

That idiot—that beautiful, spacey, one-person wrecking team—was the one who beat his entrance scores? It didn't bear thinking about.

So, why couldn't he stop thinking about it?

Currently, he was face to face with the idiot in question, and the kid was clearly not stupid. He may have watched the boy tie his own shoe to his backpack strap, but Eli had managed to stumble into an advanced math class he'd been expecting to be a 101 course and then not only followed along, but was actually able to keep up with Haruka, who was always at the top of every class he was in.

The last thing Haruka wanted right now was for the boy to run. Not when he'd just made things interesting.

Especially when the fake smile Eli was wearing was causing something deep inside Haruka to stir unpleasantly.

"You should be in this class."

Long, dark lashes blinked in confusion. "I think we've already established I shouldn't."

"You kept up better than most of the other students here. You'll be wasted in a 101 class."

Eli didn't look like he was about to run anymore. Now he looked tired—and annoyed. Haruka could work with that. It was far better than the lost child expression he'd had moments before.

"I don't need a challenging class right now—especially

in geometry. I'm in the language department, no one cares what math classes I take."

Which was a fair point, except . . . Haruka wanted to be in a class with him now. He wanted an excuse to watch Eli closely. Maybe then he could figure out what secrets those expressive eyes held. Then he could get on with his life and go back to being the center of his own attention again. Otherwise, his agenda might get sidelined, and that wasn't an option.

"Maybe, but an advanced math course could be the difference between getting your dream job and getting stuck with whatever you can find."

Eli bit his lip and tugged on his hoodie strings. "I don't know . . ."

"Haru! There you are, man. I was waiting outside forever. Did you forget our study group?" Bryan, his self-proclaimed best friend, burst into the room on a wave of energy.

Without thinking, Haruka put himself between his friend and Eli. "Just give me a second, Bryan." Haruka turned back to Eli to see him frowning at his phone. He reached out and plucked it out of the boy's hands.

"Hey!"

Haruka ignored him and looked at the screen. Eli had been texting with someone named Berry who seemed very concerned about whether Eli had eaten enough today.

He could see there were only three other people Eli texted with and one of them was named Mom. Haruka's mouth softened into a small smile. He opened up a new message window and sent his own number a quick text. Then he handed the phone back to Eli.

"If you decide to switch classes, let me know and I'll help you get in. Professor Burke likes me."

"I didn't ask—" Eli sputtered, turning a brilliant shade of red. "Why are you so annoying?"

Haruka laughed. The red in the boy's cheeks was much better than the pale, sallow color they been earlier.

"Who's your pretty friend, Haru? Introduce us." Bryan stepped forward and winked at Eli.

Before Haruka had a chance to decide whether to tell his friend to piss off or to simply drag him out of the room, Eli went through another startling transformation. His cheeks went pale, and he pulled his hood up over his hair. He seemed to shrink back into the oversized hoodie, and he looked like he was trying not to be sick.

Something burned inside Haruka's chest. "He's no one," he said, sharply and grabbed Bryan's arm. "Let's get out of here."

He dragged his friend out of the classroom, trying to give the poor, anxious boy some space from whatever it was about Bryan that had triggered him.

"I don't think I've ever seen you smile like that before, Haru." Bryan kept trying to look back into the classroom, but Haruka continued to tow him out of the building with a tight grip on his arm.

"Fuck off."

CHAPTER 7
ELI

"He's no one."

One simple sentence echoed inside Eli's mind as he skulked back to his room. Thank god, he didn't have any more classes today.

He *was* no one. He already knew that. Getting a confirmation of it shouldn't mean anything.

Honestly, he should be glad he was no one to Haruka. The man had done nothing but tease and torment him at every turn. If Eli was no one, then it meant he could slink away gracefully from this whole stupid day. Especially since it was highly likely Haruka would ignore him the next time they ran into each other.

It was better this way. Really.

His hands were shaking as he unlocked the door to his room. He needed something, but he couldn't remember what it was. There was something he did for panic attacks, but his taffy-like brain wasn't letting him focus enough to remember it.

Last time, he'd had friends to redirect his energy, so he hadn't needed—

Eli's eyes landed on his desk where he kept his anxiety meds. That was what he was missing. How could he forget something so simple? He snatched up the bottle and dry-swallowed a pill then plopped down in his desk chair. His desk was tidy and well-organized, so he had plenty of space to lower his head onto it and focus on breathing.

He really needed a distraction, but Alice and Nate were both in class right now and Jace was at the gym.

Actually, working off a bunch of nervous energy sounded perfect right now. Did he dare ask Jace if he could join him?

All he had to do was ask. It was one little thing. Of course, it was one little thing that was now massive because Eli had his nervous system go haywire on him twice in one day.

He knew he'd completely overreacted when Haruka's friend showed up. Chances were good the guy was perfectly harmless, but Eli had been such a bundle of nerves, his already-taxed system had taken it as an attack.

Seriously, he should be grateful for Haruka calling him no one. Eli couldn't have handled any more surprises or socialization at that point.

He wasn't entirely certain he could deal with it right now, but he really needed to burn this energy off. It was definitely a better alternative to sitting alone with his trash fire of a brain.

He sent the text before he could think himself out of it.

Eli: Want a gym buddy?

. . .

SpaceJace: Sure! Get over here man! It'll give me the motivation not to slack off.

Eli continued with his no-thinking policy as he threw on some workout clothes. The light, long-sleeved T-shirt he pulled on might look out of place in the summer, but it would make him feel safe. And that was what mattered.

He slunk his way to the gym, head down, headphones on, blaring K-pop louder than the thoughts in his head.

By the time he made it inside, he was entirely convinced this was a terrible idea and that he should go home immediately for a time out so he could think about what he'd done. Then Jace saw him and waved like a maniac.

"Don't even think about getting out of it, man. Get over here." Jace jogged over and ushered him to the ellipticals.

At first, Eli was self-conscious, but Jace kept up a steady stream of random nonsense that began to soothe Eli enough to get into the zone.

The zone was a nice place. It was a place where movement and music synched up and allowed him to have a lovely state of no-mind. All he had to do was nod or say uh huh to Jace at the correct intervals.

It was exactly what he needed. After thirty minutes on the elliptical, Jace signaled for a break and handed him a bottle of water.

"You want to talk about it?"

Eli considered playing dumb, but Jace had done him a solid by being his gym buddy today. "Missed the first day of my geometry class because I went to the wrong classroom and gave myself a panic attack over it."

"That fucking sucks, man." Jace grimaced.

Eli waited for platitudes, but none were forthcoming.

Just Jace agreeing with him that indeed, he'd gone through a raw deal. It actually allowed Eli the courage to elaborate.

"And then I panicked when someone new tried to introduce themselves to me." Eli smiled just thinking about the absurdity of it.

"The sheer nerve of them," Jace said, deadpanned.

Eli swatted him with his towel. "Right? What were they thinking?"

"I hope you taught them a lesson." Jace smirked.

"I almost threw up on them, so they'll definitely think twice before doing it again."

They both stared at each other and then burst out laughing.

And it was good. It was so, so good to let all the fear and stress and self-loathing go on a wave of laughing his stupid ass off with a friend.

"Jesus." Eli snorted and wiped away tears of mirth. "I swear, next time this happens I'm coming with you to the gym."

"Okay, so now I'm put in the awkward position of wanting you to have frequent attacks, so I'll have a reliable partner."

Eli tilted his head and gazed at his roommate. Jace was acting like he actually wanted Eli around. "Well, I'd hate to make you feel awkward. I suppose I could just come here with you regularly." That sounded normal, right?

Jace's easy smile told Eli he'd nailed it. "What a guy. You're a real giver."

"Jace, what poor soul have you suckered into being your partner today?" A young man with damp, sun-streaked brown hair and a dark tan ambled up to them as he rubbed his head with a towel.

Jace lifted an eyebrow at Eli as if to say, *Is this okay?*

Eli smiled and nodded. He had enough endorphins in him right now for just about anything. Ah, the joyful highs of the bipolar brain.

"This poor soul also happens to be my roommate, god save him."

"You have my sympathies." The man doffed an imaginary hat and held it over his chest soulfully. "I'm Ash—"

"Short for Ashley." Jace injected merrily.

"Because clearly my parents hated me." Ash finished.

Biting back a smile, Eli nodded. "I'm Eli. Nice to meet you." And it was nice, which was downright shocking in and of itself. Maybe college wasn't going to eat him alive after all.

The phone in his pocket buzzed. The screen showed an unknown number and the message:

Unknown: Have you thought about switching classes? –Haruka

Eli covered his face with his hand. But it might just annoy him to death.

Later that night, fluffy black hair poked out from the top of a blanket nest as Eli burrowed in, trying to hide himself from the truth.

He'd scrolled though page after page of advice about how to pad a college transcript. He hated to admit it. Loathed it to the very bottom of his soul, but Haruka had been right. Having an amazing GPA was a must—obviously

—but every advanced class he took would be another feather in his cap. And if he wanted to work for the UN, he was going to need to stand out. Eli thought he'd been so meticulous when planning out his transcript, too.

This was going to be so annoying . . .

Before he sent the text he'd been putting off all evening, he cheered himself by changing the unknown number in his phone to HotJerk.

Eli: Fine, I'll do it.

HotJerk: Took you long enough.

Eli: I'm going to hate every minute of it.

HotJerk: No one is making you do it.

Eli: And yet somehow it feels that way .

HotJerk: It won't be so bad. I'll help you.

Eli frowned at his phone. Was he in Bizarro World now? Why the hell would Haruka want to help him?

Eli: It's ok, I'll be fine on my own.

. . .

HotJerk: So fine you'll hate every minute of it? That sounds like a great plan. Try to market it and see how far it gets you.

Eli: ...

HotJerk: You'd be an idiot to turn down help that someone is freely offering you. Even if you don't like them.

Eli: No more of an idiot than someone who offers to help someone they don't like.

HotJerk: Then we can be idiots together.

Eli: Fine.

Eli sighed and threw his phone out of his blanket nest. Then swore as he fought his way free to find it again to put it on do not disturb.

Eli *was* an idiot. He had to be if he thought adding more work to his plate was a good idea. His only consolation was that the more he had, the more exhausted he would be, and the more exhausted he was, the less he remembered his dreams at night.

CHAPTER 8
ELI

Hauling himself out of bed the next morning was such a chore he nearly gave up and flopped back down to let sleep take him. The only thing keeping him upright was the fear he'd get sucked back into the restless dreams he'd been having all night. He kept drifting on the edge of sleep all night, occasionally slipping into dreams, like a rock skipping across a pond.

All he could remember was an endlessly boring grayscale world. Portraits of people Eli had no memory of scrolled past, each one emanating a heavy burden of responsibility. The only tolerable thing about the world was the ever-shifting ribbon of blue that threaded its way through his dreams.

Last week, Nate had told Eli his abuelita believed if you scratched your head after you got out of bed in the morning, you'd forget your dreams. Eli scratched until his scalp hurt.

His memories were still there, but he cared more about the pain now, so he decided to call it a win.

The shower was still closed for repairs, so if Eli wanted

his friends to be willing to be within four feet of him today, he was going to have to go downstairs again.

He crept into the shower room and then stopped himself when he realized he probably looked like a pervert. He took a deep breath, dug his nails into the palms of his hands, and entered.

The room was empty.

All the tension flowed out of him, and Eli nearly flopped to the floor in relief. Of course, *he* wouldn't be here now. It was way later than it had been when Eli took a shower yesterday.

He still hurried his way through showering and had just finished getting dressed when he heard the door open. His shoulders immediately began to creep in the direction of his ears.

But instead of the stylish black ponytail he'd been fearing, it was shaggy sun-streaked blond that adorned the head of the person who came around the corner.

"Hey, it's you! Are you on this floor too? Or are you a tourist from upstairs?"

"Tourist, I'm afraid." Eli admitted with chagrin. "Hopefully our shower will get fixed soon so we can stop encroaching on yours."

"Don't sweat it, man." Ash began to strip down with an ease that showed the guy had never been anxious about anything a day in his life.

Eli's gaze hit the floor, and Ash kept talking. About everything. He'd been chatty when Eli had met him the day before, but from his performance now, Eli had a feeling it was the guy's natural state.

He talked about his major—physical education—his dog back home, his favorite pair of shoes . . . anything that popped into his head seemed to be free game.

As Eli began gathering his bath supplies to leave, Ash said, "If you leave here in the morning, word to the wise, go by the north entrance, not the south. Every morning the bubble tea girls are there."

"Bubble tea girls?"

"That's what I call them anyway. Every single morning a group of girls meet up and get their caffeine fix outside our building and they get so hyper one of them always ends up spilling their drink everywhere. I've gone through two pairs of sneakers this week. It's brutal."

"Sounds that way. Thanks for the advice." Eli vowed to never, ever, ever leave by the south entrance again, whatever time of day it was. What if someone spilled something on him? What if (shudder) they tried to help clean him off?

Hard pass.

It occurred to Eli that he was standing in a room he really shouldn't be lingering in if he wanted to avoid a certain person.

"I gotta go, bye!" Eli shouted as he raced from the room.

He didn't want to wait for the elevator and chance getting caught, so he took the stairs back to his floor. He didn't stop looking over his shoulder until he reached his room.

Today was Saturday, and he was planning to check out the club fair with Alice and Nate. None of them had any idea what clubs they wanted to join, but they had agreed it would be nice if they could join one together so they could spend more time with each other. Alice had one class with Eli and one with Nate. Otherwise, there was no overlap for any of their trio.

Today he decided to go with the lightweight, linen pullover he got on his last shopping trip. It had a hood—just in case—but he thought sunglasses would be enough protection. He'd be with a group of friends, which usually helped counteract the effects of the Thing.

What would his life be like if he didn't have to spend so much time and energy managing his various quirks? He'd have more fashion options at the very least.

Leaving through the north entrance, he hurried to the main quad where the club fair was being held. He probably should have set a meeting place with Nate and Alice rather than assuming he'd find them easily. Silly him, assuming things.

Once at the main quad, he realized his mistake. Easily half of the 22,000 people on campus were milling around, poking through booths, and enjoying exhibits. How the hell was he supposed to find his friends?

Just as anxiety began stirring in his stomach, he laughed at himself and smacked his forehead. He had a phone, duh.

After several minutes of using it for its originally intended purpose, however, he was beginning to wonder if either of his friends ever bothered to use theirs.

He tugged on a hoodie string.

Well, he could always look around until one of them decided to call him.

A delicious smell caught his attention, and he was about to chase it when he realized with all the excitement and stress of being at the fair, the likelihood of him actually being able to eat something was nil. He'd wait until he was with friends and try then.

A cheer went up from the crowd, and he followed it, using his small size to dart between people until he reached a makeshift fence. It was an archery exhibition, which was too much for his little geek heart to resist.

He'd tried archery a few times, but with his little noodle

arms and extreme dislike of repeatedly getting wacked in the forearm by a bowstring, he didn't get far.

The crowd cheered again when the archer—a tall, willowy blonde woman—hit the center of the target. People pressed against his back.

Too Close! Wrongwrongwrong.

One hand clung to the railing too keep his balance and the other yanked his hood up over his head. What was he thinking diving into a crowd like that? Of course, people were going to accidentally touch him if they were packed this close together.

He squeezed back out and found a small, empty area near a fence post. His view was partially blocked, but at least he had some space to breathe.

Part of him wanted to get the fuck out of there and run all the way back to his room, but another, louder part of him—the part that had sent him running toward the archery event in the first place—was begging him to stay, to watch, and to have fun. He patted the anxiety pill he had in his pocket. He could always take it if he needed to.

He would stay.

His phone buzzed in his back pocket, and he reached for it, praying it would be his friends coming to rescue—ahem—find him, but he stopped midmotion.

The next archer took to the field. Eli could only see the back of him, but something about his long, muscled lines and the way he walked was familiar. Half of his upper torso was bare and glistened with sweat from the hot sun. His black hakama pants fluttered in the breeze. Unthinking, Eli inched away from his secluded position to get a better view.

The way the archer's hands moved to position the bow was sheer art. His arms lifted the impossibly long bow and settled it into position as he took aim. Eli reached a better vantage point and held his breath, spellbound as the archer centered himself.

It was Eli's favorite form of archery—kyudo, the ancient tradition of Japanese archery. He could have ten panic attacks today and still consider it worth coming out.

Tension built around the archer. Eli waited, sharing the tension, his heart beating loudly. The energy shifted, and the archer released the arrow. When it hit the center of the target, Eli felt like he'd been struck in the chest.

The archer turned, and Eli got a look at his face.

It was Haruka.

And he was staring right at Eli.

CHAPTER 9
ELI

Eli jolted backward and realized too late he'd climbed the railing to get a better look at Haruka's performance.

He fully expected to eat dirt, but strong arms caught him before he hit the ground.

Wrongwrongwrong.

Eli pulled away as soon as he righted himself and rubbed his arms trying to rid himself of the sensation.

"Sorry, Eli. I thought you'd prefer being touched over falling."

It was Nate.

The wrongness faded, and he stopped shrinking away from his rescuer. "No, it's fine. Thank you." He nodded his head in appreciation.

"Next time find a safer place to sit before you succumb to the thirst, Eli." Alice grinned at him shamelessly.

"Wh-what?" Eli's face felt like it was going to burst into flames. "I was just watching the exhibition."

"Sure, I always watch archery with my mouth open. Don't you, Nate?"

"Depends on the archer." Nate put his hands behind his head and smiled at the blonde archer from earlier.

Eli was not blind to the fact that his friends had created a small pocket of space around him, protecting him from the crowd. And now they were teasing him to distract him, just like his sister did. In his chest, a warm, glowing sensation began to form.

His hands dropped from where they were strangling his hoodie strings.

"Are you okay?" A very familiar voice asked from the other side of the fence.

Eli froze. He gave his friends a pleading look, but for some reason, his usually supportive friends were immersed in what looked to be a very intense conversation about a nearby trashcan.

He was going to have to turn around now, wasn't he?

He set his shoulders and turned to face Haruka.

Was he always that big? Eli felt like he couldn't have been that tall the last time they'd talked.

His eyes traced Haruka's arm from his mitsugake—a three-fingered archery glove—to his smooth, well-muscled forearm, up his bicep and toned shoulder to his clavicle. All just hanging out for the entire world to see.

Eli blinked slowly.

What were they talking about?

"Do you need to go to the nurse's station?"

Right. They were talking about Eli's magical ability to embarrass himself at any and all times.

"No, I—this is actually par for the course for me."

"Par for the what?"

"Sorry, English idiom for normal." Eli bit his lip. Haruka's accent was so faint, he'd forgotten English wasn't his first language. Idioms were a major bitch for language learners. Every time you started to think you'd mastered something, one would pop up and ruin your confidence.

Except Haruka didn't seem to care.

"Falling off things is normal for you?"

Oh, Eli really wanted to be anywhere else but here right now. "Sometimes?"

"That's not a good thing." Haruka put a hand on the railing and vaulted over to Eli's side of the fence.

"What are you doing? Don't you have an exhibition?"

"My part's done." Haruka stepped forward, invading Eli's personal space. "Are you okay?" His voice was quiet, and his eyes searched Eli's body, looking for signs of injury.

"I'm fine. No harm done, see?" He spun around in a circle to prove everything was in perfect working order and that Haruka was free to leave.

For some strange reason, Haruka leveled a stare at Nate then turned back to Eli to say, "Wait here." And popped back over the fence as easily as he had the first time.

"Show off." Eli muttered. Then to his friends he said, "I could do that too if I was taller."

"Oh, are you two done? I was running out of things to say."

"I don't know, Al, I think you were doing a fine job of describing the campus waste removal procedures."

Alice flicked Nate in the forehead. "Don't call me Al."

Nate rubbed his head. "The abuse! Why do I put up with you?"

"You two abandoned me! I thought we were friends!"

"We are, which is why we *abandoned* you all the way over here." Alice pointed to the five feet of distance separating them.

"I thought *you* liked Haruka. Didn't you say you wanted me to help you meet him?"

"I did, but then something interesting happened and I changed my mind."

"What happened?"

"I think I'll wait to tell you. It's too early to say."

Eli looked to Nate for clarification, but he was busy trying to get the blonde archer's attention.

"Right. Okay, well, let's go look at the other booths. We didn't come here to join the archery club." They already decided collectively as a group that none of them were interested in being in an athletic club.

"Hold on for"—Alice's eyes flicked to somewhere over Eli's shoulder—"one more minute. I need to check something on my phone." Then she pulled out her phone and started typing.

"How did you two find me? This place is crazy busy." Eli asked Nate, pulling his friend's attention away from flirting.

"When you didn't text me back, I decided to look for pockets of chaos. After that, it didn't take long to find you."

"I'm not that bad."

"You are that bad."

"You seem like you're that bad." Haruka had magically materialized beside Eli. He hadn't made a sound coming back over the fence and was no longer sporting the off-the-shoulder top of his kyudo attire. In its place, he wore a white tank top, though he still had on the black hakama.

Eli could only wish to ever look half as cool in his lifetime. Even if he had the exact same outfit, he would somehow manage to look more like a toy gotten out of a claw machine than the *casually wandered out of a historical J-drama* Haruka effortlessly pulled off.

The looks Haruka was drawing from the crowd said they agreed with Eli.

"What are you doing? Why did you come back?"

Haruka had plenty of admirers on the other side of the fence—not that Eli had been paying attention. The man didn't need to come over here and get more.

"Coming with you to make sure you don't fall off something else."

"I don't see how that's your problem." Eli was going to die of embarrassment long before that would be a possibility.

"It's everyone's responsibility to make sure our fellow students are safe!" Alice had emerged from her phone and took Haruka by the arm. "And the more eyes the better for Eli."

"Alice!" Eli hissed. Betrayal. This was betrayal on the highest level.

Alice ignored him and continued being the worst friend in the history of ever. "We need advice on what club to join anyway. Let's go, everyone." Without looking back, she dragged Haruka away, leaving Eli and Nate with no other option but to join them.

For the next hour, they roamed the quad, going from booth to booth, sometimes staying at one for a long time before finally deciding against it and moving on to the next. Alice didn't want anything packed with people—reasoning that it would be easier to make new friends in a smaller club. Nate flat out refused to join any club that had more men than women.

That left out the Pride club—it had nearly a thousand members—which almost had Alice breaking her rule. "But the rainbow lifestyle flows in my veins!" Alice wailed and shook her bag in Eli's face. It rattled with an assortment of bi, trans, and LGBTQ rainbows.

Eli would have felt odd joining anyway. Since he was

undecided on his sexuality, would he even be welcome? "You don't have to join the club to live the lifestyle, Alice."

Haruka gave no input on the decision-making process at all. Eli would have forgotten he was there, except for the quiet aura he radiated that drew every eye around him. He should have come off as intimidating, or annoying, but he didn't. He just *was.* And every now and then, he would focus all that quiet intensity on Eli, as if Haruka was trying to convey something. For the life of him, Eli couldn't figure out what.

"What about the baking club?" Alice asked. "Plenty of girls in that one, Nate."

Eli bit his lip and said, "I'm not the best at baking." It was an understatement. "Massive fire hazard would not be an exaggeration of my talents."

"Next booth, then." Haruka said and walked toward a tent that had hanging scrolls on one side.

Eli joined him, he loved calligraphy. He wasn't very good at it, but he loved looking at the curling swoops and swirls and taking in the personality of the artist. Every scroll was different, even if some had the same characters. Whatever was on the scroll was a reflection of the soul of the artist at the time they made the piece.

"This one is wrong." Haruka pointed at a drying scroll on the table. Eli recognized what he assumed was the kanji for kindness. It was missing a stroke from the base of the first symbol.

A young woman hurried up to them from the back of the tent, looked at it, and then at Haruka. "What did I do wrong?"

Haruka took a brush out of a jar, dipped it in ink, and completed the stroke.

"Thank you. How embarrassing!"

Eli didn't think she looked embarrassed. More like thrilled.

"You're welcome." Haruka nodded to her.

"Would you like to make one of your own?" She held out an empty scroll.

"No, thank you. I already have a club. They're still looking, though." Haruka took the scroll and handed it and the brush to Eli just as Alice joined them.

"You have tea!" Alice's eyes took on an unholy light as they locked on to the tea sets on the other side of the booth.

"We do! We're kind of a quirky club. My friends and I formed it three years ago when we found out we all shared an extreme love of tea and calligraphy."

Alice went to the tea display. "Do you buy it, or make your own?"

Another young woman joined her friend and answered. This one was a redhead with a cute little mole next to her eye. "A little of both. We like to find unique blends from all over the world and then come up with something new, inspired by our favorite ones."

"What's the difference?" Nate materialized in front of the redhead. "Doesn't all tea taste the same? It's just leaves in hot water, right."

Everyone on both sides of the table stared at Nate in various stages of shock and horror.

Eli didn't even get a chance to make his opinion known on the matter, Alice and the two women from the booth all began to talk at Nate at once.

"Nate, how could you grow up to be a monster without me noticing?"

"Who do you think you are? Zuko?"

"There are so many different kinds of tea plants out

there, not to mention the various fruits and herbs you can use to add flavor to them . . ."

"That kid is a genius." Haruka observed quietly, bending low so only Eli could hear him.

"How so? He got everyone angry at him."

Haruka's only response was to jerk his chin toward Nate.

At first, all Eli saw was his friend getting badgered on all sides as two more women who'd been lingering in the back of the tent came up to join in the heated discussion.

Then he noticed it.

At the very corner of his mouth, Nate was sporting a sly little smile.

"He did that on purpose?"

Haruka shrugged. "Draw something." He nudged the scroll he'd thrust into Eli's hand earlier.

Since he wasn't particularly interesting in getting caught up in Nate's bizarre flirting ritual, Eli decided to go with it. What should he write? His character formation wasn't the best, but he'd memorized at least four thousand kanji by this point. He had a lot to choose from.

On a whim, he asked, "What characters do you use in your name?"

Haruka went still and got that thoughtful look on his face again. Then he said, "My given name is written using the kanji for distant."

Eli snorted. "That figures. I didn't take you as a spring fragrance kind of guy." Which was another way Haruka could have been written.

Haruka raised his eyebrows playfully. "Are you saying I smell bad?"

"N-no, not at all, you smell great!"

"So, you like how I smell?" Haruka's mouth curled into

a smile that was very reminiscent of the one Nate was still sporting.

Eli was all too aware of how amazing Haruka smelled at the moment. After baking in the hot sun all day, he should have the decency to smell sweaty like other mere mortals, but instead he smelled like fresh laundry hanging outside combined with a hint of lavender. Eli had been doing his best to ignore it.

Instead of responding, Eli rolled his eyes and focused on the scroll in front of him. "What's your family name?"

"Yamada."

Eli didn't need to ask how to draw it. It was a common surname in Japan—like Smith, or Jones were in America. He held the brush perpendicular to the page and drew the kanji for mountain （山） and field （田） placing mountain on top, field underneath, and then distant （遥） at the bottom.

He looked it over and bit his lip. As usual, he managed to splatter ink on the page, rather than the achieving the efficient, tidy strokes he'd been aiming for. He could definitely use some practice.

"That's really good." One of the women had drawn away from the group surrounding Nate. It was the redhead with the mole.

"It's okay, you don't have to compliment me, I know it needs work." Eli scrunched his nose ruefully.

"Maybe a little, but we could help you get better if you joined our club. My name is Kate." The woman held out her hand to shake his.

Eli paused. He'd been having a good day. It probably wouldn't be the end of the world to shake one hand. Besides, he actually thought he might want to join this club and hurting the feelings of one of the club members wasn't the best way to go about joining.

Eli lifted his hand slowly but stopped when Haruka placed Eli's brush in Kate's hand.

"Thanks for letting us borrow this."

Kate looked surprised but smiled. "You're very welcome."

Alice sidled up to Eli, coming just shy of touching him. "Eliiiiii, can we join this club, please? I need to up my tea-making game."

"What does Nate think?"

Alice pointed to Nate, still surrounded by women and chatting cheerfully. "I think he's about three seconds from signing the paperwork with or without us."

"Then I guess I'm in."

The Tea and Calligraphy club. It sounded like the perfect stress-free club Eli had been hoping for.

Kate handed him a piece of paper to write his information on, so they could add him to the club register. "Can you put your number at the bottom? I know there isn't a line for it, but it's better to have more than just an email to get in contact with you."

"Sure."

"I'm hungry." Haruka was standing so close to Eli he could feel his body heat.

Eli swayed a little. He must be getting hungry too.

"Hold on, I'm almost done." Eli scribbled his number at the bottom of the page and handed it back to Kate.

"Welcome to the club! I think you guys will like it."

"Thanks! I—"

"Food."

Haruka was practically breathing down Eli's neck. Goosebumps raced across his skin.

"I'll see you later then. Nice to meet you." Eli waved and stepped away from the table. "Do you guys want to eat? We're gonna grab something."

"No thanks, I want to stay here a little longer. They're going to make me some tea. We can meet up later." Nate made a shooing motion at Eli.

"I'm staying too, you two have fun!" Alice stared pointedly at the spot between Eli and Haruka for some reason.

"Okay then."

Eli allowed himself to be herded away by Haruka. For someone who hadn't shown any interest in the fair, he was oddly eager now.

"What do you want to eat?" Haruka asked.

Eli took in the line of food trucks. It was almost as long as the rows of club booths. How was he supposed to choose? "I have no idea. I didn't even know I was hungry until you said something. Maybe an apple?" He pointed to an organic fruit truck.

"An apple? That's all you want?" Haruka looked at Eli like he had suggested they eat mud. "You just lost the right to have input on food. Follow me."

Eli followed Haruka to a falafel truck and watched as he ordered an obscene amount of food. Where was he planning on putting it all? The man didn't have an ounce of fat on him—from what Eli had observed, anyway.

When Haruka finished, Eli stepped up to order, but Haruka waved him away. "I ordered for both of us."

"Oh." That made more sense. Though Eli thought Haruka was overestimating how much Eli could eat. "How much was my share?" Eli reached in his pocket for his wallet.

"Nothing."

"But—"

"Put it away. You can owe me."

"But I don't want to owe you."

"Too bad."

Eli stood awkwardly with his wallet in his hand before finally putting it away. "I'll buy you lunch next time, then."

The smile Eli got in response was like looking at the sun.

CHAPTER 10
ELI

"How does it feel to have everyone here call you Haruka instead of Yamada-san when they first meet you?"

"Probably about how it would feel to be called Talosa-san instead of Eli."

"So, different, but not bad?"

"More or less."

Eli had been peppering Haruka with questions about what it was like to live in a different country. Since he'd only left the country once—for a weekend school trip to Montreal—Eli had a never-ending supply. For someone who had come off as a total jerk the first time they'd met, Haruka had surprised Eli by patiently answering every single question.

"So, when you—"

Haruka placed a kabob stick on Eli's already full plate.

"Thanks. Anyway, what do you do when—"

"It's not there to look at. It's there to eat."

"I already ate."

"You ate one beef skewer."

“It was really big.”

“I had five.”

“You’re bigger than I am,” Eli said grudgingly.

“No more questions until you eat more.”

“But—”

Haruka pushed Eli’s plate toward him. Eli didn’t pout. It was definitely a manly frown he leveled at the plate in front of him. Definitely.

He took his fork, stabbed a grilled vegetable, and stuffed it in his mouth, chewing with exaggerated motions all while maintaining a very manly frown. Which, for some reason, made Haruka look like he was doing everything he could not to laugh.

“Hey, you two, I finally found you!” Alice sat down next to Eli with a massive pink smoothie in one hand and a slice of pizza in the other.

“We weren’t gone that long.”

“What are you talking about? The sun is going down. Nate and I have been texting you for over an hour.”

Eli pulled out his phone and saw he’d missed fifteen texts and five calls. “Oops.”

“We were starting to wonder if Haruka had kidnapped you and smuggled you back to Japan.”

Haruka rubbed his chin and narrowed his eyes thoughtfully. “You are small enough to fit in my suitcase, chibisuke.”

“I’m not—you’re—ahhhh, you both suck.”

“You think *I* suck? Just wait until Nate gets here. He freaked out when you vanished on us.” Alice picked up her phone, and Eli peeked over her shoulder to watch her type a message to Nate.

. . .

mAlice: Found our lost nerdling! We're at the picnic table under the big pine trees

"Is he mad at me?"

"No, I don't think it's you he's mad at."

Eli took a bite of the pita bread Haruka had just placed in his hand. While he chewed, he scrolled through his missed messages. The ones from Alice were fairly cheerful inquiries about his location, but the ones from Nate went from curious to concerned to the final one that just said:

NatetheGreat: Where the fuck are you????

"Hey, are you okay? Why didn't you answer your phone?" Nate dropped his backpack onto the table with more force than necessary, then dropped down on the other side of Eli.

"I'm fine, I just forgot to check my phone." A lump of prickly rock began to form in Eli's stomach. What was going on? Nate never got mad—at least, not that Eli had seen. "Are *you* okay?"

"No, I don't think I am." But Nate wasn't talking to Eli. He leaned forward, put his hands on the table, and faced Haruka. "We were being nice and giving you a chance, not giving him away to you."

Eli's fingers started to harass the first hangnail they found. "Wait, Nate—"

Nate spoke right over Eli and pushed himself up until he was halfway across the table and looming over Haruka. "You don't know him. Not like we do. Events like this aren't good for him."

Haruka gave him an impassive stare. "I don't think you should be speaking for Eli."

Eli's cheeks were so hot, he was surprised they weren't glowing. He dug a nail into the sad, abused hangnail and felt it grow wet. "Really, this isn't a big deal, Nate."

Haruka pushed a water bottle over to Eli, nudging him with it until he took it in his hands. Eli immediately got to work dismantling the label.

"It is a big deal, Eli. I've seen how you are in crowds. You need someone with you who knows you and can help you if something happens. I never should have let you go with him. What if something happened?"

"Calm down, brother bear." Alice got up and put a hand on Nate's shoulder.

"If something happened, I would have helped him like I did last time," Haruka said, evenly.

"Last time?" Alice and Nate said at the same time and turned to Eli.

"What happened last time?"

"Why didn't you tell us?"

This was too much. Everything was suddenly way, way too much to handle.

Eli stood up. "I'm not a child. I know I have, um, problems, but I don't need someone with me all the time. I can actually take care of myself." He carefully placed the water bottle down in the shredded pile that used to be its label. "I like having friends, Nate. Friends are good, but I don't like when people talk over me or for me."

"I wasn't . . ." Nate trailed off and stopped. His lips were a thin line.

"Eli, I'm sorry."

"It's okay, Alice. Please excuse me, everyone. I'm going back now." Eli bowed slightly then turned and fled.

He made it just out of sight before the hyperventilating started. He leaned against a tent pole, slid down, and just let it happen. It was dark enough now that no one would notice him having a tiny breakdown—hopefully.

He'd done a fan-fucking-tastic job of things just now. And he'd been having the best day, too. Now, he may have just alienated his new friends all in one go.

Perfect.

And he'd just begun to think Haruka might not be a jerk after all.

But . . . he hated it when people treated him like he was helpless.

His throat tightened and burned.

Breathe. Just focus on breathing, Eli. You can do this. You've been here before.

He fumbled in his pocket for the pill he'd put there for emergencies, but it was gone. It must have fallen out when he took out his wallet earlier.

He closed his eyes, leaned his head back, and tried to allow himself to fall into the rhythm of the ambient sound around him. Vendors closing up their trucks, students discussing where to go next, faint music from across the quad. He could do this. He was a pro.

For a time, he worked to lose himself in the soft sounds of nighttime and the not-so-soft sounds of humanity as it bustled around, cleaning up the fair.

When he opened his eyes again, his breathing was much steadier and no longer high in his chest. *Good job, Eli. Well done.*

Movement down the mostly empty aisle in front of him caught his attention. Even if it was too dark to recognize faces, Haruka's outfit was distinctive enough to make out and his gait was impossible to mistake.

Haruka had gone back to the Tea and Calligraphy tent.

Eli watched as he spoke to someone in the tent for a time. It was too dark to tell what he was doing, but when Haruka finally turned to go, a flash of light from a passing car illuminated Kate's face.

He'd been talking to the redhead with the cute mole.

Eli pulled himself off the ground and headed for his dorm. He was so done with this day.

He didn't want to think about Haruka, or Nate, or anyone, so when his phone buzzed, he didn't look. He just turned it off. He was a big boy and could take care of himself for the ten minutes it took to walk back to his room.

So what if his legs felt like rubber? So what if random noises in the dark caused him to jump? He was oversensitive right now. He knew how to deal with it. All he needed was a good night's sleep, and he'd be fine.

:*Fucking dammit.*:

For once, Eli didn't startle at the Voice. Instead, he couldn't help but agree.

"Me too, Voice . . . me too."

CHAPTER 11
ELI

Sunday was a sleepy day for Eli. All the excitement and stress of the past week caught up to him and said *stay the fuck put*. So, he did.

He didn't even bother stirring from his bed until the sun was high in the sky and when he did, his head felt light and floaty, so while he did technically get up, Eli decided the bed was really the best place for him today. He got out for exactly as long as it took to use the bathroom and procure snacks from the tiny fridge he and Jace shared, then he got back in bed.

Jace had left already, or else Eli might have created a tent over his bed.

Actually, that wasn't a bad idea—Jace or no.

He set to work, draping sheets around his bed. It was touch and go for a while, but eventually he chose against his classic Voltron sheets for a nice neutral blue. Besides, what if he tore the Voltron sheets while making the tent? Perish the thought.

By the time he was settled into his fortress with his laptop—not his phone, today was also a no-phone day, and he could deal with the repercussions of that later—Jace came back.

His roommate took one look at the new setup and smiled. “Is there room in there for two? Or do you want to be alone?”

“That depends on your feelings about Stargate SG-1.”

“Extremely pro. Scoot over.”

It was a good day. No one asked him about his feelings or treated him oddly. It was just junk food and 90s sci-fi until way too late in the night.

The next morning, something was terribly, terribly wrong. The worst noise Eli had ever heard was blaring through the room. It was like a dying whale giving birth to a minivan. He jolted up, causing his laptop, his roommate, and a pile of discarded snack wrappers to go flying.

“What the hell is that?”

“It’s the fricking fire alarm.” Jace moaned from the floor. He tried to get up but slipped on an empty Dorito bag and crashed down onto the bed, narrowly missing Eli’s leg.

Stumbling and half asleep, the two of them managed to get down all ten flights of stairs to the meeting place outside the building where various RAs were doing headcounts.

“You have something on your face.” Jace reached out and peeled a Warheads wrapper from Eli’s cheek. And then snatched his hand back. “Shit, sorry man, I wasn’t thinking.”

“It’s okay.” Eli yawned and stretched. “I think my issues are still asleep. Plus, I think you sleeping on top of me for half the night has made me immune.” Though chances were good his defense system would count Jace as an intruder before the end of the day.

Jace’s eye’s flicked to something over Eli’s shoulder, and

his eyes widened momentarily. Then his face became cool and watchful.

"Where were you yesterday?" Haruka's deep voice rumbled behind Eli.

Eli jumped. "Christ! Warn a guy next time." His hand clutched his chest, trying to keep his heart from escaping.

"You didn't answer your phone." Was Haruka annoyed? Or just sleepy? It was hard for Eli to tell.

"I was taking a me-day. No phones." Eli was incredibly proud of how steady his voice sounded considering the party going on inside his chest.

"With him?" Haruka looked Jace up and down, eyes lingering at his feet. A scowl began to form on his face.

"Well, he's my roommate, so, yes?" What was up with all the questions?

A gust of wind reminded Eli it was early morning, and that he was only wearing a pair of thin shorts and unfamiliar flip-flops. He shivered and wrapped his arms around himself. Going inside would be wonderful right about now.

Haruka's eyes narrowed. Then he shrugged off the black hoodie he was wearing and held it out to Eli wordlessly.

"Um . . ."

"Take it. Even without it, I'm still wearing more than you." Haruka gestured to the tight black T-shirt and sweatpants he was wearing.

Eli looked at Jace, who shrugged. Haruka's scowl deepened.

Another shiver helped Eli make up his mind. "Okay, then. Thanks. I'll bring it back to you in class."

The hoodie was far too big for Eli, but it was warm and soft and smelled amazing.

"I need it back before Friday."

"Oh." It made sense. If Haruka lived in Japan, he probably went back and forth a lot, which would mean having a lot of stuff would be a pain. Maybe he only had one hoodie. "I can wash it today and give it back to you this evening."

"Don't bother washing it, give it back to me at lunch. I'll text you where." Haruka turned and walked away without giving Eli a chance to answer.

Jace whistled. "That guy is intense. Did we do something to piss him off?"

"I honestly have no idea. He always looks a little irritated."

"Hey, switch back with me. These things are tiny." Jace pointed at Eli's sandals on his feet. He grunted as he worked to peel them off. He wasn't much taller than Eli, but his feet were way bigger.

"That's because you have giant monster feet." Eli slipped off the flip-flops and stepped into his own sandals. "I nearly killed myself coming down the stairs in these."

Eli's shoulder blades prickled.

"Your friend is giving us the stink-eye right now."

"Maybe he needs coffee? I know I do. Hey, the RAs are letting people back in. Come on."

After a nice hot shower—on his own floor, thank god—Eli got dressed and made for the nearest coffee cart. Since his laptop told him it would be in the 90s that afternoon, Eli decided to wear Haruka's hoodie over a long T-shirt, so he didn't have to lug it and his own hoodie around in his backpack when it got hot.

After his first class finished, he fished his phone out of his pocket. He hadn't turned it on yet, and he really didn't want to, either. But yesterday had been his no-phone day and that was his limit. He couldn't have two no-phone days in a row, it was against the rules he'd agreed to with his mom and sister. If he didn't answer after twenty-four hours to a phone call or text from his family, they had the right to make him come home.

It was the only way they'd agreed to let him go to school so far away. Which was a bit excessive in Eli's opinion, but he'd agreed to it to keep them from worrying. He did wonder what they were going to do when he got a job and left the country, though.

He shook his head at his overprotective family. Then he steeled his nerve and turned on his phone. He was past the agreed upon twenty-four hours, but hopefully no one had thought to message him until last night.

Once his phone booted up, his lock screen lit up with notifications. Ten missed calls and thirty-seven texts.

Eli pulled his hoodie up, and his spiking anxiety ratcheted down several notches—something that didn't usually happen when he used his own hoodie. He was lucky if it calmed him down at all. Maybe it was the smell. He should ask Haruka what laundry detergent he used.

Taking a deep breath, he checked the thing he was most afraid of first—the missed phone calls. The first had been from Haruka. He hadn't left a message, but Eli could see from the time stamp that it had been Haruka who had called him last night right before Eli had turned off his phone. The rest of the calls were from Alice and Nate, none from his family. He breathed a sigh of relief.

No matter what his text messages had in store for him, at least he didn't have to deal with needing to convince his mom not to drag him home.

The spike of adrenaline in his gut told him avoiding the voicemails from Nate and Alice was in his best interests.

Instead, he'd read their texts. It would be easier to be friend-dumped by text.

mAlice: I'm so sorry Eli, forgive me! I got carried away. Nate will apologize too when he stops freaking out.

NateTheGreat: I'm not freaking out, just worried. We don't even know that guy, Eli. I'm just trying to look out for you

mAlice: He really does mean well, Eli. He just gets overprotective sometimes

Eli hit his head on his desk softly. He was the one who had overreacted and now *they* were apologizing to *him*. He forced himself to keep going, even though most of his brain was telling him that the end of the chat would be them telling him to go fuck himself after ignoring them all day. He tugged absently at a hoodie string.

mAlice: Eli?
Eli?
Eli?
Eli?
Eli?

NateTheGreat: You should answer her, man. She can get way more annoying.

. . .

mAlice: I caaaaaaaan. And I will

Instead of the feared friend dumping, the rest of the messages were Alice spamming his phone.

Huh.

As soon as he'd finished reading everything, another message popped up from Alice.

mAlice: He read it!!!!! Ok, talk to us Eli, or I'll spam your phone until you cry

Eli's fingers hesitated over the screen. What was he supposed to say? Apologize for having a broken brain? That was such an old and tired exercise, and he was done apologizing for being himself. But that didn't mean he shouldn't apologize for his actions.

Eli: Um
I overacted
I'm sorry for turning off my phone
I needed a day off from thinking
I'm sorry for ignoring you, that was super shitty

mAlice: Only because you scared me! I thought you hated us now!

. . .

Eli: Actually I thought you'd hate me for yelling and leaving.

NateTheGreat: Alice and I would have split long ago if that was our style. My last class is at 3:30. Can we meet after that?

mAlice: Yes please!

Eli: 4:00? By the duck?

mAlice: I'll be there!

NateTheGreat: Me too.

Eli breathed a sigh of relief and ran his hands through his hair, knocking his hood back. He still had friends.

Though Haruka *had* been acting oddly this morning. He should read his texts next. There were only two. One asking, *Are you ok?* And then another several hours later saying, *Just don't forget to eat something.*

Huh. Maybe Eli was overthinking things.

His sister had sent him a single text the night before, and it was a pirate meme. He gave the picture a heart, and then he was done.

So much buildup over nothing.

Stupid brain.

He shoved himself out of his desk. If he hurried, he could hit up another coffee cart before his next class.

"Jesus, you're pretty. Are you a boy or a girl under those layers?"

Eli had been seconds away from shedding Haruka's hoodie on his way out of class. Now he found one of his hands reaching for the hood to pull it up, but it was caught midmotion.

Wrongwrongwrong

He tried to snatch it back, but it was held fast. Eli gritted his teeth and looked up. Not one, but two Chads loomed over him. Fan-fucking-tastic.

Wrongwrongwrong

Eli twisted his wrist and yanked down, freeing his hand. "None of your business."

"I don't care what you are, I'd like to make it my business." Chad number one, all blonde hair and blue eyes, leaned in close, forcing Eli to back away.

"Pass." Eli tried to go around, but Chad number two stepped in his way.

"I'd still like to know what's under the hood first, personally."

Gross.

Eli's phone rang, and he clicked answer without checking who it was.

"Where are you?" Haruka's voice was clipped, and he sounded pissed.

"Um, by the Old Chapel, near the main pond." An irritable Haruka was better than two touchy-feely Chads any day.

"I'm almost there." Haruka hung up.

Eli stood staring at his phone for a second until he realized he still had to ditch the Chads. He turned his attention back to his harassers, but they seemed to have lost interest. Maybe they heard both sides of the conversation and preferred easy prey over prey with imminent backup.

"Some other time, pretty." Chad number one said, pulling his friend's arm to get him to follow.

Eli let out a sigh of relief. That problem was sorted out, but depending on how far Haruka had been from him when he hung up, Eli might only have seconds to compose himself. He didn't have time for his normal methods, so he went for an old, not entirely healthy, but tried-and-true method for feigning normality.

He dug a metal pencil sharpener out of his bag and squeezed it in his palm. Not hard enough to pierce the skin, but enough to give him something else to focus on other than the fantastic bit of evil his brain chemistry was concocting.

CHAPTER 12
HARUKA

It had been a good morning, all things considered. He'd finally gotten to check in on Eli since his abrupt departure from the fair, which had been weighing on Haruka's mind. Something about the kid kept tugging at him.

At first, it had been the clumsiness and those beautiful blue Bambi eyes. Both were impossible to ignore. But the intelligence and the obvious battle the boy was fighting had kept Haruka's attention.

And there had been the other thing.

It took a lot to faze Haruka. In the gray, boring world he lived in, curious things might catch his attention briefly, but they inevitably faded into the grayness along with everything else.

The first time Haruka heard the voice, it was enough to capture his entire attention. The speech he'd prepared for orientation had escaped, and in its place was panic—a stranger's panic. Someone nearby was terrified, and it struck Haruka like a fist to the gut.

It never occurred to him that it might have been his

imagination—Haruka wasn't imaginative. He dealt in absolutes, and the panic the voice radiated had been so strong, it was impossible for Haruka to believe it was anything other than real. He'd tried to find the person in the crowd, did his best to listen using whatever he'd used to hear them in the first place, but he couldn't find them. All he had was a lingering sense that there was something he was missing.

Since that was normal for him, he decided to let it go. Until it happened again. And again. Over the next week, Haruka began to get used to the random stabs of panic flooding his system. Perhaps he should have been bothered by them, but he was more concerned with the person experiencing them firsthand.

He got his first clue it might be Eli when they'd shared a class together. The panic that flickered through Haruka as he watched Eli break down seemed tiny in comparison to what the poor boy was going through.

It might not have been Eli, though. Maybe somehow Haruka had tapped into panicking people in general and could hear everyone near him who was having their own personal crisis. But each incident seemed to have a flavor to it—something he couldn't quite place.

Saturday at the club fair, Haruka had watched as Eli fell from the fence. Had seen Eli's face when his friend had caught him at the exact same moment *Wrongwrongwrong* had rung out inside Haruka's chest.

It was obvious to him the boy didn't want to be touched. Was his aversion enough to cause the panic Haruka had just felt?

He had to know. Was Eli the source of all the distraction in Haruka's life? Or only the main one?

So, he'd spent the day with him. Haruka had followed

Eli and observed him and his friends, and it hadn't been what he'd expected.

Haruka wasn't bored, nor was he mildly annoyed—something he had become accustomed to when spending a long period of time with a person. It had been . . . soothing.

Eli was nothing like the person he'd shown Haruka until then. He'd been as happy as a child, flitting from booth to booth, coming more and more out of his shell as the day progressed.

The hunched posture and hunted demeanor the boy wore like a second skin had vanished, and in its place was something Haruka could only describe as enchanting.

When Eli had written his name in calligraphy, Haruka couldn't have left his side if he'd been told to.

But the voice stayed quiet, so that particular mystery was still unsolved.

Now Haruka had a new problem. He couldn't stop thinking about Eli—or the way he attracted the gaze of other people. The more he'd blossomed by Haruka's side, the more other people had noticed. Anxious Eli was beautiful, but cheerful, relaxed Eli was transcendent.

All of Sunday, Haruka had been restless. Eli had been upset when they'd parted—not with him. Haruka knew he'd done nothing wrong. He was fully capable of helping and protecting Eli if something happened, and—he suspected—so was Eli.

The boy was battling demons most people didn't have to face, but he was also clearly capable of handling himself, even if he was accident-prone.

So, why was Haruka so uneasy about having Eli out of his sight? And why had it bothered him to see Eli acting so free with his roommate this morning? He'd seemed unfazed by the touch of the other boy, and it didn't sit right with Haruka.

Haruka reached for his phone to text Eli about lunch when it happened.

Wrongwrongwrongwrongwrongwrong

Haruka nearly dropped his phone from the intensity of the voice.

Without thinking he called Eli and didn't wait for the boy to speak. "Where are you?"

There was something very wrong with Eli's voice when he answered, "Um, by the Old Chapel, near the main pond." His voice was tight and laced with something that tasted exactly like the remnants of second-hand anxiety lingering in Haruka's chest.

Haruka was only minutes away. He didn't actually need to meet with Bryan right now. He could wait, but it didn't sound like Eli could. "I'm almost there."

Haruka texted his friend about the change of plans while he hurried toward Eli. He didn't run, but only barely.

He slowed his pace before reaching his destination. If something was wrong, he didn't want his own worry to pile on top of Eli's.

It was clear as soon as he saw Eli there was something wrong. His hood was up, string pulled tight, and his arms were wrapped around his body, both fists clenched so tightly they were white. He was smiling, but it looked like he was holding a razorblade in his mouth. "Hi, did you want to have lunch? It's a little early, but—"

"Don't." Haruka couldn't bear it. Eli's razorblade smile was cutting Haruka right to the core.

"Don't what? Have lunch?"

"Don't pretend like you're okay when you're not." Haruka stepped right into Eli's space. He wanted to shield

Eli from whatever was happening inside of him. Needed to. Even though the boy had never asked him for a single thing.

Instead of skittering back, like Haruka had seen him do countless times with other people, he stood his ground, eyebrows scrunched together adorably. “I don’t—I’m not—”

“You don’t have to tell me what happened if you don’t want to.” Even though Haruka really, really wanted to know so he could go hurt someone. “But don’t lie to me.” Haruka leaned in to make his point.

Eli bit his lip, worrying at the same ragged spot Haruka had seen him assaulting on Saturday shortly before he’d bolted.

Haruka should have eased back to give Eli room to breathe, but something in his gut wouldn’t let him. It wanted him to scoop the boy up and take him somewhere safe. And that scared the shit out of him.

Haruka didn’t do things like this. He didn’t get invested in things or people. He had his agenda, and everything he did was solely for the purpose of furthering it. He was looking for something, and he would find it or die trying.

Except . . . the pull to find that something didn’t have the same hold on him as it had before. Either Eli’s situation was so loud it was blocking out the pull, or something about or near Eli *was* the thing Haruka had been searching for.

Whatever the case, Haruka wasn’t going anywhere until he’d figured out which one it was. Even if he was wildly out of his comfort zone.

“Fine. I wasn’t okay, but I will be. And I don’t want to talk about it.” Eli’s eyes darted to either side of Haruka as if he were looking for tigers in the trees. “So . . . lunch? Or do you just want me to give your hoodie back." He continued to avoid Haruka's gaze.

There was no way in hell Haruka was taking his hoodie back. Not with the way Eli was burrowing into it like it was his only friend. "Keep it."

When Haruka had given it to Eli this morning, it had been for a multitude of reasons. Aside from the obvious, he'd needed to do something about the way everyone had been surreptitiously ogling the half-frozen boy. Wrapping Eli in something belonging to him had been a great solution. If it were up to him, Eli would wear it forever.

"Let's go eat." He motioned for Eli to follow him. He'd like to take the boy back to his room, but had a feeling Eli would balk, so he led him to the closest cafeteria and piled his own tray with food, noting that—once again—Eli had chosen next to nothing for himself.

The boy was whisper-thin, and something needed to be done about it.

CHAPTER 13
ELI

Okay, so maybe Eli's old method of feigning normality hadn't worked, but shortly after Haruka had arrived, Eli's anxiety levels had dropped to something much more manageable—even if he did feel like he'd swallowed a jar full of butterflies.

Which was why he couldn't even begin to keep up with how much food Haruka kept trying to shove at him. "I'm fine, really!" Eli's hand blocked his plate when Haruka tried to put a slice of grilled chicken on it.

"You've only had five grapes."

He'd been counting? Even Juniper wasn't that weird.

"I had a big breakfast." Eli lied. He'd had coffee and the muffin he'd gotten with the coffee lay uneaten in his backpack.

Haruka raised an eyebrow.

Eli glared at him and ate another grape. Haruka took the opportunity to slide the chicken onto Eli's plate.

Even if there hadn't been a flock of butterflies throwing a rave inside his stomach, he wouldn't have eaten much. He still had the pencil sharpener in his hand. He didn't need it anymore, but he'd gotten overzealous in squeezing it and was pretty sure he'd cut himself enough that it would be hard to hide the blood seeping out. So, he was eating one-handed.

He shoved another grape in his mouth and wrinkled his nose. Ugh, it was sour.

A clatter from across the table made Eli look up. Haruka had dropped his fork on the table but made no motion to pick it up. Instead, he watched Eli with a strange look on his face.

"Are you okay?"

Haruka blinked a few times then nodded and continued eating.

Weird.

But then that was Haruka, as far as Eli could tell. Eli didn't mind weird, though. It made him way less conscious of his own oddities. Maybe that was why he'd taken so quickly to Nate and Alice. They were their own giant buckets of weird, and Eli knew it was a privilege to be included.

Haruka's brand of weird was intense, but also quiet. And very soothing—even if he was a bit of a pushy jerk.

Once Eli had consumed enough food to satisfy Haruka—enough to make him feel like he was about to explode—Eli said, "I've got a class in a few minutes, let me give you back your hoodie." Even though he wanted to keep it. Wearing it made him feel like there was a lovely barrier between him and the world. Nothing constricting, just a nice, soft buffer to wallow in.

Haruka held out a hand, motioning him to stop. "Keep it, I have another just like it."

"You do? Why did you tell me you needed it back?"

"Because I wanted to have lunch with you." Haruka's

eyes were soft, and there was a hint of a smile at the corner of his mouth.

"Oh." The butterfly rave had officially become an army. "Okay." What was he supposed to do with his hands right now? What was he supposed to do with his body? Why did every part of him feel so large and awkward right now?

He squeezed the pencil sharpener on reflex and winced. Haruka's eyes flicked to Eli's hand, and his own hand twitched as if he wanted to reach out but stopped himself. "I'll let you go."

Was it just Eli's imagination, or was there a big fat *for now* that Haruka had left off the end of his sentence? He swallowed hard.

"O-okay."

"Call me, if something happens."

Eli nodded, knowing he would one hundred percent be willing to lose an arm before taking Haruka up on his offer. He turned and fled.

Eli scratched at the bandage on his palm for the twentieth time that evening. For some reason, *The Tale of Genji* wasn't capturing his attention like it had yesterday. And today had been so good, too. Well, the second half had been.

Alice and Nate didn't hate him even a little bit, and—even crazier—Nate apologized for being overbearing and promised to try and rein it in next time. Though he had expressed reservations about Haruka.

"You don't actually know anything about him, Eli."

"I'm not marrying him, Nate, just taking a class with him."

"And wearing his clothes?" Nate plucked at the overlong sleeve hanging past the tips of Eli's fingers.

Eli didn't have an answer for Nate. He still didn't have one several hours later as he sat at his desk diligently working his way through his assignment. Though at the rate he was going, he might be better off going to bed now and waking up early to finish it.

His phone rattled against the glass of his desk. When he picked it up, he saw a text from Jace.

SpaceJace: I gotta go home for a bit, be back tomorrow night

Eli: Is everything okay?

SpaceJace: Not sure yet. I'll let you know
Are you going to be okay on your own?

Eli: Don't worry about me, I'll be fine
Good luck with your family!
See you tomorrow

Eli winced at the sudden pain in his mouth and tasted blood. Dammit, he'd chewed his lip to pieces again.

It was only one night alone. It shouldn't be a big deal, especially since he'd need to become an actual adult who could sleep alone without nightmares at some point in his life.

And it was somewhat shitty of him to worry more about himself than Jace, who seemed to have an actual crisis to deal with.

Eli mentally pulled up his big boy pants and went back to his book.

Ten minutes later, the *Tale of Genji* took a short flight across the room when Eli realized he'd been staring at the same page since he'd gotten Jace's text.

He crawled into his bed, made a little cocoon, curled up with his phone, and pulled up his bedtime playlist. Rather than songs, it was filled with background recordings from home. He turned it on and closed his eyes, listening to the low murmur of his mom and Juniper as they made food in the kitchen.

He was almost asleep when the face of Chad number one flashed in his mind. Eli bolted upright, blankets clutched around him, his breath coming harsh and fast.

Fuck.

He'd really been hoping the oddness of Haruka and the fun afternoon with his friends would let him sail right past the unpleasantness of the Chads.

No such luck.

He scrolled through TikTok until his eyes were heavy, but when he tried to sleep, another, older, face popped into his mind. Not the Chads.

Someone much worse.

He got up and turned on every light in the room, then climbed into Jace's bed—apologizing silently to his roommate. He'd make sure and change the sheets for him before he came back.

Once he'd made a new cocoon, he dove back into his phone again, but instead of social media, he found himself scrolling through his contacts. It was way too late to text anyone now but looking at the names made him feel less alone.

He clicked on the contact labeled HotJerk and read through the short correspondence he'd exchanged with Haruka over the past week. The guy was laconic to say the least, but something about the words soothed Eli. His eyelids began to feel heavy, and he allowed himself to drift asleep.

Rough cloth covered his face, blocking out his surroundings. He'd been here before. Or was he still there now? Had he never left?

Eli tried to rip the bag off of his head, but his broken arm slowed him down, forcing him to struggle one-armed until he fell off the cot he'd been left on. He hit the floor, and a small avalanche of stacked cans rattled as they scattered across the floor.

Heavy footsteps pounded down the hall, and Eli froze. He'd woken him up!

He wiggled and twisted trying to shove his small body under the cot, but his arm was screaming, and the fall had left him disoriented. He couldn't figure out which way to go.

The door slammed against the wall.

"The hell are you doing in here?" The hungover voice of his captor slurred loudly.

Eli didn't answer. Instead, he curled into a small ball and waited for what would come next.

RRRRRRRRRRRRRR!

Eli gasped and flailed trying to get his bearings. For a moment he wasn't sure where he was, or how old he was.

His heart was beating so loudly his ringtone didn't even register at first.

It was still dark outside, but the brightly lit room gave Eli a fighting chance to find his phone in the tangled mess he'd made of Jace's bed.

It took so long to find it, he was certain the caller would give up, but when it went to voicemail, it began to ring again almost immediately. His lock screen read HotJerk.

Why would Haruka be calling him so early?

"Hello?"

"Are you okay?" Haruka's voice was husky, as though he too had just woken up.

No, he really wasn't, but he wasn't about to admit it. "Well enough for someone awoken from a dead sleep."

Something Eli was extremely grateful for. He really didn't like it when his nightmares progressed past that point. He would have been skittish all day if it had. Still might be if he didn't do something to get his mind off of it.

"Actually, I'm glad you called."

A pause. "Really?"

"I fell asleep before I could finish my reading assignment for today." Eli glanced at the clock. It was five o'clock. Three hours before he needed to get ready for class. "Now I have time to finish it."

"Hn." There was a rustling sound. "What's your assignment?"

"*Tale of Genji*."

More rustling. "Want me to read it to you?"

"Um . . ."

Yes.

Right now, all Eli wanted was to sit in bed and have someone read to him to keep the shadows away, but he didn't have it in him to verbalize it. So, he did what he usually did when he was nervous. He got bitchy. "You have a copy? Seems a bit cliché."

Haruka snorted. "No, but I have access to the internet. It's not like it would be hard to find."

Eli heard the clicking sound of fingers on a keyboard.

"English or Japanese?"

Eli sucked in a breath and his stomach got all tingly. Why did the idea of Haruka reading to him in Japanese make him feel so dizzy? "Ah, my Japanese isn't good enough for me to follow along, especially since it's for a class," Eli lied. He didn't speak it well, but years of watching anime made him very good at understanding the language. But the tingly feeling inside was too much to process right now.

"English then." There were a few more clicks on Haruka's end, then, "Where did you leave off?"

"I just started section two."

Eli listened to Haruka's voice as he narrated the marriage of Onna San no Miya to a commoner. It was deep and rich and sent slow, lazy swirls of sensation through Eli. It washed away the terror he'd been steeped in when he'd first awoken.

After a while, Eli's eyes started to drift closed, but he forced them open—he didn't want to miss anything. "You should be a voice actor."

"What?"

Shit, had he said that out loud?

"Nothing. I didn't say anything." Eli buried his face under the blankets and silently screamed into the mattress. Stupid mouth saying stupid things without stupid permission. "Keep reading."

"How far do you need to read for class?"

"Part four chapter 8." Which they had passed some time ago. "Sorry, I spaced out."

"No, it's okay, it's just . . . it's getting late. You should eat breakfast before class. Do you want to go get something?"

Yes. He very much did, but Eli was also a massive chicken. "No, it's okay. I'm not much of a breakfast person."

"You should become a breakfast person." There was an edge to Haruka's voice. What was up with him and food?

"I should take a shower though." Eli deflected. With the way his stomach felt right now, there was no way he'd be able to bring himself to eat anything.

"What room are you in? I'll bring you something."

Yeah, that wasn't happening. Just the idea of Haruka in his room sent Eli's stress level to an eight. "Oh crap, my phone is on one percent battery, I gotta go, bye!"

He clicked end call and threw his phone across the room like it had burned him. The power cord he'd plugged in half an hour ago caused it to halt halfway through its journey and slam to the floor with a clatter.

"Oh shit!"

Eli lunged for the phone and hit the floor in an undignified sprawl. His feet had been tangled in the sheets so thoroughly he was now hanging from the bed by one leg. His free foot had left a sock behind. He groaned and looked at his phone in sympathy.

"And that's what instant karma looks like."

He kicked his leg until it was free, somehow managing to retain that sock. Then he reached for his phone. He really didn't want to turn it over.

"Listen. If my head isn't cracked from taking a dive, your screen can't be cracked, okay?"

Eli flipped it over.

Oh, thank god. Undamaged.

Eli punched a fist into the air and rolled to his feet.

Okay. Time for maximum effort.

He wasn't exactly in a rush, but if he didn't want to look and smell like a hobo *and* get coffee before class, he needed to get going. What should have been a long morning of hugging his knees in a corner had gone by in the blink of an eye.

If he kept going—and was very lucky—he might not spend the entire day hiding under twelve layers of clothing.

He made his way to the shower room and found Ash rubbing a towel through his hair in the changing area. "Hey, what are you doing here?"

"Well, I'd like to say it's a social visit, but our shower room is busted. I guess it's my turn to visit your floor."

Eli laughed awkwardly. "If you ever do decide to make social visits to the shower room, warn me first so I can be in Florida."

"You're not my type, dude." Ash snapped his towel at Eli, who yelped and ran, nearly losing his bath supplies in the process.

Eli had reached his usual shower stall when a thought hit him. Haruka and Ash lived on the same floor, and if their shower was broken . . .

It was like someone hit fast-forward on Eli. He found himself taking the quickest shower of his life. He was shrugging his shirt onto his wet body and sliding on bare feet through the changing area before Ash had even finished getting dressed.

"Where's the fire? Or did you miss me?" Ash yelled to him over the sound of the blow-dryer he had aimed at his head.

"I forgot I had something to do!" Eli yelled over his shoulder as he ran out the door. If he ran into Haruka right now, he wasn't sure he could handle it. His heart was already going crazy just thinking about it.

He finished getting dressed in his room, managing to keep it down to only a green hoodie, a white long-sleeved shirt, and jeans. Then he put in his earbuds, cranked up his Distraction playlist, and took the stairs instead of the elevator—just in case.

CHAPTER 14

ELI

His morning went by at warp-speed.

Just because he'd narrowed down the number of classes on his schedule didn't mean he wasn't still taking a stupid number of classes.

He was planning on having lunch—he really was—but made a quick U-turn when he spotted Haruka in line at the counter.

Nope nope nope.

What the hell was up with his body today? Why did it go crazy every time he even thought about Haruka?

He pulled out his phone.

Eli: Can one of you grab me something to eat and bring it to the club meeting?

I'm not going to be able to grab lunch today

mAlice: Sure, babe, I got you. Anything wrong?

. . .

Eli: Nope! Just busy

It wasn't a complete lie. He wasn't going to be able to get lunch because he didn't have time to hit up another cafeteria and make it to his next class. And that counted as being busy, right?

He gave the cafeteria a wide berth—just in case he was spotted from a window. Not that he thought Haruka would come sprinting after him, wielding a burrito, but one could never be too careful.

By the time he made it to the club room for his first official meeting of the Tea and Calligraphy club, his stomach was punishing him for depriving it all day. He really should have grabbed something from the coffee cart other than coffee, but he'd been too keyed up to even think about eating.

When he spotted Alice waving a bag at him from a table, he could have hugged her.

"I'm ready to propose marriage if that's what it takes to get that bag, Alice." He slid into a seat beside her, hands clasped together, pleading. He didn't know what was inside the bag, but the smell was torturing him.

"Don't give me those puppy eyes. Of course, this is for you. You're too skinny as it is." Alice pointed to his baggy sleeves. "And don't go proposing to just anyone. Someone might take you up on it and steal you away from us."

Eli didn't respond, he was too busy stuffing the grilled cheese sandwich he'd discovered into his mouth as fast as it would go.

"And definitely don't make those sounds in public." Nate said from across the table.

"I'm hungry!" he said between bites.

"And whose fault is that?"

Eli kept his eyes glued to his food and continued to eat so he didn't have to answer. It was clearly Haruka's fault, but he'd pick never eating again over mentioning that piece of info to his friends. Nate already had issues with the man. If Eli said he made him too nervous to eat, he doubted it would make his friend less worried.

The sound of clapping filled the room. Everyone turned to see Kate standing at the front of the room with a wide smile. "I think everyone is here, so we can get started."

There weren't a lot of people in the club. With the addition of Eli and his friends, it brought the total number of members to eleven. Eli and Nate were the only guys, and it was easy to see by the sparkle in his friend's eye exactly how he felt about it.

"First, I want to start by welcoming our new members. Raise your hands and introduce yourself, guys!"

Eli poked a few fingers out of his sleeve and gave a quick wave but didn't say anything. He was there to get better at calligraphy and hang out with Alice and Nate—not to make more friends.

Alice wasn't as reserved though, she raised both hands and cheered like she was at a football game. "Nice to meet you everyone! I'm Alice and this shy cutie here is Eli. Don't be afraid if he runs away the first time you introduce yourself to him. It's his way of saying hi."

"Alice . . ." Eli whispered through gritted teeth. Not that she was entirely incorrect, but she didn't need to make a big deal about his sad lack of social skills.

Nate stood up and waved. "I'm Nate—as most of you already know. I'm glad to see some new faces and look forward to meeting you and learning everything you all have to teach me." He cocked his head to the side and gave a charming smile—one Eli knew for a fact he practiced in the mirror. "And if Eli runs away from you, I promise to catch him and bring him back for a proper introduction."

When Nate sat back down Eli leaned forward and hissed. "You two planned this, didn't you?"

"It's for your own good, sweetie." Alice patted the table next to his hand.

Nate, on the other hand, merely grinned and pointed his attention back at Kate.

"Usually, we start off each meeting by going around and asking everyone what their goals are for the week. It gives members with less experience a chance to get advice and support from everyone in the group. Even new members are welcome to give advice if you have any insight. We're all here to learn and have fun, after all.

"We only have one rule here, and I'm going to clear the floor for Raina who is the enforcer." Kate bowed theatrically and stepped aside for a tall young woman with a long, black braid, a ripped black crop top, and motorcycle boots.

She topped Eli by half a foot. Hopefully the rule would be easy to follow. Getting on Raina's bad side wouldn't end in his favor.

"Hi everyone." Raina's voice was quiet but strong. Something about it reminded Eli of Haruka. "Rule number one is easy enough to follow, so I'm not anticipating any trouble. Simply put, just don't be a dick."

Alice laughed. "I knew I was going to like this club."

"Everyone here has a right to their opinions as long as they don't trample on anyone's right to be themselves. We welcome everyone for who they are and respect their thoughts. And"—one by one, Raina made eye contact with all of the newcomers—"we expect all of our members to do so as well."

Eli breathed out a sigh of relief. He could do that.

"I think we picked the right club, guys." Alice's soft smile made the ball of anxiety that had a near-permanent home in Eli's chest unravel a bit.

"I think you're right."

"I know we were right," Nate said, with his eyes on two women sitting at the table next to them.

"Be polite." Alice warned. "I'm not having your lecherous ways get us kicked out on the first day."

"I'm always polite." Nate put a hand on his chest, offended. "I save all of my rudeness up for you, dear."

Alice gave him the finger.

The next half hour went by as each member talked about current projects and the progress they had made so far. The only other new member, a small, mousey girl named Helen, said she was mostly interested in making snacks that paired well with tea. She looked at the floor when she said this, as if half expecting to be kicked out.

"Finally!" Kate pumped a fist in the air and exchanged happy looks with a club member whose name Eli had already forgotten. "We've been waiting for a snack-maker! I've been keeping room in the budget for this just in case."

Helen's eyes left the floor. "Really?"

"You have no idea." The nameless club member jumped in eagerly.

Eli tuned out of the conversation as they chatted happily about what equipment they could afford to buy to aid Helen in her quest. It was his turn next—he had to prepare himself for what was about to happen.

It was really a crapshoot whether or not he'd be able to say anything coherent in a large group of people. Sometimes the stars aligned properly, and he'd be able to control what came out of his mouth. Other times he froze up so bad he'd barely be able to say anything.

Finally, the conversation died down, and it was Eli's turn. He tucked his hands deep inside his sleeves and dove in. Sometimes if he just started talking without thinking the problem sorted itself out. "Hi."

. . . And then other times his entire English vocabulary deserted him.

Like right now.

Desperately, he cast around the room, and his eyes fell on Alice who smiled broadly, gave him two thumbs up, and mouthed, *You got this!*

He took a deep breath and tried again. "Um, I'm a language major and . . . I like to write."

Excellent job, Eli. Keep it up.

"Right now, I want to improve my skills in writing kanji, but . . ." And the words were gone again. Stupid fear of public speaking. He pushed forward. "Sometimes I get stuck in thinking that I'm wronging the Japanese language by writing it so badly, and I give up. But when I do it right, I'm really happy so . . ." He trailed off. That was it. He'd used up all of his words at the moment. Hopefully it was enough.

For a few nerve-wracking heartbeats no one spoke and then . . .

"H-have you tried practicing what you want to write in English first?" Helen asked, eyes just to the left of where Eli was sitting.

"Actually, no. Usually I just dive into it and get frustrated halfway through when it doesn't come out right." Eli's fingertips peeked out from his sleeves.

"Helen's got a good idea, Eli," Raina said. "Try practicing what you want to write in a language you're comfortable in first. Once you feel confident, switch over. Or you can do what I did. I had the same problem when I first started learning hanzi. I treated it like I was transcribing something sacred, and my Chinese teacher teased me saying he'd given me his grocery list to practice with. When I started treating it like a utilitarian function instead of art, it got easier. It's all about reframing."

Eli let out a small laugh, surprising himself. "Thanks." He liked Helen's idea more. Kanji was too pretty to ever be utilitarian to him.

Once the group broke up to work on projects, Eli scrolled through Pinterest, looking for something that inspired him. If a project wasn't interesting, he wouldn't finish it.

He scrolled past cute kitten videos—reluctantly—and various K-pop stars—even more reluctantly—until he came across a quote that stopped him in his tracks.

He ran to grab a brush and paper and hurried back to his seat. As soon as his brush hit the paper, he lost himself in the peaceful dichotomy of brisk motion and stillness. The background noise fell away. He didn't have to think about anything else, only the gentle swoop of the brush and the slight resistance of the paper as it gave way to the ink.

When he was done, he leaned back to examine his work.

I cannot remember exactly the first time your soul whispered to mine, but I know you woke it. And it has never slept since.

~ JM Storm

It wasn't perfect, but he hadn't left a bazillion little splotches in his wake, so he was counting it as a win.

"Jesus, Eli." Alice breathed, alerting Eli to the fact that she was hovering over his shoulder. "I had no idea you were so romantic. Maybe I should have accepted your proposal after all."

"Um, I'm not, really. This just caught my attention."

How could it not have? He had his own private mystery voice living in his head—one that had been oddly quiet over the past few days.

Was it okay?

The back of his mind tingled and for a split-second, Eli was wrapped in the sensation of hot sun beating on his back and a deep feeling of satisfaction. Then it was gone.

What the . . .?

CHAPTER 15
ELI

. . . *But I know you woke it. And it has never slept since.*

Eli hit his pillow for the $5{,}789^{th}$ time that night. Yesterday, Jace had called him to let him know he wasn't going to be back that night—or the next. His dad had broken both of his legs, and Jace was filling in for him at his family's farm stand until further notice.

Which, of course, sucked for Jace's family, and Eli had assured him he would be fine—all while chewing a hole on the inside of his cheek.

He could do this. Hell, children could do this.

Juniper had been unbelievably supportive of him and his sleeping issues when they lived together. She never complained about missing out on sleepovers because her brother didn't have his shit together enough to sleep on his own. Which was a miracle since she never hesitated to give him shit when she had the chance.

He owed her and everyone in his life to overcome this issue.

It was now night three of him sleeping in a room by

himself. Not that he had actually done much sleeping. Mostly he drifted in and out of a light doze until jerking awake at the first hint of the shadow man appearing in his dreams.

He'd gotten to the point where he was afraid to close his eyes. He didn't want to get trapped in another nightmare. It wasn't like he would get lucky again and have Haruka call and wake him from it before it got bad.

He'd never asked Haruka what he'd called for either. It must have been important if he'd had to call before the sun rose.

The urge to call him now was sudden, like a punch to the gut. Eli had his phone in his hand before he even considered what he was doing. Until he saw in blinding glory, the big, fat 3:19 a.m. on his lock screen. It was way too late to call anyone right now.

Especially someone he'd been actively dodging for the past two days. What was he going to say? *I'm sorry I keep running away every time I see you, but when I do I feel like I'm going to throw up and explode all at the same time?*

Eli rolled off the bed with a groan and did all the push-ups he could manage before his arms rebelled and dropped him to the floor—a sum total of fifteen. He should probably work on his upper body strength. It wasn't like he had anything better to do at night.

He pressed his cheek to the floor. It was half on the rag carpet his mother had made him and half on cold concrete. The contrasting textures gave him something to contemplate until the poem he'd copied shoved its way into his brain again.

. . . *And it has never slept since.*

The Voice had been intermittently active all day that day, but it was never anything concrete. Just random swears and unconnected phrases. The last one had been shortly before Eli tried to go to bed and was as enigmatic as all the rest. :*At least tomorrow . . .* :

Tomorrow? Tomorrow, what, Voice?

As far as Eli knew, there were no school events planned for tomorrow. So, unless it was personal, tomorrow was nothing. Though just to be on the safe side, Eli decided he'd stay away from any and all clock towers just in case the voice in his head decided to go on a killing spree.

He'd reached a new low point in his life if he was lying on the floor at ass-thirty in the morning wondering about the potential mental instability of the voice in his head.

But what else was he supposed to do? He only had two tomorrow—well, at this point he might as well call it today —and thanks to his newfound free time, he was caught up on all of his class work. He'd even studied the first two chapters of the advanced geometry class he had later today. Most of it had even made sense.

He climbed back onto his bed and fumbled around until he found his phone. 4:00 a.m.—two hours before the library opened. All he had to do was kill two more hours, and then he could go and take a nap at the library.

He'd discovered this useful loophole a couple of years ago. Something about the peace and quiet of the library made him feel like nothing bad could ever happen to him there. So, at the very least, he could guarantee himself enough sleep to be able to keep up with his studies.

There was something wrong with his feet. Or possibly the door. Maybe both.

Whatever the case may be, actually entering his geometry classroom was proving more difficult than Eli would have guessed. It was only the idea of getting caught hesitating on the threshold that got him motivated enough to go through the door. Into a completely packed classroom.

Was it this full last time?

He cast around the room looking for a vacant spot, but there was only one.

Cool, mahogany eyes warmed as soon as Eli met them. The shivery thing in his stomach flared and then doubled in size when Haruka tapped the desk next to him.

Eli didn't realize he was still standing in the doorway until Haruka raised an eyebrow. With the sun behind him and his head tilted just so, he looked like a pop star at a photoshoot.

Eli's bag fell off his shoulder and hit the ground with a thump.

He briefly considered leaving it there and making a run for it, but the playful challenge in Haruka's eyes had him scooping it off the floor and heading for the empty desk.

When he sat down, his shoulders instantly began to creep up to his ears as he waited for—well, he wasn't sure, but he was certain something was about to happen.

Except it didn't. Haruka didn't tease him or ask why Eli had been hiding from him the past few days. Instead, he gazed at Eli with a thoughtful expression—much like he had at the fair.

Maybe Eli had been better at hiding from him than he'd thought? Though on at least two separate occasions, Eli could have sworn they'd locked eyes before he'd fled.

He sat frozen with Haruka's quiet eyes on him. At first, he thought he was going to vibrate right out of his skin, but when he realized Haruka wasn't going to say anything, his shoulders relaxed.

"Thanks." Eli ventured. "For saving me a seat."

Haruka nodded but said nothing.

And then continued to stay quiet for the entire class.

Outwardly, he seemed to have completely forgotten about Eli's existence from the moment class started. But there was a subtle energy about him that made Eli feel like Haruka was very aware of his existence. It was as if Haruka was leaning toward him without moving an inch.

Which made it very difficult for Eli to focus on what the teacher was saying. He challenged himself to write down every word she said so that, even if he wasn't able to process it now, he could look at it all later and try and take it in then.

When the class ended, Eli hurriedly stuffed everything back into his bag, but before he left, he couldn't stop himself from glancing over at Haruka. It was just a quick peek through his bangs, but it was long enough for him to be stunned once again.

Haruka had his head propped up on one hand and tilted to the side. Once again, a lock of hair had escaped his short ponytail and fell charmingly over one eye.

And every single ounce of his attention was locked onto Eli.

Before Eli had a chance to say or do anything, Haruka stood, plucked Eli's bag out of his hands, and headed for the door.

Eli blinked, then scrambled to his feet, and ran after him. "Hey!"

Haruka didn't acknowledge his shout, but instead continued walking, leaving Eli no choice but to follow him out of the building.

He fell in step beside Haruka and tugged at his hoodie strings. "Um . . . I'm going to need that back at some point."

"You'll get it back."

"Planning on telling me when?"

"Eventually."

Well, if Haruka could play at being mysterious and nonverbal, so could Eli. He bit his lip and promised himself he wouldn't say another word, even if it killed him. If he had to, he'd wait until Haruka became distracted then grab his bag and run.

He did a rather excellent job of being quiet until the kitten happened.

The sound he made was very manly. In fact, he didn't make a sound at all. He was certain of it. But if he had, it would have been an incredibly manly one.

The little paws that perched on his foot were so painfully cute, he immediately didn't let out a few more very manly sounds.

He crouched down. "What are you doing here?" Eli ran his fingers through soft, gray fur and found a tag. "Dakin? Isn't that an animal shelter near here? Did you run away?"

The tiniest little pink nose nuzzled against his hand and green eyes stared into his. He reached out his other hand and gently scooped it up.

Tucking it against his chest, Eli stood and said, "I think I've found a quest."

He looked up from the stripy, gray ball of fur in his arms to see Haruka giving him an inscrutable look. Eli took a step back from the intensity of his gaze.

"You don't have to come with me, I can find"—he lifted the kitten's tail—"his home by myself."

Haruka blinked slowly, looked down at the kitten, then back up at Eli's face. "I'll help you."

"Oh."

What was Eli supposed to do right now? If it were Alice

he was talking to, he had a feeling he wouldn't be having such a hard time trying to figure out what he was supposed to say or do next. What was it that made Haruka so different?

It couldn't be that he sometimes liked to tease Eli—Alice did it all the time. But when she did it, it didn't make his face hot or make his hands and feet feel like they were suddenly five times larger than usual.

"Okay then . . . I think the first thing we should do is call the shelter to see if they have any information on this little guy."

Haruka pulled out his phone. "I'll look up their number."

Eli nodded and turned his attention back to the kitten who had busied himself in trying to nurse from his armpit.

"You found him!"

A girl about Eli's age ran toward him at full speed, her long hair trailing behind her like a streamer—there was no way she was going to stop herself before she smashed into him. Eli closed his eyes, wrapped his arms around the kitten, and braced himself for impact.

He heard an *oof*, but nothing happened. Eli opened his eyes to see Haruka standing in front of him with an armful of flailing girl.

"Sorry! I just got so excited when I saw Rocky. I thought I'd never see him again."

Eli narrowed his eyes when he noticed the girl's hands pressing against Haruka's chest. "What was he doing running around a college? He's only a baby." Was that his voice? Jeeze, he sounded bitchy even to his own ears. Maybe he needed to eat something.

Haruka steadied the girl and stepped back, nearly bumping into Eli, but dodging to the side at the last second.

Ugh. Surprise, random people. So stressful.

Eli fished around in a pocket until he found his earbuds, put them in his ears, and hit play on his phone. He kept the volume low enough that he could hear what was going on, but still loud enough to give him a small barrier between himself and the situation unfolding in front of him.

"He darted out of the door when I stopped to pump gas. I think maybe his carrier wasn't closed properly, and he busted it open and ran. Poor little guy must be terrified. I just got him today." None of this was said to Eli because the girl couldn't seem to keep her eyes off of Haruka.

Bad manners notwithstanding, Eli had no reason not to give the kitten back to the girl—especially since he had no home to give him. "Just keep an eye on him better, okay?" He pressed his nose into the kitty's fur in a silent goodbye, breathing in its one-of-a-kind kitten smell. He really needed to have his own cat someday.

He made to pass the kitten to the girl, but Haruka intercepted. He held his hands under the small bundle, waiting until Eli released him into the larger man's care. Then he passed the kitten to the girl who proceeded to touch Haruka far more than the situation warranted in Eli's opinion.

Then for some unknown reason, she didn't leave. "So, what are you two up to today? I hope I didn't keep you from anything important?"

"We have class soon," Haruka said shortly

Eli fidgeted with his hoodie strings. He didn't have any more classes that day, but he had no trouble keeping quiet about it if it meant the overly friendly girl would go away.

"Oh, okay then." She continued to linger as she stared at Haruka. For a moment, Eli thought he was going to have to abandon his backpack to escape the increasingly awkward situation, but Rocky squirmed and tried to jump out of his person's arms. "Ack! Stop it, Rocky! I'd better go before he gets away again. Can I call you so I can thank you properly? I'm Amanda, by the way."

Eli was certain the girl hadn't looked at him once the entire encounter. Hopefully, Rocky wouldn't starve to death under her care. Maybe Eli could hide the kitten under his bed? It wasn't too late to grab him and run.

"No thanks necessary. Come on, Eli, let's go." Haruka turned and walked away without so much as a glance at the girl or her kitten.

Eli waved goodbye to the surprised girl and jogged to catch up with Haruka. They walked in silence for a few minutes until Haruka tugged on Eli's earbud cord and placed the bud in his own ear.

"Thai pop music? Meung poot passa Thai, reu bplau?"

Haruka had just asked—somewhat rudely—if he spoke Thai. Eli's grin could have split his face. He politely answered in Thai. "Yes, but I think your accent is better."

Haruka switched to Japanese. "How's your Japanese?"

Eli responded in kind. "I understand it better than I speak it. It's a work in progress, but I'm getting there." Eli switched to Hindi, "I've been told my accent is better in Hindi, but my vocabulary is limited. What about you?"

Haruka snorted. "It's garbage." He switched to Mandarin. "This is my best language, after Japanese."

"Seriously? Even better than English? That's completely unfair."

"I've had longer to practice. I am older than you, after all."

"I had, in fact, noticed that."

What Eli hadn't noticed was how close they were to each other as they walked. It wasn't until his sleeve brushed Haruka's jeans that he realized. Eli could have moved over to gain some space, but since his body wasn't making him do it, maybe he could just relax a little.

Would it really be the worst thing in the world if they accidentally touched? He'd touched Nate the other day by accident, and it hadn't been the end of the world.

They continued playing Eli's favorite game in the world until Haruka stopped in front of the main cafeteria.

"What's with you and food?" Eli asked.

"You're not hungry?"

Eli's stomach growled loudly. "Maybe a little?" He rubbed the back of his neck sheepishly. "Will you give me my bag back if I eat lunch with you?"

Haruka's mouth curved into a devilish smile. "Eventually."

As they got their food, Eli learned there was only one language where they didn't overlap—Eli was studying Vietnamese while Haruka had chosen Russian. Haruka planned on adding in Norsk as well, but only recreationally.

Eli totally got that. He'd occasionally flirted with Tsalagi—the Cherokee language—as a nod to his father's side of the family and to pay homage to the days he spent as a child going to pow-wows and moon circles before his family had moved north. But there was very little opportunity for him to interact with the language—there were only a handful of speakers in the world and very little media in Tsalagi—which meant he had never made much headway with it.

Halfway through lunch, Alice plopped herself down next to Eli, announcing, "You're both massive nerds, by the way. If you keep this up no one will ever be able to understand either of you."

That was when Eli realized they'd never really stopped playing their game.

Haruka smirked. "As long as Eli can understand me, I'm good."

"Oh really?" Alice shot Eli a look loaded with meaning. "You two are moving fast."

Eli's cheeks heated, and he threw a breadstick at Haruka. "Knock it off. You're going to give her the wrong idea."

Haruka deftly snatched it out of the air and put it back on Eli's plate. "Am I?"

"That was stupid hot, Haruka. Eli, how do you feel about sharing?" Alice asked, because she was a terrible, horrible person.

"You'd better be talking about food right now, Alice."

Alice clapped her hands and broke into giggles. "Don't make this too fun for me, Eli, or I'll never be able to contain myself."

"Make the attempt, Alice, or my hand might slip when I bleach your hair later."

Her hands flew to her head protectively. "Okay, fine, but only if you let me dye your hair magenta."

"No deal."

"But . . ."

"No buts!" Eli shoved back from the table. "Are you finished eating?" Eli asked Haruka.

Haruka nodded and then looked pointedly at the contents of Eli's tray.

"I'm full! You and your weird food fixation. Did you not have enough to eat when you were younger?" He froze. Eli knew nothing about Haruka. What if he grew up poor?

Instead of getting offended, Haruka chuckled. "Whatever you're thinking, you can stop. I had plenty of everything growing up." He stood up, snatching Eli's backpack before he could even think about it. "Come with me, I need to go shopping."

"I am not your errand boy!" Eli shouted, but Haruka had already walked off.

"I'm really starting to like him, Eli!" Alice called to his back as he chased after Haruka for the third time that day.

CHAPTER 16
ELI

"Are you sure you're a college student?" Eli asked as Haruka placed a bag of green onions in the shopping cart. "Because I'm pretty sure there's a rule somewhere that says it's against the law for college students to buy anything green that isn't candy."

Haruka ducked down an aisle, only to come back a moment later with a bag of apple-flavored gummy bears. "Better?"

"Yes, actually. If you were perfect, I'm not sure I'd be able to stand you."

"Can't have that."

"Um." Eli pulled his hood up to hide what he was certain were very pink ears. "Are you finished, or is there anything else you need?" He eyeballed the mostly full cart. How much food did this guy need, anyway?

"Nearly done. If you go get your car and pull it to the front, I'll meet you there."

They'd taken Eli's car to the store because Eli wasn't entirely sure Haruka wouldn't decide to drive them cross-country just for groceries. Just because he acted friendly didn't mean Eli trusted him any further than he could throw him.

"You're not worried that I'll ditch you?"

Haruka tapped the strap of Eli's bag currently hanging from his shoulder. "Nope."

The drive back to the school was filled with an intensive Q&A session—Haruka's this time.

"What was it like growing up in Massachusetts?"

"Boring." Which was the biggest lie Eli had ever told, but he wasn't planning on sharing that story. To divert from a topic most likely to ruin Eli's day, he brought up his sister. People always grabbed onto that particular tidbit when they learned he was a twin. "My twin sister was far more outgoing than me."

"Hn. Did you ever live anywhere else?"

"I was born in North Carolina and lived there for a few years until my dad got a job up north."

"Your dad is where your Cherokee came from, right?"

Eli nodded, not certain why he'd revealed that information earlier. He was a bit sensitive talking about it considering his extreme outwardly white appearance. He was doing a shitty job not oversharing today.

"What was that like?"

"Growing up Cherokee? Uh, it was only for a little while, but I liked it. I mean, I was really little, so all I remember are fragments. Falling asleep by a bonfire at a powwow, using my sister as a pillow. Dancing like a crazy person. The smell of sage. Oh, and the taste of fry bread." He'd never forget it as long as he lived. As far as Eli was concerned, it was the food of the gods.

"What's fry bread?"

"Something I'd make you try if it were available up here. It's so freaking good. But it's not something you can buy easily. You have to make it and I'm a menace when it comes to hot oil." Eli did his best to describe the delicious, flaky treat, but when he got to the part where the best kind was fried in bear lard, Haruka began to look decidedly pale.

Eli pulled into his parking spot in the garage next to his building. "Do I get my bag back now?

"Just let me put my groceries away, then I'll drop you off at your room. You can have it back then."

"No way, if I show you my room, I'll come back from class one day to find it full of bran muffins or something. I'm onto you." Eli pointed at his eyes and then Haruka's.

"Oh no. You've discovered my evil plan," Haruka said evenly as he got out of the car.

When Eli popped the trunk, the first thing Haruka grabbed was Eli's bag, then he took everything else minus one bag of groceries. "You can get that one."

"I'm not your servant." Eli grumbled as he took it.

When he hefted it, he realized it weighed almost nothing.

He followed Haruka silently all the way to his room—he would get his backpack back without revealing the location of his room by any means necessary.

When Haruka unlocked his door, he said, "Follow me." And ignored the plastic bag Eli tried to thrust in his face.

"I promise you hell will freeze over before I go into your roo—Oh my god, you have a guqin." He was across the room and hovering over the instrument without even registering how he got there, noticing only vaguely how Haruka had plastered himself against the wall to avoid being run over. "Can you play it?"

"A bit," Haruka said as he busied himself putting groceries away.

"I've always wanted to learn but could never afford

one." Eli's fingers twitched as he gazed longingly at the simple, but bold design painted onto the enamel. He'd never even touched one before. "And then there's the near impossibility of finding someone to teach me."

"I could teach you." Haruka reached for the bag Eli had carelessly thrown onto the bed as he'd passed by.

"Really?" Eli stepped away from the instrument and sidled over to where Haruka was stowing the last of his snacks in his small refrigerator.

"If you let me walk you back to your room."

Eli leaned against the counter in Haruka's tiny makeshift kitchen. "I could do that, but then I'd give up my right to a muffin-free room."

"Do you have something against muffins?" Haruka placed a large hand on the counter next to Eli's hip.

"Nooo, but I like having the option to decide when muffins come to visit me." Eli pulled his hood down. Would it be weird if he took his hoodie off right now? Because it was getting a bit warm.

"I could give you one lesson so you can see if it's worth letting muffins into your room." Haruka leaned in slightly.

"W-we could do that."

There were little flecks of gold in the brown of Haruka's eyes.

Haruka pulled away abruptly, walked over to the guqin, took it from its stand, and sat with it on the floor. "You coming?"

Eli did his best not to skip from enthusiasm on the way over and plopped down in front of Haruka.

Haruka's eyes flicked to the hoodie Eli placed on the floor next to himself.

"Sorry, is there somewhere I can hang it up?"

"No, it's fine," Haruka said as he worked on tightening the strings on the back of the instrument.

Eli sat cross-legged as he listened to Haruka explain the components of the guqin, how to tighten and loosen the strings, and why it was important to loosen them after you finished playing. Then he showed him a few simple chords and encouraged Eli to try.

It didn't go well.

"Why doesn't it sound the way it does when you do it?" Eli's eyebrows knitted together, and he bit his lip in frustration.

Haruka blinked.

"What am I doing wrong?" When he tried again, it sounded even worse.

"You're pressing too hard. You have to be precise when touching the strings in order to make the sound you want." Haruka reached out and held his hand over Eli's. "Can I touch you?"

Eli looked at Haruka's hand, poised over his, noting the contrast of size and skin tone. Something low in his stomach did a slow roll, and the shivery feeling that he'd forgotten all about kicked into overdrive. His eyes went to Haruka's, and he swallowed hard.

"I . . ." Eli's voice caught in his throat.

Could he? Technically, the answer was yes, of course he could. The real question was whether or not he should.

He searched the other man's face, looking for answers. Haruka looked back at him with patient eyes and a soft expression. There was no pressure there.

But . . .

"Maybe next time?" Eli's eyes went to the floor and landed on his hoodie. His fingers traced one of the strings.

He hadn't meant to say that. He looked up to gauge Haruka's expression.

Instead of showing irritation as Eli half expected, Haruka lips curved in a slight smile and pulled his hand away. "Next time."

"I, um, should probably go. I have homework." On a Friday evening. Could he have come up with a more obvious lie? It was all Eli could do to stop himself from smacking his forehead.

Haruka's lips quirked, but he nodded and stood. "Do you want me to walk you to your room?" He went over to Eli's bag and held it out. Eli took it silently and stared at the floor. What was he supposed to do with his body right now? Every time he was around Haruka it was like he completely forgot how to be a person.

"Maybe next time?" Eli repeated, hating how breathy his voice sounded.

Haruka went to the door and opened it. His eyes were warm. "I'll hold you to that. If you want another lesson, that is."

Haruka stood half in the doorway, which meant Eli would have to pass by closely. He was small enough to do it without touching the large man, but it would be close.

Haruka cocked an eyebrow, and there was a challenging look in his eyes. Almost as if he were asking Eli if he trusted him enough to let him pass.

He could have scurried by, but something made Eli pause halfway through. He turned toward Haruka, leaned against the doorframe, and forced himself to look up.

After what felt like an eternity, Eli heard himself say, "You have gold flecks in your eyes."

All traces of gold vanished as Haruka's eyes went dark. "Do I?"

Eli nodded.

"Is that good?" Haruka placed his hands behind his back. Distantly, Eli was aware of the sound of creaking wood.

He nodded again. "I think so."

Why was it so hard to walk away? Eli should really be going right now, but something was stopping him. He couldn't have looked away if his life depended on it. Everything about Haruka invited him in.

Eli tongue darted out, and he licked suddenly dry lips.

The doorframe behind Haruka creaked again.

"I—" Eli began, but was cut off by a loud clatter down the hallway.

They both turned to see Ash kneeling by a pile of books and swearing.

"I have to go, bye!" Eli turned and ran.

CHAPTER 17
ELI

He had to skid to a stop to keep from crashing into Ash, who was in the middle of sorting through papers and books in front of the elevator. Eli crouched down to help.

"Hey man, that was one hell of an entrance. You coming to my rescue, or something?" Ash reached out for the book Eli held out.

Ash's fingers brushed his, and a resounding *wrong-wrongwrong* rippled through Eli's skin. He suppressed a shudder and stood up. "No, just trying to catch the elevator before someone calls it away." He hit the up button, and the doors opened. Score.

"Too lazy to take two flights of stairs?"

"Way too lazy. This muscle mass wasn't made for hard labor." Eli pointed at his body.

:*He knows*?:

Eli's head snapped up as the Voice startled him, and he saw a glimpse of Haruka's shoulder as he went back into his room. The door closed with a bang.

The Voice had never been so loud before . . . Eli

narrowed his eyes, taking in Ash where he kneeled in front of him. "Knows what?"

Ash paused, hand lingering over the last piece of paper on the floor and said slowly, "I know lots of things. You're going to have to be more specific."

When he'd realized the Voice wasn't planning on going away anytime soon, Eli had begun compiling a mental list of everything it said. If there was a real person behind the Voice, he needed to find them. Otherwise, he was going to have to invest in a new therapist.

Ash had mentioned getting his shoes wet every morning because of the Bubble Tea Girls. The Voice had said something about wet feet, hadn't it?

Eli frowned and chewed on his bottom lip. Was the voice Ash?

He shook his head and laughed at himself. What was he going to do? Ask him if he heard voices in his head? That was a great way to send him running for the hills.

"Nothing. Just wondering if you knew a way to help me get more muscles."

Ash sat back on his heels. "Sure, if that's what you're looking for. Meet me at the gym tomorrow at six, and I'll come up with a program for you." He looked Eli up and down and winked. "Personally, I wouldn't change a thing."

If Ash hadn't said he wasn't into guys, it would have seemed like flirting, but Eli was starting to see that it was just Ash's default setting. Charming, all the freaking time.

Great. Now he had to exercise instead of sleeping in. Eli backed into the elevator and summoned a smile. "Th-thanks. I'll be there." Crying internally the whole time . . .

Ash's eyes met his as the door began to close. "See you then."

He leaned against the elevator wall as it began its

journey to his floor. Maybe he could spend the time with Ash finding out if he was the Voice.

There was a ding and the doors of the elevator started to close. Eli darted through them, realizing he'd spaced out and nearly missed his floor. He made it, but his bag didn't. The doors bounced back open when he tugged on it.

Eli ran his hands over his backpack to make sure it had escaped unscathed, and his fingers closed over something odd. A closer inspection showed him that, at some point, someone had attached a tiny, gray stuffed cat to the zipper.

His finger stroked the soft fur.

For a second—just the tiniest, briefest little moment—he allowed himself to entertain the idea that Haruka could be the Voice.

But that would be even crazier than the idea that the Voice was anything more than a loose wire in Eli's brain. Haruka had given Eli no reason to think it was him, and he'd rather run naked through the quad than ask.

No, Ash was a far more likely candidate at the moment. Tomorrow, he would see if he could find a way to collect more clues without getting thrown into a psych ward.

Hell. Eli was in the deepest and darkest of hells. There was no other way to describe what it felt like to force his body to do grueling work while his brain struggled to process its surroundings first thing in the morning.

And Eli was positive it was making sure to punish him extra right now. It wasn't a fan of how little sleep he'd been getting. After he got a shower, he was going to sleep in the library so hard his desk was going to get a dent.

"Crying isn't going to get you the results you're looking

for Eli." Ash said from where he was doing squats. "Even if it does make you look cute."

"You can go fuck yourself." Eli gasped as he fought to keep up with the treadmill.

Ash laughed and came over to Eli. "I think you're all warmed up now." He pushed the button for the cool-down sequence on Eli's treadmill. "Now for the hard stuff."

Eli needed a stronger word than fuck. Like, three times stronger, just for cases like now when a sadistic asshat had the audacity to smile so broadly while Eli was busy dying.

Once the treadmill stopped, Eli hauled himself after Ash, following him to the weights and allowed the bastard to punish him some more. "I noticed when you were working with Jace that you were using the lowest setting. I'll let you get away with that today, but on Monday, I'm bumping you up by five pounds."

"Monday?"

"If you want gains, you have to come here at least three times a week. Don't worry, I'll keep you company." He slapped Eli on the shoulder.

Wrong!

Eli bit through his cheek and tasted blood.

He'd never noticed what a touchy-feely guy Ash was, but over the next half hour, he'd poked and prodded Eli like he was a puppet. Correcting his posture, moving him where he wanted him to go, checking his form as he lifted.

"Your form is terrible. You're going to get injured if you aren't careful," Ash said as he ran a hand down Eli's spine, shaping it as he went.

Eli suppressed a gag. If this kept up much longer, he was going to throw up all over Ash.

On the plus side, it would likely get him out of being the

man's gym buddy—though he would lose the chance to find out if Ash was the Voice.

All morning, Eli had tried to prod at the spot where the Voice lived to see if he could hear anything. The only thing he got was a mounting sense of frustration—which could easily be his own from being over touched.

When Ash finally let him go, Eli barely managed to rinse himself off in the shower before dragging himself in the direction of his building.

Ash kept in step beside him as they walked. "I noticed you've gotten close to that Haruka guy."

Eli stumbled over a loose rock on the sidewalk, and Ash caught his arm.

Wrongwrongwrongwrongwrong!

Instead of getting used to it, his internal alarm was only getting louder. Ugh. Exhaustion was such a bitch.

"I wouldn't say we're close. We share a class together."

"Classmates go shopping for food together?"

"Um . . ." Eli swallowed. Had Ash been watching them?

Ash held his hands up to ward off whatever expression Eli had on his face. "Listen, it's your business what you do and who you do it with. I just thought you needed to know something about him."

"Such as?"

"He's kind of a player. No, don't come at me, I saw the look on his face while you two were together—he's into you. And if you aren't careful, you're going to end up eaten up by him and then thrown to the side like the rest of his harem."

Something hard and cold formed in Eli's stomach.

"You don't need to worry about it," Eli heard himself say distantly. His voice sounded thin and brittle. "I barely know him."

Ash shrugged and changed the topic to the horrors he was planning to inflict on Eli on Monday.

Eli wasn't paying attention anymore, but he continued to nod and make vague noises, hopefully in the right places and waved goodbye when Ash stepped off the elevator to his floor.

His heavy, aching legs got him to his room, and he flopped down onto his bed. This was stupid. *He* was stupid.

There was no reason at all for him to be disassociating over such a trivial thing. He really didn't know Haruka at all. They weren't close. In fact, they'd only hung out a handful of times.

Besides, it was only a rumor. Ash was a freshman like Eli. There was no way he could know for sure what Haruka's dating life was like.

Not that Eli even cared. He wasn't planning on dating him.

He could really go for coffee and a muffin right now.

CHAPTER 18
ELI

He didn't budge from his room for the entire weekend. Not even for a trip to the library. Instead, he dove into his studies. He finished his geometry assignment in a depressingly short amount of time and decided to try and get ahead in all of his classes. If he could test out of future classes, so much the better. Besides, there was no such thing as knowing a language too well.

And when his brain began to flag, he put on a C-drama and let it play in the background while he dozed fitfully. The noise served as a filter while he napped. He was more likely to dream about long-haired cultivators flying through the air having epic sword battles than shadowy assholes who liked to go around kidnapping children.

At least that's what he told himself. Sometimes it even worked.

He prided himself on responding to everyone who texted him—including Haruka. Not that he said much to anyone. Instead, he told them he was buried under his course load and needed the weekend to focus.

When Monday rolled around, he managed to sweat his way through another workout session with Ash. But got no closer to figuring out if the Voice was Ash or not. Eli really hoped it wasn't him. Something about the guy was beginning to ping his creep radar.

The Voice had been silent all weekend. Sometimes, however, Eli got an impression of frustration and worry. He'd almost convinced himself that he was projecting his own feelings onto a creation of his own mind—a kind of imaginary friend to help him deal with the stress of leaving home, but then frustration spiked hard when Eli shuddered his way through Ash helping him stretch his hamstrings.

Eli could have sworn to a jury that he heard the sound of glass shatter against a wall.

He checked his phone when he got back to his room and saw he'd missed seven calls from Haruka while he'd been at the gym. His phone buzzed in his hand while he was checking. It was Haruka again.

"Hello?"

"Where are you?" There was a growl in Haruka's voice.

"Good morning to you too, sunshine."

". . ."

"Did you sleep dial me?" Juniper did that sometimes. He was used to getting bizarre calls from her that she later claimed to have no memory of. Maybe Haruka was the same way.

"Why didn't you answer your phone?"

"I was at the gym. I leave it behind, so I don't get it all sweaty."

"Put it in a plastic bag next time and take it with you."

"You're incredibly bossy first thing in the morning. And in the afternoon . . . also the evening. You should look into that." Eli put his phone on speaker so he could get dressed to go out for coffee.

"What are you doing right now?" Haruka's voice sounded a little softer. Maybe he was starting to wake up?

Eli pulled his shirt over his head and tossed it in the laundry basket. "Getting ready to go out."

"Get breakfast with me."

It was on the tip of his tongue to say yes, but then the memory of Haruka visiting Kate at the end of the club fair flitted into his mind.

"I don't have time for breakfast this morning."

"I'll bring it to you, just tell me where to meet you."

"Sorry, you're breaking up. I'm going through a tunnel, bye!" Eli ended the call.

External frustration spiked again.

No, no, no, not going there. Not right now.

Eli threw on the rest of his clothes and raced out of his room, once again taking the stairs instead of the elevator.

He arrived in class with an extra-large coffee and the wrong book.

Why was he so pissed off right now? He was more of an anxiety kind of guy, not *a tear things apart with his bare hands until he calmed* down sort of person.

Though angry didn't quite cover it, did it? Instead of spikes of annoyance, it was a gestalt of worry, frustration and something else—all simmering together, building in intensity until . . . Until what?

Eli's pen tore a hole in the paper he was scribbling pathetic, incoherent notes onto. He might have had too much caffeine this morning.

When his class finished, he shoved everything back into his bag haphazardly, not caring whether everything ended up in a crushed, disorganized mess or not.

At this rate he wasn't going to make it through the day. Shit. In his haste to get out of his room this morning, he'd completely forgotten to take his meds. At least he'd taken them yesterday . . . right?

He took a detour to the bathroom and washed his face with cold water.

History of Japanese Religion was next. He loved that class because he got to see Alice and hear all of her hilarious, whispered commentary on which religious leaders were queer according to some surprisingly in-depth research she liked to do in her free time.

He took a deep breath and made his way to class.

"Hey, man! I see you survived this morning's workout." Ash waved at him from the steps of the building Eli's next class was in.

He'd forgotten. Ash was in the same class with him and Alice.

"Let me know if you need me to carry you." Ash waggled his eyebrows at Eli and then let out a low whistle. "Shit, look at that girl, she's got legs for days."

Automatically, he turned to see who Ash was talking about and saw a coed in a miniskirt hanging on the arm of a familiar figure. Eli could pick out that short ponytail in a crowd and the profile was unmistakable.

The person leaning down and talking to the beautiful girl was Haruka. Over one shoulder, he sported a light pink backpack, embroidered with a graceful pattern of purple flowers.

The girl lifted her face to Haruka's, leaving bare inches between them. Haruka wasn't pulling away.

Distantly, Eli was aware of a ringing in his ears.

Haruka jerked around and locked eyes with Eli, his gaze burning into him. At first, Eli thought he was going to charge right up to him, but the girl clinging to Haruka's arm leaned on him and stared up at him with doe eyes. Haruka hesitated but eventually turned back around and led her away.

Much like he had with Eli when he'd kidnapped him on Friday.

Only the girl with him seemed to have zero problems with touching Haruka.

All of the foreign emotions that had been swirling around inside Eli spiked, and he grabbed his stomach.

"Hey, are you okay?" Ash took Eli's elbow to support him. The wrongness that spread from his touch was muted compared to the maelstrom going on inside Eli. "I get it though, that guy makes me sick too. That's the third girl I've seen him with this week. Nice touch with the backpack, right? Must make them feel safe and protected or something."

"Or something." Eli managed. "Hey, go on without me. I forgot something." He pulled his arm free and started to walk away.

"You want me to come with? You look like crap."

Eli waved a hand absently. He needed to be alone. Now.

He picked up his phone and called Nate. "Can I crash at your place?"

He met Nate for a quick key exchange, grateful when he asked no questions. The first thing he did in Nate's room was go into his contacts list. He found HotJerk and changed the name. His phone rang in his hand right when he finished. His screen read, StupidHotJerk.

Eli hit decline call. Then he blocked the number.

His emotion storm dialed up to a ten, and he barely made it to the bathroom before his stomach proceeded to turn itself inside out.

Eli didn't know how long he spent leaning against the divider between stalls, trying to summon the energy to go back to Nate's room to lie down, but eventually he realized someone was going to call an RA if he didn't pull his shit together.

So, he did. He zipped up his hoodie, rinsed out his mouth and—bit by bit—he pulled on all of his best emotional armor. Then he made his way back to Nate's room on shaky, but resolute legs.

Guys were stupid.

Especially the hot ones.

It was good he hadn't gotten attached before finding out exactly how much of a jerk this one had turned out to be.

It wasn't like they were dating.

Or that Eli cared what Haruka got up to in his spare time.

His stomach rolled once more, but it was definitely empty now. No point in running back to the bathroom.

He went into Nate's closet, pulled out a sweater, and put it on. Then he crawled under the covers on Nate's bed.

He spent a very long time not caring about Haruka before he finally fell into an exhausted sleep.

CHAPTER 19
ELI

"*This wouldn't be happening if you weren't so pretty, boy.*" *Rough hands had Eli by the shoulders and shook him until his vision went gray.* "*Just play your role and you won't get hurt.*"

"Eli!"

"*You look just like him. So damned pretty . . .*"

Eli pushed frantically against the sweat-covered chest he was currently being crushed into.

"*My poor son.*"

"Eli! Wake up, buddy!"

Hands shook him, and Eli cried out. He opened his eyes, but the hands on his shoulders didn't fade away with the dream. Was he still there? Frantically he searched his surroundings and saw Nate hovering over him, eye's wide with alarm.

"I'm sorry, but you wouldn't wake up."

"No, it's okay." Eli panted, trying to catch his breath and slow his racing heart. "I'm glad you did."

Nate's phone rang, and he reached to shut it off. "Jerk's

been calling me all afternoon looking for you. Dude is seriously stressed out about something."

"Did you tell him where I am?" Eli's fingers clenched around the blanket.

"What am I, new? I've never given him my number, and now he's spamming my phone right when you want a place to crash. I can add two and two, you know."

Eli let out the breath he'd been holding. "Thanks."

"Do you want to talk about it?"

Eli shook his head. If he had to explain to Nate what had happened, it would mean admitting things to himself he wasn't ready to deal with. "No thanks. Just . . . block him, okay?"

Nate gave a rueful smile. "No problem there. Never liked the guy to begin with. You should hear some of the things Ash has told me about him."

Eli held up a hand. "I don't need to know."

He got up and fished through his bag. He'd forgotten his bipolar meds today, but his anxiety meds were rattling around forgotten in a side pocket. For fuck's sake, he could have taken them earlier. He shook one out and swallowed it.

"I need to go back to my room and get some things." Like the drugs that kept his emotions from seesawing like a sugared-up kid at a playground.

"Want me to come along?"

"No, it's late, I doubt I'll run into him now."

Eli knew his friend. If they ran into him, Nate was hotheaded enough to try and pick a fight with Haruka without even knowing any of the details, and that was the last thing Eli wanted.

"I'll be back soon."

Climbing ten flights of stairs got old fast. He didn't need to work out with Ash anymore, the climb alone would have him ripped in no time.

He opened the door, stepped out into the hall and—

Shit, shit, fuck, fuck, Jesus, fucking shitballs!

Haruka was camped out in the hallway with a laptop and a plastic grocery bag. He didn't look like he was planning on moving anytime soon.

Eli darted back through the door and plastered himself against the wall. At the last minute, he stuck his hand between the door and the doorframe so it wouldn't slam shut with a clang. Instead, it slammed shut with a whimper —Eli's.

He'd just broken his fucking hand because he was a massive coward.

Eli heard a faint sound on the other side of the door at the same moment worry and concern surged in his chest.

No. Haruka wasn't the stupid Voice in Eli's stupid head. He wasn't even going to entertain the idea. Because if he was, Eli was diving from the nearest roof.

Instead, he was taking himself to the school hospital to have his hand checked and never thinking about any of this ever again.

"Eli, honey, what happened to you?" Alice fluttered her hands anxiously over Eli as he attempted to eat his lunch one-handed. He hadn't broken it, but it was going to be bandaged for the next week.

"Maybe you'll have better luck than me, Al. He wouldn't tell me a thing." Nate said mulishly.

"It's embarrassing," Eli said through a mouthful of food.

"Did someone do this to you?" Alice's eyes went ice cold.

Eli sighed. "I did it to myself. Please don't make me admit how. I'm still kicking myself over it."

"As long as there isn't someone out there we need to kick over it," Alice said.

Eli gave a forced laugh. If only.

Imagining Alice kicking Haruka was incredibly satisfying, and for a moment it chased away the nightmare fog of emotions Eli was keeping at bay. He didn't have his bipolar meds, so instead he'd been going to town on antianxiety meds. Not ideal, but it was only a stopgap measure until he could get into his room.

The Voice had better not be Haruka. He had no right to be churning out these levels of worry and concern. If it was Haruka, he could go eat a dick.

Just this morning, Eli had had to fall over himself in order to duck out of sight when Haruka walked by with a swarm of women clinging to every available inch of his body.

Seriously? How had Eli missed this? Maybe Haruka had been having an off week and he'd turned to Eli for some entertainment. He'd been told he was as pretty as a girl often enough.

His throat closed, and he put his fork down, staring at his untouched plate. "I'd better go, or I'll be late for an appointment with my advisor." Eli lied. Actually, he was going to the library for a quick nap between classes, but he didn't want his friends to know how little sleep he'd been getting. They were already worried enough as it was.

No, he just needed to hold himself together until he could get back to his room, get his meds, and catch up on all of the sleep he'd been missing. Then everything would be fine.

He stood up, and the world did a lovely, slow twirl around him, forcing him to stand still until he could get his bearings.

Yes, everything would be just fine.

CHAPTER 20
HARUKA

Thunk!

Arrow after arrow went into the target. None of them even remotely close to where they were supposed to go.

"Are you okay, Haru? I've never seen you this off your game." Aaron, the captain of the archery team patted him on the shoulder.

Haruka shrugged noncommittally. "Just tired."

"I've seen you tired before, and you still make center shots nine times out of ten." Aaron stepped back and took in his stance. "Your shoulders are stiff as a board, and you're glaring at everything that moves. Dude, you don't look tired, you look pissed."

Haruka leveled a dirty look at his captain.

"See? Exactly like that. You know what? I need to . . . go over there now." Aaron took off for the shelter where the team kept their gear.

Haruka breathed out a sigh. People had been running from him all week, but there was nothing he could do about it. He didn't blame them, currently he wasn't fit to be around. The only exception was the horde of women who seemed to be tracking his every movement.

It was a very new, very recent development. He'd never been a social person, so after the initial novelty of meeting someone from Japan wore off, most people left him alone. Some continued to stare from afar, but he could ignore it and focus on his studies.

But on Monday it was like every woman on campus suddenly wanted a piece of him. He couldn't go anywhere alone anymore, and it was maddening.

Like now. The fence behind him was filled with students cheering him on even though he was having the worst practice session of his life.

All of this he could deal with. It was annoying, but after a few weeks of being ignored, they would get bored and find someone else to fawn over.

The problem was the timing of it.

Friday had gone better than he'd hoped. He knew Eli now and understood that when he encountered something too far out of his element, he ran like a frightened child. So, he couldn't push him.

All Haruka needed to do was to get Eli used to being around him. To show him there was nothing to be afraid of when they were together. At this point Haruka would rather cut off a finger than hurt him.

Eli's innocent blue eyes were hypnotic, his every movement—even the clumsy ones—did nothing but draw Haruka in more. As for the pull in his chest, it was so strong, it no longer allowed Haruka the option of staying away.

Haruka knew at some point Eli would run from him on Friday. What he hadn't expected was confirmation that Eli felt the same pull he did. When they were saying goodbye, the look in Eli's eyes matched the intensity building inside Haruka. The inexorable pull was drawing them both in.

Was Haruka a voice in Eli's mind too?

Part of Haruka was relieved Eli had run like a startled rabbit when that fucker Ash had interrupted them. It was too soon, and Eli was so shy. Haruka wouldn't push him. They had time.

Then he saw the look on Ash's face when Eli helped him clean up his mess. It was predatory. Haruka should know. Like recognized like.

And if he acted on the impulse he'd had to rip the bastard's head off when he realized Ash knew where Eli lived, it would have put a crimp in his plan to prove he was safe for Eli to be around. So, he'd left before he ruined everything.

It had been a serious mistake.

The next morning, he woke up from a nightmare Haruka knew belonged to Eli—Haruka didn't have touch issues and had never been assaulted, but the dream had been a garbled mess of images of being beaten and trapped.

But when he'd texted Eli, the boy claimed to be fine, but busy.

What was Haruka supposed to do? Camp out in Eli's hallway and wait for him to come out? He'd do it if he wasn't positive it would send Eli running all the way home.

The pull in his chest was killing him. If he'd thought it was bad before Friday, it had doubled by Saturday, then again on Sunday. By Monday morning, Haruka felt like he was walking around with a gaping wound in his chest and constantly found himself reaching up to touch it to make sure he wasn't bleeding out.

The morning was torture as he *listened* while Eli had

panic attack after panic attack. Something was wrong, but there was nothing he could do. He didn't know where the boy was, and Eli wasn't returning his calls. He'd been on the verge of destroying his room when Eli finally picked up the phone.

And Haruka had blown it. The pull had forced him to be too pushy and scared Eli away. If he'd been able to rein it in just a little, he could have seen him, made sure he was okay, and taken care of him if he wasn't. Haruka knew down to his bones that Eli was not okay.

The pull in his chest punished him brutally after Eli had hung up. All he could think about was finding Eli, protecting him, and if need be, hurting anything that threatened him.

Haruka didn't even recognize himself. Where was the calm, bored young man who'd had everything in his life come so easy? Was this his payment for all of the gifts life had given him?

Now he was a ball of worry, anger, and fear. He had to find Eli.

He'd discovered where one of Eli's classes was, so he'd decided to ambush him, hopefully without scaring the boy to death. Except when Haruka arrived, a girl had fallen down the stairs and needed him to take her to the infirmary.

The plan had been to get her there, drop her off, and get back before Eli's class ended. Then he felt something inside him rip in two and saw Eli staring at him like Haruka had shot him with an arrow.

The pull yanked him toward Eli, but the girl on his arm cried out and weighed him down.

Eli wasn't physically injured, and Haruka was planning on coming right back. He wouldn't wait for class to finish, he would pull him out, talk to him, and explain what happened.

But when he got back, it was too late. Eli had vanished, no one had seen him—or would admit to having seen him—and all Haruka could do was sit in Eli's hall, trying to keep his shit together. Because Eli needed him. His person needed him to be okay until they could fix this misunderstanding.

He kept telling himself he should be happy that Eli was jealous. And that maybe Eli felt even a little of what Haruka was feeling, but the waves of misery pouring through their bond ruined any happiness Haruka could have felt.

Especially when he'd physically felt Eli's pain. It was so intense, Haruka had to examine his hand to make sure he hadn't broken it, but the pain faded to a dull ache after a few seconds.

It still lingered on and off as the days went by. Haruka could feel it now as he sent an arrow careening over the target, missing it entirely. He should go home. His sure-fire solution to a crowded mind wasn't working today, and if he wasn't careful, he was going to accidentally shoot someone.

Kyudo had helped soothe him last week after the first time Eli started avoiding him. He'd been able to lose himself in the heat of the sun and the beautiful stillness of the moment before releasing an arrow brought him. Now he couldn't find the stillness. The hole in his chest was too loud to allow him any peace.

What else was he supposed to do? If he took a walk, his fan club would mob him again. The last time he'd tried, he'd caught a fleeting glimpse of Eli. The boy's normally brilliant eyes were dull, and his body was hunched protectively around his bandaged hand. It took everything Haruka had to not knock the girls surrounding him out of the way and chase him down.

He suspected Eli wasn't eating, and he definitely knew he wasn't sleeping—not enough to have nightmares, anyway. At this point Haruka would gladly accept any nightmares Eli sent him. At least he could be there, helping him in some way.

Eli's friends were no help. Nate glared daggers at him any time Haruka tried to talk to him, and Alice only gave him a sad smile when he'd begged her to make sure Eli ate something.

He had to do something. Anything. If Eli felt half as bad as Haruka did right now, this couldn't continue any longer. He'd scour the entire campus if he had to.

"Aaron!" Haruka called his captain to him. "I need you to do me a favor."

"Will this favor help you get your groove back?"

Groove? Haruka had no idea what a carved space in wood had to do with himself, so he assumed it was an idiom he hadn't learned yet and went for context. "Sure . . ."

"Then I'll do it."

"I need you to distract my fan club so I can get out of here."

"Is that what's been bothering you? Man, you're crazy. I would be happy to take them off your hands."

"They're all yours."

Haruka went to the back of the shelter and hid in the shadows until Aaron went over to the railing and made a big production of stringing his bow shirtless.

No one was looking at Haruka anymore. He took the opportunity to dart out the back of the shelter into the trees so he could cut back around to head for the dorms. He was about to make a serious nuisance of himself.

Two hours and several unwanted phone numbers later turned up nothing. Night was falling, and the hole in his chest had reached truly impressive levels. His hand kept pressing against it like his guts would spill out if he didn't hold them in.

Wrongwrongwrongwrongwrongwrongwrongwrongwrong-wrongwrongwrongwrongwrongwrongwrongwrongwrong-wrongwrongwrongwrongwrongwrongwrong

The blow to his psyche was staggering and nearly sent Haruka to knees, but he found his footing immediately. Eli needed him. Now.

And this time, the pull was telling him which way to go.

He followed the pull to the library at a dead run, ignoring the indignant shout from the librarian as he tore through the lobby and made for the stairs. On the third-floor landing, the pull increased and then cut off abruptly at the same time a faint cry rang out from the other side of the door.

Haruka nearly took the door off its hinges.

"Don't be a fucking tease, Eli."

Ash's voice directed Haruka to the back of the stacks.

When he came around the last bookshelf, he saw Eli crumpled across a table, cradling his head. Ash hovered over him as he pawed at Eli's shirt.

Haruka saw red.

CHAPTER 21
ELI

Why did he have to be like this? Why was he such a trouble magnet?

Eli's week already sucked far beyond the telling, and all he wanted was a few minutes of sleep before he went back to Nate's room to pretend to sleep. Now this?

He knew Ash had been acting weird that morning during their workout. He'd been even handsier that usual, and his flirting had been off the charts. Eli was completely over it and told him he didn't have time to work out with him anymore.

For a second, Eli saw a glimmer of rage in his eyes before he'd covered it with an easy smile.

He recognized that look far too well. Ash was affected by the Thing. Whatever effect Eli gave off that drew in people who only wanted to fuck him or hurt him now had a hold on Ash.

Which meant Eli now had two people to avoid on campus. Perfect.

He just hadn't expected Ash to move so quickly on his desire.

Which was why he'd been rudely awakened in the one place he'd felt safe.

One minute he'd been dozing dreamlessly and the next he was pinned on his back against the desk he'd been sleeping on.

"Ash! What are you doing?" Eli pushed against the chest pinning him down.

"Nothing you don't want." Ash gave him a smile that was different than his usual carefree grin. This one was hard and had a hint of teeth.

"I don't want this." Eli said, pushing at Ash with all his might. The man didn't budge. His inner alarm was going off the charts, sending Eli's already battered nervous system into a complete meltdown. Eli's body began to shake—a sure sign he was about to start shutting down.

That couldn't happen here. Not now. There was no one on this floor, it was late enough that most sane people were out having fun or sleeping. Only Eli was dumb enough to be somewhere he could be easily cornered alone and helpless.

"You don't want to do this. Let me go right now and I won't do anything, but if you don't, I'll get campus security."

"Once I'm done, you won't want to call them. I promise, you'll like this."

How the fuck was Ash getting any hint of desire from Eli? He'd lost touch with reality. Which meant Eli was fucked.

Which also meant he had nothing to lose, so he bit Ash. Hard.

He tried to bolt while Ash swore and clutched his hand, but Eli didn't get far. Ash grabbed Eli's injured hand and pinned it to the table. Then he slammed Eli's head against it for good measure.

Things were muffled and hazy after that. Eli felt the pressure and pain leave his battered hand and heard a sharp cry and a crash. Then nothing but numbness and a ringing in his ears.

"Eli, can you hear me?"

Yes, but he didn't want to. Not if the voice belonged to who he thought it did.

"Eli . . ." It was the worry in Haruka's voice that forced Eli to crack open one eye.

"Why?" *Why are you here? Why did you hurt me earlier? Why would you help me now?*

"Campus security is here. They're taking Ash away. You need to go to the infirmary, but . . ."

Eli tried to sit up, but his head wasn't having it. He collapsed back down onto the table.

"No, don't move. I convinced them to let me carry you." Haruka's voice was close, and the pain in it was unmistakable. "I'm sorry, but I have to do this."

Haruka's hands hovered over Eli's body as if he were steeling himself before going into battle.

"'S okay," Eli slurred. "I can walk if you jus' give me a minute."

A man in a uniform came to the other side of the table and said, "We need to go now, son. They have to check and make sure he doesn't have any internal injuries." He wasn't talking to Eli, but instead to Haruka who stood in front of Eli protectively.

"I'm sorry." Haruka apologized again before reaching his hands under Eli. His fingers brushed Eli's skin where his shirt had been torn away.

Eli's breath caught in his throat. *Oh.*

Haruka cradled Eli's head gently until he could rest it against his chest, and he put his other arm under Eli's knees, lifting him off the table.

Oh my.

Wave after wave of something incredible washed through Eli. If rainbows had a tangible form and could flood every nerve in his body, it would be a pale comparison to how he felt having Haruka touch him.

Eli burrowed into the broad chest in front of him, and his fingers traveled upward, trying to find their way under Haruka's collar.

:*Tickles.*:

:*I'm sorry.*:

Eli was not sorry. Would never be sorry. He'd gone from a pathetic, aching mess to bliss in the blink of an eye. Was this what touching people was supposed to feel like? Why did anyone ever stop?

:*This is different.*:

Wait.

It had taken a moment because of the trauma and assault followed by blissful synesthesia, but Eli realized Haruka hadn't been using his mouth to talk to him.

:*It* is *you.*: Eli stared into warm brown eyes, dumbfounded.

:*It's me.*: Haruka stared back, looking just as spellbound as Eli felt.

"Guys, we have to go. Come on." The security guard snapped his fingers between them, breaking their gaze.

Haruka looked up. "Right. Sorry."

Eli tuned out after that, simply content to drift in and out of the peaceful sea of calm radiating from Haruka. There was a moment when he roused himself—when they took Haruka away from him. He was pretty sure he cried then.

After far too long, Haruka was back, no longer holding him in his arms, but instead holding his uninjured hand. Eli settled down and allowed himself to be poked and prodded while he played with Haruka's hand.

It was a nice hand. Big and strong with a large vein Eli traced from his forearm to his knuckles. Right over a nasty bruise.

"He hurt your hand."

Haruka snorted. "With his face."

Eli's eyes went to Haruka's face. His beautiful face that now sported a split lip. Eli lifted his bandaged hand to it. "Your mouth." His eyes stung.

Haruka's eyes widened slightly. "It doesn't hurt. I'm fine."

Eli pulled away from the nurse who was busy cleaning the wound on his head. "Fix him!"

"We'll get to him next, sweetie."

"No, fix him now." Why couldn't he get his eyes to focus properly?

"You'll have to let him go for us to do that." Amusement laced her voice.

Haruka's hand tightened on Eli's, and Eli squeezed right back. He wasn't ready to let go yet, but . . . Haruka's face.

:*I'm staying. So don't ask me to go.*:

"Okay, but as soon as I'm done, you have to fix him." Eli yawned, and it made his head throb hard enough to break through the happy haze of Haruka's touch. Yawning equaled bad.

"We'll take care of him while you're getting your X-rays."

Eli grumpily conceded.

When they wheeled Eli away for X-rays, the anxiety, stress, and pain all rushed back the moment Haruka released his hand, but he forced himself not to complain because Haruka needed medical care too.

It took forever for them to finish, and they didn't even have the decency to let him sleep through it. All he was left with were his muddy thoughts and his injuries to keep him company.

As they wheeled him back down the hall, he vaguely registered words like sleep-deprived and malnourished and spared a braincell or two to be glad Haruka wasn't around. Otherwise, Eli was going to end up with food in his mouth every time he dared to open it.

"Thank you, Doctor. I'll make sure he sleeps and eats."

Haruka was there.

Eli didn't even get a chance to spin up his anxiety engines before a large hand cupped his face and peace stole over him. He was out in seconds, but not before he heard, *:It's okay. I've got you.:*

CHAPTER 22

ELI

Ribbons of blue flowed softly around Eli as he drifted. Every time he began to wake, a ribbon would wind around him and gently pull him back down.

Eventually, a particularly pressing need gave Eli the energy to fight the ribbons until he was finally able to open his eyes a teeny, tiny bit.

It had been a terrible idea. Everything was blurry and violently bright. Maybe he could hold out a little longer before actually getting up? He'd never been so content.

Eli stretched lazily and snuggled into his bed. His extra lumpy, magical bed that he wasn't ever planning on leaving. Every inch of his body was singing.

Wait, was he dead? Death couldn't be that bad if it felt like this. He ran a hand over his bed, enjoying the silky-smooth, warm texture. The bed rumbled agreeably.

Eli rubbed a cheek against the bed and buried his face in it, breathing in its intoxicating smell. He'd died and now he was in heaven. Who knew heaven was real?

"Stop thinking about dying," his bed said.

Eli's eyes came fully open, and he took in his surroundings.

The bed he was lying on was a person, and the soft, silky sheets were actually warm, golden skin that seem to go for miles.

Eli's head jerked up.

:*Ow.*:

:*Be careful.*: Strong arms came around him to hold him in place.

"What happened?" *And why am I treating you like my own personal teddy bear?*

Amusement rippled through Haruka into Eli. "Do you remember what happened last night?"

Eli scrunched his forehead. "I remember Ash . . ."

The amusement faded.

"And the hospital . . . and you." Eli summoned all of his bravery and looked Haruka in the eyes. They were soft and warm and shimmered with a thousand gold flecks. "You're the voice in my head."

Haruka nodded. :*And you're the one in mine.*:

Eli startled and tried to get up, but once again was locked in place by Haruka's arms. Did he work out or something? "How are you doing that?"

"I don't know. It happened after we touched." Haruka frowned thoughtfully. "It doesn't work when we aren't touching. At least not yet."

"Yet?" According to all the laws of Eli, he should really be freaking out right now. So why wasn't he?

"That's really disorienting." Haruka poked Eli in the nose. "Just say everything you're thinking out loud. You'll be saving me a headache."

"You can hear everything I'm thinking?" How unfair! Eli

wasn't picking up anything other than what seemed like deliberate thoughts.

"You're still doing it," Haruka said in a pained voice.

"I can't say everything I'm thinking."

"Why not?"

Because then you'll know what I'm thinking! Eli just managed to keep himself from saying.

Haruka burst into laughter, rocking Eli's body with the intensity. His arms hugged Eli close to him and he buried his face into Eli's hair. "But I like what you're thinking." His voice was a low purr.

Eli's entire body burst into flames, and he blurted out, "I have to go to the bathroom!"

Haruka relaxed his hold and let Eli sit up. "I'm sorry for teasing you, but you make it so fun." Haruka ran a finger across Eli's cheek, and a million shooting stars followed in its wake.

Eli scrambled off the bed at top speed, which turned out to be a mistake for many reasons.

"Ow." He clutched his head, then his hand, then his stomach. "What the . . .?" Why was he such a mess?

Haruka reached out a hand to steady Eli, and the pain receded. "You have a mild concussion and a few bruises. You didn't reinjure your hand though. How did you hurt it in the first place?"

Like hell Eli was going to tell him he'd busted it while running away from Haruka when he was camped out in the hallway of Eli's floor.

"You've got to be fucking kidding me." Something dark pulsed from Haruka to Eli. It was guilt, worry, and something Eli couldn't put a name to. Maybe Eli couldn't hear all of Haruka's thoughts, but he was getting something from him. "You were that close, and I let you get away. And you were injured running from me . . ."

Eli was drawn toward Haruka and placed a hand on his cheek. "It wasn't your fault, it was me being stupid, as usual."

"You're brilliant, Eli. I only call you stupid when you refuse to use your brain." Haruka lifted Eli's injured hand and pressed his lips against it, eyes staring intently into Eli's. "I wouldn't let someone else call you stupid. Do you think I'll let you do it?"

"Bathroom!" Eli tugged his hand free and winced when the pain from all his injuries slammed back down on top of him. "How are you doing that?" he asked as he staggered toward the door.

"Doing what?"

"How are you making everything stop hurting when you're touching me?"

Haruka's eyebrows raised a notch, and he got up from the bed. "I'll carry you."

Eli's back hit the wall as Haruka advanced toward him. "No way. You are not carrying me bridal style down the hallway where everyone can see."

Again, Eli got a hint of amusement from Haruka. It was fainter now that they were no longer touching, but it was definitely not coming from Eli.

"And if no one could see?"

"Not then either!"

"If you're hurting, I want to help."

Oh my god, was Haruka pouting? Eli looked away before he caved.

"Eli . . ."

Eli kept his face turned away. Everything was extremely

weird right now, and Eli was so far outside his comfort zone he couldn't even see it.

Haruka sighed. "There's a small bathroom in my room. No shower, but it has a sink and a toilet. Just let me help you get there." Haruka pointed to what Eli had previously thought was a closet.

"I'm not letting you carry me four feet across the room either."

"Then lean on my arm." Haruka held out his hand.

Eli looked at it, then at the door to the bathroom and tried to assess exactly how dizzy he was. If he made it, then his pride got a gold star. But if he didn't make it, Haruka was going to scoop him up. Then Eli would have a companion in the bathroom with him, and that was *not* going to happen.

He stretched out his hand and lightly placed it in Haruka's. So conditioned to suffering from physical contact, Eli braced himself, but was unprepared at the ecstasy that raced up his arm. He groaned in pleasure and almost fell into Haruka's waiting arms.

But he stopped himself. Instead, he glared at Haruka's hand and tugged on it until he followed Eli to the bathroom.

Eli opened the door and pulled his hand free. The pain slammed back down on him like a cat with its prey, and he had to take several deep breaths before his vision cleared enough to go inside.

"Don't even think about waiting outside."

"I'm not that weird." Haruka was smiling, but there was something about the way he hovered by the door that made Eli think he was asking himself if Eli should be alone right now.

"I seriously doubt that," Eli said and slammed the door in Haruka's face.

He was in and out as fast as humanly possible, partly because he was half afraid if he took too long, Haruka would barge in to make sure he was okay, and partly because there was something inside Eli that was begging him to go back to Haruka.

When he opened the door, Haruka was a few feet away in his tiny kitchen—not technically standing next to the door, but it was close.

Haruka came to him holding a muffin. A bran muffin. "I have blueberry too, but . . ." He trailed off with an enigmatic smile.

Eli didn't know whether to laugh or cry. "I'm not hungry right now, but—" He held out a hand when Haruka stepped closer. "But I'll take it, so I won't have to find out if you'd actually cram it inside me if I said no."

Haruka smirked and handed Eli the muffin. Then he took him by the hand and led him to a low Japanese-style table. Eli's eyes nearly slid shut on contact and followed docilly.

"You don't have to be so pushy, you know," Eli said when he sat down.

"And you don't have to be so stubborn." Haruka eyed the muffin sitting in front of Eli.

"Do you have coffee?"

"I have milk."

"Milk is coffee's evil cousin. And not an acceptable substitute." Eli tore off a bit of muffin and popped it in his mouth. His knee was just brushing Haruka's.

"I could get you coffee, but I'm not leaving you alone."

"And I'm not letting you carry me through the campus."

"Then no coffee for you."

There was another option.

"Which is?"

"Stop reading my mind!"

"It's difficult when you're sitting in my lap," Haruka said calmly.

"I'm not sitting—" Eli began hotly until he realized that somehow, he'd scooted from his side of the table to Haruka's and was, in fact, half in the man's lap. "Anyway, before I was interrupted—"

"I didn't interrupt you . . . until now."

"You—" Eli made to get out of Haruka's lap, but an arm came down like a seatbelt, locking him in place.

Haruka nuzzled Eli's hair. "At some point we should talk about all of this."

"Yes . . . but coffee, first." Eli didn't want to talk. He wanted to crawl back into bed and wallow in Haruka until the next forever.

"We can do that after we talk."

"Just because I want to do something, doesn't mean I intend to do it," Eli muttered.

"But when they're good ideas, I plan on fully supporting them."

"You're intolerable. Did you know that?"

"Somehow I don't think that's true." Haruka's arms tightened around Eli. "You're tolerating me very well right now."

"Anyway, back to the coffee." Eli had his priorities. "I have a few cans of Starbucks in my room."

"You're finally going to let me in your room?"

"I think at this point I can trust you not to assault me, Haruka."

"Eli." Haruka lifted Eli by the waist and turned him around until they were eye to eye. Eli shifted until his legs straddled Haruka's, but he didn't know where to put his hands. Haruka took them and put them on his chest. "I will never hurt you. I don't think I could if I wanted to."

Eli felt his cheeks heat and watched in horror as the blush went down his arms, all the way to his fingertips. He nodded without making eye contact and pushed on Haruka's chest until he let him get up.

Eli made sure to keep a hand on him until he was steady, preparing himself for the pain when he let go, but Haruka unfolded himself neatly and easily, rising at the same time Eli did, so they could continue holding hands.

"I'm not holding hands with you in the hallway."

"I could carry you."

". . . but it's early enough that I doubt anyone will notice us holding hands," Eli said through clenched teeth.

"That's the spirit."

Eli pulled on Haruka's arm and led him out into the hallway. "You are so much better at English than I am at Japanese. Your idioms trip me up constantly. How do you do it?"

"Well, I've been in your country for three years, I'm older than you—"

"Yeah, you are, ojiisan."

"I'm not *that* much older than you." Haruka tugged lightly on Eli's hand and pushed the elevator button. "But if you want to practice, I'm happy to help."

"Will you help me so I don't have an accent?"

"No."

"Why not?"

"Because your accent is adorable."

Eli spent the elevator ride to his floor staring resolutely in the opposite direction of Haruka, but when the doors opened, he realized he was all but draped over the man when Haruka dipped his head and whispered in Eli's ear, "Are you sure you wouldn't rather me carry you?"

Eli took off down the hall, dragging Haruka behind him and didn't stop until he reached his door.

"You very fast for someone who's—"

"I'm not short." Eli wrestled his door open using far more force than necessary.

"I was going to say injured. You're supposed to rest for the next few days until your next appointment."

That's it. He was going to die. If it wasn't from embarrassment, it would be from throwing himself down a flight of stairs.

"That's not funny."

Eli dropped Haruka's hand, and his head immediately began to throb.

"Private thoughts are supposed to be private."

"How often do you think about dying? Because several times in less than a day is alarming. Is this normal for Americans?"

"It's not—I'm not . . . It's called having a fatalistic sense of humor." *And you won't have to hear it if you stay out of my head!* Eli waited a beat and then smiled when Haruka didn't react.

Excellent. Coffee time. But first . . .

Eli made for his desk to grab his bipolar meds, tapped out his dose, and swallowed it.

"What are those for?"

Eli reached into his fridge and grabbed a can of coffee, opened it and drank half its contents in one go. "You want one?" When Haruka shook his head, Eli shrugged. More for him. "I'm bipolar. These help me manage it."

"What happens if you don't take them?"

"Eh . . . it varies." Eli hedged. Having a fatalistic sense of humor was one thing, but if it was followed by an in-depth discussion on manic depression, Haruka was likely to bolt. And while he wasn't about to run around and tell everyone he met about it, Eli really wanted him to stay.

Haruka propped a hip on Eli's desk and motioned for him to continue.

"If I don't take them, my brain chemistry can't regulate itself, and I'll start swinging from happy to unhappy."

"How unhappy?"

"Very unhappy, okay!" Eli's head pounded, letting him know he'd gotten a bit louder than he'd planned.

"When was the last time you took them?"

"Um . . ." Actually, he couldn't remember. "I'm not sure."

"So, you haven't been taking the medicine you need to take every day to be okay." Haruka's eyes narrowed.

Eli didn't like where this was going. He'd only admitted what they were because he wasn't ashamed to be bipolar and hiding it would be like hiding a part of himself, but Haruka was acting oddly invested considering it was Eli's business. "I've been distracted lately."

Haruka nodded, and a furrow between his eyebrows started to form.

Was he judging Eli?

"And for the last few days I haven't had access to them." Eli blurted out. He gasped as a lance of pain shot through his chest. What the . . .?

Haruka's eyes dulled. "That won't happen again."

Eli's chest throbbed again. "What?"

"If you'd told me you needed something that badly, I would have left you alone."

Eli rubbed his chest. "It's okay. If I'd been smart, I would have asked Nate to get it for me. It's my fault." In hindsight, he probably hadn't thought about it because he was sliding down a nice, deep depression well.

"It's not your fault if I scared you away from something you needed."

Ow, okay. The chest pains were really starting to get old.

"Is . . . is that you?"

Haruka's eyes shuttered. "Is what me?"

Eli pointed to his own chest. "Are you hurting right here?"

Haruka looked away. "I'm fine."

Eli didn't know where the courage came from, but for some reason he found himself walking over to Haruka. Slowly, hesitantly, he reached out and touched Haruka, placing his hand right over the taller man's heart.

The effect was instantaneous, all the tension building up in Haruka over the past few minutes melted away. His shoulders loosened, and his face relaxed.

"It's not okay for you to be hurting quietly," Eli whispered. "Just tell me. I won't break over something like that."

Haruka chuffed a rueful laugh. "You're terrifyingly fragile."

"I'm stronger than I look." Eli shoved Haruka's chest, and it was like pushing a stone wall.

"I can see that." There was no trace of a joke on Haruka's face. He meant it.

"See, now you're just contradicting yourself."

Haruka reached out and wrapped his arms around Eli slowly, giving him a chance to protest if he wanted to. He didn't.

"Even if your body is fragile, it doesn't mean your heart is," Haruka said into Eli's neck.

Warmth trickled down Eli's cheeks. "I'm not fragile," he said over the lump in his throat. "I'm just . . ."

He had no idea how to finish that sentence. Small? Different? He didn't like any of them, but it didn't make them less true.

So, he left it unfinished and burrowed into Haruka's arms. Here was safety, here was where all the good things lived. His eyes began to drift shut and his body went boneless.

An arm went under his knees and Eli's feet left the floor. His eyes flickered open to see that Haruka had begun to carry him to a bed.

"No, that's Jace's bed."

A flicker of disgruntlement passed from Haruka to Eli, and he patted him sleepily.

"Over there." He pointed to the neatly made bed with a Xxxholic butterfly embroidered on the duvet.

He set Eli on the bed and tucked him in. When his head hit the pillow, he began to drift off until Haruka moved away, pulling Eli back to the shores of wakefulness.

Such a terrible prospect made Eli whimper. "Nooo . . ."

The bed sank, and warmth and calm rushed back in to envelop Eli, driving him back into blissful oblivion.

CHAPTER 23
ELI

The next time Eli woke, he didn't have to fight his way free from sleep. His aching head demanded attention, and it wasn't taking no for an answer.

"Yuck, my mouth tastes like ass."

The sun was high in the sky and pouring through the window, highlighting a glass of water and a bottle of Tylenol. Before he could reach for it, Haruka handed them to him, not quite touching his hand as he passed the items over.

Eli took them gratefully. His head didn't hurt half as bad as it had that morning, but his body ached like he'd been tossed around like a ragdoll.

He turned to Haruka, who was staring pensively at something in his hands. Eli leaned forward for a closer look.

"You found my kitty!"

Haruka nodded, still staring down at the small stuffed cat. "It was on Jace's bed. With this." He picked up a familiar hoodie and tossed it to Eli.

His cheeks heated. This looked so bad. There was no

way he could disguise the fact that he'd taken Haruka's things to bed with him as part of his nest.

"It's not what it looks like . . ." He began nervously. How was he going to explain it in a way that didn't make him seem like a complete weirdo?

"What does it look like?" Haruka's voice was a thin veneer of ice over a rushing river—which didn't make words come any easier to Eli.

"Um . . ."

"Do you sleep in his bed?"

Well. This wasn't going in the direction Eli had been expecting.

"Sometimes?" Only when Jace was away—which was every night, currently. Eli knew it was an incredibly childish thing to do. "Is that bad?"

Haruka didn't say anything, instead he kept turning the little cat over in his hands.

What was happening right now? Earlier, Haruka had seemed fine with how weird Eli was. Was it really such a surprise that Eli had a fucked-up sleep situation? Maybe it was one thing too many.

He chewed on his lip and tasted blood, which reminded him . . . "Do you want help with your face?"

Haruka looked up from the cat. "My face?"

Eli scooted forward for a closer look at the cut on Haruka's mouth. It looked small, but he knew it was probably painful, "Your cut. Did they clean it for you at the hospital? I can help you with it if you want."

"Okay." Haruka's pensive expression transformed into something Eli couldn't read.

Eli stood up gingerly, testing to see if his head was planning on cooperating with him. Everything acted the way it was supposed to, so he hunted down his first aid kit and brought it back to where Haruka sat at his desk.

"This might hurt a bit." Eli dabbed an alcohol pad on Haruka's lower lip and stopped when he heard a hiss of pain. "Sorry, I'll be done in just a second." He finished as quickly as he could—or at least he tried to, but he kept getting distracted.

Haruka's mouth was perfect, how dare Ash damage it?

"You have to ask that after what he did to you?"

Eli started, then realized he had a hand on Haruka's chin, which meant Haruka could hear his thoughts. "Perfect can mean a lot of things, you know. Like a painting, or a flower." Eli snatched his hand away before he embarrassed himself further. "I'm all done."

"So, I'm like a flower?" Haruka leaned backward in his seat and put his hands behind his head.

Eli was just happy the weird mood had dissipated, but he couldn't stop himself from saying, "Oh, shut up."

There was a loud pounding on the door, and Eli jumped about a foot into the air.

"Eli, you get your tiny ass up and open this door right now before I break it down."

Holy crap, Eli had forgotten all about Nate. He was halfway to the door before a hand on his arm pulled him back.

"I'll get it," Haruka said, tucking Eli behind him before opening the door.

"What the fuck are you doing here?" Nate tried to push his way past Haruka but was blocked by his arm.

"Taking care of Eli."

"Taking care of—Eli, why haven't you been answering your phone? What's going on?" Nate tried to look over Haruka's shoulder at Eli, but since they were both shorter than the man between them, Eli only saw the top of his head.

"It's okay, Nate's not going to do anything." Eli pulled on Haruka's arm. It resisted him, but after a few seconds, Haruka dropped it and took Eli's hand, sending tingles of delicious sensation up his arm.

Eli tugged at it, trying to get free without drawing attention, but Haruka tightened his grip. Unless he made a big deal out of it, Eli wasn't getting his hand back right now.

Nate stomped into the room and dropped down onto Eli's bed. "I've been calling you since you went missing last night. What the hell happened to your face?"

Eli smacked his forehead, which turned out to be a terrible idea. "Ow . . ."

Haruka glared at Nate.

"Don't look at me, he did that to himself," Nate said.

"I'm sorry! Last night was really weird, and I think I lost my phone. I would have called you but I—"

Haruka pulled Eli's phone out of his pocket and handed it to him.

He had thirty-eight missed calls from Nate and thirty-two from Alice.

"You got a call from the police station, too. They want you to come in and make a statement today if you're up for it," Haruka said, choosing the worst possible time to be helpful.

"The police station? What the actual fuck, Eli?"

"It's a long story." One Eli wasn't looking forward to telling.

"And you." Nate turned his ire on Haruka. "Why didn't you answer Eli's phone when I called?"

Haruka shrugged and pulled Eli closer. “You didn’t answer when I called you earlier this week.”

Nate was back on his feet, and Eli hurried forward to get between his friend and Haruka, holding out both arms. “Jesus, chill, guys.”

Nate growled and sat back down on the bed, glaring at both of them.

Eli collapsed into his desk chair. Haruka followed, sitting on the edge of the desk, keeping his body between Eli and the bed and allowing his hip to bump against Eli’s arm.

Nate gaped openly at the easy contact between the two. “You need to start talking, Eli. When did this happen?” He waved his hand at the nonexistent space between Eli and Haruka. “No, wait, tell me about the police station first.”

“Umm . . .” What was the best way to spin this?

“Don’t dumb it down, Eli. Your friend deserves to know the truth.”

“I wasn’t going to dumb it down.”

“Yes, you were.” Haruka lifted Eli’s chin and forced him to look him in the eye. “Ash hurt you. He deserves to be punished for it.”

“*Ash* did this?”

“It doesn’t look that bad, does it?” Eli hadn’t looked at himself in the mirror yet, but if he looked as bad as he felt, it probably wasn’t pretty.

“You look like someone slammed your face into a wall!” Nate exclaimed.

“It was a desk, actually.”

Nate got up and began to pace, while Eli explained what happened. He tried to leave out the gory details, but when he did, Haruka stepped in to fill the gaps.

"And Haruka stopped him?" Nate looked at Haruka appraisingly.

"He did."

"And the two of you . . .?" Nate pointed between the two of them with an eyebrow raised.

"Aren't fighting anymore," Eli said hurriedly. He wasn't ready to try and explain the complicated and unbelievable connection he had with Haruka to someone else, especially since they hadn't discussed it yet.

"Oh." Nate deflated a bit as his anger began to leave him. "What a fucking asshole. I hope you beat the hell out of him, Haruka."

Haruka's face darkened. "Not as much as he deserved, but yes. I gave him many good reasons to never come near Eli again."

"You're going to press charges, right?" Nate asked.

"Yes," Haruka answered.

"I can answer for myself, thank you," Eli said coolly. "If I pressed charges on everyone who shoved me around, I'd spend my entire life in court."

Court wasn't his favorite place. He'd spent far too much time there when he was a child, dealing with the fallout of his kidnapping.

The room went deadly quiet, and the steady hum of Haruka's presence cut off abruptly.

He was still touching Haruka, but he couldn't feel anything from him.

Oh.

He'd been touching Haruka while thinking about the Incident.

"Nate, I think Eli needs to rest now." There was something wrong with Haruka's voice.

There was a beat of awkward silence before Nate stood.

"I'll go tell Alice what happened, just . . . stay with Eli for me, okay?"

"I'm not going anywhere," Haruka said solemnly.

Nate went to Eli and crouched down. "You should use your friends more than you do. It's what we're here for." He reached out slowly but was blocked by Haruka's hand. Nate gave a wry smile. "I think you're in good hands right now. I'll talk to you soon."

Nate's departure left a vacuum in the room.

"I don't need to rest right now."

"Hn," Haruka said noncommittally, but Eli took it as an acknowledgment that he'd used Eli's injuries as an excuse to get rid of Nate.

Eli picked up the little gray cat and poked at its feet. Haruka's gaze was a tangible force pressing against him, but he didn't look up. "I can't feel anything from you right now." Eli nudged Haruka's leg with his arm.

"Good."

"Good?"

Haruka sighed. "I don't want to hurt you more than you've already been hurt. You don't need the weight of my reactions right now."

"So, it's okay for you to deal with my stuff, but I'm too fragile for yours?" Eli rolled his chair away. "I don't know what this"—he pointed back and forth between them—"is, but I don't think it's here just for me. I may not pick up as much from you as you're getting from me, but I've seen some of your dreams. You aren't any happier than I am. You just deal with it better."

"You've seen my dreams?"

"Some of them. You've seen mine too, right? That's why you called and woke me up last week?" Now that Eli knew Haruka was the Voice, everything seemed so obvious.

"Hn."

"So, what do we do now?"

Haruka's eye's darted to Jace's bed before answering. "What do you want to do?"

The bed thing again. It was as good a place to start as any. "Jace is gone right now. If you wanted to stay with me for a few days while we figure this out, I wouldn't mind. I'd . . . rather not sleep alone."

Haruka frowned. "My room is more comfortable."

Eli couldn't dispute that. It was bigger and had a bathroom. "But all my stuff is here."

"I'll help you move it."

"What about when Jace comes back? I'll just have to move everything back again."

"He can get a new roommate," Haruka said with a hint of a growl.

Maybe Eli would address the whole *moving back to his old room* thing when Haruka was in a better mood.

"Normal people are supposed to be able to sleep alone," Eli said forlornly. He really had tried to make it work and look where it had gotten him.

"Normal people who have gone through what you've gone through don't handle it half as well as you have."

"You've got an answer for everything, don't you?"

"If you ask, I will answer."

Eli laughed. "Fine. Let me grab a few things, and we can go back to your place."

CHAPTER 24
ELI

Moving to Haruka's room took longer than Eli had anticipated. Originally, he'd intended to take the bare essentials, but Haruka took all of Eli's clothes out of his closet, cleared out his desk, and emptied his refrigerator. When he began to fold Eli's duvet, Eli said, "You have a comforter already, we don't need this one."

Haruka had given him an odd look before dropping the comforter and moving on to Eli's toiletries.

He had also refused to let Eli carry anything, which Eli protested, but secretly loved. Moving was high on his list of least favorite things to do.

By the time they had Eli moved in to Haruka's room and stopped by the police station to give his statement, Eli was ready to collapse, but he wasn't allowed to because Haruka was there, demanding he eat first.

"You're a tyrant," Eli said as he covered his plate, shielding it from the chicken skewers Haruka was attempting to load onto it.

"I don't know what you have against food. You need it

to live. Some people actually like it." Haruka took a bite of the rejected chicken.

"I like it just fine in moderate doses. I'm not a giant like you are, so I don't need to eat as much." Eli patted his poor stomach. He'd eaten more today than he had in the past three days. If this kept up, he was going to get fat.

"I'd like to see that."

"Well, I wouldn't." Eli grumbled. He was starting to get used to having his unspoken thoughts answered, even if it was incredibly annoying. He kept trying to maintain enough distance between them to keep his thoughts private, but anytime he stopped paying attention, he found himself draped over Haruka. So far, the man had been surprisingly tolerant of it.

"Hey, why do you think you can hear my thoughts when we touch, but I can't hear you?"

Haruka's face shuttered. "I wouldn't know."

"Earlier, I wasn't able to feel you at all, either."

"Weird." Haruka stood and began to clear the table.

"Haruka."

No answer.

"You know how to block me, don't you?" Eli took his plate over to Haruka.

Haruka continued to put their leftovers away without looking at Eli.

"Haruka." Eli poked him in the side. "Don't make me tickle it out of you."

"You say that like it's a threat."

"I'm tougher than I look." Eli poked Haruka in the side again. "Spill. If you know how to keep me out of your head, you have to teach me how."

Haruka cocked his head to one side. "Do I?"

"Yes! It's only fair."

When Haruka failed to respond, Eli narrowed his eyes. His sister was particularly ticklish at her armpits. Maybe Haruka was too? He dove in without even considering that what he was doing might be a bad idea.

Eli got the pleasure of seeing Haruka's eyes go wide with surprise when he made his attack. He enjoyed two whole seconds of victory before Haruka had Eli's wrists trapped in one large hand in a move so fast, his head spun.

"Life isn't fair, Eli."

Eli twisted, and Haruka tightened his grip, his eyes never leaving Eli's.

He was pretty sure he should be freaking out right now. Normally, Eli would be screaming at the top of his lungs, or on the verge of passing out, if someone grabbed him like this.

But he wasn't doing any of those things. As soon as Haruka squeezed Eli's wrists, his mind went still and quiet. It was like being wrapped inside something soft, warm, and safe. Like nothing bad could ever touch him there.

Haruka pulled Eli closer, and Eli tugged, testing. The room was so quiet, Eli could hear his own heart beating.

"Don't . . ." Haruka closed his eyes and took a deep breath.

"Don't what?" Eli was having trouble remembering what they'd been talking about. Haruka's hair was free from its usual ponytail and had fallen over his face during their struggle. It was shiny and looked silky smooth.

Eli's fingers wiggled.

A shudder went through Haruka.

In the quiet, soft space Eli floated in, the words :*So innocent . . . I can't.*: drifted past him.

Then Haruka opened his eyes, and they were full of mischief. "Don't tickle me."

Then he scooped Eli up and tossed him over his shoulder.

"Wait! No! I'm injured! My head hurts!" Eli lied. His head had stopped throbbing hours ago, and Haruka was being more than gentle enough to keep from agitating it past their bond's ability to soothe any lingering pain.

"No, it doesn't." Haruka said over his shoulder as he walked over and deposited Eli on the bed. "But I'll be nice this time. Next time you won't get off so easy."

Eli peered up at Haruka through his tousled bangs. The odd tension between them was broken, but Eli was breathing like he'd run up five flights of stairs. He chewed thoughtfully on his lower lip, wondering if this was another effect of the mental connection they shared.

Haruka took a step toward the bed, stopped, turned around, and went to his closet. "I'm taking a shower. You go to bed."

Eli watched as Haruka slung a towel over his shoulder and walked out of the room stiffly.

"Guess I'm going to bed then," Eli said to himself.

He stripped quickly and put on the first set of pjs he could find, a limited-edition Sailor Moon set. The top was a white, long-sleeved shirt with Luna, Sailor Moon's cat, winding around the torso. The shorts were black with Artemis, Sailor Venus' cat curving around one hip.

He crawled under the covers and expected to pass out as soon as his head hit the pillow. The day had been long and exhausting—even with his impromptu nap. But his mind wouldn't stop spinning. Flashes of Ash, pinning him to the desk, chased him as he sought oblivion. As soon as he banished them, thoughts of today's classes jerked him to full wakefulness. Eli flipped over and buried his head under a pillow. He hadn't even contacted his professors!

He threw the pillow across the room then had to get up and retrieve it.

Haruka was taking a long time, wasn't he?

Eli scooted to the middle of the bed and began tucking pillows and blankets around himself, then curled up in a ball. He clutched the small gray cat in his hands and breathed in Haruka's unique scent from his pillow. Only then was he able to slide into sleep.

In his dreams, he felt hands rearrange his body until he was draped over something warm and safe. Something *his.*

There was a light touch on the top of his head, and Eli sank deeper into oblivion.

Eli wandered through a gray world. He turned around to see how far he'd travelled and saw blossoms of color in the shape of his footprints. He kneeled down and traced a finger over a gray flower and marveled at the way it burst into a vibrant red. He ran his hands over everything he could reach, enjoying the greens, blues, and yellows that rippled out like waves at the brush of his fingers. Every color of the rainbow was his to command, and he couldn't get enough of it.

Music broke into his world and pulled at him. Eli tried to cling to the beautiful landscape he'd created, but the music grew louder and more persistent.

Eli opened his eyes and glared in the direction of the music. It was across the room, and if he wanted to make it stop, he'd have to get out of his cocoon—which was a terrible idea because it held traces of his dreams and the comfiest blanket in the world.

He groaned and tried to burrow further under his blanket. If he went far enough, maybe the music would go away.

Then his blanket moved. And it was poking him in the hip.

That was when Eli realized he had a bigger problem than shutting off the alarm he didn't remember turning on.

He didn't need to panic. It was a totally normal guy thing—he should know since he was currently experiencing the same issue.

He tried to wiggle out from under Haruka, but the arm around him pulled him in closer, and Haruka buried his face in the back of Eli's neck. Eli gasped as his hipbones were pushed intimately against the mattress. He ground against the friction without thinking.

Eli felt Haruka freeze, then sit up slowly, prying himself away from Eli's back. He propped an elbow on one knee and yawned as he rubbed his eyes. His hair curtained most of his face. "Sorry, I just woke up," Haruka said in a voice thick with sleep.

"M-me too." Eli sat up, facing the edge of the bed. He tried to stand, but one of the sleeves on his baggy sleep shirt was trapped underneath Haruka, causing the neck of his shirt to slip over one shoulder.

Haruka gazed at him for a long moment before shifting his weight to release Eli.

Eli got up and pulled the hem of his shirt down. "I have to go to the bathroom!"

He ran for the bathroom, making sure to keep the front of his body facing away from Haruka.

CHAPTER 25
HARUKA

Haruka was supposed to be paying attention in class. He was supposed to be taking notes and listening to the lecture on what to expect on their midterm, but his attention kept straying to the bewitching creature sent into his life with the sole purpose of torturing him to death.

It had taken every ounce of self-control Haruka possessed this morning to allow Eli to leave his bed unscathed.

The image of Eli's slim hips, barely covered in his sleep shorts haunted him. Thinking about the little cat tail wrapped around the curve Haruka had been pressed against this morning had been all it had taken to get off when he'd jerked off in the shower—for the second time in less than twelve hours.

He was torn between the urge to burn those shorts and the desire to enshrine them.

Haruka wasn't used to *wanting* like this. All his life, he'd been given anything he wanted. Anyone he desired, Haruka could have. He'd lost count of the number of men and women who had propositioned him over the years.

None of them stirred him like the boy sitting next to him, chewing on the end of a pencil like his life depended on it.

His lips were swollen from the constant abuse Eli put them through, and they glistened in the morning light. Did he put something on them to make them look that way? Knowing how much the boy hated drawing attention to himself, Haruka doubted it. He was just naturally beguiling.

Haruka had walked Eli to his first class that morning—he couldn't have stopped himself if he'd tried—and he had personally pulled Eli's hood up before he'd left him at his desk. The boy's large Bambi eyes had nearly done him in, but Haruka had somehow managed to drag himself away and leave the classroom.

He was fortunate Eli's class was half an hour longer than Haruka's, so he could be back to wait for him.

Haruka scrubbed his hands over his face and suppressed the urge to hit his desk. If he could, he would keep Eli in his room where no one could see him or hurt him. Or steal him.

Not for the first time, Haruka was glad the boy had a tendency to hide himself in loose clothes. Not that it made much of a difference. There was something about him, some ineffable quality that shined through anything Eli wore, something that announced to everyone that he was special, someone worth knowing more about.

And Haruka wanted to know everything. His favorite food, his favorite movie, his favorite hoodie—everything. Anything that could help Haruka capture and keep the boy's attention all to himself.

He was such a selfish creature, but he couldn't bring himself to care.

Eli was his. The boy just hadn't realized it yet. And if Haruka wasn't patient, he would scare him into running away again and leave Haruka with a hole in his chest that made the first one look like a pinhole.

For Eli, he would wait as long as it took for the boy to want him back. Even a fraction of how Haruka felt would be enough. As long as he knew he was Haruka's and Haruka was his, everything would be okay.

This morning had been a good sign. Eli hadn't run back to his own room after spending forever in the bathroom, like Haruka had half-expected. Instead, he'd stayed and continued to alternate between clinging to Haruka and pulling away like he had the day before. He'd even eaten most of the food Haruka had bought him for breakfast. Maybe someday soon, Eli would let him feed him personally.

And now he was staring at Eli's mouth again.

"Are you ready to go?" Eli asked, tilting his head to the side adorably. He was like the sun, brilliant, blinding, and something Haruka couldn't take his eyes off to save his life.

He nodded and closed his notebook on the empty page in front of him. He trailed after Eli, unable to do anything else.

When the boy's phone chimed, Haruka wanted to ask who messaged him. Who it was that brought the soft smile to Eli's lips. But he knew better than to act like a caveman. If he was lucky, he would find out on his own. Patience was the key with Eli.

"Alice wants to have coffee with us. Do you think she'll notice the bruise on my face?"

Haruka scowled at the reminder of what Ash had done

to Eli. He'd never been as close to killing someone as he had that night. His aunt would have changed her mind about not wanting to recruit him for the shady side of his family's business if she'd seen him in that moment.

"You don't want to?" Eli's hood slipped back off his face.

"No, it's fine." Haruka pulled Eli's hood back up, covering the livid bruise. It had transformed into a truly impressive array of green and blue. "If you keep this on, she won't notice anything."

And it will be easier to stop myself from hunting down the person who gave it to you.

"The police said he's being held without bail for the time being. So, we don't have to worry about seeing him yet." Eli answered Haruka's unspoken thought—seemingly unaware he hadn't actually said anything out loud.

Damn it. Haruka had been working hard to keep from spilling over into Eli's mind. He used the space of no-mind he'd learned to slip into while practicing archery, but apparently, he still needed to work on it. Hearing Eli's thoughts could only help Haruka, but hearing Haruka's thoughts would only damage Eli.

It was better for Eli not to know too much about the predator he had at his side. Especially since he seemed unaware of the reality of situation he was in.

Haruka had never known exactly what his soul had been searching for all these years, but he had known one thing. That once he found it, he would never let it go. And after knowing first-hand what losing Eli would feel like, Haruka was willing to do anything it took to make sure it didn't happen again.

Eli felt something for him, Haruka was sure of it. The problem was, he had no idea what those feelings were. And there was the issue of Eli's roommate Jace. Haruka could ask him point blank if there was anything going on between them, but he was afraid the skittish boy would run if he did.

Instead, he'd chosen to wait and see if Eli's thoughts would shed light on the subject. It was tricky, though. Eli's mind was a fascinating puzzle Haruka hadn't even begun to understand. He was an odd mix of self-deprecation, optimism, and oblivious innocence.

Every bit of his mind worked overtime to weave a complex tapestry of protection around the gaping wound of his kidnapping—something Haruka only discovered by accident. It had been a nothing more than a faint whisper on the edges of Haruka's mind, but when he'd heard it, Haruka knew it was the source of Eli's nightmares.

They reached a large maple tree by the pond, and Haruka sat at the base of the tree, content to be left with his thoughts.

Haruka observed quietly as Eli interacted with his friends. Both Alice and Nate worked to entertain and distract Eli, but it didn't escape his notice that they each took turns asking subtle questions, trying to figure out the nature of Eli's relationship with Haruka.

"Eli, when we're done eating, can we go back to your room? I want to borrow the copy of the *Escaflowne* OVA you found last week." Alice smiled sweetly, but her eyes darted to Haruka.

He didn't know what she was trying to do, but if she wormed her way into Eli's room, it would be obvious he didn't live there anymore. Haruka had done his best to make sure Eli had no reason to go back to his room when packing the boy's things.

"Um . . ." The bridge of Eli's nose began to turn a charming shade of pink.

"I just borrowed it. When I'm finished, I can give it to you," Haruka said. It was the first words he'd spoken beyond a simple greeting.

The reason for the subtle questioning—that none of them were talking about—was due to the fact that shortly after everyone sat down on the grass, Eli began scooting over to Haruka. When he propped his head on Haruka's thigh, both Alice and Nate's eyebrows shot toward the sky.

Haruka had motioned for them not to say anything. It was better to just let the boy do his thing. He'd had a hard week after all.

And he was in a good mood right now.

Haruka could feel it like a sweet song, threading through every aspect of his mind. Every now and then, he would catch snatches of Eli's thoughts.

Right now, he was wondering if he picked where they ate tonight, if he could get away with not being overstuffed like a turkey.

Haruka smiled. Eli could pick where they ate every night, but Haruka would continue to push food at him until he stopped looking like a strong wind could steal him away.

He closed his eyes and leaned his head against the tree propping up his back and let the sounds of the campus, and the chatter of Eli and his friends wash over him.

This was good.

"I should have made you carry me back here. I think I'm going to explode." Eli leaned against the doorframe heavily while Haruka unlocked their door.

"Do you want me to carry you inside?"

"I think I can manage a few more feet."

"Suit yourself." Haruka pushed the door open and motioned for Eli to enter first.

The boy toed off his shoes, stumbled over to the bed, and dropped himself on it like a bag of rice, landing face down, groaning.

Okay, maybe Haruka had fed him a little too much.

Eli sat up and began to unzip his hoodie. "I think I'm going straight to bed."

Haruka nodded and peeled off his shirt.

"W-what are you doing?"

"Going to bed," Haruka said simply then went into the bathroom to brush his teeth.

When he came out, Eli stood outside with a small bundle of clothes hugged to his chest and darted past him, closing the door firmly behind.

Haruka changed into a pair of sweatpants and climbed into bed, making sure to leave room for Eli.

Then he waited.

And waited.

He took out his phone and scrolled through YouTube videos until Eli finally emerged, wearing an oversized gray T-shirt and black pajama pants with the Batman logo down one side. His eyes were large and uncertain.

"There's only one bed."

Haruka nodded and put his phone away. "Just like last night, and the night before."

He'd been expecting this. In fact, when Haruka had been helping Eli pack, he'd fully intended to go out afterward and buy another bed. A plan he'd immediately scrapped when Eli told him to leave his comforter behind because Haruka already had one.

"Right."

Haruka watched as Eli visibly steeled himself to climb

into bed. Halfway there, he stooped to pick up a long throw pillow from the floor, crawled under the covers, and wedged the pillow between them, glaring at Haruka as if daring him to say anything.

Haruka put his hands up and bit back a smile. Then he turned out the light and settled back, preparing himself for a long, sleepless night of lying next to someone he craved but couldn't have.

Ten minutes later, the pillow shifted and rolled onto Haruka's stomach and a small, warm bundle of sleeping Eli pressed against his side. The boy's arm went over his chest and knocked the pillow onto the floor. Haruka pressed his nose into wavy black hair and breathed in Eli's scent.

This.

If he could have nothing more, this would be enough.

CHAPTER 26
ELI

Eli had a Problem.

Scratch that. He had multiple problems, and he needed to start tackling them. And the best way to deal with them was to start at the bottom of the list and work his way up.

Because if he started at the top, he was pretty sure he'd end up screaming into the abyss.

First up, was that he couldn't go anywhere alone. Initially, it had been comforting having his friends go with him when he needed to be out of his—their—room, but it had been two weeks since the attack, and Eli was getting twitchy. The only alone time he got was in the bathroom, and even then, he had an escort.

Like now. Currently he was taking a shower, but he knew without even needing to look that Haruka was parked in the changing area, playing on his phone. Which made it difficult to take care of certain, ahem, things he tended to do on his own. And it was becoming more pressing as the days went on.

Eli halted his train of thought. He was edging too close

to priority one on the top of Eli's Big List of Problems, and he wasn't ready to go there yet. He needed to ease his way into it.

Next up was a tricky one—acting normal around other people. You'd think Eli would have mastered that a long time ago, given his endless opportunities to practice, but he'd only ever been able to manage a weak facsimile in the first place. Now he had a weird mental bond with Haruka to throw into the mix.

He was trying to maintain some semblance of personal space between the two of them, but any time he stopped paying attention he found himself acting like Haruka's own personal human scarf.

At least he didn't have to worry about not answering unspoken thoughts like Haruka did—not that he seemed to have any problem with it—because after the first couple of days, Eli stopped picking up anything more than the odd snippet of thought or pulse of emotion from time to time.

Eli scrubbed his head in frustration. Wait, had he already shampooed his hair? He'd better do it again, just to be on the safe side.

And they hadn't even really talked about their connection. Both of them had acted like being stuck together was a done deal. It had seemed so obvious to Eli. He hadn't given it a second thought. The hollow space inside of him had filled. Now he had Haruka there, and that was all he needed to know.

But he was having second, third, and fourth thoughts now. They should be talking about it, shouldn't they? But any time Eli brought it up, Haruka's face got all shifty. He'd either change the subject, or tease Eli until he forgot what they'd been talking about.

He couldn't let that keep happening.

And then there was Haruka's fan club.

They were everywhere. Students of all ages camped outside their building in the morning, staking out Haruka's classes, following him as he walked through the campus—usually at a discreet distance. Usually.

According to Alice, the reason for Haruka's sudden popularity was a post made by an anonymous person on a college singles forum. The poster claimed to be close friends with Haruka and said that he was lonely, but shy. They posted a picture of him and asked everyone who saw him to introduce themselves.

Alice made another post on the same forum claiming it was a prank, that Haruka was definitely not looking for new friends, and anyone approaching him was doing it at their own risk, but the damage was already done. He now had a loyal following dogging his every step.

Fortunately, at this point, Haruka was well known for having a short temper with anyone who got up in his business, but there was always a brave soul willing to get close and take a chance to shoot their shot. And it was . . . irritating.

Maybe it was because of their connection, but Eli wasn't a fan of people getting touchy-feely with Haruka. And all of the brave ones were like that. It didn't feel wrong the way it did when someone touched Eli, but it didn't feel right either.

Eli was just glad Haruka didn't seem to like it any more than Eli did. Everyone who came to him was brutally shot down and dismissed. It had become a normal part of their day.

And their days *were* normal. It was crazy, the idea of Eli having a semblance of normality in his life. But after the first few days, they'd just clicked and everything became smooth—aside from Eli's list of problems, that is.

Being together was the easiest thing Eli had ever done. Talking with Haruka was as simple as breathing, and not talking was easy too. They could spend hours quietly immersed in their own projects, being alone together.

It was only when going outside that they came across issues.

Haruka defended Eli's personal space far more vigilantly than Eli did, even to the point of rudeness. Eli was used to allowing small breaches of his defenses as a normal part of daily life. When Haruka was around, it simply didn't happen.

Like yesterday when one of Eli's classmates had tried to throw their arms around him from behind, Haruka had straight-up body checked her, knocking the girl to the ground when she bounced off of him.

After dealing with the dirty looks of onlookers and consoling a tearstained girl with scraped palms, Eli wasn't sure if maybe it would have just been better to have let her glomp him in the first place.

He sighed and scrubbed his arms until they were bright pink.

And then there was the very top of the list of Eli's Problems. And it seemed to tie in with all of the others in some way or another.

There was a tension between them Eli couldn't explain. He'd never felt anything like it before. Mornings were . . . intense. Every night, Eli did his best to create a barrier between them before they went to sleep and every single morning, he woke up draped over Haruka like a second skin. And they never talked about it.

Was this normal?

What a ridiculous question. There was no way of knowing what normal was in their situation because, as far as Eli knew, no one had ever dealt with something like this before.

All Eli knew was that there was this pull inside him, growing stronger every day, urging him to get him even closer to Haruka than he already was. Sometimes he thought Haruka felt it too.

There were moments where Haruka stared at him, and Eli was reminded of a small fish being circled by a shark. Instead of being scared, it made him think of the time Haruka had squeezed his wrists together in one hand. It made the shivery sensation in his stomach kick into to overdrive.

Eli's hands ran down his body as he covered himself in soap. His skin tingled in the wake of his fingers.

Alice had teased him at the beginning of school, intimating that Haruka was into Eli. Wouldn't he have done something by now if he were? Maybe he was waiting for Eli to do something first—which was *not* happening.

What if he shot Eli down with the same brutal efficiency he'd used on all the others? That would make their bond go from the best thing in Eli's life to the worst in the blink of an eye.

No, Eli would continue to be like a quarter of the people on campus and enjoy the phenomenon of Haruka's grace and beauty from afar.

But not as far as everyone else.

Eli got an up close and personal look every single morning, and the only reason Haruka didn't know about Numero Uno on Eli's list was all thanks to a discovery he'd made on the Saturday after the attack.

Eli and Haruka had been sitting back-to-back while working on homework, and Haruka pulled away.

"You're giving me a headache."

"Huh?"

"Whatever you're doing is making my head hurt."

"Sorry, I'm memorizing Vietnamese verbs, but it's a little boring, so I'm comparing them to Thai verbs as I go to make it more interesting."

Haruka had looked at Eli like he was insane. Maybe he was, but he now had a way to keep Haruka out of his head. Anytime Problem Number One showed up, Eli began translating random phrases from one language to another, and Haruka would give him a dirty look and pull away.

Unfortunately, Problem Number One was popping up more often as the days went by. This morning Haruka's skin seemed to glow in the early morning light when Eli had opened his eyes. He'd been mesmerized as he traced the hard lines of Haruka's chest with his eyes. The smooth curve of his bicep had been so tantalizing, Eli hadn't been able to stop himself from reaching out and running his fingers over it.

Eli's hands gripped the base of his cock, and he squeezed.

He couldn't keep doing this.

But he also couldn't seem to make himself stop.

He stroked himself as he imagined Haruka waking up to catch Eli touching him. Fantasy Haruka flipped him over, reversing their position and pressed Eli's hands down against the bed.

His hand sped up as he imagined Haruka taking both of his hands in one of his, while thrusting against Eli and . . .

Eli came with a choked gasp. Fuck, it didn't take much to get him there anymore. All he had to do was think about

Haruka and he was done. If Haruka ever actually touched him like that he'd probably ruin his pants in a matter of seconds.

And to think he'd actually believed he had no interest in sex. Well, there was no doubt about his sexuality now. He was Haruka-sexual.

And he had no clue if the guy was even into dudes.

"Eli," Haruka's voice intruded on his thoughts, and Eli jumped, nearly killing himself on the slick tile as he struggled to stay upright. "Breakfast is going to be over in the caf soon. Hurry up."

"I'll be right out," Eli squeaked, hurrying to clean up the mess he'd just made of himself.

When he finally emerged, he knew his whole body was bright pink with embarrassment but hoped Haruka would think it was because of the steam rather than guessing Eli had been jacking off furiously in the shower.

He was going to quit his bad habit.

Starting tomorrow.

He rubbed a towel through his hair and started for the door only to be stopped by a hand on his shoulder. "What's wrong?"

"Get dressed first."

"Whoops!" Eli laughed in embarrassment and rubbed his head harder.

He'd almost gone out in a towel and nothing else. Haruka's room was only a few feet away from the shower room, but still, dashing mostly naked through the hall wasn't his idea of a good time.

"Thanks."

Eli grabbed his clothes and ducked behind a curtain to dress. "We don't have to hit the cafeteria, you know. There are plenty of other places to eat."

"Hn." Haruka always got monosyllabic when he wanted something, which meant he probably really wanted to eat in the caf today.

"Fine, I'll hurry." Eli shoved his head through the neck hole of his T-shirt and opened the curtain, stuffing his arms through the holes as he came out. "Okay, I'm ready."

"You forgot your hoodie."

"I left it in the room. Don't worry, I can live without it until we finish eating."

"Hn." Haruka walked out and Eli followed him, but instead of heading toward the elevator, he went back to the room and grabbed a hoodie—the black one he'd given Eli—and handed it to him.

"Thanks." Eli put it on as fast as he could and made for the door, only to be stopped by Haruka who pushed him gently against the wall in the narrow entry.

Haruka crowded into Eli's space and began to zip up his hoodie.

Eli began to translate the steps of making instant ramen into Hindi.

Haruka's eye twitched, but he still zipped the hoodie all the way to Eli's neck. When he moved to pull up the hood, Eli touched his hand to stop him.

"I'm good, really."

It was thoughtful for Haruka to remember, but Eli found he didn't need it as much as he used to.

Haruka stepped back. "Okay."

Once at the cafeteria, Eli waited at a table while Haruka got food. He'd given up choosing things for himself because no matter what he got, he always ended up eating food from Haruka's plate. Also, it was nice not to get jostled and pushed around in the sea of people swarming the place.

"Can I sit here?"

Eli lifted his head from his phone to see Bryan, Haruka's friend, standing next to him. "Go for it. What's up?"

Bryan put his tray down and sat next to Eli. "Just looking for Haruka. I haven't seen him around much lately, and when I saw you, I knew he'd be nearby."

On cue, Haruka materialized behind Bryan and kicked the leg of his chair. "Move."

"Like I said." Bryan winked at Eli and moved to the other side of the table.

"What do you want?" Haruka asked as he slid a plate in front of Eli.

"I saw Aaron, and he asked me to find out why you haven't been coming to practice."

"I've been busy."

Eli looked up from his plate in surprise. He'd assumed Haruka had been going to his club activities while Eli was in class. Apparently not.

"The captain said he didn't want to kick you off the team, but you haven't been returning his texts for the past two weeks. He'll have no choice if you don't show up today."

Haruka nodded and continued to eat.

"Well, anyway, I've discharged my responsibility. It's all on you now." Bryan turned his attention to Eli. "As for you, what's up with you stealing my best friend?" His voice was playful, and he nudged his water bottle against Eli's plate.

"I'm not stopping you from hanging out," Eli said, frowning. "He's free to do whatever he wants."

"Claws in, kitty. I'm just teasing you." Bryan leaned forward on his elbows, then yelped and gave Haruka a dirty look.

Haruka didn't look up from his plate.

"It must be nice having your own personal bodyguard." Bryan reached down and rubbed his shin.

It *was* nice, actually. Very nice. And he wasn't planning on giving him up anytime soon, so Bryan needed to shut up about it before Eli gave him a kick too. He tried to convey this via glare.

"I see why you stick close to him, he's so cute I could eat him." Bryan braced his hands on the table and shoved his chair back. "Missed me that time." He waggled his eyebrows.

"Why are you friends with him?"

"He's convenient."

"You're lucky to have me, and you know it." Bryan affected a wounded posture.

They finished breakfast while Bryan filled them in on all the department gossip. Haruka and Eli were at the top of the list, but Bryan seemed to tire of getting kicked so he moved on to the next best thing and regaled them with everything he knew about the department head secretly hooking up with the professor of Korean Literature.

Eli was never going to look at either of them the same way again.

Once Bryan left, Eli jumped on Haruka. "You can't skip archery practice." If Haruka got kicked off the team, Eli wouldn't get a chance to see him in hakama again and that would be a crime.

"Why not?"

"Because . . . extracurricular activities look good on a transcript. And quitting them for no reason doesn't."

Haruka shrugged then stared down a boy in a football jersey carrying a tray toward their table until he changed direction. "Your friends have class during practice."

"I'm not going to get murdered if I'm alone for two hours."

Haruka gave him the stink eye.

"Whatever. I'm going to the archery field to draw this afternoon. You can do whatever you want."

Haruka grunted, but Eli got the feeling he was pleased.

CHAPTER 27
ELI

Coming to the field was a terrible idea.

The fence was lined with Haruka's fan club, and they actually cheered when Haruka stepped out onto the field with his bow. That was when it dawned on him that if Eli could see all of the skin Haruka's outfit displayed, so could everyone else.

He wanted to throw a blanket over him or perhaps find a shovel. Just in case anyone got any ideas.

Eli had started out at the fence, too—enjoying the sun with the rest of the onlookers—but the comments and whistles started getting on his nerves, so when Haruka had come up to him and suggested he sit in the shelter under the shade, he'd taken him up on it.

And if he'd enjoyed the complaints as Haruka walked away without paying attention to his fan club, it was nobody's business but his own.

Now, he sat perched on top of a table, drawing quick sketches of Haruka as he sank arrow after arrow into the target.

"Those are really good," Aaron said, leaning against the table to get a closer look.

Eli frowned at his sketches. He only had a very modest talent in art. If his drawings were good, it was more likely due to his subject matter than anything else.

"They're okay."

"No seriously. Can I take a picture for our Facebook page?"

"Sure." There was no reason not to. They were only warm-up sketches. It wasn't like anyone would be able to tell who he was drawing. He handed his sketchbook to Aaron.

Then he proceeded to stare at Haruka until he realized he no longer had an excuse to do so.

Ugh.

He fished in his pocket for his phone and sent a few TikToks to his sister, so she'd know he was still alive. During his search, he came across a clip about soulmates.

Huh.

It wasn't particularly well done, or informative, but something in the clip stuck in his head. *You'll know your soulmate because you'll be drawn together like magnets.*

It was a little too close to what Eli was experiencing for him to ignore, so he opened a page in his browser and typed soulmates into the search bar.

He found a link to an article on soulmate myths, scanning through it to see if he could find anything useful. He read several different red thread myths. So many Asian countries had their own version. The one from Japan claimed that each person had an invisible red thread tied to their pinky. The other end of the thread was attached to the pinky of their soulmate.

He stared at Haruka's hand as it released another arrow,

but he didn't see a hint of red on his pinky. Eli's either, for that matter. He went back and found another link on soulmates—one about bored ancient gods and how they had a tendency to fuck with soulmates, but it sounded ridiculous, so he didn't bother clicking on it.

"Hey!"

Eli looked up from his phone to see Haruka snatch Eli's sketchbook out of Aaron's hands.

"I wasn't done posting those yet."

"Too bad." Haruka tucked the sketchbook into his bag, then sat on the bench next to Eli's table and began to unstring his bow. "I'm done."

Eli clicked his screen off. He could look into it later.

The next afternoon, Eli found himself sitting in front of Alice, doing something he'd never thought he'd do.

"You are going to be so beautiful when I'm done!"

"I don't need to be beautiful." He grumbled. "I'd be more impressed if you made me more masculine."

"Hush, you."

It had started out as a silly idea. Alice had brought her makeup kit with her, claiming that, since she was using brushes, refining her makeup skills was technically something that fit in with the club's motif.

"I'll allow it," Raina had shouted from the other side of the room.

And since Eli had been the only person not currently enmeshed in a project, he got to be her victim.

"Are you going to at least tell me what you're doing to my face?"

"Nope!" Alice chirped.

"Remember I'm washing this off as soon as you're finished."

"After I've taken a picture for posterity, yes, you may."

"Just don't post it anywhere."

"Oh, I'm posting it everywhere." She promised merrily.

He pulled away from her brush. "Alice!"

"Don't move! You're going to ruin it." She held out against Eli's pout for twenty seconds. "Okay, fine. I'll only post it on the club Facebook page."

Their club was small, maybe nobody would see it?

Eli presented his face again. "Deal."

He was proud of himself, actually. Alice wasn't touching him, but her brushes were. Unlike when he'd dyed her hair —where he also used a brush and only really ever touched her hair, not her skin—this time he wasn't in control of the touching, so he hadn't been sure if it would be okay. However, when he closed his eyes and allowed her to do her thing, it turned out to be surprisingly soothing.

He let out a small hum of pleasure as Alice traced a soft brush over one cheek. His phone buzzed, and he ignored it. Whoever it was could wait. This was nice.

"Okay, bear with me here, Eli. I'm going to try not to touch you, but I might slip."

Eli nodded, not really listening. He was half asleep in his chair.

Until she started sticking things to his face.

Wrong

Eli twitched.

"Sorry!"

Eli felt a few more dots of sticky cold touch his face as Alice applied more things to his cheeks.

Wrong

Eli's fingers twitched.

Wrong

"I swear I'm not doing this on purpose." Alice said, there was a hint of panic to her voice. "Do you want me to stop?"

"No, it's fine. You can keep going." It really wasn't that bad. It was only Alice, after all. His internal defenses were barely kicking up a fuss.

"And one more . . ."

Wrong

"I'm finished!"

His phone rang, and he answered it.

"Who keeps touching you?" Haruka asked. His voice was arctic.

"I'll be right back," Eli said to Alice and went out into the hall.

"Don't smear anything before I can take a picture!" She called after him.

"Aren't you in a class right now?" Eli hissed into his phone.

"Do you need me to come over there?" Haruka was a master of ignoring questions he didn't want to answer.

"I'm fine. It was just Alice." Eli smiled softly. Overprotective didn't begin to describe Haruka.

"Alice? What is she doing?"

"Honing her makeup skills."

". . . on you?"

"I thought it would be a good way to test my boundaries. It wasn't that bad, actually."

"Your boundaries are fine. I'll see you soon."

Eli's phone beeped, informing him that Haruka had hung up.

What a pompous fuck.

He closed his eyes and tapped the back of his head

lightly against the wall behind him. They had such a strange relationship.

Eli took a deep breath and went back inside.

"Okay, Alice, show me what you've done to me," he demanded, reaching for the mirror she held in her hand.

"Be nice, I'm sensitive," she said before handing him the mirror.

Alice? Sensitive? She seemed so sturdy and unflappable. Whimsical, yes, but not sensitive. Eli looked at Nate, who nodded subtly.

He braced himself. No matter what he looked like, he'd find something nice to say about it. Then he turned over the mirror and looked at himself.

Alice had made liberal use of her eyeliner, making his eyes look much larger than he was used to, but he couldn't deny it looked good. She'd also gone to town with the color blue. She'd put an asymmetrical dusting of light blue eye shadow over his right cheek and layered it with darker shades of blue. The effect spread up the side of his face and curved over his eyebrow, spreading over most of his forehead. On his left cheek she'd written the word 'beauty' in a swirling cursive Eli couldn't help but be envious over. On top of it all was an artful smattering of sparkling, opalescent sequins.

The effect was stunning. "Wow."

"I know, right?" Alice clapped her hands happily.

"Holy crap, Alice, nice job!" Kate came over to examine Eli and reached out a hand to tilt his chin. Eli backed away —one more *wrong*, and Haruka was likely to ditch the rest of his class. "Oops! Sorry, Eli, I got carried away."

"No worries."

He took another look in the mirror. His face was absolutely beautiful.

Eli's fingers crawled into his sleeves. How long did he have to wait before Alice would let him take it off?

Whoof

Eli grabbed his chest. What the . . .? He felt like he'd just been punched.

"What do you think, Haruka? Did I do good?"

Haruka stood next to Alice, his face devoid of all expression. "Hn."

"He's going to be beating people off with a stick when they see him."

"Hn."

"You know I'm washing it off before I leave this room, Alice." Eli went up to Haruka. A curl of anxiety twisted in his stomach. He didn't want Haruka think he looked stupid.

Eli's fingers found the edge of his hood.

"Don't." Haruka pulled his hand away. "I want to see it."

Click

"Alice! You have to warn people before you take a picture. Haruka might not want to be on the club page."

Haruka took Alice's phone.

"What are you doing?"

"Sending myself a copy."

"No, don't delete the original!" Eli tried to grab Alice's phone, but it was too late. "She's just going to take another one."

Alice snatched her phone back and snapped three more pictures, then stuck out her tongue.

Haruka huffed.

He still had no idea if Haruka thought he looked stupid or not. Bond or no, he was still a bit of a jerk sometimes. Like . . .

Eli's mouth dropped open.

"Hey . . . you called me a beautiful moron!"

"Um, Eli, he didn't call you anything."

Haruka burst out laughing. It lit up the room like a roman candle—or maybe that was just how it seemed to Eli.

No, he wasn't the only one who thought so. Everyone in the room turned to watch as taciturn, cool-as-ice Haruka laughed so hard he had to lean on Eli for support.

"You are a beautiful moron." Haruka wiped a tear from his eye.

"Yeah? Well, you're a hot jerk."

Alice snapped another picture, and Haruka and Eli both turned to look at her. "Don't mind me. Please, feel free to keep providing us all with quality entertainment."

"That's enough pictures, I think. Makeup wipes please." Eli held out his hand and wiggled his fingers.

Alice took one more picture, then handed him the box. "Do you need help?"

"I've got it—hey!"

Haruka plucked the box from Eli's hand and took his chin in one hand. "Hold still."

"Haruka's showing off," someone said from the back of the room.

"What qualifications does it take to get into Eli's inner circle? Is there a class you can take?" Alice teased.

"It's an exclusive club. Only one member," Haruka said as he gently, but thoroughly, cleaned Eli's face.

Eli wanted to pull his hood down over his entire head. "You all suck. Hey—ow!"

"Sorry." Haruka frowned at the sequin he'd pulled off of Eli's cheek. "Is there a better way to get these off?"

"Just time and patience. I'm sorry, Eli. I got a little carried away there at the end."

"I'll just—don't pick at it—try to wash them off in the shower later." Eli pushed Haruka away to stop him from poking at his face. Then he pulled up his hood and said to Alice, "You owe me!"

"And I appreciate it! Love you!!!"

Eli snatched up his bag from the table seconds before Haruka could take it. Ha! Score one for Eli.

"Bye, Eli!" The rest of the room chorused.

He waved a hand as he made a hasty exit, Haruka in tow.

"Did anyone else see you?"

"I don't think so, why?"

"No reason."

"I don't need any more attention than I already have, thank you. Unlike some people, I don't need a fan club."

"I would sell my fan club for a dollar, and you know it."

"I wonder."

"Eli . . ."

Eli's phone rang. "It's Jace."

He hadn't talked to his friend in over a week. The last he'd heard, Jace would be stuck on the farm until harvest season was finished, and that was still about two weeks away. He hit answer eagerly.

"What's up?"

"I hate to do this to you, but . . . I'm not going to be back until the spring semester."

"Really?" Eli chewed on his lower lip. Jace's dad must be doing worse than he'd thought.

"They need me for the Christmas tree season too. There are only a few weeks between harvest season ending and the beginning of the Christmas rush, so there's no point in going back."

"What about your classes?"

"I've worked it out with my professors. Some of it I can do online, and the rest I'll just have to play catch-up with in the spring."

"That sucks."

"It does, but, hey, at least I'll get to see you when I come to pack up my things next month."

Eli smiled. "That's better than a kick in the ass, I guess."

Jace laughed. "Try not to get any weirder while I'm gone, okay?"

"I doubt I could get weirder than you, shrink-boy."

"Whatever, shorty."

"You're only two inches taller than me, shorty."

"If I'm short, that makes your height truly tragic."

"Shut it, or I'll shut it for you."

"Try it, shrimp. I'll take you down."

There was a woman's voice in the background, calling Jace to dinner, so Eli said, "Okay, I'll let you go. Take care of your family."

"Thanks, man. Are you going to be okay without a roommate?"

Eli's eyes flicked to Haruka. "Don't worry about me, I've worked something out."

"Good. Now I don't have to feel like crap."

"Right, you can focus on feeling short instead." Eli ended the call on Jace's cry of faux outrage.

"He is literally the only adult male I can do that to," Eli said. "And he's still fucking taller than me."

Haruka pushed the button to call the elevator. Eli had been so caught up in his conversation with Jace, he hadn't noticed they'd entered their building.

"So Jace isn't coming back?"

"Not for this semester. I guess you're stuck with me for the foreseeable future."

The elevator dinged, and they went inside. No one else got on with them, but Haruka still stood close enough to Eli that he could feel the man's body heat. He tugged at his zipper. "Is it hot in here?"

"That doesn't seem so bad."

"What does?" What were they talking about?

"Being stuck with you." Haruka leaned over him and put an arm on the wall above his head.

Eli's throat went dry, and he gave a little cough. "I guess we already kind of are, right?"

"Right."

Haruka wasn't moving away. If anything, he was boxing Eli in further.

"Are you going to miss him?"

"Who, Jace? I mean, I guess so? I didn't know him very well, but he's a cool guy."

"Hn."

Eli was getting lightheaded. Something about the way Haruka smelled was driving his hormones into overdrive.

And he kept getting closer.

If he got any closer, Eli was going to have to start translating furiously—at least until he could get to the shower room to relieve some tension. And Haruka had given him so much material to work with yesterday, showing off all that gorgeous, golden skin.

"I got you." Haruka's eyes flared, and in their depths, Eli saw something primal staring back at him.

"Got me? What did you catch me doing?"

The door dinged and opened onto their floor. That was when Eli noticed Haruka's arm was lightly touching the top of Eli's head.

"You . . . you were listening?" He shrank back, ready to bolt, but there was nowhere for him to go.

Haruka gripped his arm firmly and hauled him out of the elevator. “Since you don’t like being carried in public, I suggest you come with me.” The glint in his eyes told Eli he fully intended to carry him kicking and screaming down the hallway if necessary.

“I’m coming, you don’t have to pull my arm off.”

“And if I don’t, you’ll escape.”

Escape? From what? Being coldly brushed off like everyone else? If Eli got the chance, you better believe he would.

“You really are a moron.” Haruka opened their door and shoved Eli inside.

CHAPTER 28
ELI

Eli tripped through the door and almost ate dirt, but Haruka caught and steadied him before he could hit the ground.

"That's why you've been so busy translating nonsense at me?"

"It's not what you think."

Haruka rubbed a hand over his face, while still keeping a firm grip on Eli's upper arm. "I've been a moron too. Just as badly as you."

"Is name calling really necessary?"

He hadn't called any of the other people names when he'd dismissed them and their feelings so easily. Eli must be special.

Someday, Haruka would find someone he didn't want to drive away, and it wasn't going to be a tiny little twink like Eli. It would probably be a much taller blonde girl with massive—

"I take it back. You are much dumber than me."

"Hey, I—mmph!"

Haruka had cut Eli off.

With his mouth.

On Eli's mouth.

Holy shit, what was happening right now?

Haruka pulled away just enough to say, "I don't want a blonde girl with big tits. I will never want one, no matter what color her hair is."

"Are you sure? Because there are so many of them out there, and they all seem to want you."

"I'm very, very gay, Eli. I'm sure."

"Oh." Eli said in a small voice. "Well, there are a lot of guys in your fan club too . . ."

"Most of them aren't there for me, but even if they were, I wouldn't want them either." Haruka nuzzled the side of Eli's face with his nose. "Do you know what I was thinking when I saw you this afternoon?" His voice sent goosebumps up Eli's neck and down his arms.

"What?" Eli's heart was beating so fast he thought he was going to pass out.

"Mine." Haruka growled into Eli's ear. "When I saw you, I thought *he's mine.* I wanted to hurt everyone in the room for seeing you like that."

A curl of pleasure swooped low in Eli's stomach. This didn't seem like rejection at all. Haruka wanted him too?

"You've been torturing me for weeks, but I—" Haruka drew back just enough to look Eli in the eyes. "Eli, you're beautiful without makeup, but when I saw what Alice had done to you, I thought I was going to go insane."

"Oh." That explained why Eli had felt like he'd been kicked in the chest when Haruka had shown up.

Haruka's thumb traced Eli's lower lip just like he had in Eli's fantasy.

"Ahh . . ." Eli breathed.

"You made me wait for too long. Don't make me wait

anymore." His hand trailed down, and his fingers traced Eli's Adam's apple. He dropped a kiss on it, then another.

Eli swallowed hard.

His mind was a kaleidoscope of conflicting thoughts and emotions. Was this really happening? Was this a terrible idea? Should they slow down?

Dear god in heaven, he really didn't want to slow down.

Eli pressed his hands against Haruka's chest and pushed. "Wait!"

"I know you don't want me to wait, Eli. And I know you don't want me to stop." Haruka said, teeth grazing against Eli's collarbone.

Everything was going so fast, he needed to stop and think, just for a few minutes.

"No waiting. No thinking." Haruka took Eli's wrists and pressed them against the wall and bit the spot where Eli's shoulder met his neck. "Say yes, Eli." He growled and tightened his grip.

It was like magic. All the warning bells, shoulds, and what ifs shut off, and Eli was left with blissful silence inside his head. All he was left with was need and a body that ached for one thing. Haruka.

"Yes," Eli whispered. "Please."

His feet left the floor as Haruka lifted him and carried Eli to the bed. He didn't toss him there like he usually did when they played around. He laid him down slowly, reverently, like Eli was something precious to be treasured.

"Are you going to be good for me, Eli?"

Eli nodded. There was no other answer inside of him to give.

"I need to hear you say it out loud." Haruka kneeled beside him with sin in his eyes. He slid a hand into Eli's hair and pulled, just hard enough for Eli to really feel it.

When it slid away, long fingers traced a line over Eli's pulse.

"Yes . . ." Eli would be so good. As good as he needed to be as long as Haruka didn't stop touching him.

"Good boy."

Haruka sat back on his heels and for a long moment, all he did was allow his eyes to wander over Eli's body. As if he were deciding where he wanted to start. He looked like he wanted to eat Eli alive.

Eli shivered and his tongue darted out to wet his lips.

Haruka's eyes tracked the movement, and he shifted until he was straddling Eli's body. Trapping him securely on both sides. "Do you do that on purpose?"

Eli meant to ask what he meant, but when he opened his mouth, Haruka ran his thumb over his lower lip again.

Was it supposed to feel this good? Eli gasped as Haruka played with his lower lip, stretching it slightly as he ran his thumb back and forth. Then he swooped down, like a bird of prey and captured it between his teeth.

"You don't know how many times I've wanted to do this," Haruka whispered against Eli's mouth. "I've seen you do it a hundred times, chibisuke, and each time I wondered if it was as much fun as it looked."

Eli's head was swimming from delicious, sensory overload, but somehow, he managed to ask, "Was it?"

"It's so much better." Haruka pushed himself up, and his hips pressed into Eli's.

Eli watched, mesmerized, as each and every one of the gold flecks went out as Haruka's eyes got darker.

Shouldn't he be scared right now? He'd never done anything like this before—never even *kissed* anyone before.

Haruka's hands dug into the covers on either side of Eli. "Never?"

Eli shook his head. "I never wanted to." But he wanted to now.

Weeks of watching Haruka simply exist near Eli, had him in a near permanent state of want. He wanted to do all the things he'd been too afraid to do when he woke up wrapped around Haruka each morning. Wanted to touch. Wanted to feel. Wanted to taste . . .

Eli's hands snaked up to twine around Haruka's neck, and his hips lifted on their own accord, searching for friction.

Haruka's shivered. "I'm trying to go slow right now, but you aren't making it easy."

"When have I ever tried to make things easy for you —mmph."

Haruka's mouth descended, stopping Eli from talking, thinking, or remembering how to breathe. His tongue traced a hot path along the seam of Eli's mouth, urging it to give him access. Eli gasped and let him in.

Haruka held Eli's jaw, controlling the angle of the kiss as he slid his tongue into the boy's mouth, exploring and plundering as he went.

Eli bucked against Haruka's thigh and held on for dear life as Haruka devoured him, pressing kiss after kiss into his mouth, fucking it over and over again with his tongue.

When he finally pulled back, Haruka's eyes were night black, without a star to be seen. In the depths, something dark stirred, like a jungle cat twitching its tail right before it pounced on its prey.

What had Eli gotten himself into? A shiver of fear went through him. Not fear of Haruka, but fear of the unknown.

"Thinking again?"

Eli nodded, unable to catch his breath enough to speak.

"Want me to help you stop?"

"Y-yes," Eli managed to say, afraid that if he didn't answer out loud, Haruka wouldn't help.

The world moved as Haruka switched their positions, rolling until Eli straddled his hips.

"Off." Haruka pulled Eli's hoodie off his shoulders and helped Eli lift his shirt over his head.

Eli covered his chest, shyly, very conscious of the pink flush spreading across his body.

"I want to see you." Haruka said and took Eli's hands away, pinning them behind his back.

Eli struggled, wanting to cover himself, but Haruka held him firmly, not allowing him to move an inch. Eli's mind went white.

He wanted to live here, in this quiet, lovely space full of softness and safety.

"So beautiful." Haruka tucked Eli's wrists into one hand so he could touch Eli's chest, lingering on the pink buds he found there. He licked a finger and trailed it wetly over one stiffening peak.

"Ahhh . . . don't . . ."

"Don't what?"

"Don't . . . stop." El rocked against the hard ridge of Haruka's cock when it pulsed against his ass.

"Oh, I don't plan on stopping." Haruka promised as he unzipped Eli's jeans and released his cock. Eli watched as it strained against his stomach, pink and leaking slightly at the tip. When Haruka grasped it in one large hand, Eli saw stars.

"Hah . . ."

He'd been right. There was no way Eli would last long with Haruka touching him like this. The man's hand covered him completely—just looking at it was enough to make Eli's vision go sparkly at the edges.

"You said you'd be good, Eli. I think you can last a little longer for me." Haruka gave him a few slow strokes and then ran a thumb over the tip, spreading the wetness he found there in lazy circles.

"I'm . . . trying."

"Try harder." Haruka gripped him tighter and sped up the pace.

Eli couldn't speak, all he could do was rock himself back and forth against the heat of Haruka's cock, while the man had his way with him.

"If you hold out, I'll put you in my mouth."

Just the thought of Haruka's mouth on him had Eli coming hard, covering his stomach and Haruka's hand in white.

"That . . . was . . . evil." Eli panted and slumped bonelessly, held up only by Haruka's hand, still binding his wrists behind his back.

Haruka smirked. "Next time."

Eli shivered and focused on getting enough air into his lungs. After a minute he asked, "What about you? I've barely had a chance to even touch you."

Haruka released his hold on Eli's arms and lifted the boy's hips, scooting him back to reveal the damp spot spreading across his jeans. "I wanted you for too long, Eli. Just watching you . . ." Haruka closed his eyes. "You are intoxicating. I was afraid I would hurt you if I let you touch me."

"I don't believe you would hurt me." Without Eli's permission, anyway.

Haruka's eyes flashed.

"How are you so perfect for me, Eli?" He mused, pulling him close and kissing him softly. Then he rolled Eli over and pressed him into the mattress, kissing him less softly.

Eli was panting when they finally came up for air. "I feel sticky."

Haruka looked down at the mess they made. "Shower."

"Separate showers," Eli said firmly. There was no way he was doing sexy things where anyone could hear. It was bad enough they'd done it behind such thin walls. He had no idea what kind of sounds he'd made, but he doubted they'd been quiet.

"Hn."

They didn't have separate showers.

Once he'd ascertained they were alone in the shower room, Haruka backed Eli into a stall, closed the curtain, and turned on the water. Before he had a chance to protest, Haruka already had Eli pressed against the cold tile wall and was rutting against him.

"Wait . . ."

Haruka covered Eli's mouth and whispered in his ear. "Be quiet if you don't want anyone to hear."

Then he soaped every inch of Eli's body—pressing the boy's hands against the wall any time Eli tried to reciprocate.

"Please . . . I want to touch you." Eli thought he would go crazy if he had to go another minute of seeing Haruka's wet, muscled body without touching it.

"I know." Haruka laughed darkly against Eli's neck where he was in the process of sucking what Eli guessed was going to be an impressive bruise tomorrow. He was going to be a mess, but right now he couldn't find it in him to care.

Eli strained against the hands pinning his against the

wall, biting his lip hard to keep from making any noise, but every time he did, the quiet place took over, and he forgot what he was doing. Finally, he relaxed and allowed Haruka to do whatever he wanted.

As soon as he quit fighting, Haruka released his hands.

"Good boy." Haruka kissed him hard and stepped back to lean against the wall.

Finally, *finally*, Eli was allowed to touch. He allowed his hands to run greedily over Haruka's body. He couldn't have stopped himself if he tried. This was all his. His to play with, his to touch, his to lick . . .

Eli's tongue lapped at a brown, pebbled nipple. Then he nipped it with his teeth. Haruka grunted and wrapped his arms around Eli, pulling his body flush against him.

Eli wanted to wallow in this man. He rubbed his small, soapy frame against Haruka, but it wasn't enough. He wanted to be closer, so much closer than he already was.

Something hard as steel pressed against his stomach, and Eli's hands went to it. He should wash Haruka as thoughtfully as he'd washed Eli.

So, he did.

Now it was Haruka's turn to try to stay quiet as Eli stroked his length. It was so different than Eli's. His hand barely fit around it. What would it be like if he put it in his mouth?

He locked eyes with Haruka and got on his knees. The large man's pupils flared, and he placed his palms against the wall.

Keeping his eyes on Haruka's, he nudged his cock with his nose and ran his tongue along the seam, from the base all the way to the tip. He wrapped his lips around it and heard Haruka swear in Japanese. Eli's own cock was painfully hard and leaking furiously, but he ignored it in favor of getting as much of Haruka in his mouth as possible.

He didn't get far. His mouth was too small, and the tip hit the back of his throat long before Eli's lips reached the base. He choked, and Haruka pulled Eli back by the hair. Tears pricked the corners of his eyes as he looked up at Haruka.

Haruka's hands tightened in Eli's hair. He tugged against the hold on his hair and tried to put Haruka back in his mouth, but he couldn't reach. A whine escaped him.

He'd never felt anything like this in his life. It was like Haruka's skin sang to him, calling him closer so it could fill up all the hollow and empty spaces inside him. He couldn't imagine ever getting enough of this.

Haruka hauled him up by the shoulders and pressed Eli against the wall, face first. Haruka's heat against his back combined with the cold tiles touching his chest made Eli's body go crazy.

"Haruka, please . . ."

"I've got you." Haruka took Eli's cock in his hand. It was slippery with soap, and Eli let out a high-pitched whimper. Haruka covered his mouth. "I don't want anyone else to hear the noises you make."

Eli was enveloped again in the lovely, soft world of quiet. He was a creature of pure sensation as Haruka thrust his cock between Eli's soapy thighs while stroking Eli.

When Eli came, Haruka's hand muffled his cries, and he bit down on Eli's neck, stifling his own cries as he released between Eli's thighs.

Eli stayed in the lovely soft place while Haruka cleaned them both off. He barely noticed as he was bundled into a fluffy robe. If there was another person in the room, he couldn't have cared less.

CHAPTER 29
ELI

Late again!

Holy flying shit, they'd slept in, and now both of them were going to be late for class.

"We didn't set an alarm!" Eli shoved Haruka's arm off of him as he tried to scramble off the bed.

He almost made it, too.

He got all the way to the edge of the bed before Haruka grabbed his arms and rolled Eli underneath him. Then he kissed Eli breathless, taking his time to remind Eli of everything they'd gotten up to last night.

"Good morning." Haruka bit the edge of Eli's jaw lightly before moving away. "Now you can get up."

Eli blinked at the ceiling for a minute or two, struggling to process the past twelve hours. How was this his life?

A few minutes later, Haruka poked his head out of the bathroom with a toothbrush in his mouth. "You might want to get up now."

Eli threw a pillow at him, and Haruka dodged back into the bathroom.

If Eli wanted coffee, he was going to have to skip most of his morning routine. His toothbrush made a brief appearance in his mouth, and he didn't even bother to look in a mirror. Instead, he shoved on the first shirt he saw, grabbed a random pair of pants and shoved his sockless feet into his shoes.

He was halfway to the door when Haruka grabbed him by the back of the shirt and shoved a glass into one hand and his meds into the other.

"Thanks." Eli swallowed them and tried for the door once more only to be stopped again and bundled into Haruka's black hoodie.

"It's going to be cold until this afternoon." Haruka said as he zipped it up. His fingers brushed the hood like he was going to raise it, and a smile ghosted across his face before he dropped his hands, leaving it to lie on Eli's shoulders. "Okay, let's go."

Eli danced impatiently while Haruka ordered them both coffees, growling when he slowed the whole process down by getting them each a cheese croissant.

Eli made *gimme hands* at the coffee when it came, but Haruka held it out of reach, handing him the croissant instead.

"Two bites and then you can have it."

"Argh!!! How did you get even bossier?" Eli grumbled and tore into the croissant with his teeth. As soon as the second bite was in his mouth, he jumped for the coffee still being held just out of reach. He missed. "In our next life, I'm coming back as the tall one, and you're never getting coffee."

Haruka relented and lowered the coffee until Eli could reach it. "Our next life?"

"Yes, and you're going to be very, very short. And less

hot." Eli shot a glare at the lone member of Haruka's fan club hovering at a respectful distance.

Haruka slung an arm around Eli's shoulders. "So, your type is short and ugly?"

"And annoying."

"I promise you I can manage that last one."

"Hush, I'm trying to get this coffee inside of me, and you're slowing down the process."

Haruka dropped Eli off at his class—almost on time. Outside the door, Haruka planted a hand on Eli's chest, pushed him against the wall, and leaned in. Eli blocked his face with both arms. "Not here!"

Haruka let him go, but his low chuckle followed Eli as he hurried into the classroom.

He jerked up his hood to cover his burning face because, of course, everyone turned to see who had arrived late.

Jerk. He thought it as hard as he could, and a second later he got a brief impression of amusement.

Nate and Alice met him at the door at the end of class.

"You know you don't have to do this every day, right?" Eli said in lieu of a greeting. This had to be getting old for them. He knew he was certainly getting tired of being shepherded around everywhere he went.

"We don't have to, but we want to," Alice said.

"I know you do, but really, there's no need. The police told me Ash is out on bail, but he's gone home to Boston with a shiny new ankle bracelet until the trial." Eli kept his voice down because he didn't want everyone to know his business. His department was notoriously nosy. "At this point, it's just Haruka being paranoid."

"I don't blame him," Nate said. "You looked terrible the next day. Scared the shit out of me."

"Everyone on the campus isn't like Ash. I'm not a celebrity or a politician, guys." Ew, as if. "I don't need an escort everywhere I go."

"Oh, Eli! We've been helicoptering you, haven't we?" Alice's eyes were suddenly big and wet. "I'm so sorry!"

Any second now Eli was going to have a crying girl on his hands. He needed to do something fast.

He took a deep breath and let it out. Then he put a hand on her shoulder. No alarms sounded, nobody jumped out from behind a potted plant and dragged him off to jail for doing something out of character, and it didn't feel horribly wrong. It didn't feel good, but it was a start.

"It's okay, Alice, really."

It had the opposite effect he intended. Tears streamed down Alice's cheeks, and she began to sob. Horrified, Eli snatched his hand back.

Fuck. He was not up for hugging. Not now, maybe not ever. He looked at Nate anxiously. "I think I broke her."

"You're really okay, aren't you?" Alice howled.

"It's fine, Eli. Those are her happy tears." Nate put an arm around Alice and squeezed her shoulder. "I promise you didn't break her."

"I love you, Eli!" Alice sniffed and searched her purse, pulling out a tissue.

"I love you too, Alice." Eli looked at both of his friends. "So . . . does this mean you'll stop treating me like someone is going to drop out of the sky and kill me at any moment?"

Nate and Alice exchanged glances.

"I think we can do that, but I'm not even going to begin to speak for Haruka," Nate said.

Eli laughed nervously. "Maybe we don't have to mention this to him?"

Nate threw up his hands and backed up. "Hey, I'm not lying to the guy. He's fucking scary. I won't bring it up, but if he asks, I will definitely rat you out."

"Same. I'm staying on his good side." Alice chimed in, looking more composed than she had a minute ago, though she still had a sheen in her eyes. "Actually, this works out for me. I forgot to put on my estrogen patch this morning and haven't had a chance to go back for it."

And that was how Eli found himself with an entire hour to himself for the first time in weeks.

It was glorious.

If no one had been around, he would have spun in circles all around the pond Maria Von Trapp-style. Instead, he sat by the pond and enjoyed drinking a coffee he didn't have to worry about someone taking from him and replacing with a piece of fruit.

At first, he was able to ignore the stares. He'd gotten used to being around someone who was on the receiving end of tons of them, but after having to turn down three invitations to eat in a row, he started to get suspicious.

"No, really, I have to get to class." Eli said as he gathered his things.

A bushy-haired English major, who'd introduced himself as Forrest, trailed after him. "I can walk you to class, if you want."

Eli turned to look at him just as the wind kicked up and blew his hood back.

Forrest's eyes zeroed in on Eli's neck. "I'm sorry, I didn't realize."

"Realize what?" Eli pulled his hood back up.

"That you're not available. You're seeing someone, right?"

"Kinda, yeah." He was definitely doing something with someone, at the very least. They still hadn't managed to actually talk about it yet.

Forrest gave him a sad smile. "Figures." Then he turned and walked away—minus the spring in his step he'd had when he'd first approached Eli.

How had he known . . .?

Eli's hand slapped over his neck.

Fucking hell.

He ran for the nearest bathroom and looked in the mirror.

Christ! He looked like he'd gotten attacked by a vacuum cleaner. The only reason his friends hadn't seen it was because his morning class had the windows open, and he'd kept his hood up to keep from freezing to death.

He tightened his hoodie strings and walked to his next class hunched over his phone, searching for ways to get rid of hickeys.

Haruka picked him up at the end of class, and they went to meet his friends for a late lunch.

"Eli, I forgot to mention it, but you didn't get all of the sequins off from yesterday. Did they give you trouble?" Alice used her sandwich to point at Eli's face.

"No, I got distracted and fell asleep before getting them all." He resisted the urge to shoot a dirty look at said distraction.

"Haruka, you've got one in your hair . . . Actually, you have several. Oh, and one on your neck." Alice pressed her hands to her mouth. "Holy shit, did you two . . .?"

"Don't say it, Alice, I'm begging you." Eli rubbed his

newly throbbing forehead. He touched a knee to Haruka's and thought :*I'm not ready for this yet!*:

Haruka looked off to the side and whistled innocently.

:*You are just the worst!*:

Alice balled her hands up and made a little squeaking sound.

"Can we talk about this another time?" Next fall sounded great to Eli.

"Yes!" Alice punched a fist in the air. "I mean, yes. Yes, we can."

Nate continued to eat calmly through the entire conversation like he wasn't even surprised.

Eli wrinkled his forehead. How had he known?

~

"Are you embarrassed by me?"

Eli and Haruka were on their way back to their building at the end of the day when Haruka finally asked the question Eli had been dreading.

"Only a blind moron would be embarrassed by you."

"Are you afraid of people thinking you're gay?"

"No more than I'm afraid of people knowing I'm short and bipolar. Whatever this is, whatever we are? This is all part and parcel of being me, and I'm done with being ashamed of being myself."

"Then what is it?"

Eli sighed. "I don't like the attention." He tugged hard on his hoodie strings. "You're fucking beautiful, Haruka. If everyone knows I'm dating you, I'm going to get dirty looks and hate mail and who knows what else. And everyone is going to be watching us. If you don't mind, I'd like to ease into it instead of jumping in with a massive splash."

“People were paying attention to you before you met me.”

“How do you know that?”

“Because I watched you.”

Eli nudged Haruka with his elbow. “Stalker.”

Haruka’s lips curved into a half smile. “Hn.”

“You’re lucky I seem to be into creepy guys.”

“Only this creepy guy.”

“One of you is more than enough.” Eli let his arm slip around Haruka’s waist and snuggled into his side. When Haruka dropped a kiss on top of his head, he didn’t protest—he was tired of fighting the desire to wrap himself around Haruka just because he was afraid someone would see.

It was dark. No one was watching. He could have this small moment.

CHAPTER 30

ELI

The staring thing turned out not to be a figment of Eli's imagination.

"What am I looking at, Alice?" Eli stared at Alice's phone in horror.

"It's a forum for the campus, mostly for bored people who like to gossip, but they also post pictures, or in your case, pictures and videos."

"I didn't post these!"

"Neither did I, Eli. I swear. I only put one picture on the club Facebook page. I don't know how someone got these shots of you."

"I thought no one else saw Eli like this," Haruka said to Alice with an edge to his voice.

"I didn't think they had," Eli also said to Alice, pointedly ignoring Haruka. "How many people are in this forum?"

"Um . . . let me check. It says 6,547."

"That many people saw this video?"

"And the pictures, too. Possibly more if people shared it."

"That's almost a third of the student body!"

Eli hadn't worried much about the looks he'd been getting until someone came up and asked him out while Haruka was walking him to class this morning.

It hadn't gone well for anyone. The guy was upset because his shoes were ruined. Eli was mad at Haruka for throwing the guy in the pond, and it seemed like Haruka was mad at Eli for daring to exist in front of other people.

Okay, that last one was probably a little unfair. But the end result was that they currently weren't speaking to each other.

"How did someone even take this video?" Haruka finally deigned to ask Eli.

And now they were back on speaking terms, which was progress, but Eli was still planning to be grumpy about it.

The video in question was only a few seconds long, but something about it seemed to resonate with people. Eli didn't get the appeal, personally.

"I think it was when you called me. I went out into the hallway because that's what polite people do. I didn't realize anyone had noticed me." He'd been preoccupied at the time.

"So, it's Haruka who put that dreamy look on your face?"

"Stuff it, Alice."

"I think it's sweet!"

"Can you get them to take them down?" Haruka no longer looked like he was sucking on lemons for some reason.

"It's too late for that. This is even bigger than the post Ash made about you. This is just where it originated. It's trending on TikTok now."

"What?! Why are people so interested in me talking on the phone?"

"Aside from my fabulous makeup skills on your lovely face? It's the energy you give off. You're so happy here." She gestured at the video on her phone. It was paused on a frame of Eli. His head was tipped back against the wall, and he had a soft smile on his face. "It's like you're in your own little world, thinking only about the person on the other end of the phone. Everyone who sees it is going to want to be that person. You are the embodiment of boyfriend material here!"

"Yes, my boyfriend," Haruka snapped.

"You don't need to look at me like that, I'm not going to take him from you." Alice ducked behind Eli.

"No, but half the school is about to try." Haruka was back to scowling.

Eli had gotten a little hung up on the whole boyfriend comment, so he didn't respond.

"This is the part where you tell him not to worry," Alice said in a stage whisper.

"Huh? Oh, yeah, no. I don't even want people noticing me, why would I want them hitting on me?"

"I think you should switch to online classes," Haruka said firmly.

"And I think you need to switch to decaf." Eli stood up. "Thanks for telling me about this, Alice. I'd better go if I'm going to make it to my next class."

Eli left the empty classroom and heard Haruka say to Alice, "No more painting Eli," before he followed him out.

They walked in frosty silence before Eli finally broke down and said, "I didn't ask for this."

"Hn."

"You realize you can pack more meaning into one sound than most people can in a five-minute monologue, right?"

"Hn." Haruka's lips quirked.

"I'm not taking online classes."

"Fine." Haruka unzipped Eli's hoodie and pulled his collar aside.

Eli zipped it back up and glared, hastily looking away when a pout began to form on Haruka's face.

No, no, nope. He wasn't falling for that trap. The bastard didn't know the meaning of sadness or remorse, and he only acted cute when he wanted Eli to cave. And he totally would if he looked at Haruka right now.

"Eli." Haruka had drawn close when Eli looked away. His voice was soft and butter smooth in Eli's ear. "I don't like that everyone thinks they have a chance with you."

Eli suppressed a shiver, but his body swayed toward Haruka. This was completely unfair.

"You are not available."

Eli closed his eyes tight. *Don't look. If you look at him, it's all over.*

"No, I'm not available, but—"

A finger lifted his chin, and Eli's eyes opened automatically. The pout was gone, in its place was a serious expression.

"I don't want to cage you. I want to keep you safe. If I could be around you all the time, it would be different, but I can't do that."

"No one is going to hurt me, Haruka."

"Someone has already hurt you." Something dark stirred in Haruka's eyes.

Several someones, in fact, but Haruka didn't need a reminder of Eli's tragic backstory right now. Not if Eli wanted to be able to go around campus with any sort of dignity.

"I don't think walking around looking like I got mauled is going to change anything."

A flash of hurt surged through Eli—not his, but Haruka's.

All the irritation from this morning vanished.

He didn't want to hurt Haruka. They loved to snark and snip at each other, but it was only play. Actually hurting him was simply out of the question.

"You don't have to tell people who you're dating as long as it's obvious that you are." There was no trace of pain on Haruka's face, but Eli could still feel it burning in his chest. Then it cut off abruptly.

Eli tugged his zipper down. "Three days."

Haruka pulled Eli's collar aside. "Until your video stops trending."

"Don't push it."

Three weeks. It had been three goddamned weeks, and Eli still had people trailing after him. He'd become an expert at dodging into empty classrooms and around corners to avoid his fans. It was November and cold every day now, so Haruka had stopped insisting he display his love bites to the world. He didn't want Eli to get sick.

Not that it stopped him from giving Eli new ones every chance he got.

For a few days after Eli's new burst of popularity, his friends had begun escorting him to classes again, but when nothing bad happened, they'd started to slack off and allow Eli to have his freedom again. So far, Haruka hadn't caught on.

It was annoying to have people constantly approaching him—every day at least one representative of the Theater club tried to badger him into joining. He'd also become a pro at declining potential suitors with a simple, "Thank you, but I'm already dating someone."

But having a modicum of personal autonomy was worth being mildly irritated.

Eli propped his elbows on the fence and watched Haruka as he practiced kyudo. Since it was colder, he'd stopped showing off so much skin, but he was still poetry to watch.

Right now, he stood stock-still, waiting until he found something only Haruka could sense. He'd explained it to Eli as right action. When it was time, right action would flow through him, and the arrow would fly true.

Eli was pretty sure he could watch his boyfriend practice kyudo forever.

Boyfriend. He was dating Haruka.

Eli was *dating* Haruka.

It had been three weeks, and he still couldn't wrap his head around it.

Sure, they had a mysterious mental bond, but what Haruka saw in anxious, bitchy, antisocial Eli was beyond him to understand.

Honestly, Eli thought he was clearly getting the better end of the deal.

Haruka was still a bit of a pushy jerk, but he was also kind and considerate and gave Eli everything he had in his power to give.

And when he shoved his way into Eli's personal space and touched him, Eli didn't care how pushy he was. Haruka shut Eli's mind down and made his body sing.

Sometimes he thought Haruka could eat him alive, and Eli would die smiling.

"What's that smile about?" Alice came up to him on one side and Nate came up on the other.

"You know exactly what he's smiling over, Al. Please don't make me listen to the dirty details."

"Like I'd tell you." Eli snorted. "Come on, let's go."

He waved to Haruka, so he'd know Eli's friends had come to walk him to class. Haruka lowered his bow and waved back.

Instead of walking Eli all the way to his class, Alice and Nate parted ways as soon as they were out of sight of the archery field, leaving Eli free for the next two hours.

He swung his arms happily as he walked down the sidewalk. He hadn't realized how physically constricted he'd felt by constant companionship. It wasn't like he didn't love being around his people but being forced to do so was getting to him. It was time to talk to Haruka about how overprotective he was being.

Tonight. After class, he'd find some way to get the man to relax and let him go back to being a free-range Eli. One who didn't have to contact someone before he poked a toe out of his room.

It was funny. At the beginning of the year, Eli could barely get himself to leave his room unless it was absolutely necessary. Juniper would be so proud of him.

He felt easier in his skin now. The shadows that haunted him constantly had faded to mere whispers he could shrug off. Hell, he could probably even sleep alone now.

Maybe he could let that last one go untested. He had the best body pillow in existence. It would be insane not to use it.

"Hey, pretty," a familiar, slimy voice called to him. Where did he know this voice?

Eli had been so lost in his thoughts he'd abandoned the vigilance he used to wear like armor. Having a constant escort must have lulled him into complacency because standing two feet away was Chad number one.

How had he forgotten that guy? Just hearing his voice made Eli's stomach churn. And now he had to deal with him alone.

"Fuck off, Chad." Eli tried to keep walking and was unsurprised when he was blocked.

"Don't be like that. And the name's Hank, not Chad."

"Figures," Eli muttered. Hank was still a very Chad-like name in his opinion. "I'm going to be late for class, get out of my way." Start strong, finish strong. If he didn't act like he was about to throw up from fear, he might get out of this unscathed.

"I'll walk you there." Hank moved to the side and fell in step with Eli, who started walking the second his path was clear.

"I don't need someone to walk to class with me." And if he did, he had far better options than this guy. Maybe he should have stuck with Alice and Nate after all.

No. He didn't need a bodyguard. He'd been dealing with the Chads of the world long before the Eli Protection Squad had formed. He could take care of this on his own. All he had to do was walk fast and ignore Hank until he got to class.

"Maybe not, but my services are free." Hank's voice went low and suggestive. "I never get complaints."

Hard pass.

"I'm sure somehow I'll survive." Eli let his tone drip with venom. He wasn't doing great on the ignoring part of the plan. He gotten too comfortable speaking his mind—when he got his freedom back, he'd have to watch that.

Unfazed, Hank tried to put an arm around Eli, and he dodged to the side. Score one for Eli!

It would have been an excellent boost of self-esteem if he hadn't tripped. Hank caught him by both arms and force-marched Eli backward.

Wrongwrongwrong rang out inside Eli's head as he was pushed into a space between two buildings.

"What is your problem?" Eli tried to jerk his arms free, but Hank held him fast against a wall.

"My problem is you. Flaunting your ass around campus like you're the hottest thing out there. I just want a taste to see if you're worth the hype." Hank's face was so close Eli could feel his hot breath against his cheek. He twisted his neck to the side to get away.

His internal alarm was going berserk, which meant there was no way he was going to be able to hide this incident from Haruka. He could kiss his free time goodbye.

Not that he really cared about his precious free time right now. The only thing going through his mind right now was the hope that Haruka would arrive before Hank did something to ruin Eli's entire week.

"Back the fuck off, asshole!"

That . . . was not Haruka. Or any other voice he recognized, for that matter.

"Consent is a thing, buddy. Google it," another unfamiliar voice said.

Hank turned to look at the people interrupting his fun, allowing Eli a chance to see that the entrance of the alley was lined with students. He might not recognize their voices, but their faces were very familiar. They should be. They'd been following him and Haruka around for weeks.

He looked closer. And some of them were people who'd asked him out.

While Hank was distracted, Eli tried to squirm free, but

Hank threw a forearm across his chest, keeping him pinned in place.

"Get lost. He wants it, and you're interrupting."

"Keep dreaming. Eli doesn't like to be touched by anyone but Haruka," an unknown girl said.

A boy held up his phone. "I've been recording since you shoved Eli into the alley. I don't think a jury will think Eli wants it."

"I don't!" Eli twisted hard, and Hank relaxed his hold, allowing Eli to finally get free.

He bolted for the line of Haruka's fans. They opened a space for him, let him slip through, then closed back up, forming a wall between Hank and Eli. He didn't fail to notice that they all kept a respectful distance from him, giving him a nice, safe bubble of personal space.

A chest pressed against his back that didn't feel even slightly wrong. Haruka had finally arrived.

Hank backed up. "It was just a joke."

"It didn't feel like a joke," Eli said.

"We've got several camera angles to work with, so the police can see whether or not they think it was a joke," the first girl said.

Eli looked around and realized several people had their phones out recording everything.

Hank backed up again. Then he turned and ran.

"Should we go after him?" Phone Boy asked.

"Let him go. Somehow, I doubt the police are going to believe I'm enough of a siren to have two separate men attack me in my first semester. I'd rather not be known as the campus floozy, if you don't mind."

Eli felt a low growl in Haruka's chest. He hadn't said anything yet, and it was making Eli feel a little nervous.

"W-what are you all doing here, anyway? I thought you

were Haruka's fans, not mine." Yes, he was stalling for time, but he still wanted to know. His rescuers had shown up at a very convenient time.

"We were, but we decided to combine forces with your fans when we saw how devoted you two are to each other," Phone Boy said.

"You're so cute together!" A short girl—who was still taller than Eli—clenched her fists together in front of her chest and jumped up and down happily.

There were several dreamy sighs and squees from the gathered crowd.

"Ah . . . I don't, I mean, we're not."

Haruka wrapped his arms around Eli from behind in a hug.

"How did you know?" Eli finished lamely.

"I hate to break it to you, Eli, but you two are pretty obvious. The way you look at each other, the fact that he's the only person who can touch you. You're always together, he feeds, you, I mean, come on. We're not blind." This came from a tall, waif-like girl Eli didn't recognize at all—though she seemed to know plenty about him. He really needed to start paying better attention to his surroundings.

Haruka put his chin on Eli's head.

"You've been watching us?" Eli wasn't sure how he felt about that.

"What can I say? You guys are a much-needed distraction from the stress of schoolwork and grades," the first girl said

"Don't worry though, we won't get up in your personal business. We're just happy to watch from afar," Phone Boy said.

"And discuss you on our Discord server," another girl put in. "And we can make sure nobody bothers you."

“There’s a Discord server?” Eli tried to take a step back, but there was a giant, clingy wall behind him, so all he accomplished was making everyone around him sigh again. “How many of you are there?”

Phone Boy frowned and looked thoughtful. “At my last count, I think it was nearly nine hundred.”

“Nine hundred?!”

“It’s a good thing, Eli. If someone messes with you, one of us is always around, so we can tell everyone else you need help.”

“Always around . . .” Eli rubbed his face. “Thanks? I think.”

It wasn’t just him, right? This was super weird. But also, kind of sweet? He decided to go with sweet. He hadn’t gotten molested, which was a serious plus in his book, and their new fan club had said they wouldn’t get too personal.

“Thank you,” he said again, only more firmly. He jabbed Haruka in the gut.

“Thanks,” Haruka said grudgingly.

“You’re very welcome.”

“Okay everyone, let’s give them some space so they can go be”—Girl Number One giggled—“together.”

“Bye Eli, bye Haruka.” The group chorused and began to disperse.

Haruka tightened his arms around Eli, making him squeak.

“You’re squishing me!”

“Good,” Haruka said, grumpily, but relaxed his grip a notch.

“So, I should probably go to class . . .”

“You still have an hour before it starts.” Haruka released his death hold on Eli and took his hand. “We need to talk.”

Well, it had been worth a shot.

Eli allowed himself to be dragged to a secluded bench. He would dearly love to have coffee right now. It was cold, and he needed something to compensate for the adrenaline crash that was about to happen.

Haruka opened his jacket and pulled Eli close, tucking him under an arm to keep him warm.

"You ditched Nate and Alice."

"I did." This was so weird. He should be shaking right now, or having some kind of trauma response, but being pressed against Haruka's side was better than any coffee ever. Even if they were about to have what promised to be a nasty fight.

"It's not going to be a nasty fight." Haruka pulled Eli into his lap and pressed his face into his neck. "You scared the shit out of me."

Eli didn't even put up a pretense of struggling. After having Hank's hands on him, all he wanted was for Haruka's touch to wash it away.

"I'm sorry, I just—" Wanted to be alone for a few minutes? Had gotten so used to feeling safe around Haruka that he'd forgotten the world was still full of predators? "I wasn't thinking. But I feel suffocated. I was going to talk to you about it today, but then Hank showed up and ruined everything." Once Alice and Nate found out, he'd have to move schools if he ever wanted time to himself again.

Haruka's pulled him in closer. Eli's back was flush against his chest, and he wrapped his jacket around him. "Don't switch schools. I know I can be . . . overprotective, but when I can't see you, I'm on edge. I can't get over the feeling that someone is going to hurt you or take you away."

Eli shook his head. "I don't want to leave. I like it here. And I like your clingy, octopus ways—obviously. But this isn't sustainable. You can't be with me all the time—" He smiled when Haruka huffed irritably into his hair. "And I can't live my life with someone always stepping on the back of my shoes."

"I'm not being irrational, you're a trouble magnet. Let me protect you from the bad things. I want to do it."

Eli wiggled until Haruka loosened his hold enough for Eli to turn around so he could straddle his legs and face him. Haruka's face wasn't sullen like it was when he was trying to get his way. He looked lost.

He stroked Haruka's cheek. "I like when you protect me. Haruka, I've never felt this safe before. Not since"—Eli's throat closed briefly, but he pressed on—"I was kidnapped. But we need to work out a compromise we can both live with." Soon, before Eli caved to the look on Haruka's face, and he ended up with a backpack leash.

"It's not the worst idea." Haruka's eyes glinted, a hint of his evil side peeking through.

"I'm not putting on a bondage show for the world to see."

"But if no one is watching, it's okay?" Yep, the evil side was definitely taking over.

Eli flushed and fought not to think about Haruka tying him up. They were in the middle of an important conversation, and now was not the time to get sidetracked.

"If this wasn't about your safety, I would definitely be getting sidetracked."

Eli cleared his throat. "Anyway, moving on . . . Seeing as how I'm not interested in getting assaulted by random people, I admit you have a fair point. But I think we're forgetting something important here."

"Such as?"

"Our newly combined fan club. They're always around,

and today they came in super handy. They even said they've been keeping an eye out for me. Maybe we could ask them to help?"

Haruka hummed in acknowledgement. "I still don't like it."

"You aren't going to like anything short of me taking online classes in our room." Eli held up his hand to forestall any argument. "And that's not happening."

"Fine." Haruka didn't look happy, but the lost expression was gone from his face. "But I'm still walking you to class when I'm free."

"But you're not leaving class early or showing up late anymore."

Haruka scrunched his nose and pouted.

"Grades are important, Haruka."

"Not that important."

"They're important to me, so deal with it."

"Fine."

CHAPTER 31
HARUKA

He had planned to ease out of bed as soon as Eli fell asleep, but it was so soothing to feel him slip from the waking world to the dreaming one, that Haruka lost time holding the small, fragile boy close to him.

Too fragile. Too easy to hurt or to pick up and run off with. It was effortless for Haruka to carry him around, and there were plenty of other people in the world who could do the same.

Like Hank.

Haruka lifted Eli's head off of his chest and placed it gently on a pillow.

There were plenty of other people in the world who could see many of the wonderful qualities Eli had to offer. Ones with no morals.

Like Hank.

He closed the bathroom door and made a phone call. It took longer than he'd planned because he'd forgotten about the time difference—right now his aunt was in the middle of her pre-lunch meeting, which meant her assistant was busy too. He was willing to wait.

When he'd finished his call, he padded quietly back to the bed and climbed in, very ready to be wrapped around Eli once more.

He was certain his heart had stopped beating the moment he'd felt Eli's fear when Hank grabbed him. It wouldn't happen again—not with Hank, at least. Haruka had just made sure of it.

He brushed the hair back from Eli's face and caught a glimpse of shadows in his mind. Haruka pulled him onto his chest—usually holding him was enough to banish the bad dreams that plagued Eli.

"No . . . please don't." Eli whimpered.

"It's okay, Eli. I'm here."

Haruka rubbed Eli's arms to wake him, but he didn't respond. Instead, Haruka's mind was flooded with images of a small, dark-haired boy getting flung across a room, slapped, beaten, and abused—all by the same man.

"Eli!" He tapped him on the face. "Wake up."

Eli's eye's fluttered open, but they were unfocused. Haruka was ready for the fist that came toward his face, so he caught it, held it firmly, and pressed a kiss into it.

"You're safe, Eli. No one's going to hurt you anymore." Haruka fought against his own set of shadows as they rose. They wanted him to rend and tear, but Haruka couldn't fight memories.

He held Eli's struggling form in his arms and spoke softly in Japanese, hoping it would wake him up and make him realize where he was.

When the boy finally stopped fighting, he pressed his face against Haruka's chest, and let out a ragged sob. "He called me pretty."

Haruka went quiet and began to stroke Eli's hair.

"When he was lucid, he told me he took me because I was pretty like his dead son. When I acted like his son did, he would give me candy, and when I didn't, he hurt me. I tried, but I didn't know what his son was like, so . . ." Eli curled up into a ball.

"So, he hurt you a lot." Haruka finished for him.

Eli made a choking sound and nodded into Haruka's chest.

Eli hadn't talked about his kidnapping before. Haruka had only caught glimpses of it in his mind, but they'd been bad enough for him not to push. He wanted Eli to tell him about it when he was ready.

It took a while for Eli to tell his story, but Haruka was nothing if not patient. When the boy choked or froze up, Haruka spoke to him in Japanese. He didn't say anything important, just that Eli was safe and good and that no one could hurt him here. It seemed to work because, after a minute or so, Eli would relax and continue.

When Eli was ten, he was taken from his yard by a man who had recently lost his family to a fire. It wasn't planned. The man had snapped when he saw Eli and took him. No one saw him do it, and since the man had no connection to Eli or his family, the police had no way to find him.

He'd spent eight days being tormented, beaten, and pampered depending on how well Eli had managed to act like the man's son. On the eighth day, the man had overdosed, and Eli had crawled past his body to freedom.

Eli had been dealing with nightmares about his kidnapper ever since.

"I've managed to overcome most of the trauma, but I can't sleep alone and . . . I don't like when someone calls me pretty."

No one ever would again if Haruka had any say in the matter.

After all of that—and being attacked twice on the same campus—Eli was still fighting to be able to live a normal life.

"You are very strong, Eli."

Eli let out something that was half laugh and half sob. "Yes, I'm very strong. So strong I had a nightmare because someone called me pretty."

"It was more than that, and you know it, baka." Haruka loved every millimeter of Eli, but he wasn't going to coddle him. "Don't belittle how hard you worked to get here."

Eli blinked up at him with his big Bambi eyes. Then the corners of his mouth twitched. He sat up and kissed Haruka hard. "You really just fucking get me."

"I do."

Haruka caught a flash of Eli thinking about his sister and how she was the only other person who knew his whole story and didn't treat him like a sad, wet puppy. It was why he loved her more than anyone. And now he had Haruka too.

"You have every bit of me, Eli."

Eli's mind shined happily for a moment before the remnants of his nightmare dragged his thoughts back to his kidnapper.

"Where is he now?" Haruka asked.

Eli flinched and pressed his face into Haruka's chest again. "He—his name is Liam"—his voice cracked, but he kept going—"but I don't like to say it. He survived because I was able to tell the police where he was after I escaped. He was in a mental institution for a few years, but then he was transferred to prison. I . . . haven't heard anything about him in a while. My mom usually takes any calls related to him."

And from what Haruka was picking up from his mind, Eli wanted things to stay that way.

"I will make sure you never see him again." Haruka vowed.

"You're crazy enough that I almost believe you."

"And I've been working so hard to keep you from noticing the crazy," Haruka said lightly.

Eli laughed. It was a small, pale ghost of Eli's usual laugh, but it was a start.

Having a fan club turned out to be far more interesting than Haruka had anticipated.

When they'd first begun to show up in his life, they'd been nothing but a barrier between him and Eli—which meant they had to go. So, he did what he did when he'd first arrived at the school and coldly ignored them. This time it hadn't worked.

Now he knew why.

He didn't blame his followers for becoming enamored of Eli—who wouldn't be? And, while he didn't understand the fascination other people had developed with their relationship, he was fully prepared to use it to his advantage.

Haruka had had an unconventional upbringing, but it was coming in handy now. Just because he hadn't willingly participated in the family business, didn't mean he hadn't paid close attention to everything going on around him.

Now he was having as much fun as he was capable of without Eli actively participating.

He had spies.

The day after their fan club had stepped in and protected Eli, Haruka had joined the Discord server devoted to the club and gotten to work. Over the next few weeks, he'd taken them from a loosely organized group of students to a well-oiled machine.

He'd arranged people into groups depending on what their major was and what part of the campus they tended to spend the most time in. If he wanted to know what was going on in a certain part of the campus, all he had to do was contact the group responsible for the area.

And all he'd had to do in return was give them signed pictures of him and Eli.

Eli had been resistant until Haruka told him the club had agreed not to take pictures of them any other time. Then he was all for their weekly photoshoot.

He'd even created a private Instagram page for members of the club and would upload candid shots when the mood struck him. Anyone caught taking screenshots would be removed from the club.

It had been a compromise for him. Haruka didn't want anyone having pictures of Eli, but if they were devoted to the cause of keeping him safe, and Haruka could control which pictures were posted, he was willing to unbend a little.

The shots of Eli that were particularly cute were only for Haruka.

The whole situation had immensely improved Eli's mood. If Eli had begun to come out of his shell before, now he had truly started to shine.

His rare, shy smiles had turned into laughter, and Eli almost never needed to pull his hood up to feel safe. Now he did it to hide the evidence of Haruka's ongoing mission to make sure everyone on campus knew exactly who Eli belonged to.

It was his favorite mission, by far.

At the moment, Haruka was in the library, studying for an exam when his phone buzzed.

Redpheonix: Stranger approaching Eli

Caligirl: Holy shit, he's going to hug him

Haruka: Send picture

There was only one exception to the no-picture rule, and that was if Haruka asked for one. It was probably for the best that Eli not know exactly how well protected he was. It would only worry him.

Caligirl: It's ok, he stopped at the last minute. Eli seems to know him

Haruka: Picture. Now.

Haruka was gathering his things when a picture popped up in his messages. It was only a profile of the stranger, but Haruka recognized him. It was Jace.

The only person Eli trusted at school other than

Haruka, Nate, and Alice. The person whose bed Eli used to sleep in when he was away. The person who'd actually slept in the same bed with Eli. Haruka was not a fan.

Haruka: On my way.

Let me know if they leave the area.

Caligirl: Roger

Redpheonix: You got it, boss

He recognized the cafeteria behind them in the picture, and it was close enough that he wouldn't have to come up with an excuse for being there. He was always hungry.

Eli was chatting easily with Jace when he arrived. When he spotted him, Eli's face lit up in a sunshine smile that never failed to make Haruka's heart skip a beat.

Haruka went right up to him and draped himself over Eli, putting his arms around him and propping his chin on his boyfriend's head. Then he gave Jace his best *get fucked* stare.

Jace jaw dropped, and he looked back and forth between Eli and Haruka, "Jesus, Eli, when did this happen?"

"It's a recent thing."

"And you're really okay with this?" Jace narrowed his eyes at Haruka, seemingly immune to Haruka's glare.

"Yeah, it's kind of nice, actually."

Haruka could practically hear a blush forming on Eli's

cheeks. He'd like to see it, but from a tactical standpoint, he was better where he was. It was important to start out strong and make his point clear.

Jace wasn't touching Eli ever again.

"Is this the other arrangements you told me about on the phone?"

The reminder that Jace had Eli's number made shadows stir restlessly in Haruka.

"Ummm, yes, actually."

It wasn't a denial of their relationship, but it also wasn't the resounding, *yes, I belong to Haruka and Haruka alone* he would have preferred. Fortunately, he could sense little flutters of joy from Eli from the small admission.

It was good enough for now.

"Does this mean I can hug you now?"

"No." Haruka pulled Eli in closer and cranked up the glare to maximum.

"It's ah, actually still in early development right now, so maybe not. Oh, I did touch Alice the other day, and it wasn't too bad."

"You did?" Haruka asked. Alice was in his *harmless, but good ally* column. Did he need to rethink that assessment?

"That's great! Keep up the good work." Jace looked far more overjoyed than Haruka felt. Good for him.

Eli ducked his head, and Haruka got a flash of Eli patting the shoulder of a crying Alice for roughly two seconds. Alice could stay in her current column for now.

"I'm glad I ran into you though. I was actually about to call."

So, they hadn't planned to meet up. Good.

"I noticed when I was packing that your stuff is all gone. Did you move somewhere that made you feel safe?"

"He did."

"I can answer for myself, thanks." Eli poked him in the gut with his elbow. It was like being hit by a teddy bear. "I moved in with Haruka."

"And you're okay with that—and all of this?" Jace made a show of eyeing the way Haruka was wrapped around Eli.

"We're dating," Haruka said flatly. No point in dragging it out.

Jace looked like he'd just eaten something rotten. "Really?"

There it was. Haruka had had a feeling Jace was into Eli but couldn't be sure. Now that he was, he could keep an even closer eye on the guy.

"Y-yes. We are."

"And you're sure?" Jace stepped closer. "About him?"

"He's nicer than he looks. You're just freaking him out right now."

Haruka was, in fact, not freaking out. He was planning.

Planning to make sure Jace never came close to being alone with Eli ever again.

"Come with me to get coffee," Eli said suddenly and grabbed Haruka's hand.

He willingly allowed himself to be led away.

As soon as they were out of earshot, Eli said, "I know what you're thinking."

Haruka highly doubted that. He'd worked hard to make a solid barrier between his thoughts and Eli's. Was it fair? No. But it was necessary. It wouldn't be in either of their best interests for Eli to be intimately aware of just how obsessed he was with the boy.

It would only scare him.

No, things were good the way they were. All Haruka needed to do right now was keep the Jace situation contained until he went back home.

The way Jace was currently trying to stare him down as they walked away let Haruka know he wouldn't make it easy.

That was fine by him. Haruka's day had suddenly become completely free.

"What am I thinking?"

"That you think Jace is going to sprout fangs and claws, throw me over his shoulder, and make a run for it the second your back is turned."

Haruka scowled. Maybe he was being a bit obvious.

"He's had dozens of opportunities to do so if he wanted to, and he's been nothing but friendly and understanding of my quirks."

"I like your quirks."

Eli's neck flushed red. Haruka wanted to bite it.

"Jace won't be here for long. He only needs to pack his things. I'd be surprised if he didn't leave tonight." Eli chewed on a hangnail. Haruka took his boyfriend's battered hand and placed it safely in his own, then offered him a piece of gum. "No, thanks, that's not going to go well with coffee. Anyway, you won't have to deal with him for long. Do you think you could at least try to be nice?"

"No." It was hard on Haruka when Eli asked for the impossible—he rarely asked for anything, and it made Haruka's day to be able to give him what he wanted. "But I can try not to be mean."

Eli scanned his surroundings and then went on his toes to kiss Haruka on the cheek. "Thank you." His face was bright pink.

Haruka rubbed his cheek. He almost never got public Eli-affection. It was worth the promise of trying not to be mean.

CHAPTER 32
ELI

Haruka was being extra clingy—even for him. Ever since their fan clubs had combined to create an überclub, he'd become more affectionate in public. It was a little embarrassing sometimes, but it wasn't uncomfortable. In fact, it was a little too comfortable.

Eli had spent too long secretly thinking he might be broken in some way other people weren't. That he might never find someone he loved *and* was attracted to.

Love?

Did he love Haruka?

He wasn't even sure what love was. How could he know if what they had together was love? It was intense, whatever it was. When they were apart, he couldn't go more than a few minutes before feeling a tug inside him that insisted they reunite as soon as possible.

And he thought about the man constantly. Anytime Eli saw something he thought Haruka might like, he found himself texting him. Any object that might make him smile was something Eli did everything in his power to obtain. Haruka smiles were a gift to the world.

Now that he had the freedom to leave Haruka's side, he found little desire to do so. And maybe he didn't initiate affection in public the way Haruka did, but when the man had barnacled onto Eli in front of Jace, Eli's insides sang as loudly as they ever did, whether they were behind closed doors or not.

Everything Haruka did told Eli he was wanted, needed, and an important part of his life. So, if he was a bit possessive and territorial, Eli could live with it.

Eli was still a little touchy when Haruka and Kate were in the same room together even though he'd never given Eli any indication he remembered who she was. Haruka visiting the club tent at the end of the fair had made Eli feel territorial too.

All that being said, if Haruka stepped on the back of his shoes one more time today, they were going to throw hands.

"I'm not going to vanish if you aren't up my ass, you know," Eli said after the second time he'd had to stop and fix his shoe.

"Hn." Haruka handed Eli back his coffee and moved to walk beside him rather them loom over him from behind.

When they reached Jace, Eli said, "Sorry to keep you waiting."

"No worries, I'm well aware of the love affair you have with coffee."

Haruka reattached himself to Eli's back, creating a lovely wind barrier. He was also super warm, way better than the hand warmers Eli usually carried around in November.

"So, what are your plans today? I'm finished with classes. If you want to hang out, I'm free."

Haruka's fingers dug into Eli's sweater, but he didn't say anything. He was keeping his promise. If it wasn't Nate or Alice, Haruka had a tendency of being stingy when it came to sharing Eli's time with other people.

"That's perfect, I brought a show I know you're going to love. We can watch it in our room. You know, one more time, in case we don't get to again."

"Sure! Though if you're going to be back in the spring, we'll definitely get a chance to geek out again."

"True, but we might not be roommates. Let's have one last night together, just you and me."

"No." Haruka's arms went from gentle to steel bands around Eli's chest.

Eli tapped his hands and wheezed. "Breathing isn't optional for me."

"I'm not taking him to a strip club, we're just watching *Battlestar Galactica*."

"The original?" Eli asked.

"Obviously."

"Yes!" Eli had mentioned during their first week of living together that he'd only seen the reboot but wanted to watch the first one. "Haruka, you've got an exam tomorrow, you can't come and binge a show tonight."

"But—"

"It's just Jace. He's not going to eat me."

"He might," Haruka muttered.

"Don't be that guy, man. Healthy relationships are based on trust. You trust Eli, don't you."

"Of course."

"Then trust his ability to choose the right people to hang out with."

"Yeah . . ." Eli said weakly. Jace didn't know about Ash, otherwise he would have known not to use that particular argument.

"Fine."

It had worked? Nice.

Haruka unwrapped himself from Eli but didn't look happy about it.

Eli jumped on the chance before Haruka changed his mind and decided to forget his promise. "Great, let's go," he said to Jace, already walking down the path toward their dorm. "I'll text you later." He promised over his shoulder.

Jace filled Eli in on what he'd been up to on the farm until they got to their room.

Once they were inside, his face grew serious. "I'm sorry about being so pushy, but I wanted to talk to you away from him to make sure you're okay."

"Me? I'm great, why do you ask?" If Eli got any happier, he was fairly certain rainbows would start shooting out of his ass.

"You couldn't stand the guy before I left. You do remember that, right?" Jace moved the boxes off of his bed so he could sit down. "I just want to make sure you don't have Stockholm Syndrome, or something."

"No, it's nothing like that. Actually, there's something I should tell you."

Ash was Jace's friend, after all. He had the right to know.

He told Jace everything—minus the mental bond he shared with Haruka.

"Are you fucking kidding me? I'm going to kill him." Jace jumped off his bed and started to pace. His hands twitched like he wanted to strangle someone.

"He's looking at jail-time, no need for murder."

"It would make me feel better." Jace folded his arms and sat on the edge of his desk. Eli's was no longer beside it, having been moved to Haruka's room weeks ago.

"Well, it wouldn't make me feel better, otherwise Haruka would probably have already done it."

"He does give off that impression, doesn't he?" Jace rubbed his chin.

"Come on, he isn't that bad." Eli patted his bed. "Come on, let's watch this show, I want to get as far as we can before you have to leave tonight."

"I don't have to go tonight. We can watch all night if you want to," Jace said hopefully.

"Don't push your luck."

The show was cheesy as hell, and Eli loved it—once he forgave the original Starbuck for not being a girl.

He didn't even realize Haruka hadn't bombarded him with texts until three episodes in when his stomach began to rumble. It had been so long since he'd had a chance to get hungry—Haruka usually stayed on top of feeding them both.

A bag of Doritos and two episodes later, Eli started to get downright worried. Had something happened?

"I think I'm going to turn in, man. Want to have breakfast in the morning?"

"Already? It's only ten o'clock."

"I had an early morning." It was true-ish. Haruka had an early morning, and Eli had woken up long enough to watch him get dressed before going back to sleep for another hour.

What he really needed was to know why his clingy

boyfriend hadn't been texting him all night long. Even when Eli was with Alice and Nate, he still got a reminder to eat or an update on where to meet afterward.

Eli climbed off the bed.

"Wait. Before you go, I want to say something."

"That's a serious face."

"Well, I have a serious thing to say."

"Well, say it before I get anxious, serious boy."

"Give me a second, I've been working up to this all night, okay?"

"Not making me any less anxious, here." Eli wasn't joking anymore. His shoulders were already starting to tense.

"Sorry, it's just . . . Okay, here goes." Jace took a breath and let it out. "I like you. No, wait, don't say anything yet. I've liked you since we met, but I didn't want to make you uncomfortable. We lived together and it was really good, so I thought I would be fine leaving it there for a while. Especially since you didn't seem interested in anyone.

"But finding you with Haruka . . . I can't help myself. I needed you to know. You don't have to settle for that jerk—"

"Hey!"

"I'm sorry, but it's true. He looks like he's ready to kill someone at a moment's notice. If you picked me, things would be easy—we would be easy." Jace finished with a hopeful expression.

Eli was frozen to the spot. This was not how he expected his night to go.

"Jace . . ." What was he supposed to say?

"Don't answer now. Think about it tonight and tell me at breakfast tomorrow morning." Jace reached out like he was about to touch Eli's hand. Eli put his hands behind his back and moved away.

"I'm sorry, Jace, but I don't need to wait." There was no contest. Eli wanted Haruka and only Haruka. And he wanted him right now, so he needed to get out of here ASAP —but without hurting Jace's feelings. "You're fun and easy to be around, but I need to be with Haruka. I can't explain it. I just—all I know is that the thought of not having him makes me unable to breathe."

"That's not the healthiest sign—"

"I don't care. I'm happier than I've ever been. He takes care of me in a way I didn't even know I needed. And I take care of him too." On the outside, maybe they looked codependent, but from the inside, they just made sense. And that was what really mattered—it was their lives after all. Not anyone else's.

"Eli . . ."

"I'm sorry Jace, I care about you, but as a friend. Only a friend." Eli reached out, thinking to pat Jace on the shoulder, but stopped. He would only be forcing himself in order to try and make Jace feel better. It wouldn't feel good for him to do and might even give off mixed signals. It was better for him to be clear. "I have to go now."

Jace closed his eyes. After a long moment, he nodded. "Okay. I don't have to like it, but I'll accept it. Just, if anything goes wrong—anything at all—I've got your back. Even if we're just friends. Understand?"

"I understand." Eli left the room. As soon as the door closed behind him, he sprinted for the elevator. He'd been surprised enough by Jace's confession that Haruka should have picked up on at least some of what just happened, but he hadn't called.

Something was definitely wrong.

CHAPTER 33

ELI

He got to their room in under two minutes, phone in hand, ready to call if he didn't find Haruka there.

The door slammed against the wall when he opened it, but when he got inside, he found Haruka sitting on the floor, playing his guqin. He looked up at Eli's dramatic entrance.

"Uh, hi! Have you eaten yet? I'm starving." Eli asked, feeling awkward as hell. Had he been overthinking things?

Haruka pointed to the table next to him. There was an open pizza box with half a pizza inside.

"Great, thanks."

Eli sat down. It didn't seem like anything was wrong. How was he supposed to ask why Haruka hadn't been his usual, possessive self this evening? Was he finally getting sick of Eli?

"So . . . how was your evening?"

"Good."

"That's good." Why Eli so awkward all of the sudden? "Did you finish studying?"

Haruka nodded and continued to play.

"So, why did you decide to learn to play the guqin?" Oh no . . . he was so stressed out he was doing the random babbling thing.

"I like historical C-dramas so—"

"Jace asked me out." Eli said, half hysterically, jumping to his feet. He couldn't sit still right now. Not when he felt like he was about to explode.

The music stopped, but Haruka didn't say anything. He didn't look at Eli either. Instead, he was motionless.

"I said no and he was really nice about it and then I came home and also why haven't you texted me?"

"Did you want me to?" Haruka slid the instrument off his lap.

"No . . . I don't know . . . maybe? Why are you asking hard questions?"

Haruka said nothing in the eloquent way only he was able to achieve.

"Didn't you pick up anything when it happened?"

"I noticed you were surprised a few minutes ago, but I thought it was from the show you were watching. You've been feeling things all night long."

"So, you were paying attention?"

Haruka gave him a Look.

"Don't look at me like that. I can't read your mind." Unlike some people. "Are you mad?"

Haruka shook his head.

This wasn't helping with the anxiety that had been creeping up on him for the past few hours. Jace's announcement had made it worse. Right now, Haruka was turning it into torture.

Was Eli subtle enough to get his antianxiety meds without drawing attention to himself? Did he even know where they were? It had been weeks since he'd even thought about them.

"What's going on then?" Eli asked in small voice. "Are you tired of me?"

Haruka went very still. "How can you ask me that?"

"I don't know you as well as you know me. For all I know, you could get sick of me and decide to be with someone else." His stomach was a wasteland of a million stabby little knives. Eating wouldn't be happening anytime soon.

"Tell me you're joking."

"Tell me what you were doing at the booth with Kate after the club fair." Eli slapped both hands over his mouth. It was literally the last thing he'd wanted to say, and yet there it was, out and about like a park pervert in a trench coat.

"After the club fair." Haruka tilted his head thoughtfully. "You saw that?"

"Yes," Eli said miserably. Usually when he felt this bad, he'd crawl into Haruka's lap. What the heck was he supposed to do when he felt this way because of Haruka?

There was a long, horrible moment where Haruka did nothing. Then he gave a small laugh. He reached under the table and opened a drawer Eli hadn't even known existed, pulled out a rolled-up piece of paper, and handed it to Eli.

"What . . .?"

"Open it."

Hesitant fingers unrolled the paper to reveal the messy, splotchy kanji Eli had written that day at the fair. Eli traced the character for Haruka. "You kept this?"

"I went back to the booth to ask for it. That's all."

"Oh." Eli's mouth tasted like blood, and he realized he'd chewed the inside of his cheek to shreds. "Why?"

"You know why."

"So, you're not into Kate?"

"I don't even know which one Kate is."

"Then you're not tired of me?" Eli's feet brought him a step closer to Haruka.

"Never."

"Then what happened tonight?" Everything around Eli felted warped and surreal. He was actually interrogating his boyfriend on why he wasn't acting like a stalker, like it was a bad thing.

"I was trying to be supportive . . . and to show you I trust you." Haruka unfolded himself from his position on the floor and stood up. "But it's been challenging."

"Why? I mean, supportive is great, I love support, but why all of a sudden?"

"Because I don't want you to leave me."

Ohhhhhh.

Now that was more like the Haruka he knew. His stomach stopped trying to claw its way out of his throat, which allowed Eli a chance to calm down enough to really look at his boyfriend. Up close he didn't look as relaxed as Eli originally thought when he came home. His eyes were tight at the corners and his fingertips were white, like he'd been clenching his hands recently.

"Leave you? I love you, why would I leave you?" Just the idea made him sick. "You might as well ask me to chop off a hand—" Eli stopped as Haruka's eyes turned predator bright.

What had he said? He rewound the past few seconds in his head. Eli's cheeks burned when he realized what he'd just confessed to. Until that exact moment, he hadn't fully realized exactly how true they wore.

Eli loved Haruka.

"Say it again." Haruka drew so close his toes were nearly touching Eli's.

"Well, I do!" Eli stuck his chin out. "Love you, I mean."

"And here I thought you were going to make me say it first . . ." Haruka whispered, closing the distance between them, stopping when there was only a hairsbreadth of space between his face and Eli's.

English was too limiting sometimes. Japanese had several ways to confess—from the cute *suki* that meant I like you, or *daisuki* which sort of meant love, but was closer to *I'm super into you and want to get more serious.* Then there was the term that meant a lasting, forever kind of love.

"Aishiteru." Eli touched Haruka's chest, willing him to hear that Eli understood exactly what he was saying."

Haruka placed a hand over Eli's. "Watashi mo aishiteru."

I love you too.

It was so simple and incredibly sweet.

They were simply two college kids confessing to one another in their dorm. It should have felt anticlimactic—their beginning had been rocky and at times even explosive. So, this felt right. Like they'd found a balance.

"And I'm going to rip Jace's arms off next time I see him."

"There's the Haruka I know. I was wondering where he was hiding." Eli went on his toes and nudged Haruka's cheek with his nose.

"I wasn't hiding, I was being respectful."

"You're so respectful. Should I go back upstairs so you can keep practicing?" Eli teased.

Haruka growled. "Don't push me, Eli."

"Or what?" Eli was suddenly very interested in knowing what would happen if he kept pushing.

They'd had a lot of naked fun together, but they'd never gone further than getting each other off. There were more fun things they could get up to—Eli had done extensive research on the matter. But Haruka had never pushed for anything more. What if he was only being respectful?

There was such a thing as too much respect.

"You don't like thinking about me being with someone else?" He was going too far, he knew he was, but he couldn't seem to stop himself. Haruka was so contained. Eli wanted to see what it would take to make him lose control.

"Don't even joke about it." Haruka grabbed Eli's arms and hauled him against his chest. Eli's toes were barely scraping the ground.

"You're always so careful with me. Aren't you afraid I'll get bored?" He wasn't bored, not even a little, but he was curious. Curious enough to ignore the fire igniting behind Haruka's eyes and the warnings he kept giving and continue to push to see what it got him. And since Haruka was touching him, he trusted the man would understand that Eli was actively trying to provoke him rather than suggest he was actually bored.

I want this. Show me the fire you keep trying to hide. Eli gazed into Haruka's eyes as he thought the words at him.

Haruka's fingers dug into Eli's arms with bruising force, and Eli gasped, but not in pain.

"Fire burns, Eli."

"I trust you." There was no world where Haruka would continue to do something if Eli wanted him to stop.

Haruka nodded, as if it were a contract they'd just agreed on. "I will never break your trust. If your heart asks me to stop, I will, but if your mouth does, I will find it something better to do." The fire in his eyes had transformed into a flaming tiger, pacing back and forth, waiting for its moment to strike.

"Game on, then," Eli whispered.

Eli closed his eyes and took a breath. Then another.

"Let me go, Haruka." Eli opened his eyes and gave him a little push.

Eli's toes left the floor. His feet dangled in the air as Haruka brought Eli's mouth to his.

"I don't think so," Haruka said between one kiss and the next.

"Put me down." Eli twisted, trying to get free. The burn against his skin as he fought the hold on his arms was fucking perfect. How did he make Eli feel like being small was such a good thing?

"No."

How far could they go?

"As far as you want to go, chibisuke," Haruka said as he began to nip his way along Eli's jaw. "You can't even imagine some of the things I want to do to you."

Eli thought sticking him in a cat-maid costume was somewhere on the list.

Haruka pulled away from Eli's neck. "You're not wrong."

Eli took the small distraction as an opportunity to shove Haruka's chest as hard as he could and twist his lower body to gain the momentum to tear himself loose—gambling Haruka would choose not actually hurting him over holding on.

His feet hit the floor, and he sprinted for the door. He made it two feet before Haruka grabbed him by the waist, dodged his flailing arms, and threw him over his shoulder.

"Clever kitty. But not fast enough." He tossed Eli onto

the bed and pinned him with ease. "Now that I know you might run, I have to do something about it."

Haruka reached for his nightstand and pulled out something fuzzy that clinked faintly as he brought it out. He held his hand up, making sure Eli got a good look at two sets of fur-lined, padded cuffs.

Eli's heart skipped a beat. When did he get those? "Don't even think about it." He hissed.

For a split-second, Haruka paused, and the fire in his eyes banked. He raised an eyebrow at Eli.

Oh my god, fucking yesssssss. Eli shouted in his mind.

Haruka's mouth twitched, and the hesitation was replaced with smug amusement. Then the flames turned into a bonfire.

Eli fought as Haruka trapped both hands in his and expertly put the cuffs on, then attached each to the bed posts.

Eli pulled at his restraints as hard as he could, but they didn't budge—he was splayed out and vulnerable. Haruka could do anything he wanted now. White misted over his mind, and he hovered on the edge in the delicious space between busy thoughts and blissful peace.

Haruka took the collar of Eli's shirt in both hands and tore it down the middle.

Eli tipped over the edge, spiraling into a world where he didn't have to think or make decisions. Haruka was in charge now. All Eli had to do was be good for him.

Hands unzipped his pants and pulled them down his legs, leaving him in nothing but a pair of thin boxers and the remnants of a torn shirt. A small needy noise escaped him as his cock sprang free from the opening in his boxers.

"You're already so hard for me," Haruka said as he took Eli in the palm of his hand. "What a good kitty."

His grip tightened.

"Ahhhhh . . ." Eli keened, arching his hips up into Haruka's grasp, desperate for friction.

A large hand wrapped around his hip and pressed him back down.

Haruka took his hands off him completely and sat back on his heels, one knee on either side of Eli's legs. He wasn't crushing Eli, but he had him thoroughly pinned.

Haruka looked Eli in the eye and gave him a saturnine smile. There was a tearing sound, and Eli's boxers became a thing of the past.

His breath came in short little pants as he watched Haruka free one of Eli's thighs and press a kiss onto it. He traced his tongue up the soft, sensitive skin of Eli's inner thigh and sank his teeth in right before he reached the apex.

The first bite was light, testing.

The second one was not.

Eli's world whited out, and he nearly came on the spot.

"Be good, Eli. I haven't given you permission yet."

"T-trying . . ." Eli panted.

Haruka kissed the abused spot and moved onto the other thigh to give it the same treatment.

Eli was ready for it now and rode the waves of pleasure and pain until he could barely breathe.

His cock was leaking steadily, and Eli would have given anything if Haruka would just touch it—or let him touch himself.

"Anything?" Haruka had moved until his mouth was poised over Eli's aching member, his warm breath on it amplifying the already unbearable torture.

"Anything you want, I promise." Eli begged.

Hot lips descended on him, and it was like the heavens

had opened. If this was what dying felt like, he was fully onboard.

"Haaaaaa . . ."

Haruka's tongue swirled around the head and dipped briefly into Eli's weeping slit. Then he pulled away.

"No dying, Eli. I'm not done with you and won't be for a very long time."

:*Not ever.*: Haruka's mental voice was loud and stamped onto Eli's mind like a brand.

His mouth engulfed Eli fully, swallowing him to the base.

"Fuck!"

Eli slowly lost his mind to the way Haruka devoted every ounce of his attention to wringing every bit of pleasure he could get out of the boy's body. Eli was like his own personal instrument, and Haruka seemed to thrive on each noise he couldn't hold back.

And if he didn't slow down Eli was going to lose control.

"Please, please, I'm close, just let me . . ."

Haruka hummed and picked up the pace.

"No . . . stop . . . I'm—"

Haruka's sucked harder and gave just a hint of teeth, and Eli went over the edge. He watched Haruka's throat work as he swallowed every last drop.

The world went a bit slow and a bit soft for a while as Eli struggled to pull his brain back together. Finally, he said, "You did that on purpose."

Haruka ran his tongue over his lower lip and smiled lazily. "My mouth was occupied, or I would have given you permission."

"You're still going to punish me, aren't you?" Why did his heart rate pick up like that?

Haruka's smile went positively feral. "Would I do something like that?" He prowled his way up Eli's body slowly, and the buttons on his shirt dragged against Eli's skin. "Is it a punishment if I make you beg me to do it?"

Eli couldn't take his eyes off of the curve of Haruka's mouth as he spoke.

"Wh-what are you going to do?"

"Wait and see."

Haruka locked eyes with Eli and began to unbutton his shirt. He seemed to love having Eli's eyes on him and only him. Nearly every time they played together, he would make sure Eli was naked and quivering below him before he removed a stitch of his own clothing.

It wasn't that he didn't want Eli to touch him. It was because he wanted Eli to be gagging for it before he did.

Eli was already gagging for it, and he only wanted it more as more smooth, glowing skin was revealed. But he had a strong feeling Haruka wouldn't allow any touching this time.

"You're very smart." Haruka pulled his shirt off one arm and then down the other before letting it fall to the floor.

Dude had a sadistic streak for someone who spent so much of his time taking care of Eli.

"I'm planning on taking very good care of you tonight, Eli."

The dark promise Eli found in Haruka's eyes made him shiver in all the right places.

Haruka traced a finger over Eli's lower lip, dipping into his mouth briefly to wet it. Then he trailed his hand down Eli's chest and ran his spit-slick fingertip over one of Eli's nipples.

His eyes were half closed, and he watched Eli writhe under him with a gleam of satisfaction.

"Sometimes I want to keep you here, just like this. My toy. Mine to use and use and use until you beg me to stop."

Eli was finding it difficult to think through the beautiful haze, but it didn't sound like a bad thing to him.

Haruka laughed darkly. "Don't tempt me, Eli.

:*Mine. If anyone ever tries to touch him like this, I will kill them.*:

It wasn't as loud as the last time Eli heard his mental voice, but it was still crystal clear. Haruka's iron control over their bond was slipping.

Good. Eli wanted Haruka to fall apart for him too.

Eli bit his lip and didn't try to hold back a moan when Haruka pinched his nipple cruelly. When he knew he had Haruka's full attention, he ran his tongue over his lower lip slowly, taunting him.

:*I'm going to fucking wreck him if I'm not careful.*:

"Yesssss . . ." Eli didn't care what happened to him anymore, all he wanted was to be closer to Haruka, to be possessed and claimed, to be owned so fully, he'd never doubt how much Haruka wanted him.

Haruka made a strangled sound in his throat, closed his eyes and turned his head away, inhaling deeply. When he turned back, his eyes were calmer.

That wouldn't do. The soft haze Eli had been drifting in had morphed into something primal when Haruka's control started to break. He wanted—no, needed to know what would happen when it did.

Eli did a slow roll of his hips and arched into Haruka and got the pleasure of watching something akin to lightning flash in Haruka's eyes.

"You're not being good for me, Eli." Haruka warned.

Eli laughed. "Would you want me this much if I was always good for you?"

"I will always want you . . . but if you want to play this game,"—Haruka leaned forward, released Eli's hands from the headboard, and flipped him over effortlessly—"you have to be prepared for the consequences."

"Wait—" If he couldn't see Haruka's eyes, how would he know when he pushed him over the edge?

Hands went over his, covering them and pinning them once more. "Oh, you'll know . . ." Haruka's breath was hot against Eli's neck.

Eli cried out as teeth clamped down on the back of his neck. They held him firmly, and Eli's body went limp as the fight began to drain out of him. He struggled, trying to fight off subspace. He couldn't give in so easily, or he wouldn't get what he really wanted. He bit his lip in order to focus.

Haruka released his neck. "Let go, chibisuke, you know I'm going to win. Make it easy on yourself." The heat of Haruka's body left Eli's back, and he felt his hands being drawn together behind his back and heard a click as the cuffs were connected.

Haruka's weight shifted, and Eli heard the nightstand open. "What are you doing?"

"You said anything I want. I want everything." Haruka's hand smoothed over Eli's ass.

They'd never done that before. Eli was so small and Haruka so big, it had been too daunting—until now.

Right now, Eli wanted it so badly his mouth watered.

So, of course he said, "Get fucked!" and struggled to reach the end of the bed.

Haruka laughed softly and stopped him by grabbing the links between Eli's cuffs and pressing them against his back. "You first."

Eli felt something cold and wet press against his back entrance, and he tensed.

Haruka's restraining hand shifted from Eli's hands to the back of his neck. "Be good Eli, or you'll get hurt. I'd hate to have to stop now." His hand circled Eli's small throat and tightened his grip.

Eli went boneless.

"Good boy."

Haruka continued to slide a finger inside him. Eli hissed at the slight burn and tensed again. Even with lube, it still hurt. He was rewarded with soft laughter.

"You'd better relax, you've got a long way to go."

"Asshole," Eli said into the pillow, but did his best to relax.

More laughter and another finger made an appearance.

"Ahhhh . . . mmhh!"

How fucking big were Haruka's fingers? And how was Eli's cock this hard after coming his brains out only a few minutes ago?

Haruka spread his fingers apart slightly.

"Fuck!" Eli ground his hips against the bed and knew he wasn't far from making a mess of the comforter.

Haruka clicked his tongue. "Not yet, chibisuke. There's so much more I want to do to you first."

"You arc just . . . the worst . . ."

"If you can still talk, I'm not doing my job properly."

He worked a third finger inside Eli, forcing him to keen loudly the whole time.

As Eli panted and cried his way through the third finger splitting him open, he felt something night-black roil inside Haruka.

When Haruka withdrew his fingers, all Eli could do was breathe into the comforter.

There was a crinkle of foil behind him, and he made for the edge of the bed again. He wasn't being a brat anymore;

his body was trying to escape all on its own now. He knew first-hand how big Haruka's cock was, and if it was too big for his mouth . . . Fucking hell, what had he gotten himself into?

Fire-edged shadows rolled through him, wave after wave battering him down as firmly as the hand on his neck had. Eli's body went loose and plaint, welcoming the shadows and letting them fill him. They were Haruka's shadows. Somehow that made them different than the ones Eli had to deal with. Instead of being overwhelming, they felt right. He felt hands lift his hips and a pillow was placed under them.

When Haruka pushed into him, Eli couldn't have fought him if he wanted to. All he could do was make small cries that seemed to egg the shadows on as they swirled through him, making the soft place their own.

It was better than anything, and Haruka wasn't even all the way in.

"Haaaa . . ."

Haruka's hands tightened on Eli's hips pulling him backward slowly, splitting him open inch by inch until Eli's ass was flush against Haruka's hips.

"Please . . ." He didn't even know what he was asking for, all he knew was he never wanted this to end. If the flashes Eli kept getting from Haruka of Eli chained to his bed were any indication, Haruka didn't want to stop either.

:*You'll be lucky if I ever let you leave here.*:

Haruka pulled out most of the way and slammed home harshly.

Eli only kept from coming by biting his lip until he tasted blood.

Haruka fisted a hand in his hair and pulled Eli's head

back until he could kiss him on the mouth, licking at the spot Eli had bitten.

Then he drove into him again. And it *hurt*. It hurt so bad? Good? Eli didn't have a hope of bracing himself. All he could do was take it as Haruka took Eli's bound hands and pulled Eli back onto him, setting a brutal pace. Tears flowed freely down Eli's cheeks, and his surroundings drifted away from him. He couldn't have told anyone his name right now if his life depended on it. All he knew was that he felt alive. More than he ever had in his entire life.

Haruka found a spot inside Eli that made every cell in his body sing.

Eli cried out so loud his throat hurt, and Haruka paused, pulling Eli back further and further until he was almost touching Haruka's chest.

He held him there, on the brink of heaven and hell, keeping Eli's arms safe and secure in his hands.

"You're mine, Eli." Haruka growled into Eli's ear.

Tears streamed down Eli's face. It was so much, so good, but he wanted—no needed—more.

"Say it."

". . ."

"Tell me you're mine, and I'll give you everything you want."

He knew Haruka wouldn't move until he did, and Eli was pretty sure he would die if he had to wait any longer. "Y-yours . . ." He panted.

A deep shudder went through Haruka's body, and the fire inside him took Eli completely. Haruka lifted Eli's body up until he was almost off his cock and then brought him back down again brushing against the spot that made Eli soar. He lifted him again, but this time slammed him back down harshly. Eli cried out, nearly blacking out from the sensation.

Time lost meaning as Haruka drove into him over and over again using Eli like a toy made for his own pleasure, just as he'd promised.

Haruka let Eli's knees drop back to the mattress, gathered the boy's hands in one of his own, then took Eli's poor neglected cock in the other.

"Sing for me, Eli," Haruka pounded him from behind while stroking him in the front. Eli gave him everything he asked for, crying out as he emptied himself onto the bed.

Haruka fucked into his abused hole, hands on Eli's hips with bruising force, until he came a few seconds later.

Eli dropped toward the bed, and Haruka followed him down, breathing hard, shifting at the last second so he didn't crush him. He rolled onto his side and wrapped himself around Eli.

Shadow and fire had combined with soft light to make a nest for Eli to rest in—safe from anything that would ever dare try and hurt him.

"I will always keep you safe, Eli." Haruka murmured into Eli's hair.

Eli's body trembled as he tried to turn over and curl up against Haruka's chest. But something was stopping him. His hands were still cuffed behind his back.

"Um . . ."

Haruka huffed into Eli's hair and sat up so he could release him. When the cuffs came free, Eli's arms flopped to his sides.

"Ow." He was going to have so many bruises.

His sense of Haruka cut off so quickly it was like a switch had been flipped.

Haruka ran his hands down Eli's body, moving him this way and that as he examined every inch of his body.

"I'm fine." Eli protested weakly, face burning when Haruka inspected his ass for tearing. He swatted at the larger man's hands, but they were brushed aside until Haruka was satisfied Eli was undamaged.

Haruka left for a minute and came back with a wash-cloth and a bowl of warm water and cleaned Eli off, his gentle hands a strong contrast to how he'd been handing Eli moments ago.

When he finished, he cupped Eli's bright red face and forced him to look at him. "Are you okay?"

Words like, *amazing, brilliant,* and *completely fucked out, but great* jammed up inside his head, and Eli found it impossible to speak. So, he nodded.

Haruka's face softened from the worried frown that had been building.

Eli found his words again. "The comforter isn't though. I should have let you pack mine after all."

Haruka cocked an eyebrow. "I can go upstairs and get it now if you want."

"Don't you fucking dare." Eli punched Haruka's chest with the strength of a kitten.

CHAPTER 34
ELI

The next morning was not his friend. Waking up was a terrible idea, even if he was having the best cuddle of his life.

"Oh my god, what did I let you do to me? Everything hurts!" Even his toes. Dear god, why did his toes hurt?

"Pretty sure you begged me to do it." There was a kiss on his head. "You might want to skip class today."

"I'm not skipping class."

Shouldn't Eli not be in pain right now? Like, he was pretty sure being plastered to Haruka meant he shouldn't be hurting anywhere. And Eli was clinging to him like they were glued together.

But if he didn't hurt anymore, then maybe the happy little glow in his chest would stop singing as loudly as it was right now. He wouldn't feel as owned and protected as he did if his body no longer carried the reminder of last night.

Crap, he was supposed to have breakfast with Jace this morning!

"Skip it. No wait, go to breakfast with Jace. I'll come too."

Eli could hear the smugness in Haruka's voice.

"You suck so much."

"At an expert level, yes."

Why did he love this jerk so much?

"Don't know, but I'm not going to complain."

"Stop reading my thoughts!"

"Nope." There was another kiss on his head.

Eli tried to sit up, but all he did was flop around weakly for a minute before giving up.

"Do you want me to get you breakfast?"

"No. If I don't go to breakfast with Jace, I'll officially be the worst friend in the history of life." Eli tried to sit up again and met with partial success—he managed to smush himself face-first into Haruka's broad chest. He was up-ish, but not under his own power.

"You want me to carry you?"

"I will end you." Eli tried to sound fierce, but his ass was yelling at him for daring to sit on it. Maybe it wouldn't be so bad if he was in slightly less pain.

Haruka lifted him onto his lap and cuddled him. Nope. He definitely didn't manage fierceness, but all of the pain in Eli's body dropped by fifty percent. The odd quirks of his and Haruka's bond continued to astound him.

"Try again in a minute. I'm sure you'll destroy me." Haruka kissed the top of his head.

Eli nudged his nose against Haruka's chest and let himself have this moment. "I will. You'll cry."

Haruka's arms tightened around him, causing every inch of Eli's body to rebel.

"Urk."

"Sorry, I couldn't stop myself." Haruka stroked his back. "Stay here as long as you want."

Eli nodded and nuzzled Haruka's chest again. He needed to get up, but none of him wanted to. He just wanted to stay here in bed with Haruka and enjoy the lingering remnants of the soft, hazy place for the rest of the day.

"If we did that, I think you'd be even more sore by the end of the day." Haruka's voice rumbled in his chest under Eli's ear.

"I would murder you and bury you in Jersey," Eli said with feeling.

"Why does everyone hate Jersey so much? Is it that bad?"

"I've never actually been, but I've driven through. The traffic is a nightmare."

"You're not going to like Tokyo then," Haruka said, like it was a given Eli would go there with him someday even though they'd never talked about it.

"As long as I'm not driving, I'll love it."

Okay, no more procrastinating. It was time to get on his feet like a big boy. He pushed himself off Haruka's lap and pretended like he didn't notice the boost his boyfriend gave him.

He was up. He wanted to cry a little, but he was standing. That was better than he'd thought he could do, so he was going to call it a victory.

Breakfast wasn't as hard on his body as Eli had feared. Once he'd moved around a bit and had a shower, his body seemed to forgive him for what he'd put it through last night—which was good because he definitely wanted to do it again.

Haruka joined him for breakfast and glared at Jace the

entire time. One might think after last night, he would have chilled out, but if anything, he'd gotten even more possessive. He'd even had the gall to suggest Eli wear one of his shirts out in public.

Eli had imagined himself wearing the black cashmere V-neck sweater Haruka had offered him and laughed in his face. His hands would get lost in the sleeves, and he'd be lucky if it even managed to stay on his shoulders for a minute before slipping off completely. With his brand-new bruises, he'd look like a battered child.

When he'd said as much, Haruka turned a little green and rescinded the offer.

"You've already won, you know. You don't have to keep looking at me like you're going to rip my head off," Jace said to Haruka after the two of them had been engaged in a stare-off for the past five minutes.

Haruka snorted but didn't respond.

Having decided to ignore how childish both of his tablemates were acting, Eli said, "I'll clean the rest of my stuff out this evening, and we can let our RA know the room is empty." He had little more than his comforter and a few random bits of furniture left in the room, so it wouldn't take long.

"Actually, why don't we keep the room, in case you end up needing it again." Jace narrowed his eyes at Haruka.

Haruka bristled at the implication, and Eli squeezed his leg in warning. With the way his ass felt right now, if he had to fish Jace out of the pond later, he was going to kill his boyfriend.

"I'll keep it for now." Eli felt Haruka's leg tense under his hand, and he patted it. "But only so you can come back to it in the spring. It's a great location, after all."

Haruka relaxed, but only a little.

On second thought, maybe it would be better if those two didn't live in the same building.

"That's what I would have said if you'd asked me," Haruka answered Eli's unspoken thought in Japanese.

"Don't be rude," Eli responded in English.

Jace flashed Haruka a shit-eating grin.

Haruka told Jace to fuck himself in Japanese.

Eli sighed.

Somehow, they made it through breakfast without anyone being maimed or thrown into the nearest body of water. But by the time they reached Jace's car, Eli was torn between the overwhelming desire to tear his hair out and the need to crawl back into bed.

Jace decided to fire a final parting shot before he got into his car, because apparently, he thought Eli should get a chance to experience what having an ulcer felt like before he turned nineteen.

"You aren't good enough for him," Jace said with one hand on the door frame of his car. "But you're what he wants, so I won't get in your way. If that changes—"

"It won't." Eli jumped in to assure him.

"If that changes," Jace repeated. "Or if you ever hurt him, you better believe I will get in your fucking way."

Instead of getting annoyed like Eli expected, Haruka nodded. "I will never hurt Eli."

"You'd better not." Jace got in his car and drove away.

Eli clapped his hands together once. "Excellent, you're both horrible, and I'm going back to bed." He turned toward their dorm and left Haruka to follow him or not. He was already done with this day, and it wasn't even nine thirty.

Eli skipped his morning class but sent Haruka to his since he had an exam. Rather than sleeping, he spent the morning texting with his sister who had suddenly decided now was the perfect time to grill Eli on every aspect of his life.

Berry: You've been too damn happy lately. What's wrong?

Are you failing all your classes or something?

Eli: As if that would happen. Ask a less stupid question

Berry: No question is less stupid than you, love.

So I have to try and accommodate for your extreme disability

Eli smirked and sent her a picture of him flipping her off.

Berry: Seriously, what's wrong?

Making me act worried isn't nice

It'll trick people into thinking I care or something

Eli: I know it's hard to believe, but have you considered that I might actually be happy?

Berry: Really?

No joke?

. . .

Eli: Really.
No joke

There was a long pause before Juniper finally texted back.

Berry: If you're not fucking with me, then I'm happy for you. If you are then prepare for me to kick the crap out of you when you come home this weekend.

Eli: This weekend?

Berry: It's Thanksgiving, doofus

Crap. He'd totally forgotten he'd planned to come home during Thanksgiving break. At first, it had been something he wanted so badly he could have cried, but now? What was Haruka supposed to do without him?

Berry: Doofus?

Eli: Sorry, I've been caught up with studying, I forgot what week it was

Berry: Just don't forget to come home, ok?

. . .

Eli: Of course not, but . . . I might bring a friend with me

Berry: Oooooooooo
Tell me everything!

Eli: Fuck off

Berry: No way, I want to know!!!!!!!

Eli: Forget it, harpy

He loved his sister, but he wasn't planning on coming out to her via text. She'd have to find out the old-fashioned way —via video chat from Antarctica because she was going to be the biggest pain in the ass ever about it.

He rolled onto his back and his ass twinged, forcing him to amend. She was now second biggest. Nothing could compare to Haruka.

Juniper had finally been dethroned.

CHAPTER 35
ELI

Classes were over for the day, and Eli skipped his way down the sidewalk. He was going home!

Which was, of course, fraught with plenty of anxiety inducing issues, but still, he was going home!

And Haruka was coming with him—hence the issues. When Eli had tried to bring it up, he'd been nervous as hell because what if Haruka didn't want to come? Or even worse, what if he did want to come? His mind was spinning, and his heart was racing as he tried to summon up the nerve to text Haruka and ask him to meet him so he could ask, but then his phone buzzed.

StupidHotJerk: Of course, I'm coming. Sit down and breathe

Everything is going to be fine

I promise

. . .

Eli: You heard?

StupidHotJerk:
I did

Eli: And you're coming with me?
To meet my family?

StupidHotJerk: Yes
And if it stresses you out too much, you don't have to tell them about us. Just enjoy being home

Eli had immediately opened his contacts and edited Haruka's name to WonderfulHotJerk.

And now he was free for the next week. He could take Haruka to all of his favorite places in Eastern Mass. He had to take him to Salem—especially now that it was post Halloween craziness. It wouldn't be as lively, but Eli couldn't have handled lively anyway.

Haruka tried to play it cool, but he was just as much of a nerd about American culture as Eli was about Japanese culture—which was probably one of the reasons they fit.

As he made up a list of all of the places he wanted to go next week, Eli realized he'd made a fatal error. He'd stopped paying attention to where he was going and had subconsciously taken the quickest route back to his dorm.

Every other time of the year, there was nothing wrong with taking this path. It was the quickest, most efficient way to cut through the campus, but October through November it was the worst possible route to take because it was directly under the flight path of all of the migrating geese from the north. They would take off from the pond and thoroughly befoul the sidewalk on their way out. After a few weeks of such treatment, the inclined path became a nightmare slide to the worst day of your life.

Eli had gotten lucky. He'd watched an entire pack of freshmen learn the hard way why the normally crowded walkway was suddenly empty. The previously chipper group of coeds ended up at the bottom of the hill in a sad, disgusting, tangled mess. The spark of life was gone from their eyes. Clearly, the experience had left an impact on their souls they would take years to recover from.

Eli recognized his mistake, but only because his feet had begun the long slide down the hill.

"AHHHHHHHHHHH!!!!!!!" He screamed gracefully and with much dignity as he skated down the hill, arms waving and praying to every god he knew that he wouldn't fall down in the horrible mess.

Halfway down, he started to spin until he was going down ass first, still on his feet. When he reached the bottom, he stood frozen, unable to believe he'd made it unscathed.

Other than his shoes. They were disgusting.

Applause drew him out of his daze as onlookers cheered his success.

Eli took a bow. *Hey, any accident you can walk away from, right?*

His phone rang. It was Haruka, so he answered, but had to pull his ear away from the ear-splitting laughter on the other end. He waited until Haruka began to laugh so hard he was making choking sounds. Eli hung up, shoved his phone in his pocket, then pulled it out again and texted:

Eli: If you kill yourself laughing, you won't get a chance to miss out on all the head you won't be getting ever again

The first chance he'd gotten, Eli had gone on TikTok to research ways of getting rid of his gag reflex. He'd spent an afternoon practicing each method until he found one that worked. Then he tested it out on Haruka.

Fucking Eli's throat had instantly become his new favorite pastime, so it was no surprise when Eli got a short *Sorry* in response.

Haruka had better hope Eli took his shoes off before he kicked him in the shin. He shouted the thought as hard as he could.

Not that he actually would, but when someone was short, people tended to underestimate them. Threats help keep people in line.

When he reached his building, he toed his shoes off before entering. Gingerly, he picked them up—once he'd located a spot not covered in goose shit—and pitched them into the closest trashcan.

He entered the building in his socks, ignoring the stares at his feet. By the time he'd reached his room, he'd cycled between grumpy scowling and hysterical laughter enough times that he was certain everyone in the building was going to give him plenty of space for the rest of the year.

He wiped a tear from his eye and looked up, realizing someone was standing in front of his door.

"Juniper?"

Arms went around him as his sister proceeded to try and squeeze the life out of him. He tried to reciprocate, but he'd long ago given in to the fact that his sister had beaten him thoroughly in the genetic lottery. She wasn't as tall as Haruka, but she wasn't much shorter.

"Eli!" An angry, confused voice rang out down the hallway. Haruka was frozen in the act of rubbing a towel through his hair, but only briefly.

He let the towel drop onto his shoulder and began stalking toward them. There was a mixture of emotions on his face, but the only one Eli paid attention to was the sharp stab of fear he felt emanating from him.

"Haruka, this is my sister, Juniper," Eli said hastily. While he loved to fuck with Haruka to get a rise from him, fear was never an emotion he wanted to inspire.

The fear cut off, and Haruka's face rearranged itself into its usual *too cool for everything* expression as he met them at the door.

He flicked his wet hair at Eli and turned to give Juniper a bow. "Nice to meet you. I'm Haruka."

"Is this the friend you're bringing home?" Juniper poked Eli in the chest, causing Haruka to flinch. Juniper eyed his reaction with interest and did it again. This time Haruka didn't react, but somehow, he managed to do it loudly. "Interesting."

Eli waved a hand in her face to bring her attention back to him. "What are you doing here? We were going to see each other tonight. I'm already packed—well, mostly."

Juniper's eyes shuttered. "Why don't we go into your room, and you can finish packing while I explain."

"Ooookay."

She knew. Eli didn't know how she knew, but she did. Stupid insightful twin sister! Well, he wasn't going to let her be the one to bring it up. Fuck Antarctica, they were doing this now.

The second the door closed behind them he blurted out, "I'm gay and he's my boyfriend and if you give me any shit about it, I'm going to hit you with the bag of old Chinese food we have in the refrigerator."

Juniper blinked at Eli.

Haruka blinked at Eli.

Eli dropped down in the closest chair and concentrated on breathing.

Haruka came around behind him and rubbed his back using large, slow circles. "It's okay, chibisuke. I'm here."

Which made Juniper's eyes nearly pop out of their sockets. "You're . . . He's . . . What the fuck, Eli?"

Haruka made to stand in front of Eli, but he put a hand on the man's arm.

"She's not mad, just confused. Give her a minute."

Juniper needed more than a minute. She plopped down on the bed, making Eli doubly glad they changed the comforter after their morning's recreational activities. Then she sat there for an eternity, letting her eyes dart back and forth between Eli and Haruka. The longer the silence drew out, the closer Haruka got to Eli. Each passing second seemed to make her eyes grow even wider.

Finally, Eli got sick of waiting. "Come on, Berry. You had to know this was going to be a possibility. The odds of me being straight weren't good."

Tears welled in Juniper's eyes.

Oh no. Crying. He wasn't prepared for crying.

"I'm just so happy for you!" She flung herself off the bed

and onto Eli's lap, nearly crushing him. Eli saw Haruka flinch out of the corner of his eye.

"You're happy? Really?"

"Of course I am, stupid! I was so afraid you'd be too stressed out to make friends, let alone have a boyfriend. And one who can touch you—who I will kill if he ever bad touches you." Juniper did the thing where she became terrifying in the blink of an eye and then shifted back to friendly like nothing had happened. "I just can't stand it." Then she hugged Eli until he squeaked.

"Breathing . . . I like breathing."

Juniper thumped him on the head, and Eli was fairly certain Haruka was on the verge of a nervous breakdown from the amount of twitching he was doing.

"You should have told me!"

"I would have when I was ready, but—hold on, didn't you already know? I thought that's why you came here."

Juniper's face went pale, and she climbed off his lap. "I came because I needed to tell you something important."

The relieved smile that had been working its way across Eli's face faltered. His eyes went to Haruka, who knelt beside him and took his hand. It was like a hit of instant serotonin. Whatever his sister needed to say, it couldn't be that bad.

"What happened?"

Juniper's eyes darted around the room like she couldn't bring herself to look at him. Then she took a deep breath. "There's no easy way to say this, so I'm just going to say it. Liam—the guy who kidnapped you. He's out on parole."

There was a ringing in his ears, and his sister's voice became muffled. Eli had to focus to understand his sister.

". . . at first Mom didn't want to tell you, but he missed his meeting with his parole officer . . ."

There was another moment where things got a bit staticky, but he tuned back in to hear his sister say, ". . . you hear me, Eli? His house was empty. The police said it looks like he never stayed there after his first night back. They found a recent picture of you . . ."

And that was the last thing Eli heard before the static took him.

CHAPTER 36
HARUKA

Eli was still in Haruka's arms. And quiet. So terribly, horribly quiet.

Haruka was vaguely aware of the red marks his hands were making where he clenched Eli's hands and tried to relax, but he couldn't bring himself to loosen his grip.

He'd gotten so used to roaming freely in Eli's mind when they touched. The silence he found there now was terrifying. Haruka was afraid if he didn't hold on as tightly as possible, Eli would slip away from him forever.

"Eli!" Juniper's voice was edged with hysteria, and she reached out to strike Eli's cheek.

Haruka caught her by the wrist before she could make contact. "Don't." He had no way to explain to her that striking him was pointless. The boy had retreated so far inside himself even Haruka couldn't reach him. Hitting him would only make Haruka want to hit her back.

And once Eli had recovered, he would be mad at Haruka for doing so. It was the only reason Haruka had been able to restrain himself earlier when Juniper had manhandled Eli.

She was his sister. He knew that, but he'd gotten used to being the only one who was allowed to touch Eli. When he saw someone try to touch him now, all he wanted to do was hurt them.

And as much as Eli seemed to like Haruka's overly possessive nature, he knew better than to unleash it on the boy's sister.

But if it would bring Eli back from wherever he had retreated to, Haruka would slap her across the room and apologize later.

He shook his head.

If it didn't work, it would cause too many unnecessary complications. He was going to need Juniper's cooperation for what he was about to do next.

"When was Liam released?"

Juniper stared wordlessly at her wrist, still trapped by Haruka. He released it but kept an eye on it in case it got any ideas. When she didn't respond, he snapped his fingers in front of her face. "I need you to focus right now. How long as it been since someone has seen Liam?"

"Two, no, three days."

Haruka's chest tightened, and his skin prickled as adrenaline shot through him. Three days was more than long enough to find out where Eli was. Liam could have already taken him, and Haruka would have never seen it coming.

"You should have told us." He snapped. His fingers twinged in pain, and he realized he was slowly crushing Eli's hand. He'd nearly broken the boy's hand, and Eli's mind hadn't given him so much as a whimper.

Juniper looked at Haruka like he'd turned into an alien before her eyes. "Us? I didn't even know there was an *us* until five minutes ago."

Haruka forced himself to soften his tone. He needed her on his side. "There is. I would do anything for him. Whatever you think, I need you to believe that."

"Every time I talk to Eli, or text with him, he always spends half the time deliberately not telling me about something. I know my brother better than anyone, so I know that whatever he was hiding from me, he was completely over the fucking moon about. It was you, wasn't it?"

Used to. Juniper used to know Eli the best. That honor was Haruka's now, and he was never letting it go.

He nodded.

Juniper puffed out her cheeks and blew out a breath. "I had a feeling that if Eli fell for someone, it was going to be dramatic as fuck."

Haruka snorted. She no idea. "I need you to help me get him out of here."

"Of course. He can't stay here, especially like this. Where should we go? The hospital?"

"No," Haruka said quickly. They might get separated at a hospital, and it would make Eli worse. "I'm taking him home."

"That's the first place Liam will look for him!"

Haruka looked at Eli's blank face and stroked his cheek. "No," he said softly. "My home."

It had been almost too easy to convince Juniper to give Eli to him. Whether it was from shock or not, it made Haruka know he was the best choice for keeping Eli safe. People would die before Haruka let them be separated.

They left in a matter of minutes. Eli had already packed a little, and Haruka would buy him anything he'd missed.

Haruka was busy on his phone making preparations—pulling his old assistant out of her bed to get them the quickest flight to Japan—while Juniper drove them east to their house to grab his passport.

She'd been instrumental in keeping Eli's mother from stopping their plans. In only a few minutes, Juniper had turned her mother from a nervous, emotional wreck to someone who was fully on board with getting her son out of the country as fast as humanly possible.

It was only when they got to the airport that she gave him trouble.

"Of course, I'm coming with you two. He's my brother! I'm not sending him to a foreign country alone." Juniper squared off in front of them at the ticket counter. Eli was tucked against his side, as limp and compliant as a puppet.

"He won't be alone. He has me." He would always have Haruka. Always. He took a gamble on Juniper loving her mom as much as Eli did. "But your mother has no one. You stay with her, and I will keep him safe."

Juniper's lower lip trembled, and Haruka finally saw the resemblance to her brother.

"I promise." He willed her to let him take her brother away.

When she lowered her eyes and whispered, "Take him."

Haruka was torn between being glad she'd stopped resisting and scornful she would let her only brother go so easily.

"Is he okay?" The woman behind the ticket counter spoke up finally, looking at Eli with concern.

Juniper stepped in. "My brother is afraid of flying, so he

gets tranqed before he flies." She shook a prescription bottle in front of the woman, then tucked it into Eli's bag.

The woman frowned sympathetically. "Poor sweetie." She reached over the counter as if to pat Eli, and Haruka pulled him away and gave her a *look.* Her hand stopped like it had hit a force field. She gave an embarrassed laugh and looked back at her screen then gave it a double take. "We'll take good care of the two of you, Mr. Yamada."

Juniper mouthed *mister* at him with her eyebrows raised.

"Someone will be here shortly to escort you to the lounge."

Juniper's eyebrows disappeared under her bangs. "Who are you?"

"Someone who can keep Eli safe."

Haruka tolerated it when Juniper hugged an unresisting Eli. She waved at them, looking as though she could change her mind any second as they were led to the first-class lounge.

While they waited for their plane, Haruka kept Eli tucked safely against him, glaring at anyone who paid them any attention. When it was time to board the plane, Haruka ended up carrying Eli because the boy's knees kept buckling.

He took one look at the small, but luxuriously decked out cubicles they each had and squeezed himself and Eli into the nearest one.

There hadn't been so much as a flutter from Eli since he'd learned about his kidnapper's release, but when an attendant tried to force Haruka to leave Eli's seat and go to his own, he'd sensed . . . something. It was small and fleeting, but Eli had definite feelings about sitting alone.

Haruka paused, ignoring the flight attendant as she

fluttered nervously around them. "Eli?" He tilted the boy's face so he could look into his eyes, but there was nothing there.

"Sir?"

Haruka sent the woman scurrying with a snarl. He'd buy the fucking plane if he had to, but he wasn't budging.

Haruka wasn't able to relax even when the plane was in the air.

No, he wouldn't be okay until Eli was himself again and somewhere Haruka could keep him safe.

CHAPTER 37
ELI

The first thing he noticed was how warm he was. The second was a rumbling sound that seemed to surround him. The third was—

"Squished." Eli pushed against the firm body he was plastered against. "Haruka, you're crushing me."

He only noticed the hand in his hair because it stopped stroking him.

"Sorry."

The pressure on him eased a little, and Eli opened his eyes. Wherever they were was dark and cozy. He buried his face in Haruka's shirt and breathed in his warm, soothing scent.

"We should get ready to go, shouldn't we?" He wasn't sure what he was saying, but he had a nagging feeling they were supposed to be doing something.

Eli felt Haruka kiss the top of his head. "You can stay here as long as you want."

"Oh good." He sighed happily and was about to drift back to sleep until he heard a soft cough in the distance. He lifted his head and looked around. "Um . . . are we on an airplane?"

A pause. "Yes."

"Haruka."

"Yes?"

"Why are we on an airplane?"

Another, longer, pause. "What is the last thing you remember?"

The hand in his hair began to pet him once again, and Eli lost a minute or two enjoying the sensation. Wait, he was supposed to be remembering something.

Eli frowned and bit his lip. "I was at school . . . nearly killed myself on goose poop . . . You were such a jerk! How did you even know about it?"

Haruka's arms tightened around him briefly, and he bestowed Eli's head with another kiss. "You broadcast it so hard, I was able to see everything." His voice was soft, and there was a touch of sadness to it.

Why was Haruka sad?

Eli sat up and searched his face, but all he saw was Haruka's default expression—cool and composed.

"What happened?"

"You really don't remember?"

"Remember what?" Something about the current situation tickled his memory. He'd felt this way before, hadn't he? Only he hadn't been as chill the last time.

"I . . . lost time, didn't I?" Eli turned his face away as shame crept over him.

It had been a long time since he'd fugued out. Years, actually, otherwise his family would never have let him leave home for college.

A hand on his chin brought his attention back to Haruka, but Eli couldn't bring himself to look at him.

"You don't have to look at me, but I can't let you believe I would ever think less of you over that—or anything."

"Anything?" Eli tried to shove a note of levity into his voice. "What if I liked to hit people with my car for fun?"

Haruka buried his face in Eli's hair and said, "I'd get you a better car."

Eli laughed and finally allowed himself to look at Haruka. "You're obsessed." He brushed a strand of hair away from his boyfriend's face.

Haruka shrugged as if he couldn't be bothered to deny it.

"Do you know why I blanked out like that?"

Haruka nodded.

"Does it have something to do with why we're on an airplane?"

Haruka nodded.

"You're afraid if you tell me, I'm going to freak out again, aren't you?"

"Yes."

Okay, that was fair. He didn't like it, but it was a reasonable reaction to have. Especially since Eli hadn't told him it was a possibility. It must have been scary as hell.

"Scary, yes." Haruka nodded as he followed Eli's train of thought.

"Is there a time when you'd be comfortable telling me? Because I really should know at some point."

"I'd rather wait until we get to Japan."

"We're going to Japan?!"

Eli had thought maybe they were going somewhere close-ish, like Montreal, or Florida, but he hadn't taken into account Haruka's extra-ass personality. How stupid of him not to take that into consideration.

"You really should have." Haruka agreed. "And you

should keep your voice down if you don't want people to think I've kidnapped you."

"Feel free to kidnap me to Japan any time you want." Eli shifted his weight because the side of the cubicle was digging into his left ass cheek. "This thing is a bit snug for two people, isn't it?"

"Do you want your own?" Haruka asked carefully.

Eli considered. "How long do we have until we land?"

Haruka checked his phone. "Three hours until we change planes in London."

The next cubicle was diagonal and seemed far away, but the newly forming bruise on Eli's ass made him think it was still a solid option, even if for a little while. "Is that one mine?"

Haruka nodded, not looking particularly enthused about Eli crawling out of his lap, but he didn't protest, until they parted and—

Wrongwrongwrong

They locked eyes at the same time, both with twin looks of surprise. Eli scrambled back into Haruka's lap at the same time Haruka reached out to drag him back down. As soon as they touched, his internal alarm cut off. He was engulfed in the same warm, happy feeling he'd been enjoying when he'd woken up.

After a minute, Eli said tentatively, "So . . . that was new."

"Hn."

Haruka shifted Eli's body until he was draped over him monkey style. It was a much more ass-friendly position, but he was going to get a neck cramp eventually.

But that was future-Eli's problem. Now-Eli was content with the way things were. Besides, he could always go back to the other position if he needed to. After all, he had gotten a lot of practice with ass-bruises lately. Sometimes he even liked them.

Haruka's hand cupped the offended cheek gently and gave it a little squeeze.

"Pervert."

"Hn."

~

The *always needing to touch Haruka* thing hadn't been as awkward as Eli expected when they switched planes. No one looked at them twice, not even their attendants—they had attendants!—as they ferried them from a private lounge to their next plane.

No, the problem had been when Eli needed to use the bathroom.

He'd had to bodily shove Haruka out of the small, but fancy bathroom and lock the door. He could use the bathroom alone, thank you very much, even if he was shaking all over by the time he'd finished.

Haruka's face was dark when Eli came out, and he snatched Eli right off the floor and carried him back to their seats. "Don't do that again."

"Oh, I'm doing it again." Eli scooted off his lap but stayed curled against Haruka's side. Laps were not a good battleground.

Haruka glared at him, and Eli glared back.

Haruka rubbed his forehead—still managing to scowl at Eli. "That was awful."

"And it'll be even more awful when I stop being able to have sex with you because you hugged me while I was trying to pee, so deal with it."

Haruka pulled Eli back onto his lap and made a grumpy, grumbly noise.

It was good they had the room to themselves, otherwise any onlookers would have been baffled watching them fight and cuddle at the same time.

They'd stopped talking after that.

Their next plane was from a Japanese airline, and if Eli had been surprised by the way they'd been treated before, it was nothing compared to now.

They had an honest-to-god room with a bed. It was tiny, but much better than what they'd had before, and the service was insane. He'd been told by their personal attendant three separate times that if they needed anything to just push the button by the bed and someone would come right away.

Currently, they were sitting facing opposite sides of the bed, each with a hand stretched behind them so they could still touch.

He couldn't take it anymore. He had to know.

Eli turned around. "Okay, seriously who the hell are you? Yakuza royalty?"

Haruka turned to look at him and gave a shrug with a glint of amusement in his eyes. "You're better off not knowing."

"Are you kidding me?" Eli tugged on Haruka's hand, encouraging him to come to the center of the bed.

Haruka moved to where he was led and sprawled out on his back like a big cat. "Yes."

"Assbutt." Eli heaved himself on top of Haruka and was rewarded with a grunt. "I am going to find out eventually, right?"

"Eventually." Haruka flipped their positions—now Eli

was the one getting squished. "But I wish you didn't have to. It's an annoying situation."

"So, it's not that you don't want me to know?"

Eli had realized early on Haruka had money, but not this much. His dorm room was sparsely furnished, but spacious. The few possessions Haruka had were all expensive, and every item of clothing he owned was designer.

"No. Or rather, I don't want you to *have* to know, but I'm not going to hide it from you."

"That's not terribly reassuring, you know."

Haruka hummed in agreement. Then he yawned so hard his jaw popped.

Haruka let all his weight settle on Eli, and he buried his face in Eli's neck. "Tired."

"Don't fall asleep on me!"

"Haven't slept since yesterday," Haruka said into Eli's neck.

It was like getting hit with a bucket of ice water.

All the warm, tingly feelings his body had been wallowing in now that he and Haruka were speaking again jettisoned from the plane without a chute. Haruka couldn't endlessly give to Eli. He needed to be taken care of too.

Eli retrieved an arm from where it had been pinned and stroked Haruka's soft, silky hair. "Sleep then. But not on me."

"You'll run away."

"Silly. Where am I going to run off to? We're on an airplane."

"Stay anyway."

"Why don't I sleep with you? I'm tired too."

Haruka rolled over just enough that he was no longer crushing Eli, but he kept an arm and a leg over him.

Eli wiggled until he was comfortable and allowed

himself to be lulled to sleep by the sound of the plane's engines.

~

"What are you doing?" Haruka's sleepy voice pulled Eli's attention from the computer screen.

"Studying." He pointed at screen covered in kanji. "I realized when I woke up that I haven't prepared at all for a trip to Japan. So, I'm brushing up on common phrases and —hey!"

Eli reached for the laptop Haruka had just stolen and was stopped by a hand to the face.

"You're a language major. All you do is study."

Eli tried to get around the giant hand blocking his view and failed. "But I might forget something."

"You won't."

"But I haven't been studying Japanese as much as other languages lately. I might be rusty."

"You aren't rusty."

"How do you know?"

"Because we've been speaking Japanese since we got on the plane, dork." Haruka finally let go of Eli, but only because he was too busy laughing at the poleaxed expression on his face.

"Oh." Eli's face went hot, and he covered his cheeks.

Haruka closed the laptop and put it behind his back. "You are just too cute."

"Arghhhhh." Eli tipped over on his side and buried his face in the blanket. When he did, the contact he had been maintaining with Haruka's leg broke.

Nothing happened.

"Hey!" Eli waved his hand wildly and pointed to the

inch of space between them. "I can use the bathroom alone!" Just like every other human past the age of five.

Haruka's eyes were blank for a moment, but then he smiled. "That's one less thing to fight over, at least."

"I'm sure we'll find something else soon enough."

Eli missed the way Haruka went still because he was busy stealing his laptop back.

"I have a list of all the places I want to go. You're taking me to every single one of them." He brought up a document he started four years ago. It was over ten pages long now.

"Hn."

Eli stopped mid scroll. "I'm not serious. We don't have time to go to all of them. But I want to see Osaka Castle. Oooo! And can we go to Nara? I want to feed the deer."

"They aren't as cute as you think—they're all a bunch of ass-biters."

"Then you better get a picture."

Haruka ruffled Eli's hair. "Deal."

CHAPTER 38
ELI

Everything was a bit of a blur when they finally touched down in Japan. Eli would have expected it to be something akin to a religious experience, visiting the country he'd been obsessed with since he was little. Instead, jetlag had joined forces with the stress of suffering a blackout and having a fight with Haruka to create a surreal bubble around his mind.

He allowed himself to be led through customs and responded automatically when given the perfunctory questioning by airport security. It was only when he was bundled into the back of a massive black limo that he came back to himself.

Haruka was buckling him in, lifting his arm out of the way like a doll when Eli asked, "Where are we going?" He tried to tug his arm out of Haruka's grasp, but it was held in a gentle, but iron grip as he finished buckling Eli in.

"Home." Haruka took Eli's chin and lifted it, placing a light kiss on his lips. Then another one that lingered and grew until Eli's head was spinning and he'd forgotten what they'd been talking about.

Haruka didn't pull away until Eli was gasping. Unconsciously, Eli reached for Haruka to draw him back in and grumbled when he didn't budge.

"I'm sorry. I shouldn't have done that," The twinkle of mischief in Haruka's eyes didn't make him look sorry at all. "I think it's better to stop before I forget where we are." Haruka motioned toward the glass divider between them and the driver. "I don't want anyone else to hear the sounds you make when I fuck you."

"Oh my god, Haruka." Eli groaned and tried to bury himself in the seat cushions. He failed because Haruka had been too thorough when he'd belted Eli in. How the hell had he forgotten they were practically in public?

"I promise to make it up to you when we get home." Haruka leaned back, and the heat that had been building in his eyes banked and went dormant.

Something about how easily he'd regained control irked Eli.

He really shouldn't. He knew he shouldn't, but there was something in him that wanted to knock down the walls Haruka so effortlessly built around himself, and it made Eli say, "You'll be lucky if I ever let you touch me again."

Haruka's eyes flashed, and he raised an eyebrow. He leaned in until his forehead was touching Eli's. "You say that like it's a deterrent. But we both know you like it when I hold you down and make you cry."

Eli hissed as all the blood in his body tried to get to his dick at the same time.

Haruka cocked his head to the side like a bird of prey when it saw something interesting. "Don't look at me like that unless you want me to forget about not wanting other people to hear you." His thumb ghosted over Eli's lower lip.

Words stopped being a part of Eli's toolbox of abilities.

How quickly Haruka could take him from a thinking, rational person to a being of pure sensation. One whose sole focus was Haruka and Haruka alone.

Distantly, Eli heard the sound of leather protesting as it was crushed under Haruka's hand, now very close to Eli's head.

"If you are very, very good for me right now, I won't fuck you into screaming my name until we get to my room."

Eli was having trouble remembering why exactly it would be a bad thing if they didn't wait.

"Because I think you will be very upset with me once your head clears."

That felt a lot like future-Eli's problem. Now-Eli was positively vibrating under his skin. The way Haruka's eyes were glued to Eli's lips as his fingers flirted with the seam made him think it wouldn't be difficult to push him into doing anything Eli wanted him to.

Night black eyes watched him closely, waiting to see which way Eli would tip.

It would barely take any effort at all, one little bite, one tiny little lick, and Eli knew he'd be getting his ass pounded into the leather seat of the most expensive car he'd ever ridden in faster than he could blink.

But . . .

Haruka didn't like to share. He'd made it clear that he wanted to keep this part of Eli all to himself, and it felt wrong somehow to take advantage of the fact that Haruka would give Eli anything he asked for just because he asked for it.

"I'll be good." Eli squeaked.

Haruka closed his eyes took a deep breath and rolled his

shoulders. When he opened his eyes, the fire was slumbering once more.

They took the bullet train to Osaka, which was freaking awesome—or at least it should have been, but Eli couldn't stop thinking about what had almost happened in the back of the limo.

To distract himself from the sexual tension still buzzing under his skin, Eli looked out the window and proceeded to act like a three-year-old at Disney World.

"Look at the size of that Sanrio store!

"How is it possible for everything to be crowded and beautiful at the same time?

"Can we go to that shrine sometime?"

He wanted to see everything, do everything, and talk to everyone. Eli had never experienced anything quite like it in his life. And through it all, rather than teasing him, Haruka simply gave an occasional *hn* in response to the nonstop stream of chatter Eli couldn't keep to himself.

After about an hour, Eli's brain went a little numb from sensory overload, and he felt his head begin to nod. Before gravity could exert itself, Eli felt Haruka's large hand guide his head down to rest on his boyfriend's shoulder.

Eli woke up in another limo. Either he had suddenly become an incredibly heavy sleeper, or Haruka's magic touch was just that good.

"Good timing." Haruka's voice rumbled under Eli's head. "We're almost home."

"This is your home?" Eli sat up, and his eyes nearly popped out of his head as he tried to take in the towering chrome and glass skyscraper before them.

The limo breezed through the security of the private entrance and stopped in front of a private elevator. The driver got out and opened the door on Eli's side, took a step back and lowered his head respectfully.

Eli brushed Haruka's hands away when he tried to unbuckle his seatbelt. "I'm not three." His hands were shaking from overstimulation, but he managed to trigger the release.

"Wait." Haruka put a restraining hand on Eli, halting him before he got out of the car. He held out Eli's brain meds and a bottle of water.

"Oh." He'd completely forgotten. The change of time zones combined with his blackout had him so out of sync he didn't even know what day it was, let alone what time it was. How the hell had Haruka remembered? Eli touched his chest. There was a little glowing ball inside, and it wanted him to say mushy things. "Thank you."

Eli swallowed the pills and tried to exit the car but was stopped again until he drank the water he'd been offered. "Pushy jerk," he said, trying to suppress a smile.

"Stubborn cat."

"I'm excited, sue me. Can we go now?"

"Hn."

Eli catapulted himself from the car before Haruka could change his mind.

"Who isn't three years old??" Haruka called after him, taking roughly five hundred thousand minutes to join Eli at the elevator.

"Kidnappers don't get a say in how their captives behave." Eli's eyes darted to the driver, only then realizing his words might be taken seriously. "He didn't actually"—shit, what was the word for kidnap in Japanese?—"um, steal me, I really want to be here, I promise."

Then he realized he'd been speaking in English to Haruka, and the driver might not have understood him in the first place. He smacked himself in the forehead and resisted the urge to climb inside Haruka's jacket until the trip was over.

The driver didn't move from his position by the car door, but there was a hint of a smile on his face.

"Can we go before I die of embarrassment?" he whispered miserably.

Haruka placed a large hand on the back of Eli's neck. It was warm and grounding. All of the crazy energy that had been building momentum since Eli woke up settled, and his body relaxed. He resisted the urge to purr, but his limbs went all floppy without his permission.

When the elevator doors opened, he allowed himself to be led inside, letting the pressure on the back of his neck guide him. When the doors closed, he leaned into Haruka's side and just existed, enjoying the way Haruka folded him into his warmth, still keeping his hand firmly on the back of Eli's neck.

Fuck anxiety meds, he had Haruka.

The elevator made a soft chiming noise, and the doors started to open. Automatically, Eli sprung away from Haruka. This was his home after all. What if he wasn't out to his family?

The loss of contact with Haruka shot his stress meter to a five. When the doors opened all the way, Eli saw an older, statuesque woman smiling at them. She had Haruka's eyes, but her smile was nothing like his. Behind it was a hidden blade, dripping with poison.

CHAPTER 39
HARUKA

Haruka's entire body tensed, and without thinking he stepped in front of Eli.

It was a mistake.

He didn't want this woman to even look at Eli, and now she knew it. He forced himself to relax. It may have been a while, but he still knew how to play the game.

Haruka affected a bored tone. "You were supposed to be in Nagasaki this week, not in my building hijacking my elevator." He was nothing more than a trust fund baby. A spoiled nuisance to be dealt with quickly and kept happy. He donned it like a cloak, willing her to continue to believe the lie that had kept him free all these years.

"Haru-chan, is that how you greet your aunt after all this time?"

Haruka rolled his eyes at the childish honorific she'd added to his name and sketched an indecently brief bow—the picture of a kid who wanted nothing more out of life than expensive toys and no parental supervision.

It was too soon. Eli didn't know about the dangers of his family yet. Haruka wanted him to enjoy his first experience of Japan to the fullest, and he needed him to continue to love Haruka's country.

He'd thought he had time, but Haruka had underestimated his aunt.

Eli poked his head out from behind Haruka.

His aunt's eyes positively sparkled, and she clapped her hands together.

"Oh, Haru-chan, you shouldn't have, he's just my type. Absolutely precious. As apology gifts go, this is simply perfect." She moved forward eagerly as if to drag Eli from the elevator.

Haruka stepped in front of her, forcing her to choose between backing down or bouncing off him. She stopped in her tracks.

"He's mine, and he can understand you."

His aunt's eyes flashed in irritation. She didn't like being denied things. Too bad. This was one thing he would never unbend on, even if he had to blow his carefully crafted cover.

"It was a joke, Haru-chan. I'm not here to steal your toys."

Eli tried to go around him and was stopped when Haruka put out an arm to bar his way. He shot Haruka a cautious look of inquiry before saying, "I'm Eli Talosa. I am not a toy."

"Don't talk to this viper, I will deal with her," Haruka said in Thai.

It was a language his aunt had refused to learn. She'd been to Thailand once and had an unpleasant experience with a monitor lizard. Afterward she'd cut off all personal ties to the place—going so far as to relegate any business dealings to someone else.

She leaned down as if speaking to a small child. "I'm

Haru-chan's aunt, little one. My name is Chiba Hitomi, but you can call me Nee-san."

Haruka could feel the confusion coming off Eli in waves. He didn't want to call her big sister. Eli knew there was something dangerous about her and wanted to leave, but he also wanted to be polite.

"It's nice to meet you." Eli's bow was far more formal than the one Haruka had given.

"I love him, give him to me when you are done," his aunt said in Russian.

Haruka responded in kind. "We won't be here that long." It was true. Eli could be here for a hundred years, and Haruka still wouldn't be done with him. He switched back to Japanese so Eli could understand. His boy's obsession only extended to Asian languages. It was adorable. "Is there something you needed? Otherwise, we've got video games to play."

"Yes, I wanted to invite you to eat this evening. The both of you."

"We can't make it. Jet lag."

"Nonsense. Our CEO is finally back. It would look bad if our company didn't celebrate it.

Eli sucked in a sharp breath at the word CEO. Haruka felt a spike of anxiety from Eli before he stepped backwards, breaking their link.

Fuck.

"An hour. Then I'm leaving." And Eli wasn't coming.

Haruka stepped forward, using his size to force his aunt out of the doorway and pressed the penthouse button. The doors closed in his aunt's face.

The elevator was deathly silent as they continued their trip to Haruka's rooms.

Haruka wanted to touch Eli but wasn't sure if he'd be welcome.

It was a physical ache in his bones, the need to make sure Eli was okay and to comfort him if he wasn't. The boy was tiny and, for all his bluster, very innocent. In Haruka's eyes he was painfully breakable.

"CEO, huh?" Eli said finally. "I'm not calling you that, ever, just so we're clear."

"Are you mad?"

"I'm only mad if you were planning on not telling me."

Haruka place a hand on Eli's chest, telegraphing the movement in case his boy was feeling twitchy.

He wasn't. Instead of shying away, Eli allowed Haruka the same easy access he'd enjoyed for the past month. How he loved this tiny, enchanting creature.

More than anything, he sensed curiosity. Eli wasn't angry at all. Nor was he anxious. After the initial start Haruka's aunt had given him, Eli had suspended his reaction until he had more information. He believed in Haruka completely and was waiting for him to explain what was going on.

"I was planning on telling you." Haruka allowed a brief break in the wall he'd built in his mind so Eli could feel his sincerity.

"I'm CEO in name only. The company belonged to my parents. They died when I was very young, so my aunt took over."

He opened another small breach in his wall. :*We can't talk about this here. Wait until we reach my room.*: He tapped his ear in the universal gesture of *someone might be listening.*

He felt Eli's assent before the boy said cheekily, "So you're a like a trust fund baby?"

Haruka smiled at how fast Eli had caught on to the game and nodded.

"All right, trust fund baby, get ready to spoil me rotten."

He knew Eli didn't mean it, but he wished he did. Nothing would make him happier than to spoil him. Eli was annoyingly unmaterialistic.

Haruka pulled Eli close. "Are you going to be my sugar baby, then?"

"Only if I get my own car. A shiny one."

Haruka would buy him ten if he was serious.

The door chimed and opened onto Haruka's suite of rooms. He tugged on Eli's hand and led him inside.

"Haruka."

"Yes?"

"You have a koi pond in your living room."

"I know." Haruka's mouth twitched as he watched Eli explore.

He'd lived here for ten years, so it was ordinary to Haruka. Boring even. Everything was boring before he'd met Eli.

The room transformed into something magical as Eli poked and prodded everything in sight. Haruka followed silently when Eli ran out to the rooftop garden.

"You have a heated pool!"

"I do."

Eli ran up to him and grabbed both of Haruka's hands. "Can I swim in it?"

Haruka caught a flash of pure, childlike excitement. Eli had never had access to a private pool, so he hadn't been swimming since he was very young. There would have been too many eyes for him to be able to enjoy himself.

If they ever returned to the States, Haruka would buy Eli a house with a pool.

"You can swim in it whenever you want." Wearing as much or as little as he wanted.

Eli released Haruka's hands and made like he was going to strip down and jump right in, but his attention was diverted by the view before he took off a single item of clothing. "I can see Osaka Castle from here!"

He was weak for this boy.

Haruka reached for his phone and opened the app that allowed him to connect to a device he'd installed in his suite the last time he'd been here. Once he was assured there were no surveillance devices around, he tossed his phone onto a nearby bench.

Then he made his way to where Eli was—standing on a rock wall, trying to get a better view of the Osaka skyline.

"Tomorrow can we go-ack!" Eli was cut off as Haruka scooped him off the wall and tossed him over one shoulder.

"Yes." Tomorrow they could go anywhere, but right now they had unfinished business.

The encounter with his aunt had him feeling . . . territorial. She hadn't been kidding when she'd expressed an interest in Eli.

Haruka carried Eli inside and deposited him on top of a decorative marble table. "Thank you for being good, Eli." Haruka enjoyed the way the boy's eyes went dark at the word good. His irises were so thin his eyes were a midnight blue.

The way Eli went from a hyper ball of energy to passive and compliant in seconds stirred something inside him. Something dangerous in its intensity. Something that focused solely on Eli.

Haruka's control danced a fine line as he willed his mental walls to stand firm against the darkness in his heart. He couldn't let it taint the golden core of the boy in his arms, but he couldn't stop himself from basking in the glow.

Haruka watched, mesmerized, as mischief flared in Eli's eyes and a pink tongue darted out to wet soft lips. The boy thrust out both hands and planted then in the center of Haruka's chest and shoved hard.

Eli wasn't compliant after all. He wanted to play.

Perfect.

The impact of Eli's push was negligible. Haruka stood his ground and jerked the boy's hips sharply against his own. His cock was already hard as steel as it pressed against Eli. No one had ever affected him this way.

It was all he could do not to tear off Eli's clothes and bury himself inside the boy's tight little hole. His shadow side egged him on, telling him Eli was begging for it.

And he was. Eli might be trying to push him away, but on the inside, he was pleading for Haruka to wreck him.

What a perfect, dirty, little angel.

One that should be begging more.

Haruka stripped away the black hoodie he'd given Eli. It was the only thing he refused to tear to shreds. And since Eli was wearing his favorite shirt under it, he couldn't tear it either unless he was willing to suffer Eli's wrath later. For such a small person—or perhaps because of it—Eli was surprisingly vindictive. And incredibly creative about it.

Eli put up a good fight as he tried to keep his shirt on, but he melted like a puddle when Haruka took his upper arms and held him firmly, exerting just enough pressure for the boy to really feel it. His eyes went soft and dreamy, long enough for Haruka to free him from his shirt, but as soon as Haruka let go of his arms, he lashed out.

He was going to make Haruka work for it today, and that fit in perfectly with his own plans. They both needed this. Eli needed to release some steam after his breakdown, and Haruka needed to reassert his claim after their fight and his aunt's annoying comments. He was happy to let Eli fight as much as he wanted.

It wasn't the fight Haruka wanted though—well, not entirely—it was so much more than that. As much as he loved watching Eli be bratty, it was nothing compared to harnessing that power, taming it, and bringing it under his own will. Haruka would forever be in awe that such a beautiful creature would willingly surrender everything to him.

A vase shattered on the floor, sent there by Eli when he tried to scoot backward, kicking as he went. Eli peeked out from behind his disheveled bangs to gauge Haruka's reaction. There was no remorse there, only sly calculation—he'd done it on purpose.

Haruka bit back a smile. Words couldn't begin to describe how it felt to see Eli fully in his power, no fear or hesitation in his eyes.

Trust.

He trusted Haruka with himself, both to protect and to contain.

Haruka caught Eli by the leg and dragged him across the table, dodged the other leg when it tried to kick him in the chest and trapped it against his side with the first one.

He shifted his weight, turned the struggling boy over until he could tuck him under one arm, and grabbed the hoodie with his free hand. "I was going to fuck you on the table, but *someone* made a dangerous mess on the floor." He tightened his hold on the wiggling baggage under his arm until it *eeped*. "So, now I'm going to have you here instead."

Haruka tossed Eli onto the couch, making sure to give him a safe, if somewhat rough landing. Before the boy had a chance to recover, Haruka had him flipped over onto his stomach and straddled him, using the hoodie to bind Eli's arms behind his back.

"Get off!" Eli shouted into the couch and tried to buck Haruka off of him.

Haruka allowed most of his weight to pin the boy flat and slid a hand up his spine, enjoying the feel of the soft, porcelain skin. Eli shivered, and goosebumps sprang up in the wake of Haruka's fingers.

The shiver went deeper than Eli's body. Haruka could feel the soft, quiet place shimmering around the edges of Eli's consciousness. He was almost in the place where Eli could be free from worry, the need to fight, or the need to think. All he needed was a push.

Haruka leaned over Eli's back, braced a hand on the couch beside the boy's head, and lowered his head until his mouth brushed against Eli's neck. "It's not polite to break my things, kitty."

Haruka didn't give a single fuck about the vase, but this was too good an opportunity to pass up. He kissed the quivering flesh before giving it a quick nip.

"Ah . . ."

It was such a small sound—just a tiny sigh, really—for the amount of havoc it wrought on Haruka's system. His world narrowed down to a pinpoint, and his own mind went very quiet as something rose up inside Haruka and demanded he push into the boy right now, raw and unprepped.

His hands clenched until veins stood out on his forearms, and Haruka breathed heavily against Eli's neck, forcing himself to calm down.

He—mostly—succeeded.

"I think you need to be reminded who you belong to, kitty." Haruka sat up and turned Eli's face to the side so he could see it, then he wrapped a hand around the boy's slender neck. His thumb traced a vein, and Haruka marveled at how it fluttered. He tightened his grip just enough for Eli to know exactly who he belonged to.

This was his. Eli was his.

Haruka's eyes drifted half closed as Eli's mind shimmered and went white. He watched as the boy went limp and all the fight went out of him. Eli's eyes were dark, and his mouth was slightly open as he panted softly underneath Haruka.

Haruka released his throat and traced the boy's mouth before dipping a finger inside. A soft, pink tongue darted out to meet it, and Eli began to pant harder. He arched his back, grinding his ass needily against Haruka.

:*Pleasepleaseplease.*:

Subverbal Eli was fun to play with.

Haruka climbed off Eli long enough to pull the boy's jeans and boxers off. Then he took him by the hips and draped him face first over the back of the couch.

He stripped off his own clothes before joining Eli, pressing himself against his back and put two fingers inside the boy's mouth. "Get them good and wet, Eli, unless you want me to hurt you."

Eli groaned and ground his ass against Haruka's cock. Deep in the soft, hazy world inside his mind, Haruka picked up the thought that Eli wanted him to shove into him, to hurt him, to claim him.

Haruka laughed softly. Eli would kill him if he couldn't get out of bed in the morning. He took control of the boy's hips, spread his cheeks apart and allowed the head of his cock to brush over Eli's hole, teasingly. "I won't let you hurt yourself, Eli. I can't play with you if you're broken."

Eli strained against Haruka's hold but couldn't move

his hips a millimeter. He let out a high-pitched keening sound.

"Behave," Haruka said and gave Eli's ass a slap. Eli cried out, and a lightning strike of *pleasurepain* blossomed in his mind. Haruka watched in fascination as the pale skin began to turn pink, creating a perfect impression of his hand. He traced his fingers over the abused skin, and Eli's mind shimmered brightly.

"Beautiful," Haruka whispered. Everything about Eli was simply breathtaking. "How are you so perfect for me?"

He untied Eli's hands and placed them on the top of the couch on either side of Eli's head. "Don't move them."

Eli's face went dreamy, and Haruka stroked his cheek before resting his fingers against soft lips. This time Eli lapped at his fingers like they were covered in ice cream.

"Good kitty. Very good kitty."

Satisfied, Haruka reclaimed his hand. "You deserve a treat."

He planted a hand in the middle of Eli's back, pinning him. The glow in Eli's mind intensified.

He smoothed his hand over Eli's ass and inserted a spit-slick finger inside Eli roughly, barely giving his body a chance to adjust before giving him another.

"HaaaAh!" Eli arched against him as *pleasurepain* dominated his mindscape.

Haruka forced himself to slow down and give him one more finger. Eli's soft cries were murdering his self-control, but Haruka managed to pull himself together long enough to roll on a condom before pushing slowly inside Eli.

All thoughts of holding back fell to pieces when Eli shifted his hips and pushed back, allowing Haruka to slide all the way in to his tight, wet heat. Nothing felt like this, nothing had ever made his blood sing the way it did when he was inside Eli, feeling exactly how much the boy wanted him.

When Haruka bottomed out, Eli made a cute little sound that made Haruka grab his hips and begin to pound into him. He wanted to hear every little noise the boy could make. He wanted to make him scream.

One of Eli's hands slid down from the top of the couch, and he began to stroke himself. Haruka took his hand away and slammed it back into place, covering both of the boy's hands with his own. "Bad kitty."

Haruka drove into the boy at a punishing pace, for a few seconds not thinking about how small and fragile Eli was. But the glow inside Eli called out to something inside Haruka. Something barely leashed and better off left alone.

Before it could break free, Haruka slowed his pace and released Eli's hands. He took the boy's slim, pink cock in his own hand—it was positively dripping with precome. He knew he could make Eli come untouched, but it would be more intense this way. Haruka wanted to imprint himself onto every fiber of Eli's being so he'd never forget who he belonged to.

He stroked Eli and fucked into him, using the boy's hip for leverage so he could get in as deep as possible.

"Ha-Haruka . . . ahhhhh!" Eli bit his hand, trying to muffle his screams. "Please let me come, haaaa . . ."

He should make Eli beg more, he did it so beautifully, but Haruka was reaching his own limits. "Go ahead, kitten."

Haruka stroked Eli faster, adding a twist at the end of each stroke while driving into his sweet spot, and the boy shattered. His body convulsed around Haruka, driving him over the edge too.

Haruka was nearly feral as he slammed into Eli, forcing sexy little whimpers out of him as he chased his orgasm.

Haruka blissed out for a bit, dropping lazy kisses onto any part of Eli he could reach, just enjoying being part of Eli's glow.

"I think you're crushing my everything." A tired voice came from underneath Haruka.

He was draped over Eli, who was squashed between him and the back of the couch. Haruka gave him one last kiss before peeling himself off the boy.

"Let me make it up to you."

"How?"

Haruka swung Eli into his arms. "By giving you a bath."

If Haruka was very lucky, once Eli saw Haruka's bathtub, Eli might let him have him again.

~

Eli was curled up in Haruka's bed, fast asleep. The sun was still out, but jet lag, stress, and Haruka's undivided attention had him so exhausted, a riot could have broken out beside him and the boy wouldn't have twitched a single toe.

Haruka brushed the hair away from Eli's face and kissed him.

He wouldn't find a better time than now to do what needed to be done, so he sent a text to his assistant. He had a few things to discuss with his aunt.

CHAPTER 40
ELI

This was, hands down, the best Thanksgiving holiday he'd ever had. He'd spent three hours exploring Osaka Castle with Haruka. He would have spent every yen he possessed at the tourist stands surrounding the base of the castle if Haruka hadn't used his superior size and reach to strong-arm his way into paying first.

Eli had managed to slip away to buy two massive, baked sweet potatoes with his own money. He'd been too shy to speak to the vendor, though. Even though he knew exactly what to say, all he'd managed was a shy little *meep* while he pointed to the size he wanted and held out two fingers.

Next time, Eli. You'll do better next time.

He was back in Haruka's suite surrounded by all of his loot, sorting through it and categorizing by each person he'd bought something for.

"Is any of this actually for you?" Haruka asked.

"Ummm . . ." Eli sorted through the pile until he found the little golden maneki-neko magnet he'd bought. "I got this for our fridge. You don't have any magnets on it, and that's a crime in my country. I'd hate for you to get fined."

"I appreciate it," Haruka said solemnly.

Eli tilted his head to the side as he took in his boyfriend's lack of expression, trying to decide if Haruka had realized he was joking. The man was a mystery sometimes.

Haruka's phone buzzed, and he took it out of his pocket. "It's my aunt. I need to meet with her for a few minutes." He walked over to the mirror, took his hair out of its usual ponytail, and combed it into place.

"Do you want me to come?" Eli watched as Haruka took a blazer out of the coat closet. In less than a minute, he'd transformed from a spoiled college student to a respectable adult. A team of stylists wouldn't be able to help Eli achieve that effect in a hundred years. When he got dressed up, he always somehow came across as a preteen on his way to church.

"It's okay, I won't take long."

"While you're gone, I might try to do some more research. You know, on the whole mind reading thing." Eli tried not to look like he was holding his breath. Haruka didn't seem to care much about why they were connected the way they were and occasionally got moody when Eli brought it up.

Haruka straightened the cuffs on his jacket. "That's one of the reasons I brought you here."

"Really?"

"There's somewhere I think you'll enjoy. If you insist on researching it, you might find something helpful there."

"You mean like talking to a Shinto priest about it? Is there a local legend about mind reading?"

"No, dork." Haruka flicked Eli in the forehead. "But

there's a well-stocked library several floors down that might have something."

Eli pouted until Haruka kissed his forehead.

He immediately ruined the gesture by saying, "You watch way too much anime, you know."

"You watch almost as much as I do."

"That's how I know you watch too much." Haruka kissed him again, only on the mouth this time. "Come on, I'll show you to the library before I meet my aunt."

"Do you have time? I don't want to piss off Chiba-san. She's kinda scary."

Haruka snorted. "Don't worry about it. I'll deal with her. You focus on having fun."

Haruka dropped him off at the library, giving him a knowing look as Eli's brain short-circuited over the three-story nerd wet dream he'd been presented with.

"You might want to start over there." Haruka pointed to a corner of the room next to a thirty-foot arched window.

Eli didn't even notice him leave.

"Why am I not surprised to find you like this?" Haruka's voice pulled Eli out of one of the books he had in his lap. "You look like a book troll."

"Huh?" Eli put a finger on the page to hold his place and looked around.

He was wedged against the side of a bookcase and had several stacks of books surrounding him. Some of them were nearly as tall as he was and wobbled dangerously.

Haruka took the top off the tallest pile and started a new one, adding the top of the next tallest tower to it before he sat down in front of Eli. "You know this room has tables. Big ones."

"Yeah yeah, sure," Eli agreed absently before shoving a book in Haruka's face titled *European Fairytales*. "Look at this."

At first Eli had zero luck, mostly because he was so excited he couldn't focus, and partly because most of the books weren't in English. And the ones in languages he could read were a bit too advanced for him to be able to understand them fully. Then he found a small, leather-bound book tucked away so high, only a bona fide shelf-climber like Eli would ever think to look.

Eli chuckled as he thought about what Haruka's face would have looked like if he'd seen him dangling twenty feet off the ground while straining to snag the edge of the tiny book stuffed on top of a row of dusty old tomes.

"It would look like this." Haruka's eyes burned into his, and Eli realized their knees were touching. "There are ladders in here, you didn't have to risk yourself for a book."

"They're too heavy to move every time I need to find something." Eli moved his knees away from Haruka's. "See, this is why I need to research our bond."

"I see no problem with it."

"That's because you don't have to worry about me wandering around inside your head all the time."

"You seemed to like it fine yesterday," Haruka said, a small pout forming on his lips.

"Shut up. You know exactly how I feel about that—you don't need to go fishing for compliments."

Haruka preened. "Then I don't see what the problem is."

"It feels like you're closer to me than I am to you. I know you think you're protecting me from something scary inside of you, but did you ever consider that I might like it? If it's a part of you, then it's just more Haruka and I love Haruka—even the annoying bits. Why wouldn't I want to know everything about my favorite person?"

For a second, Haruka's cool as ice expression faltered, and Eli caught a glimpse of something vulnerable and childlike before his face closed up. "Hn."

Rather than push, it was better to let Haruka process what Eli said. Otherwise, they'd fight, and Eli wouldn't be able to show him the super cool story he'd just found.

Eli crawled into Haruka's lap so they could look at the battered book together. "I don't know why it caught my attention—maybe because it was so hard to get to." When Haruka grumbled unhappily, Eli hurried on. "But when I flipped through it, I found a story about a group of traveling merchants. They were insanely lucky—apparently they had the favor of some god. Anyway, they spent generations enjoying the god's patronage until he asked them for one of their daughters."

When Eli had reached this part of the story the first time, the hair on his arms stood on end. Kind of like it was now.

Eli shivered and continued.

"The merchant family loved their god, but they loved their daughter even more, so they politely turned him down. Unfortunately, this god turned out to be a dick and cursed the whole family." Eli pointed to an illustration of a beam of light striking a group of cowering people. "He tore each person in half and scattered the parts to the four corners of the earth, saying none of them would ever be happy until they found their other half."

"What happened to the girl?"

"Apparently the god decided to be an even bigger dick

to her. He cursed her to be drawn to herself in each life, only to be torn apart, lifetime after lifetime."

Haruka said nothing, but his fingers dug into Eli's sides.

"I know, creepy, right? Anyway, the reason why this stuck with me is because it says when a shattered soul gets close to their other half, they can hear each other. Sounds familiar, no?"

It was actually starting to feel a little too familiar for Eli's taste. It wasn't just his arms now, the hair on the back of his neck was standing up, too. Maybe calling it a super cool story was a stretch.

Haruka took the book out of Eli's hands and read it while Eli rubbed his arms. When he put the book down, Eli asked, "What do you think?"

"I think that god has too much time on his hands." Haruka poked Eli's cheek. "And so do you. Let's go eat."

Eli scooted off Haruka's lap, feeling a little disappointed, until he noticed a faint line of goosebumps going from Haruka's neck to his hairline.

After they ate, Eli called his family while Haruka went to yet another family meeting. Once again, he offered to go, and once again he was rebuffed. As much as he loved being in Japan, he was starting to look forward to going home—he had a feeling being a trophy boyfriend was going to get old really quick.

It was well past midnight before he gave up and went to bed alone. His eyes were heavy when his head hit the pillow, but before he fell asleep, a thought hit him. Haruka still hadn't told him what happened to cause Eli's blackout.

His mind naturally shied away from events like that, so

Eli wasn't in a hurry to ask about it. Was Haruka being sensitive to that? Or did he have another reason?

Sleep hit him before he had a chance to think any more.

Darkness.

Everywhere Eli turned, all he saw was a never-ending sea of nothing.

And behind the nothing came terrible, mocking laughter. "It doesn't matter where you go, I'll always find you."

"Get fucked, creep!" Eli shouted at the laughter, trying to sound anything other than the terrified ten-year-old he felt like.

He wanted to throw something at the voice, but he had nothing. He wanted to run, but there was nowhere to go. He was alone, always, always alone.

"You won't have to be alone, pretty, if you choose me. It will be easy. Don't you want life to be easy?"

Eli shivered. If he could go the rest of his life without being called pretty it would be too soon.

He curled into himself and tried to block out the laughter, but it came at him from all sides, attacking every weakness and chipping away at Eli's mind, trying to reach his core.

Howling wind joined the laughter, tearing at Eli's clothes. He curled in even tighter. He would hold on. Being alone forever sounded better than giving in to this freak.

Even if he felt so cold he might shatter.

The bleak thought was like a knife to his soul, and laughter chased after it ready to exploit any weakness.

Eli shook as he fought to hold himself together.

Just one more minute.

Just one more second.

Just one more breath.

Warmth bloomed against Eli's back, driving back the cold and forcing the laughter to retreat back behind the nothing.

Eli gasped as heat rushed back into him, lending him

enough strength to sit up. He found Haruka kneeling over him anxiously.

Through lips still numb from the biting wind, Eli said, "I don't think it's over yet."

Haruka nodded and continued to act as a shield for Eli, staring into the darkness, waiting for whatever lay behind it to make its move.

Eli pressed against Haruka, trying to ground himself. He wasn't alone, not anymore. How could he have forgotten?

"Only for now, my love." The voice from the darkness said mockingly. "Until you give me what I want, you'll never be whole."

A sharp pain lanced through his core, and Eli screamed. He tried to cling to Haruka, but his hands passed through him. Before his eyes, Haruka's form grew indistinct and began to fade away. Eli tried to meet his lover's eyes, but they were focused on something behind him. Whatever he'd seen, made Haruka look positively murderous.

When the last traces of Haruka were gone, the darkness descended, surrounding Eli and filling him with hundreds of memories—all of them of Haruka. None of them were happy.

Every memory revolved around the two of them, but it didn't show their lives together, or how they met. It only showed how they parted.

Memory after memory rolled through Eli, and he got to experience each one as though it were happening to him now. At first, it had been stupid misunderstandings that had driven them apart—all orchestrated by the vengeful, jealous god. But as time went on, their memories of each other started to awaken, and the god had to resort to more violent tactics.

And somehow, it was always Eli who was stolen, murdered, or brutalized, usually right in front of Haruka. As the nightmare slideshow of events began to come to an end, Eli recognized a pattern.

More often than not, Eli was driven to kill himself.

The god must have finally found a formula that suited him. Time after time, life after life, Eli was the one who'd torn them apart.

The last thing Eli remembered thinking before succumbing to oblivion was, so it wasn't just me. Something really is out to get me.

CHAPTER 41
ELI

His head was pounding up a storm when Eli finally managed to pry himself out of bed. Eli bit his lip when he realized Haruka was gone. He stroked the cold sheets next to him and found a note.

At a meeting. Back soon. Eat something when you wake up.

~Haruka

Eli rubbed his head furiously. It seemed like he saw Haruka even less than he did when they were in school. It may have only felt that way because Eli had nothing to do here.

He should remedy that.

Eli brushed his teeth and washed his face roughly, trying to get last night's dream out of his head. It was the first time he'd had a nightmare while sleeping next to Haruka.

Coffee. He needed coffee in order to deal with the odd thoughts his brain was throwing at him. But not the gourmet stuff stocked in the fancy-schmancy kitchen neither of them used. Eli wanted to go out and explore.

He rode the elevator down the bajillion or so floors and spent the entire time telling himself that dreams and reality were two entirely different things.

Reading fairytales before bed was a great way to give a person nightmares.

Eli reached the first floor and waved to the receptionist on his way to the door. When he got there, he skidded to a halt. In front of him were two burly security guards blocking his path.

"Um . . . hi?" Eli's fingers crawled inside his sleeves.

"Please forgive us, sir." Both guards bowed to him, but neither moved out of the way.

Eli backed up a step. Maybe there was construction outside? "Is there something wrong?"

Once again, all the guards would say was, "Please forgive us."

"Okayyyy." Eli turned around and went back the way he came.

There was more than one exit, after all. He didn't relish going through the busy parking garage, but he was sure he could dodge any incoming cars if he had to.

Except his key card wouldn't give him access to the garage.

His blood-to-caffeine ratio was not sufficient enough for him to deal with this. He went up two floors, tried the other entrance, and got the same treatment.

"We are very sorry, sir. Please forgive us."

Same for the worker's access tunnel and the emergency exits.

Eli pulled out his phone.

Eli: What the fuck did you do?

. . .

There was no response.

Eli walked up to the closest pair of security guards. "Excuse me—yes, I know you're very sorry, I got them memo." Eli pinched the bridge of his nose. "Haruka put you up to this, didn't he? No, don't deny it, the look of terror is more than enough."

Eli took out his phone again.

Eli: I am going to break something and be very loud about it if you don't call me right now

Eli waited thirty seconds and then started surveying his surroundings, trying to figure out what his best options were.

He turned to guard number one. "Which one is more expensive? That painting? Or that statue?"

The only response Eli got was a set of raised eyebrows and a hushed conversation into the guard's headset.

"No, you're right. Why choose? I'll throw the statue *at the* painting." Eli rolled up his sleeves. It was a small statue, but it looked like it would be pretty heavy. Eli would need a triple espresso after this.

His phone rang. Eli pressed answer and continued on his trajectory toward the statue. "What's up, sweetie? I'm a little busy right now, so make it quick."

"I'm on my way to our rooms. Meet me there."

"Sorry, I'm going through a tunnel, can you speak up?" Eli put his phone on speaker and tucked it into his pocket.

He grabbed the statue by the arms and lifted. "Damn, this fucker is heavy."

"Eli, let me explain."

"Sure thing, I just have this one thing I need to do first."

Lift with your legs, Eli, you can do it!

There was a scraping sound as the statue finally parted with its base.

Ha! I may be small, but I'm scrappy as hell.

He was distantly aware of the small audience he'd attracted, but he couldn't give them any attention. Not unless he wanted a broken toe out of this adventure. No, focus was the key to success here.

"Eli, put it down."

"Oh no, I think we're well past that. Now if you'd texted me back right away or, I don't know, maybe not told your henchmen to keep me from leaving? No, you're losing a statue. Hope you weren't too attached."

Fuck, that painting was far away.

"But . . . you might get to keep the painting. This thing is heavy." Eli's fingers slipped, but he managed to catch the statue before it crushed his foot.

"I don't care about the statue, put it down before you hurt yourself." Haruka sounded out of breath. "I'll smash it for you, just, put it down, please." There was a note of desperation in his voice.

Eli took a guess at how much time had elapsed and shoved the statue at the closest security guard and ignored the *WRONG* that scraped against his insides when he accidentally touched him.

He hung up the phone and ran for the farthest elevator because Haruka was probably in the closest one.

Once inside, he punched the button for the penthouse, fully planning on barricading himself inside.

He beat Haruka there by ten seconds and had the pleasure of slamming the door in his face, only to have an incredibly one-sided shoving match with the door when Haruka opened it again.

"Fine!" Eli took off his hoodie and threw it at Haruka. "Please explain. I'm dying to know why I'm being kept prisoner in my favorite country in the entire world. Use small words so I can understand." Eli sat himself on top of a marble table and crossed his legs, projecting *touch me and I'll cut you* to the best of his ability.

"It's not as bad as it looks."

"Oh really? So, I can leave whenever I want to?"

"Yes, of course." Haruka rubbed the back of his neck. "You just have to take me with you."

Eli leaned back on his hands. "Fine, then let's go right now."

"Where do you want to go?" Haruka asked warily.

"To the airport. I'm going home." Eli hopped off the table and made for the bedroom.

"No."

"Excuse me?" Eli pulled his suitcase out from under the bed only to have Haruka shove it back again. Eli left it because he knew it would be pointless. He'd known it was pointless the moment his key card refused to give him access to the parking lot—he just hadn't been willing to admit it yet.

"What are we even doing here, Haruka? Why did you bring me here? Was what happened back home so awful—"

It was like being kicked by a small horse. Eli nearly choked as the flash of memory hit him, and he swayed on his feet while his brain coughed up the details of Juniper's visit to their dorm. Haruka stepped forward to steady him, and Eli stopped him with a glare. “I don’t want you to touch me right now.”

Haruka looked like Eli slapped him in the face.

“So Li—,” His throat closed off again. He couldn’t say that name right now. “H-he jumped parole and is looking for me.” Eli clawed at his own hands so he could keep going, and Haruka looked positively wretched as he looked on helplessly. For a second, Eli thought he was going to touch him anyway, so he continued hastily. “I blacked out, you panicked, and brought me halfway around the world.”

Things had been going too well for Eli’s little slice of happiness to continue for much longer. Something like this was bound to crop up sooner or later.

Eli sighed and sat heavily on the bed. “That does sound like you.”

Haruka paced in front of him looking like a cross between a kicked puppy and a riled-up jungle cat.

“I get it, okay? I’m not mad about you bringing me here. I don’t love that you didn’t tell me why, but I’m guessing you were afraid I’d black out again if you did.”

Haruka nodded and stepped forward, only to be stopped when Eli held out a hand. The kicked puppy expression was gaining ground.

“But there’s no reason to keep me locked up here. He’s not going to come to Japan. He’s got to be on the no-fly list, and he couldn’t afford to get here even if he wasn’t. He was dirt-poor when he . . . did what he did.”

“I don’t care,” Haruka said softly. “If there’s even a chance—”

“I’m old enough to be on my own for five minutes. Jesus, all I wanted was a cup of coffee.”

“There’s coffee here.” At Eli’s glare, Haruka amended, “Or someone could go and get you any kind you want.”

"It's not the same thing, and you know it. What's going on with you?" Eli took a closer look at Haruka. He didn't look like he'd slept much better than Eli had last night. "Are you okay? Maybe you should cut down on the meetings with Chiba-san. Or at least let me go with you."

"Stay away from her. The less you know the better."

"What does that even mean? What are you keeping from me?"

Haruka examined his fingernails far more closely than necessary. "I'm working out a deal with my family to keep you safe."

"Shouldn't I be a part of it then?"

Haruka shook his head. "My family aren't good people, Eli. There are worse people out there—but trust me. Just hold on for a few more days, and they'll be out of your life. You won't have to see my aunt or meet anyone else."

"So, I can just sit here like a princess in a castle every day waiting for you to come home to spring me for a tiny adventure before you stuff me back in my tower?"

Haruka's eyes were shuttered, and he refused to look at Eli.

"Haruka, I have to go home. My family is there. I have school!" Eli couldn't help but wonder if this was all an elaborate joke, but the darkness in Haruka's eyes said otherwise.

"You can go to school here. My aunt already offered to get us private tutors if we want them. And your family can visit. I'll fly them here—Juniper would love it."

"She won't love you keeping me here."

"You'll be safe here."

"I'll be trapped here!" Eli had always wanted to live in Japan, but not like this.

“Is it so bad, Eli, being with me?” The hurt on Haruka’s face cut straight into Eli’s soul.

“No, of course not . . . but . . .” How could he make Haruka understand that safety wasn’t the only thing that mattered to Eli?

Haruka’s phone buzzed.

“I have to go. I left in the middle of a meeting.”

Haruka moved like he wanted to kiss Eli but paused, waiting for Eli to come to him. Eli turned his face away. Haruka waited, as if hoping Eli would change his mind. After a minute, he walked stiffly to the door, his expression wooden. Eli couldn’t look at him anymore.

“I only have a ninety-day visa,” Eli said to his clenched hands, listening as the sound of footsteps moved away from him. Haruka would have to let him go after that, wouldn’t he?

“We can take care of that too,” Haruka said just before the door closed behind him.

CHAPTER 42
ELI

Eli moped on the bed for exactly six minutes before jumping up and running to the kitchen. He loaded his arms with as many cans of coffee as he could carry and ran back to the bedroom. Then he came back out to grab his laptop—and its charger—and brought them in as well.

He stood in the bedroom doorway and stared at the hoodie still lying on the floor where he'd thrown it. It was Haruka's. It wasn't *the* black hoodie he'd originally given Eli—that was out getting cleaned because reasons—but part of Eli still wanted it.

Finally, he darted out of the doorway and kicked the hoodie across the room, turned around and ran back to the doorway, stopped halfway, ran back, snatched it up and raced into the bedroom, slamming the door behind him.

He locked the door, but since he didn't trust Haruka not to break the lock, the next half hour was devoted to shoving as much furniture in front of the door as he could. He had a bathroom, coffee, and his laptop. He could stay here indefinitely.

He had two hours of peace and quiet before there was a knock at the door. Eli put on his headphones and turned on his distraction playlist. The knocking turned into banging, so Eli turned up the volume and tucked his legs inside the hoodie he refused to admit he was wearing.

He ignored the dozens of phone calls from Haruka, but he'd had to switch his music over to his laptop because the calls kept interrupting his songs.

The calls stopped eventually. Then every few minutes his phone would chirp to let him know Haruka had sent him another text.

StupidStupidJerk: Let me in Eli

Or talk to me

Have you eaten yet today?

I see you took all the coffee, but not any food

Let me at least give you something to eat

I know you're reading these, so at least I know you're okay

Eli went into Haruka's contact page and turned off his read receipts. Then he added another Stupid to his name.

StupidStupidStupidJerk: Do you need anything?

You don't have to see me, I can have someone else bring it to you

Eli?

. . .

Tears pricked his eyes, and Eli turned his music all the way up.

Eli: How dare you take my best friend away when I need him the most?!

Eli threw his phone across the room so he didn't have to see Haruka's response. Then he put on the fluffiest anime he could think of and watched it until he fell asleep.

When he woke up from a long night of trash fire dreams, it was light out and the apartment was still. Eli climbed on top of the dresser he'd pushed in front of the door and pressed his ear against the door.

Nothing.

Eli gave it a few more minutes before finally getting up the nerve to push everything away from the door. When the noise didn't bring Haruka running, Eli opened the door to discover the floor was littered with bags full of all of Eli's favorite snacks—as well as new ones that looked amazing.

If Eli tried to eat now, he'd throw up, so he stepped over the mountain of snacks and nearly killed himself on a Kero-chan plushie keeping guard on the other side. He ran to the kitchen to look for more coffee and was unsurprised to see their supply had been fully restocked. Once again, Eli loaded himself down with all the coffee he could carry.

Before he closed the door to barricade himself back in, his eye caught on the Kero-chan plushie.

Eli picked up the tiny, stuffed flying lion and absolutely did not start crying his eyes out. Neither did he throw the stuffie across the room and then run after it to snatch it up to bring back into his lair.

Before he locked himself back inside, he shoved all of Haruka's offerings into a massive pile so he wouldn't be able to tell Eli had taken anything without going through the whole thing.

After popping open a can of coffee, Eli retrieved his phone. Ignoring the twenty new messages from Haruka, he typed:

Eli: Don't be toxic. You can't buy me

There was an immediate response.

StupidStupidStupidJerk: I'm not trying to buy you. I'm worried you aren't eating

Eli: Funny

Food isn't terribly appealing right now for some reason. I wonder why?

StupidStupidStupidJerk: Don't hurt yourself just to punish me

Please

At least take your meds

Shit, he'd totally forgotten to take his meds.

Eli went to the bathroom, found the right bottle, shook out two pills, took a picture, then dry swallowed them. He may be pissed, but he wasn't stupid. At some point they would work this out, and it would be better if Eli wasn't seesawing wildly between mania and depression when it happened.

He was, however, petty enough to wait thirty minutes before texting the picture to Haruka.

StupidStupidStupidJerk: Thank you

Eli: Don't thank me. I didn't want you to cut a hole in the wall

StupidStupidStupidJerk: My wall appreciates it

Eli rolled his eyes and went back to ignoring his phone.

An hour later there was a knock at the door.

"Eli, I brought you coffee and muffins."

Eli walked over to the door and loudly opened a can of coffee at it. He chugged half the can before putting his headphones back on and turning on *Eternal Love-Ten Miles of Peach Blossoms.* He skipped to the part where QianQian was locked up in her palace and being pathetic as hell. She hadn't lost her eyes yet—he hated that part and was fully planning on skipping it.

He picked up his phone.

Eli: I swear to god if you try to pluck out my eyes . . .

. . .

StupidStupidStupidJerk: Don't watch the Peach Blossom show right now

I'm begging you

Literally anything else

Eli: Kidnappers don't get a say in what I watch

Eli sent Juniper a few pictures of Osaka Castle, telling her to expect a ton of presents when he got back. He considered telling her what was actually going on but decided against it. When Haruka pulled his head out of his ass, it would be a massive pain to get Juniper to calm down if she found out his boyfriend had kidnapped him.

It occurred to Eli that a normal reaction to being locked up was fear. He'd felt plenty of it the last time.

But no, Eli wasn't the one who needed to be afraid right now. If Haruka didn't back down, Eli was fully prepared to make his life a living hell.

His stomach growled.

Eli poked it and said, "Quiet, tummy, we're winning this thing. Just hold on a little longer."

He looked at his phone, and it told him it was only a bit past noon. How long could Haruka hold out before caving? A few hours? A few days? The man was stubborn, but he had serious issues with Eli not eating. Which one was he more obsessed with? Eli eating, or Eli not getting kidnapped?

His stomach growled again.

Fuck this.

He put an ear to the door, but it was only a precaution.

Since Haruka wasn't spamming his phone, it meant he was probably in a meeting.

He dismantled his barricade and stepped into the hallway. He grabbed his wallet, phone, and the cute shoulder bag filled with fancy stationery he'd bought for Alice.

He stopped counting the stairs as he went down them. All he knew was there were way too goddamned many of them, but he couldn't afford to take the elevator and alert security that he was on his way. Haruka would pay when this was all over. He didn't know how, but he knew it would involve coffee.

Every few floors, he took a short break so he could catch his breath—and so he could write *fuck you* on a piece of paper to leave on the landing.

When he finally reached the main floor, he sat on the last step and concentrated on breathing until the corners of his eyes stopped popping with little sparks. He needed to go back to his old gym routine. His nose wrinkled when he remembered who helped him come up with his old routine. Stupid Ash.

He hoisted himself up and put on his game face. Then he opened the door and bolted for the exit.

As expected, he was surrounded in seconds.

He took a deep breath and crossed his fingers, hoping his boyfriend was exactly as obsessed with Eli as he thought he was.

"Excuse me, but you're between me and the place I want to go." Eli moved toward the door, and the security guard in front of him took a step back.

"Please forgive me, sir," the guard stammered.

Eli took another step forward. The guard took another step back, then another as Eli kept going.

In his peripheral vision, Eli could see the other guards

throwing looks at one another as Eli backed the lone guard against the door. There was less than an inch between them when he moved forward again. The guard pushed the door open, and Eli stepped outside.

"I'm sorry, that was incredibly rude of me. But your boss gave you instructions that were impossible to follow." Eli bowed low. "It's not your fault. I promise I won't let him fire you. What's your name?"

"Kamakura Keiji."

Eli watched as Kamakura's eyes darted between Eli and the other guards filing outside.

For a moment, it looked like one of them was about to get brave, so Eli said quickly, "Trust me, he meant it when he told you not to touch me. He'll be angrier about that one than letting me go." Eli bit his lip because he wasn't entirely certain it was true.

Nara sounded like a great place for lunch. But how was he going to get there?

"Kamakura-san . . . do you have a car?"

"Yes, but—"

"I know you're going to follow me when I leave. Wouldn't it be easier to do so if we were in the same car? I'll even let you drive."

Kamakura looked like he was questioning every single one of his life choices when he sighed and said, "Follow me."

On his epic list of things to do in Japan, visiting the Daibutsu in Nara was in the top five. He'd planned on dragging Haruka there, but that was out the window now. Eli would have to go on his own.

He sat in the back of a very nice car—probably not Kamakura's, since it was loaded with expensive-looking snacks, drinks, a flatscreen TV, a Nintendo Switch, and a half dozen other things Eli hadn't yet figured out the purpose for.

He bit into something that was a bit like a waffle and a bit like a cookie while scrolling through his phone, searching for other things to do in the area. A name caught his eye. Tenkawa Benzaiten.

It was a shrine he'd read about in his History of Japanese Religion class. He'd found himself doing more research on the kami of the shrine because something about her had spoken to him. The kami's name was Benzaiten, and she was the goddess of things that flowed—music, water, knowledge, and words.

Eli sat up and tapped the button to open the window between him and Kamakura. "Stop here, please." He passed his phone through the window to show his unhappy driver the location.

The shrine was breathtaking even in late fall.

Eli leaned against the car and took in the vibrant red torii—the massive gate found at the entrance of Shinto shrines.

"I'll be right back," Eli said to Kamakura.

He started toward the torii and stopped when he realized he was being followed. "I don't need a babysitter."

"Sir—" Kamakura began, looking conflicted.

"Listen, this relationship of ours is built on compromise. I recognize that I can't shake you entirely, and you understand that you can't actually stop me from doing what I want, right?"

Kamakura nodded slowly.

"Excellent. Now, I'm going inside this shrine for, hmm, about thirty minutes, and you're going to stay by the car and wait for me. I'm not going to run off. You have the car, after all."

"I don't know . . ."

"Let me—" Fuck. What was the word for rephrase in Japanese? All he could come up with was the word in Spanish—which was ridiculous because he only knew ten words in Spanish. "Say in a different way, only not so nice. I'm going in there alone, or I will hug you and take a picture of it to send to your boss. Okay?"

Kamakura went pale and stepped backward, nearly tripping in his haste. "Please don't do that."

"Great! I'm glad we've reached this compromise. If I'm not back in thirty minutes, you can come get me."

"No hugging?"

"No hugging."

Eli whistled as he walked away. Haruka's employees were going to get a very skewed idea of Eli during this trip. Kamakura probably thought Eli was a cuddle-happy touch-freak.

He burst out laughing as he walked toward the torii, startling two tourists taking a selfie. Before he entered, he remembered to bow before walking through the gate. History of Japanese Religion was really coming through for him right now.

For a time, he stood on a small, red bridge and stared unseeing at the landscape, not entirely sure what he was doing there.

It was peaceful, probably because it was late in the

season. Most of the trees had lost their leaves, and there was a bite to the air. Eli wrapped his arms around himself, snuggled into the sweater he'd stolen from Haruka's side of the closet, then moved further into the shrine.

When he reached the main shrine building, he bowed and placed a handful of yen into the offering box. Then he rang the bell, bowed twice, and clapped his hands twice. Then he pressed his palms together and lowered his head.

Hi. Um, I'm Eli Talosa from Massachusetts. I know I'm a foreigner, but I really love your country. Thank you for having me? Ugh, this is awkward, I know, sorry. It's just, you seem like someone who might get where I'm coming from. I know this sounds crazy, but I think I might be cursed by a god and . . .

What the hell was he doing? Was Eli actually coming up to a foreign god and begging for help? What else was he supposed to do? Either he was crazy, and he needed help, or he and Haruka were cursed, and they needed help. In any case the only way to get help was to ask.

If there is anything you can do to help, I'd really appreciate it. Thanks!

Eli bowed again and ran away.

Sheesh. He felt like he'd just tattled to a teacher because someone was bullying him. And all he could think about was whether he was supposed to have rung the bell and then clapped, or the other way around. He really should have paid more attention in class.

He was about to go back to the car when he realized he wasn't ready yet. As much as he wanted to be *plows boldly forward in the face of trouble Eli*, he was seriously freaking out.

So, he found a nice tree to freak out under.

His kidnapper was on the loose and probably looking for him. Haruka had gone bananas. And there may or may not be a god who had cursed the both of them to an eternity of being torn apart.

Eli put his head between his knees.

It hadn't been just a dream. Right?

It had felt so real. Dying over and over again, losing Haruka, being torn away from him countless times—it had been too horrible for it to have just been a dream.

And he was here dealing with it alone instead of having his partner with him to share the burden.

He lifted his head. Had Haruka had the same dream? If he had, that would explain why he'd suddenly gone all alpha male on Eli.

Haruka was probably hurting as much as Eli, and Eli had just ditched him to go sightseeing.

He should have talked to him.

Eli leaned his head against the tree. *So, this is what it feels like to be a stupid jerk.*

He wasn't a fan.

In a few minutes, he would pull up his big boy pants and try and fix this mess, but for now he would sit and be still.

He closed his eyes and listened to the sounds of nature. The wind swirling through fallen leaves, a lone bird chirping, a shrine maiden sweeping the pathway.

He reached into his shoulder bag and pulled out a notebook and pen.

Even if our curse
Separates us once again
I will still find you

He wasn't the best at poetry, but it seemed fitting to write something at the shrine of a kami who presided over words. And because he was Eli, he wrote the work *jerk* at the end of his haiku.

"You realize that word means jerk, right?" a young, feminine voice asked in English.

Eli looked up to see the shrine maiden looking over his shoulder. "Yes."

"And that adding it means it isn't a haiku anymore. You've got too many syllables now."

Eli smiled ruefully. "I know. But even though it doesn't fit, it's still fitting."

The shrine maiden raised an eyebrow. "If you say so."

Eli stood, bowed to the shrine maiden, and turned to go. He pulled out his phone. The Daibutsu would have to wait for another day.

He dialed Haruka's number.

A phone buzzed softly behind him.

Eli turned to see Haruka standing in the shadow of a tree several feet away. "How long have you been here?"

"Not long." Haruka's face was in default mode. Cold and distant.

"It wasn't nice to lock me up."

"Hn."

"That's not what partners do." Eli started to walk down the path, and Haruka joined him, keeping several feet of space between them.

"I'm sorry."

"I know."

"But I would do it again."

Eli laughed softly. "I know that too."

They walked quietly for a while, making their way deeper into the trees surrounding the shrine.

"I'm sorry too," Eli said finally, inching closer. "I should have talked to you, but I was so hurt, I couldn't even look at you."

Haruka stopped, and Eli turned to face him. He looked even worse than he had during their fight. The shadows under his eyes had increased, making his ethereal beauty haunting.

The space between them was only about a foot now, but it felt like a thousand miles. Eli couldn't feel even the slightest hint of his presence in his mind.

"Did you have the same dream?"

Haruka went stiff, and his face went even colder. "Someone kept taking you away from me." A shudder went through his large frame. "They hurt you, and I couldn't stop them."

Eli bridged the thousand-mile gap without thinking. His arms went around Haruka, and he held him tight. Haruka was like a statue in his arms, cold and unmoving. "Don't shut me out, Haruka. Don't be the reason we get torn apart this time."

And it would tear them apart. Maybe not this time or the next, but eventually, Eli wouldn't be able to take being cut out of the loop and locked away.

Tentatively, Haruka lifted his arms and wrapped them around Eli, holding him carefully, like he was some precious, fragile thing.

"I'll let you protect me and be as crazy as you want. Just . . . talk to me first. I don't want to be taken away from you any more than you want to lose me."

Haruka crushed Eli against his chest with bruising force, but Eli didn't care. He burrowed in and held on tight. Eli felt wetness on top of his head and realized Haruka was crying.

"Okay." Haruka whispered and rubbed his face against Eli's hair. "Whatever happens, we'll face it together."

Eli was about to tell Haruka not to use his hair as a handkerchief when he heard the sound of clapping.

"You two are adorable, really."

Haruka turned and shoved Eli behind him, but left him enough room to see a tall, blond man standing on the path in front of them.

"I thought you were going to do my work for me this time, but here you are working things out and being annoyingly clingy in the process."

"Who are you?" Haruka asked in a low, dangerous tone.

"Someone you betrayed and abandoned."

Something hot and heavy slammed down on him, locking him into place. Haruka's body jerked at the same time, and Eli felt a flash of alarm through their bond.

Fuck.

"I doubt that," Eli said shakily, trying to push through the fear lancing through his body. The story he'd read said nothing about the girl betraying the god. Also, something inside of him clashed against the claim. As if outraged by the accusation.

"Like you would know." The man sneered. "I've erased your memories so many times there must be nothing left of your first life."

"I know enough to know I'd never want someone like you." Eli peered up at Haruka's face. He'd never want anyone other than the man currently holding onto him like his life depended on it. "And he doesn't want you either."

Eli felt a strong burst of agreement come from Haruka.

:*We need to get out of here. Now.*:

:*You finally done shutting me out?*: Eli asked.

:*Yes.*:

:*Good. Can you move?*:

:. . . *No,*: Haruka said, grudgingly.

The mad god carried on, oblivious to their silent conversation. "If I put you back together, you might change your mind about that. What do you say? Wouldn't you like to know what it's like being whole again?"

Twin spikes of revulsion bounced between them.

:*No offense, Haruka. You know I love you, but I don't want to be you.*:

:*I don't want to be you either. You're more fun to play with when I can see you. Besides, I'm not sharing you with anyone, let alone this guy.*:

:*Agreed, so what do we do?*:

:*Stall, until we see an opening.*:

Eli could do that. "We don't need you to make us whole. Don't you have something better to do with your time? If it's been so long, maybe you should find a better hobby."

The god threw back his head and laughed. "How about just you then? I've always found this side of you more amusing than the cold, quiet side. What do you say, pretty? If you go with me, I'll leave this one alone."

Eli's stomach churned. Could he sacrifice himself like that? If it was for Haruka?

:*Don't even think about it. You said you wanted me to stop shutting you out, that means you can't do it either.*:

:*Together or nothing then?*:

:*Together or nothing.*:

:*It's been nice knowing you in this life.*:

:*It's not over yet.*:

"Neither of us is going with you," Eli said.

"Do you even realize how self-centered it is for the two of you to be together like this? You're lucky that I even want you."

"Then stop wasting your time on us. Go find someone else more worthy of your attention." Eli spat. He didn't care how weird they were. Nothing felt as right as the bond he had with Haruka. This god could get bent.

"Fine. If you don't want to be reasonable, I'll just reset you both again." The man held up his hands, and clouds parted overhead. The sun instantly became scorching. "Maybe next time, I'll find a way to make it so you can't meet. You'll feel differently me about me if I become your savior instead of him."

:*I hate this guy.*: Haruka's mental voice growled, vibrating Eli down to his bones.

:*I don't care what he says. There is no world where we don't find each other.*: Eli gripped Haruka so tightly his fingers went numb. He tried desperately to move his feet, but the weight pushed even harder, and his knees nearly buckled.

:*I will always find you. Wait for me.*:

:*Make sure and be a massive jerk next time so I'll recognize you.*: Eli's throat hurt from holding back tears. He refused to cry in front of this asshole of a god.

:*As long as you make sure to be a tiny brat.*:

:*It's a deal.*:

They faced the god defiantly, standing side by side, holding hands, ready for whatever was about to come.

A ball of blazing light formed in the god's hands, and Eli found a detached part of him thinking how cool this would look if it wasn't happening to them.

Eli braced himself, ready to die, ready to be torn away from Haruka, willing himself to remember everything this time. He wouldn't be fooled by this asshat. He would find Haruka, and they would figure out how to get rid of this guy in their next life.

Eli felt Haruka's wordless assent as the light flashed and sped toward them—only to be blocked by a broom.

The little shrine maiden stood between them and the mad god with a look of faint irritation. "I told you it was a bad match, Helios. I told you this hundreds of years ago when you came after my boy the first time."

"Stay out of this, Benzaiten." Helios snarled.

"Excuse me? You come into my house, attack my people, and have the nerve to tell me to stay out of it?" Benzaiten seemed to grow with every word, until she towered over Helios.

The weight vanished from Eli's body. Eli and Haruka exchanged glances and, in unison, scrambled back to give the gods some space.

"Your people? This one has belonged to me since she was born."

"We're two people now, assface!" Eli couldn't stop himself from shouting.

"Yes. Mine." The goddess said each word like an attack. Helios staggered backward. When this one was born on my shores"—Benzaiten nodded toward Haruka—"he became mine. Why do you think he kept being reincarnated here again and again?"

Helios gave her a calculating look. "Then keep that one, I don't want him anyway. But give the other one to me."

The goddess turned and fixed her eyes on Eli. "You should have been mine, Eli. I've been waiting for you to come here. You've gotten close many times, lived dozens of lives throughout Asia, but this is the first time you've made it to my shores." Benzaiten turned back to Helios. "When he asked for my help today, he became mine as well."

Haruka looked at Eli in surprise. "Is that why you came here?"

"I wasn't planning on it, but yeah. Kinda?"

"You have no power over my people, Helios. Amaterasu knows you're here, and she's not happy about it. She still has many worshipers to fuel her. Do you?"

The mention of the Japanese sun goddess had Helios dropping his hands. For the first time, his arrogant smile left his face. He looked toward Eli and Haruka "You were supposed to be mine."

"We were never yours."

The sun blazed brighter, but Helios no longer seemed strengthened by its rays. Instead, he dropped to his knees.

"She's almost here, Helios," Benzaiten said, twirling her broom artfully.

Helios gave Haruka and Eli one final look and vanished.

The sun's rays flickered as if it were disappointed.

"Um." Eli began and stopped.

"Thank you." Haruka released his death grip on Eli and bowed to the goddess.

Hastily, Eli followed suit. "Thank you so very much." He used the politest version of Japanese he could manage.

"You're very welcome. Both of you. I've wanted to do this for ages, but this is the first time you've been here, Eli. Haruka belonged to this land when he was born here. All of the gods and goddesses have been aware of your problem for some time, but we haven't been able to do anything about it until now. Do you want to belong here, Eli?"

"Yes, please!" Was that too eager? He felt like maybe he'd just been too eager.

Benzaiten laughed, and it sounded like water flowing playfully over river stones. "Good. Take good care of each other, you two. We're all invested in your relationship, so make it a good one."

The goddess touched each of them on the head. Eli's

mind glowed happily, and his internal alarm stayed silent. Apparently, it didn't mind goddesses.

"I've given you both my blessing." She held out both hands. "Here, I have one for each of you."

Eli reached out and allowed her to place a small silk bag in his hand. It was an omamori—a good luck charm usually found for sale at shrines and temples. This one was a little different than the ones Eli was used to seeing. It had three tiny bells attached to the drawstring. They tinkled softly as he turned the bag in his hand.

"If you take these with you, it should be safe to return to your home for a time, Eli, but I'm afraid you can't stay. This is your true home now. Helios can't touch you here, but my blessing will fade if you leave for too long."

"How long do I have before I need to come back?"

"You must return every two months to recharge the omamori here at my shrine, but I warn you, it isn't perfect protection. Helios can still find you and might be able to hurt you if he's clever. You will only be truly safe here."

Eli nodded and bowed again. "Thank you."

Haruka bowed as well.

The goddess turned and walked away, sweeping the path as she went. She looked smaller somehow, and Eli had the impression that if he ran after her, she wouldn't know who he was anymore.

"That really happened, right?" He held the omamori gingerly, afraid it would disappear if he wasn't careful.

Haruka gave Eli a half smile. "Hn."

Eli twined his fingers with Haruka's. "So, what now? Do we go back to America?"

Haruka squinted up at the sky, then gazed at the shrine maiden in the distance. "Maybe just for a little while. If that's what you really want."

"What about your family? It looked like something big was happening there."

Haruka heaved a big sigh.

"Full disclosure, Haruka."

"Full disclosure." He guided Eli to a bench, and they sat down. "The company is supposed to be mine, but I don't want it. My aunt runs things, and I've been happy with the arrangement. Technically, I can take over at any time though. I hold a majority of the stock. A large majority."

"What have you been doing the past few days if you don't want to be in charge?"

Haruka smirked. "I've been proving to my aunt that I'm more than capable of doing so if she doesn't stay out of my life. It backfired though. She wants me to step in and help her manage things."

"Is that something you want to do?"

Haruka shrugged. "I want to do whatever will keep me with you."

"Oh," Eli said in a small voice. "That doesn't sound fair."

Haruka took his hand, and suddenly Eli could feel the truth of Haruka's words. Everything he did centered around Eli. What he wanted most was to see Eli smile and to make sure he had many opportunities to keep doing so.

"You are so freaking soft," Eli said, trying to ignore the heat in his cheeks. "If our classmates could see you like this —" He looked down, unable to meet Haruka's eyes.

"I'm only soft for you." Haruka cupped Eli's chin and lifted it.

"Make sure and keep it like that." Eli finally allowed himself to meet Haruka's gaze. He was absolutely gone on the man. He had been from the moment they'd met, he just hadn't realized it yet.

:*I will.*: Haruka dipped his head and pressed his lips against Eli's.

Eli sighed happily and wrapped his arms around Haruka's neck. In the distance a car horn caught his attention, and he pulled away.

"Oh no, I forgot about Kamakura-san!"

Haruka narrowed his eyes. "Please continue to forget about him. Forever."

"Oh no, you don't. He was only trying to do his job."

"He did it badly."

"What was he supposed to do, chase me with a giant butterfly net? Face it, you gave him terrible orders." Eli stood up and held his hand out for Haruka. "And I may have tricked him a bit as well."

Haruka took his hand and stood. "I need smarter employees."

"You're not allowed to fire Kamakura-san. I promised him I wouldn't let you."

"Hmph."

"Promise me." Eli tugged on Haruka's hand.

"Fine. I'll just relocate him."

"That's just as bad!"

"He can work at our Russian branch."

"Is it nice there? I've never been interested in Russia, so I don't know anything about it."

"Russia, it is."

EPILOGUE

ELI

"If I wasn't the short one, I would be the one holding you down." Eli groused with zero heat. He was exactly where he wanted to be.

"You are welcome to try any time you want." Haruka emphasized the word try with relish as he kissed his way down Eli's neck.

Eli had been planning on grabbing a quick snack before hotfooting it to his next class, but when he'd opened the door to leave, Haruka was outside, keycard in hand with a mild look of surprise on his face.

Then he walked Eli backward until he was pinned against the bed and started tongue-fucking his mouth like it was his life's sole purpose.

"I'm going to be late." Eli protested weakly.

"Mn." Haruka agreed as his hands began to unbutton Eli's shirt.

"I'll just eat after class," Eli conceded and reached for Haruka's belt.

"Nope." Haruka stood up and hauled Eli off the bed,

took his backpack from the floor—where Haruka had thrown it—and pushed Eli to the door. "Food, then class."

"But— but—" Eli found himself alone, on the other side of the door holding his bag. He almost pulled out his keycard to go back in but knew Haruka was fully capable of shoving him back out the door if he wanted to.

So, class then. But first, the coffee cart.

It had taken some doing, but Eli had managed to convince Haruka to let them finish out Eli's freshman year in America—with a mandatory visit to Japan every two months, of course. And Haruka was a total tyrant about making sure Eli always wore his omamori when he got dressed in the morning.

It wouldn't have happened though, if Juniper hadn't called to tell them Liam had been found dead in a cheap motel. It had been another overdose, only this time it had been successful.

Eli tried to find an emotion other than relief at the man's passing, but there was none.

Haruka still kept most of his thoughts to himself, but sometimes when they cuddled, Eli could hear and feel every soft, sweet, somewhat obsessive thought in Haruka's head.

It was enough to make Eli's heart burst.

His class barely registered as Eli thought about everything that had happened in the past three months. Fortunately, he was able to take notes without paying much attention to them.

Okay, that was a big fat lie, Eli wasn't thinking about the past three months near as much as he was obsessing over the way Haruka had chucked him out of their room earlier. He needed to find a way to make him pay.

He continued to obsess during Tea and Calligraphy club.

"Eli, it took me weeks to perfect that green tea blend. Please don't pour it all over the table," Alice said as she ran to grab paper towels.

"Shit, sorry, I was distracted." Eli tried to right his teacup, but overcompensated, and managed to spill even more tea all over the cookies Helen had given him.

Nate snagged a soggy cookie and took a bite. "Hey, Helen, you should add green tea powder to these, they're delicious!"

Helen ducked behind Raina as soon as she heard her name. She'd always been too shy to talk to Nate, but Eli caught her peeking at the charismatic boy as soon as his attention went back to his friends.

He'd also noticed Nate tended to tease her more than anyone else in the club. Eli exchanged glances with Alice. She was definitely planning something. Eli wouldn't be surprised if he found out she'd locked the two of them in a supply closet overnight sometime over the next few days.

"What has you so distracted, man?" Nate took another cookie.

"None of your business," Eli muttered, feeling his ears go red.

"Ah, so it's a dirty thing. Say no more. Please."

"Speak for yourself, Nate. I want all the naughty details."

"Me too!" Kate said as she came up to their table. She picked out a cookie that had escaped being drowned in tea.

"Look at the time," Eli said, looking at his watch-free wrist. "I really need to go . . . anywhere but here. Bye!" He grabbed his bag and beat a hasty retreat.

It was early for either of them to be back in their dorm room, but Eli couldn't stop himself from checking.

When he got inside, he found Haruka pacing the room

as he looked over a document. Eli recognized it as one of the weekly missives his aunt sent him.

Eli took it from Haruka's hand and dropped it on the floor as he walked Haruka backward toward the bed. He planted his hand in the center of Haruka's chest, shoved him down, and straddled him.

Fear wasn't the reaction Eli had when fire kindled in Haruka's eyes.

Far from it.

"Now where were we?" Eli purred.

Sign up for my Newsletter ***or join my*** Facebook reader group ***to get a steamy extra epilogue!***

Or buy it on Amazon for a revised version with an added chapter with hints about Psync 2**.**

Afterword

Oh my god everyone, I loved writing this book so much. Thank you for coming with me to learn all about these two gorgeous, hot messes.

If you liked this world, please follow me! I currently have six more MM stories in the works for this college and, if enough people ask for it, I'll write another book about Haruka and Eli. Please consider leaving Psync a review on Amazon. If it gets 50 reviews on Amazon, I'll know you folks want another book. (Edit: Psync 2 is out now! But you can still review Psync 1 if you want to!)

GLOSSARY

I understand everyone isn't as big of a language nerd as I am, so I tried to keep the Japanese down to a dull roar. I know I didn't succeed, however, so here's a list of the words I've used and their meaning as well as a brief explanation about suffixes for anyone who finds them as fascinating as I do. Disclaimer: I'm not a native speaker, so take this all with a grain of salt. This is my understanding of what these terms mean.In Japan, unless you know someone super, super well, you don't just call them by their given name. Usually, you call them by their surname which comes before their given name. Haruka's name is Yamada Haruka.

Suffixes

Senpai - If Eli had met him at a Japanese college, he would have called him Yamada-senpai (and Haruka would have loved that) because Haruka is older.

San – If they'd met randomly without a set social situation in Japan, Eli would have called him Yamada-san.

Kun – If they'd met at work and they were the same age,

Eli would call Haruka Yamada-kun. Kun is also used for any male younger than the speaker. It's used among schoolmates as well.

Chan – Haruka's aunt calls him Haru-chan. When she uses it, it's super insulting. Chan is used for children—usually girl children. Close female friends someone times refer to one another using chan. Family members also call younger female members chan.

Nee-san – Haruka's aunt wanted Eli to call her Nee-san which would have been sweet if she wasn't trying to be a creepy perv about it. Nee-san is for older sisters and for older women you are close too and you look up to.

Japanese terms

Hakama – Traditional pleated pants often worn practicing kyudo.

Kyudo – Ancient art of Japanese archery.

Mitsugake -Kyudo three fingered glove to protect the hand.

Daibutsu – Literally means the big Buddha. It's a huge statue of the Buddha in Nara. The temple is super cool and you should visit if you ever go to Japan.

Clamp – An animation team I would willingly slap an innocent stranger for in order to be able to meet. They are responsible for creating Card Captor Sakura, Xxxholic, Tsubasa, X, and many other amazing anime.

Baka - Idiot.

Note from the Author

I am not Japanese. I was, however, a Japanese major in college. All the inner monologues about being Japanese and cultural references were taken from conversations I had with Japanese teachers and students and my own experiences when visiting Japan. This doesn't mean I got it right. Please don't assume that my thoughts and opinions are stereotypical of being Japanese. Unfortunately, Haruka is a fictional person. He does not represent Japanese people or the way they think and act.

I debated with myself long and hard over whether I should write the POV of someone who is Japanese when I myself am not. Eventually, my love of the culture and desire to have more representation in literature made me decide to try. If I have offended anyone, I encourage you to message me about it. I am here to learn and grow.

As for Eli's neurological disorders, I feel comfortable writing about them. I have lived them!

ALSO BY ZILE ELLIVEN

Enchanted University Series:

Patience

Psync 2

Quiet

Printed in Great Britain
by Amazon

36961633R00218